ASHLEY

Ashley Kath Bilsky

Between the Shadows

THE LEGION OF MITHRAS

First Edition: December 2015
Published by: Ashley Kath-Bilsky
at Create Space

ISBN-13: 978-0-989257046
ISBN-10: 0989257045

Author: Ashley Kath-Bilsky
Publisher: Ashley Kath-Bilsky
Cover Design: Ramona Lockwood
Illustration: Elissa Marie

First Edition
ISBN-13: 978-0-989257046
ISBN-10: 0989257045

ACKNOWLEDGEMENT

Special thanks to my beloved family
for their love, support, and encouragement.
I am so blessed to have you all in my life.
And to my dear readers, thank you
for taking this journey with me.
I hope you enjoy the adventure.

Dear Susan –
I am so glad we met
at Margie's class, and
to be one of your Immersion
sisters and friends.
Thank you so much for
your encouragement and
support, and for being
an "A Kath Bilsky Caraidear".
Keep smiling :)
Hugs
Ashley
18 Jan 2016

In Memory Of
Jane, Charlotte, Arthur, J.R.R. & Agatha

ASHLEY KATH-BILSKY

Between the Shadows

THE LEGION OF MITHRAS

Chapter 1

Ceòthar Innis, Scotland ~ 17 March 1813

Like a grave being opened, a surging, teeth-chattering gust of wind rose off the loch. An eerie sensation lifted from the soles of Patience Sinclair's feet to the crown of her head. And she knew the reason why.

Someone was watching her.

At once, an unrelenting, crippling pain seized the back of her head—twisting, building, as if a thousand stars were about to burst inside her skull. She pressed her right hand hard against the pain, praying the torment would soon subside.

One, two, three, four…

After eight measured counts her stilted breathing eased, and the wave of stabbing, burning daggers slowly ebbed.

It had been years since she'd felt the same heart-stopping, thought-crippling spasm. The fact it returned today filled her with foreboding.

A low growl sounded to her right. She glanced at her dog, noting the alert angle of Henrietta's head. As her beloved Irish Wolfhound stared at someone behind them, its warning grew more menacing.

Patience set aside her book, stood, and turned about. An icy wave of stunned surprise washed over her. She stared at her unexpected visitor, a treacherous fair-haired young woman from her past. Much as she'd wanted someone to visit with her, the one person she'd never hoped to see again was Anne Melville.

"Please, do not turn me away!" Anne's voice sounded panicked, shrill, like the tormented cry of an inmate at Bedlam.

Patience took a few tentative steps forward. Henrietta followed, a quiet reminder her dog was wary and ready to protect if need be. She gently stroked the coarse black hairs on Henrietta's broad head, and continued to study her unexpected guest.

"Why are you here, Anne?"

"We were friends…once."

A jagged jolt of pain ripped through Patience's body with Anne's knife-twisting reminder. Resentment and outrage ignited—a seething fury that if unleashed could catapult her up to the tower's medieval battlements. Her breath rushed forth hard and fast from her lungs. Muscles in her throat—raw and taut with tumultuous emotion—contracted.

"You must help me, Patience."

"Help *you*? I am a prisoner here because of you." Patience's heart pounded. Each beat echoed in her ears like the rhythmic stride of soldiers advancing toward their enemy.

"I know I hurt you—"

"Hah. You destroyed my life. Three years exiled by my family. Not to mention the cruel taunts and endless, malicious gossip—all because of what you said and did in London."

Patience trembled with the intensity of her hurt, humiliation, and hatred. At nineteen years of age, she should be accustomed to being unwanted, unacceptable, and unloved. But every scar that once pierced her soul had been ripped open again by Anne's presence, tearing tender flesh anew like a blade drawing fresh blood.

"Tell me, Anne, have you ever thought about the devastation you caused me? In your world of beauty, popularity, and exciting social engagements, did you ever consider what it might feel like waiting for a visit by one's family? Or, a letter saying all was forgiven and to please come home?"

"I understand *now*." Anne's voice broke into heartrending sobs. "I am grievously sorry for my actions, but I beg you, do not punish me. I have traveled so far. You are the only one who can help me. Please, you *must* return with me to London."

Refusing to be influenced by quivering desperation and the frail, pitiful sight of her nemesis, Patience ignored the sharp tug on her conscience. Still, no one knew better than she how frightening the world could be when one felt lost and alone.

"I do not seek to punish you,"—Patience paused to steady her temper— "but neither can I help you. I don't live here by choice, Anne. My stepfather made it quite clear what he would do with me if I disobeyed him or returned to England. I am a pariah. I can help no one—not even myself."

Never before had Patience witnessed such hopeless anguish and devastation in someone's expression.

Guilt prompted a defensive tone. "If you must know, I've changed. Put simply, people do not like me and...well...now, I do not like people."

"Do not say that." Anne's luminous eyes widened as if a curse had been spoken. "Even as a small child, you were compassionate and good to everyone."

Patience looked toward the 14th century tower.

Hewn from granite, its existence had been forgotten, abandoned. Her gaze drifted to what remained of the curtain walls, great hall, and holy chapel. Once proudly anchored to the ancient MacGregor keep, they were now nothing more than crumbled stone and mortar skeletal remains. Ironically, the tower's lonely fate had become a daily reminder how much her family had forgotten and abandoned her.

If only I had the courage to leave.

If only I could prove myself sane.

If only my family loved me.

A lock of her auburn hair, tugged free by the wind, danced before Patience's eyes. She swept it aside and noted the sky's mirror image reflected on the loch; its clarity drew her gaze toward the heavens.

Sun and clouds played a game of chase on the wind, conjuring changes of light and shadow in their wake. She watched the swiftly moving clouds cross the sky, racing toward the distant horizon. There, majestic mountains stood sentinel, their rocky peaks capped with lingering snow.

Much as Patience loved Scotland and the beauty of its nature, three years of banishment at *Ceòthar Innis* had all but severed kinship to the land. Like the brutal blade of an executioner's ax, her ancestral home had become a private prison.

Days lengthened into weeks.

Weeks yawned into months.

Months eclipsed into years.

And still she caught herself thinking—*if only*.

Once she dreamed of someone coming for her.

Now, she didn't.

And suddenly Patience realized if she refused to help Anne, she'd never leave Scotland. She'd never be loved, marry, or have a family of her own. Most of all, she'd never have another chance to prove she deserved to be free.

She looked back at Anne's disheveled golden hair and pale English beauty, more striking than ever. "What makes you think I can help you?"

"Because *you* understand." Anne stepped closer, her chafed hands clasped together. Delicate fingers interlocked in prayer-like fashion, perhaps hoping the gesture might add power to her entreaty. "Please, Patience, if I could turn to someone else, I would."

"Of that much I am certain," Patience murmured.

"I know what you think of me. If it brings you any satisfaction, everyone seems to have the same opinion now. I have been called selfish and manipulative, shallow and unfeeling. I am nothing but a spoiled, temperamental hoyden of a sister; a rebellious, scandalous daughter. And such a faithless friend no one will speak to me, let alone look at me."

Patience returned to her seat amidst a half circle of sacred rowan trees. She motioned toward another chair. "Come, sit, Anne. I vow I am curious what happened to cause such a popular flower of grace and beauty to descend into the role of outcast."

Once seated, Anne smoothed the fabric of her pink gown. "I know not what to do. *Everyone* has turned against me."

"Why?"

"I do not know. My father used to hate to see me cry, yet no amount of tears softens his anger toward me now. My brother, Charles, broods and ignores me altogether. As for my mother, she has taken to her bed and will not deign to look at me. I have done everything I possibly can to beg their forgiveness."

"Why would you need their forgiveness?"

Surprise, shame, and something indescribably sad flickered in Anne's eyes. She looked away. "I ran away."

"Where did you go?"

"Loathe though I am to admit the truth, to be with a man." The words were spoken in a near whisper, raw with self-recrimination. Her gaze averted, Anne stood then moved to stand beneath the canopy of a nearby tree. It seemed rather apparent she sought to hide beneath the branches, but Patience saw her all too well.

"Like a besotted fool, I fancied myself in love. Please do not ask who he was because, strange as it sounds, I do not know." Anne's voice grew strong, imbued with rising bitterness. "I have flashes of memory, but they seem more a nightmare. In truth, they make my skin crawl."

Standing, Patience approached her former friend. Slow, steady steps—very much as one might approach a frightened child or animal. "Dreams and nightmares, however painful, often help us move beyond what we want to forget but must remember. Even memories you do not understand could be an important key."

"I don't *want* to remember!" Terror etched Anne's features. "I only want to go home."

Patience could no longer ignore Anne's pain or the compassion it kindled within her heart. How could she not help someone so frightened? Perhaps by so doing, she might also prove she deserved to go home, too.

A glimmer of hope sparked to life. Challenged quickly by its obstinate twin—hopelessness.

Icy tentacles of fear gripped Patience by the throat.

Fear of those she'd encounter in London. Fear of the ominous threat of Bedlam should she disobey her stepfather. But the fear that plagued her most was what would happen to her if she remained here alone.

Abandoned.

Forgotten.

Forever.

"There are many things to consider." Her voice darkened like a dense cloud moving swiftly to block the sun. Doubt warred with tentative hope. "I cannot see my family, and none of their friends would welcome me as a houseguest. I would need to secure lodgings elsewhere."

"Please, Patience. There must be a way."

"Auntie Catherine," Patience whispered.

"Who?" Anne studied her with a wary expression.

"Lady Carlyle, my grandmother's sister. She came to see me after I first arrived in Scotland. My only living relation on my father's side, she was outraged by the actions of my mother and stepfather. She wanted me to leave with her. I refused—thinking my family's wishes must be respected. The countess wasn't pleased, yet vowed to help me if I found the courage to disobey Lord Henley and reclaim my life."

"Your Auntie Catherine is Lady Carlyle?"

Patience noted the astonishment in her former friend's voice, and the all-too-familiar, calculating gleam in the young woman's eyes. Anne may choose to not remember the man she ran away to be with, but she had a vise-like memory for titles and the names of society's most influential matrons. Apparently, Lady Carlyle was both.

Patience opted not to reply, but directed her gaze across the loch.

"For pity's sake, why did I never know Lady Carlyle was a blood relation to you? I daresay you were foolish to not leave this boorish country with her. She could have orchestrated a stellar return for you to society. Lady Carlyle rarely bestows favor or sponsorship. I can assure you, many have tried to win her patronage."

The fact Anne knew so much about Lady Carlyle buzzed inside Patience's head like an irritating gnat. In truth, she'd never met Auntie Catherine—or had any contact with the countess before being exiled to Scotland.

"I was too afraid of Lord Henley's threat if I disobeyed."

Anne moved gracefully to stand before Patience, clasped her hands together and tucked them under her chin in a beguiling manner. "Poor

Patience,"—she offered a piteous smile— "your stepfather would not have hindered you from living with a titled, socially prominent woman like Lady Carlyle. Since the countess is a family relation to you, he could have cultivated the association for himself." She made a tsking sound, then shook her head in a patronizing *'how could you have been so stupid'* manner.

"You know nothing about my stepfather, Anne."

"Lord Henley?" Anne snickered delicately. "The celebrated hero of His Majesty's Royal Navy? The man who will do anything to form an alliance with the most influential, important people of the *Ton*? Come now, why would such an arrogant, social-climbing, man deny any connection with the powerful, well-connected Lady Carlyle?"

The stark honesty of Anne's words conjured a long denied awakening within Patience. Hurt surged from the depths of her being. And what little remained of that parched, desolate field of brittle family trust she'd somehow salvaged for three years had now been set ablaze by reality's fiery torch.

"Because I am not family to him," Patience replied, her voice tight with the painful truth. "I have never been family to him. He detests me. As for garnering the good opinion of the countess, Lord Henley resents anyone he cannot influence or control."

Anne's eyes narrowed and her mouth puckered in a sour expression. "Forget Lord Henley. Return to London. Let us both put the past behind us, Patience. You shall have a strong ally if you accept Lady Carlyle's offer of assistance now."

The image of the petite, silver-haired Lady Carlyle surfaced in Patience's thoughts. "She has many estates, including a castle in Scotland—a day's journey from here. If she is not there, one of her fine coaches could transport us in privacy and safety to England. She keeps a fully staffed house in London. But if she is not in residence there…"

Tapping a finger against her lips, Patience latched onto her aunt's promise to help her like a gift of angels. "She promised her servants would serve me well in her absence. They would know how to contact her, and she would join me with great haste."

"Then you will come with me back to London?" Anticipation and hope brightened Anne's pale features, yet her posture stiffened, as if the slightest movement might work against her wishes.

"If I return with you, Anne, you must promise to do as I say and always be truthful. If you lie, or deliberately keep information from me, I shan't help you at all."

"I promise." Anne smiled with obvious relief.

"Yes, well, the truth telling begins now. Tell me why you came all this way to Scotland. Why you believe I can help you."

All joy and excitement quickly vanished from Anne's expression. Her eyes widened and her lips parted on a shuddering sigh.

"Tell me." Patience encouraged.

"Because..." Anne paused, unable or unwilling to speak further.

"I cannot help you unless you are honest with me."

"Long ago, when we were little children, you told me,"—Anne's voice wavered and thinned— "sometimes you could not play because you had to help someone who was friendless, lost, and alone. That memory beckoned me, and I knew I had to find you."

Contrary to Anne's words, an element of half-truth evasiveness hovered in the air.

"But do you know why?"

"No."

Patience said a silent prayer for guidance.

"No one is angry with you, Anne." Patience gentled her voice. "Your father's heart is not hardened toward you. Your brother is not ignoring you. Neither has your mother taken to her bed refusing to look at you. Try to understand. The reason they cannot see you, or hear you, is because...you're dead."

Chapter 2

Telling someone they are dead was never easy. Some spirits accepted the truth with stoic calm, having had some inkling of their fate. Others reacted in unpredictable, even violent ways.

Anne Melville remained silent, keeping her gaze steady upon Patience. Perhaps she thought the words had been spoken out of revenge, or a cruel jest.

Patience schooled herself to show no emotion. Neither did she say anything more, one way or another. With only the sound of the wind rustling about them, the strange staring challenge continued until, at long last, Anne lowered her gaze.

A myriad of emotions flickered across Anne's face—fear, confusion, disbelief, and finally…acceptance. She lifted her graceful arms out to her sides and obviously saw for the first time not how she remembered herself but the way she appeared to others. Her body was now nothing more than a pale, willowy fog-like substance.

She touched the skirt of her faded pink gown and frowned at the assorted stains, small tears, and fraying about the hem. "I do not understand. What happened to me?"

Patience tried not to stare at the traces of blood on one side of Anne's face. Or, the ugly marks about her delicate neck—a certain sign someone had hastened the poor girl's death. Much as she wanted to voice her suspicions, Anne's emotions were in too fragile a state.

At the same time, the longer a lost soul wandered between worlds, the greater the chance it could be doomed to become an undulating, inhuman black mass or shadow figure—forever trapped in the netherworld. The thought made Patience shudder.

For someone as concerned with appearance and status as Anne had always been, she likely needed more time to grasp her situation. Broaching the subject of what could happen to her soul next must be handled with compassion and care.

In truth, an increasingly horrified Anne seemed more preoccupied with her hands than being dead. Always the mark of a true lady, once smooth and soft as a newborn kitten, they were marred by mud splotches, scratches, and ragged, dirty fingernails.

Obviously embarrassed, she covered one hand with the other. Her chin quivered, and tears rimmed her eyes.

The essence of Anne's spirit dimmed—a telling sign.

When spirits became frightened, despondent, or weak from expending too much energy to appear, their vaporous form shimmered. Next it would dissolve into a thin mist and disappear entirely. Unfortunately, not knowing how long ago Anne died meant each time she disappeared there remained a distinct possibility she might never have the strength to reappear.

Hopefully, Anne was overwrought with sadness.

Hopefully, she'd soon grasp her mortal life had ended.

Hopefully, the fact she'd found her way to Scotland and attached herself to Patience for help meant Anne's spirit would remain nearby for the time being.

Even if she was at times too weak to manifest.

"Anne", Patience said, her tone somewhat stern. "You must focus on our conversation; not fret about the way you look. We have much to discuss about returning to England. Every moment is precious."

With a slight nod, Anne looked up, her lifeless eyes now filled with the knowledge of all she had lost. "I daresay I need your help more than ever, Patience."

Later that evening, Patience lay abed, unable to sleep. Thunder rumbled. A woeful, highland wind moaned above the rhythm of freezing rain pounding against the roof. Sitting out in the fresh air earlier that day, she'd thought spring had come at last and now—*hail.*

But it wasn't the weather that kept her awake.

As the mantelpiece clock chimed three in the morning, Patience studied a gold brooch Auntie Catherine had given her in Scotland. Oval in shape, the brooch had a unique design. Cloisonné inlays of precious stones had been used to form a blue bird in flight. The bird, feathered wings outstretched, rested against a backing of what looked like ivory set in the gold base of the piece. Upon this ivory, words in black paint had been written in Gaelic. However, the position of the bird made the lettering impossible to read.

A heavy rim of gold surrounded the brooch. Positioned as if marking points of a compass were four leafs, each a deep reddish gemstone. Most intriguing about the brooch, however, was a gold-framed miniature painting situated at its center. Carried protectively by the bird, the miniature was not the face of a person, but a ladies' eye.

The eye's color was blue-gray with flecks of white. The subject's brow and long, feathery lashes looked to be ginger-brown, much like her own dark auburn. She felt a strange connection to the piece, as if a spiritual tether existed between her and the lady.

It could be an ancestor.

Auntie Catherine and her grandmother had been twins. Both had vibrant green eyes; thus, neither one could have posed for the artist. One day she'd ask about the woman and the brooch. For now, all she knew about the object was that Auntie Catherine had given it to her with somber, explicit instructions on how and when it was to be used.

"Freedom is not something one barters, my dear," Auntie Catherine had said. *"One day I pray you decide to reclaim your life. If so, I shall do whatever I can to help. If I am not at my residence, show this brooch to Josiah Whaley, my butler. 'Tis proof of your identity, as well as your plight. Know that I trust Whaley implicitly. He will protect your privacy, do your bidding, and keep you safe until I return. Remember, Patience, I will support your decision, but it must be your choice to leave your prison."*

Hoping her aunt had not changed her mind, Patience carefully placed the brooch inside an embroidered velvet drawstring bag. After setting it on her bedside table, she extinguished a candle then scrunched down beneath the bed covers. Her thoughts turned once more to Anne Melville and how far the young woman's spirit had journeyed. No ghost had sought her out from such a distance before.

"And there is no telling how long it took her to find me either."

"Is that all ye have tae say at this hour?"

With a heavenward roll of her eyes, Patience sat up and watched a tall figure rise from the recessed stone window seat and cross the room.

"I hate it when you do that," she said.

Dressed in the faded colors of his tartan kilt, Sam MacGregor stood beside the bed, his brawny arms folded across his chest. "I am vexed with ye, lass."

"Not that I am surprised, but why?"

"A woman-child shows up after bein' bluidy murdered and ye agree tae help her? Do ye ken what will happen if yer Sassenach stepfather finds ye in London? Did he nae threaten to put ye in Bedlam? Caileag, there is mór danger helpin' this girl. Ye may find yerself dead as well."

"I have no intention of getting myself killed, Sam."

"I'm thinkin' that young woman felt the same before someone choked the life out of her."

"Her name is Miss Anne Melville, and I am not *she*. I can take measures to protect myself. In truth, I am more concerned about the dead than the living in London."

"Och, and there's another thing. What do ye ken will happen when ye go traipsin' about with some wisp of a lost spirit girl? Everywhere ye go there'll be a head on a spike, people bein' drawn and quartered, nae to mention a hangin' or burnin' at the stake and foul demons a-chaisn' ye left and right."

"I will protect myself from all that." Patience pounded her pillow to form a more desirable shape. "Now, if you don't mind, I need to sleep. Go play your pipes or rattle some chains if you're bored. Better yet, why not find Miss Melville and talk to her?"

"And what would I be sayin' tae the likes of her?"

"You may find you have a lot in common."

"Because we're dead? Ye ken she's nae like me. We've nae a thing in common. Aye, I'm a ghost but able tae think and speak. I faced death with eyes open, lass. I made a sacred vow tae stay here and protect these lands and the MacGregors for all time. And I've been hauntin' these highlands doin' jest that."

"I know," she said in a half whisper. "You're a good and true Scot, Sam."

"Aye, with nae a thing tae say tae any English lass, livin' or dead. I dinnae ken why I talk tae ye half the time."

A bubble of laughter escaped Patience. "Oh, Sam, you love me and you know it."

"'Tis only because yer a Scot and blood relation, despite bein' raised in that land of butchers and devils."

"Goodnight, Sam."

"Listen tae me, caileag." He sat down on the edge of her bed, his large, battle-scarred hands clasped together. "I dinnae like this plan tae go tae London town. Stay here where I can keep ye safe."

"I must go. I believe everything that happened between me and Anne brought us to this moment. She needs my help to move on, and I need to stop hiding and have a life. Helping her is my chance to do that. I may not get another."

Grumbling under his breath, Sam stood. "Mark my words, nae good will come of it." He waved his arm, prompting a forceful, cold breeze to sweep across the room. "Willful and stubborn, 'tis what ye are."

"You could always come with us."

He paused before a stone wall and looked back at her with a '*have you sprouted six heads'* glare. "Heed me well, I died with my head on my shoulders. I've nae desire tae put foot on English soil now."

"I have it on the best authority you cannot die twice." She offered an encouraging smile. "You might even have fun tormenting those *bedeviled Sassenachs*."

"Bah", he said with a snort before vanishing.

Despite her feigned confidence, Patience could no longer hide her trembling once Sam left. More than anything, she wanted to block out the fearful images his words resurrected.

Why did I ever tell him about the horrors I saw as a child, especially in London.

So many ghosts roamed the ancient city, from haunted homes and palaces, to parks and churchyards. Unlike Sam, most of London's ghosts were not kind or good. Many had been corrupt in life, driven by greed, power, hatred, and often unrestrained rage. In death, they were no different, and sometimes worse. Relentlessly, they pursued her, unwilling to accept she could do nothing to help them.

With a shudder, Patience clutched her woolen blankets close. Despite the comforting scent of peat and warmth from the hearth in her bedchamber, a bitter chill permeated her soul.

Against her will, a floodgate of memories surfaced, along with never forgotten images of ghosts she'd encounter again in London…namely the *droch tannasg.*

Like a haunting piece of music that never ends, they were trapped souls, doomed to repeat terrible events or choices from their lives. Unable to interact with the living, they were found everywhere. They manifested without warning—terrifying scenes from a malevolent, gruesome play.

To not show any reaction to their sudden appearance, especially in public places, meant she must keep her guard up at all times. Still, there was little she could do to prepare for—or escape—the anguished cries and torturous screams that, more often than not, woke her from a sound sleep.

God help me. Will I be able to close my mind to it all?

Did she still have the focus, strength, and control necessary to stave off the onslaught of unwelcome sounds, sights, and spirits? For three years she'd had no need to use blocking techniques…not with Sam standing guard.

Evocative notes from Sam's piping echoed into the night. Her eyes grew heavy. Sleep came, and with it, a forgotten nightmare. Fragmented images and angry words from the past taunted, reminding Patience—even in slumber—not only of the dangers she'd soon face from ghosts and mortals, but of what she'd lost and the young man she still loved in vain.

Chapter 3

London, England – 03 May 1813

She was making too much noise. Had he a hand free, Tristan St. Ives, Viscount Leighton would cover her mouth and muffle the sound. Then again, with two hands free, he might simply strangle the woman.

What the blazes was she laughing about?

The woman had the most irritating witch-like cackle he'd ever heard. Perhaps she was mad.

Nothing was worth this, especially a quick tumble between the sheets with a woman he didn't know or care about. Besides which, the last thing he needed or wanted was another scandal. For all he knew, she might have some devious plot to be discovered with him. After all, there were still mourners below stairs, any one of whom might decide to investigate the unseemly sounds coming from the bedchamber of a lady who had buried her husband a few hours ago.

Women.

Determined to leave quickly as possible, Leighton stepped away, distancing himself from the groping woman.

"What are you doing?" Lady Masterson looked stunned.

"I should think it obvious," he answered, righting his clothing.

"I thought you intended to have your way with me."

"I came to my senses."

"Well," Lady Masterson replied with an indelicate snort. "I must say I find your behavior peculiar, if not insulting."

He stared at the widow for a moment. "Madam, might I remind you that your husband is barely cold in the grave?"

"All the more reason to celebrate," she said with an amused air, but quickly sobered. "If you must know, I loathed him. In truth, the very sight of Edgar disgusted me. Mind you, I behaved the perfect wife in public, but in private I delighted proving any man was better than him—even the lowliest servant among our staff. At first I did it to disgust him then realized how much I enjoyed the game. One time he caught me with two stable boys at the same time. I had hoped his discovery would kill the old sod on the spot."

"You are quite the dedicated slut, my dear."

"Do not pass judgment on me, Lord Leighton. No one has forgotten your public debacle with that deranged Sinclair girl. Or, the foul things she said about you. I am a young widow, and see nothing wrong with finding pleasure whenever I can. As for my dead husband, he got what he wanted—a young wife and an heir, although admittedly not by his seed. I daresay his friends thought him some kind of virile demigod to father a son at his age."

She sighed like a contented cat, caressing the full skirt of her mourning gown like a prized treasure. "Now he is dead…finally. I am rich, titled, and independent. And I intend to celebrate my freedom. Seeing you at my husband's funeral today was an unexpected surprise. I have been curious whether the praise about your skill as a lover is true. Alas, I shall have to let it be known you were *unable* to finish."

If there was one thing Leighton detested, it was being gossiped about in any fashion. Indeed, for the past three years he'd taken great pains to restructure his personal life with two objectives—to never lose his heart to another woman, and to avoid scandal of any sort.

"The word is *unwilling,* not unable, Lady Masterson. I happen to be very selective about the women I bed." With a crooked brow, he added, "Alas, *you* do not meet my standards."

The look she directed at him could have melted iron.

Without another word, he left her chamber, pleased to note servants nowhere about. Exiting the town house, he glanced at his coachman, noting how dour Sanderson looked before quickly averting his gaze.

About to step into his brougham, Leighton heard a strange sound, between a growl and a whimper. Looking to his right, he saw what appeared to be a large beast of some sort sitting on the doorstep of the stately pillared home next door.

What in God's name…

Curiosity got the better of him. Walking a few steps toward the house, he stopped short. The door opened, enough to allow the beast entry. He heard a woman say, "*Do hurry before he comes over here.*" The animal obediently entered the house, and the heavy door slammed shut, followed by the sound of the lock being bolted.

With a sardonic chuckle, Leighton turned back toward his carriage. "Fear not, madam, if I never look at another woman again it will be too soon for me."

Hand to her mouth, Patience listened as the carriage next door drove away. Of all the people in town she might have encountered so soon after her arrival, why had it been Viscount Leighton? Had he seen her, the man would have wasted little time informing her stepfather.

"Why do I not remember dying?" Anne asked with a petulant tone.

Patience turned about to see Anne pacing, oblivious to the disastrous close call that had almost happened.

"You will in time." Patience returned to the drawing room. Anne accompanied, causing an icy chill to sweep down Patience's spine.

"Anne, you will tell me if you remember anything, whether you think it important or not?"

Her spectral guest nodded, but there was in Anne's expression a quality that seemed somewhat suspicious. Had Anne also seen Leighton departing from the neighboring house? And, if so, did she remember anything about the dashing friend of her brother, Charles?

Best to think of something else. I do not want to discuss Leighton with anyone, least of all Anne.

Instead, Patience studied the street map opened on a writing desk. "I daresay this hackney map is a godsend. All of London lies unfolded before me. I shall be able to find my way about town without assistance."

"Why did I not go to heaven, Patience?"

Anne's question lingered like the tolling of a bell, expectantly waiting for Patience to respond. But 'twas not in her power to understand why some spirits did not move on immediately after death. For certain, many found peace and paradise the moment they took their final breath, or soon afterwards. At the same time, there were spirits who lingered, wandering aimlessly, and others who deserved to never find peace.

Keeping her back to Anne, Patience folded the map, careful to follow the various pleats and creases in the stiff linen fabric.

"Patience, did you hear me?"

Aware she had to respond, Patience delicately cleared her throat. "Some spirits remain earthbound because they want to; others linger because there is something they must do first."

"Well, I have *no* desire to *linger,* and think it most unfair I must perform some *task*. I should like to go to heaven straightaway."

Patience bit her bottom lip, half-tempted to tell Anne that being temperamental, demanding, or haughty was not the key to paradise.

Placing the now pocket-sized folded map into its protective case, Patience decided it best, for the moment, to change the subject. 'Twas then she heard Anne laugh. Turning about she found the fair-haired spirit pointing at Henrietta.

"How is it that your dog sees me?"

"Dogs are very observant."

"I did notice in Scotland that first day how she stared at me."

"In actual fact, she knew of your presence before I did. Dogs often see spirits, cats as well. They have keen senses of sight, smell, and hearing. They also observe things humans never take the time to notice. I must admit, Henrietta is exceedingly intuitive, especially for a puppy."

"She's a puppy?"

Patience laughed at the wide-eyed expression of her ghost guest. "Yes, and you should be flattered. Henrietta finds you interesting. As a rule, she does not like ghosts."

"There's a blessing." Anne wiggled her fingers at the black wolfhound. Returning her attention to Patience, she sighed. "So, what must I do to *not* linger here longer than necessary?"

"Do not forget we have only just arrived in town." Patience motioned for Anne to join her on the sofa. "We have a mystery to solve. Unfortunately, we are hindered by two rather large problems. Your memory has been severely affected, making it difficult to piece together what happened to you. And I must not be seen by anyone who might tell my family I am in town—at least until Lady Carlyle returns."

"Then, how do we proceed?"

"Since the last thing you remember is running away from the London home of your parents, we will begin our search there. I must gain access to your bedchamber and look for clues."

"What if we cannot find any?"

"I am confident the first piece to the puzzle will be found at your home."

"How can you be so sure?"

"Shall I tell her, Henrietta?" Patience smiled as her dog rested its large head in her lap. She kissed its brow. "Because besides being able to see ghosts, I often see images when I touch an object that belonged to another. In this case, things that belonged to you. You might have saved an item gifted to you from the man you ran away to meet that night. Perhaps you wrote in a diary about him as well."

When there was no reply, Patience looked to see Anne's ghostly image shimmering, beginning to fade. "Anne, did you keep a diary?"

"I cannot remember." Anne rubbed her brow, clearly losing strength to remain visible. "I suppose it is possible."

"Then tomorrow we shall sneak into your family home in Mayfair. Whaley made enquiries. Your parents have retired to their country estate, perhaps for the entire Season. Since the town house is closed, we can conduct our search with no one the wiser."

"That's nice..." Anne's voice faded into a whisper as she vanished from sight. Henrietta circled the sofa then sniffed the spot where the spirit had been sitting.

"Come, Henrietta," Patience cooed then hugged her dog's neck for its obedience. "I doubt we shall see Anne again before morning."

Chapter 4

Mayfair, London

Patience tried not to consider what might happen should she be discovered in the darkened, unoccupied town house of the Melville family. She doubted a constable would believe the door magically opened. Neither would he believe she could see—and speak with—ghosts.

Holding a flickering candle, she followed one such spirit up the staircase. An intimidating array of somber portraits covered the wall to her right. Without question, Anne's ancestors had perfected the art of looking haughty and disapproving.

Why does no one smile in their portrait?

Had their sour countenance been suggested by the artist, or had they looked down on people in life as their image now did on canvas?

"What are you staring at?"

Patience had paused on the stairs before the portrait of an old man. With a slight shrug she turned to Anne. "I was wondering what he would look like if he smiled."

"I doubt any of them ever smiled." Anne continued to drift down the hallway.

Patience looked again at the portrait, "I bet you wish you had smiled more now."

A few moments later, she stood with the ghostly figure of Miss Melville in the center of what had been Anne's bedroom.

"It's just as I left it," Anne said.

"Often 'tis too painful for the family to touch anything, and they seal up the room." Patience circled the bedchamber, holding her candle aloft to chase away shadows and examine the room's contents.

From imported silk wallpaper with a delicate cherry blossom pattern, to the lush carpet and draperies, the room was charming and welcoming.

The bed linens looked clean and inviting. A recessed window seat still held a book Anne must have been reading before she ran away.

Patience crossed to Anne's dressing table, noting an assortment of delicate fragrance bottles and a shiny, polished silver toilette service. Picking up a hairbrush, she closed her eyes a moment then put it back where it belonged.

A startling revelation came to mind.

"This isn't the untouched shrine to a dead daughter's memory," she said in a half-whisper. "This room is waiting for you, Anne."

"What do you mean, waiting for me?" The irritated tone in Anne's voice prompted Patience to turn toward the spirit.

Patience gentled her voice and manner. "What I mean is that I do not think your parents know about your death. I suspect they left your room this way hoping you might come home during their absence."

"They must know I am dead. They *must*." Anne swept about the room, conjuring a cold breeze in her wake.

Icy tremors skittered down Patience's spine. She studied the woman's vaporous image. "The only explanation is that you are still missing to them. In truth, I suspect no one knows what happened to you except me—and the person who might have caused your death."

"You mean I was m-murdered?"

"Possibly. I do know someone hurt you badly."

The immediate high-pitched shrieking of Anne's voice prompted Patience to grimace and distance herself from the spirit. She hadn't intended to state the matter so bluntly, but the sooner they exposed the truth, the easier it would be to help Anne.

Crossing to the window seat, Patience made a pretense of examining the book of sonnets. In truth, she surreptitiously studied Anne's demeanor and movements, waiting for the ghost's mercurial mood to calm.

In short order, the room's temperature eased to a comfortable degree. Patience returned the book back to its original position then looked up with a start to see Anne hovering over her.

"Is it because I do not remember what happened to me that I have not gone to heaven?"

"Whether your injury caused your death or not, I do not know. And since we have no idea where your death happened…or when…it is imperative I help you remember as quickly as possible."

"Why is it imperative?"

Patience had to impress upon Anne the need to make haste, but the unpredictability of the ghost's behavior and her lack of control, conjured all manner of doubt. They should have had this conversation at Carlyle House, but she'd hoped Anne would remember more returning to her parents' home.

I have to tell her now. There is no other way.

Patience released a weary sigh. "The longer you do not remember what happened, the less you will ever remember. And the greater the chance your soul shall be lost forever."

"I don't want to remember someone killing me."

"You must, Anne. He is still out there. I daresay he thinks he has gotten away with what he did to you. What if he kills again? Surely, you want him punished. God forbid another girl should suffer your fate."

Anne did not respond, her expression disinterested.

Recollecting how selfish Anne had often been in life, Patience opted to try another tactic. "Do you not want your body found? Unless you remember, we cannot prove you are dead, or help your family to understand what happened to you."

"This is so unfair. You mean to say not only was I killed by some horrid fiend, but I did not have a funeral? My b-body has been hidden somewhere? Tossed aside like so much rubbish?"

"I am so sorry, Anne."

"You have to find me!" Terror laced Anne's voice as she went over to her dressing table. She peered into the looking glass; the reflection of a gaunt, pale image stared back. She covered her face with her hands and wept. "My parents must know what happened to me. You have to find me so they can bury me in a churchyard."

"I will, with your help." Patience joined Anne at the dressing table, and set the candlestick upon the polished surface. As she began opening drawers, searching for anything that might help discover who Anne ran away to meet, the mist-like spirit wandered away toward the bed.

Patience wanted to be kind, but must impress upon Anne that she needed help. "As I said, we have no time to lose. Until you remember, I need clues. This is your room, so any assistance you can give me would be most appreciated. I daresay this will likely be the only opportunity I have to search here. Did you have any secret hiding places?"

When she heard no reply, Patience looked up to see that Anne had vanished again. "For heaven's sake, now is not the time to leave me alone trespassing in your family's home."

Finding nothing in the dressing table, Patience began a more thorough but careful search of the room, trying to think where Anne might have hidden something from prying eyes. She'd already examined the book of sonnets. No inscription from an admirer; no love note pressed within the pages for safekeeping.

Remembering her grandmother favored tucking important papers behind the frame of a painting, Patience searched the art work. She also used her second sight to visualize an object's significance, but to no avail.

She pressed a hand to the small of her back and looked about the room a final time, her gaze coming to rest upon an ornate French wardrobe. Curiously, the beautiful, richly carved columns on the outer side of each door held her attention. At the top of each column were gold winged cherubs. They seemed to beckon.

Moving a chair in front of the wardrobe, she stood upon the seat to better study the cherubs, and found the left one turned slightly. Even more compelling, a current of heat sparked through her fingertips by touching the cherub. Clearly, Anne had turned the object many times.

With a click, a shallow drawer opened from the bottom left side of the wardrobe. Inside the drawer she found a gentleman's riding glove, and several letters tied with a gold ribbon. Though anxious to examine the objects, now was not the time or place. Removing Anne's secret cache, she closed the drawer.

Placing the items on the bed, she returned the chair to its place before Anne's writing desk. Blowing a stray curl out of her face, she retrieved the man's glove and bundle of letters. Just then she heard a heavy door opening and closing below stairs, followed by murmured, deep voices. Not dead voices either.

Her racing heart pounded. Afraid to breathe, she stood motionless. A quick glance to the dressing table reminded the lit candle would expose her presence in the house. Masculine laughter prompted her to look back at the still open bedchamber door.

Please don't come upstairs.

From what she could ascertain, there were two men. Since Anne's parents were definitely at their country home, one of the men must be her brother, Charles.

What are they doing? It sounded like they were walking about from room to room. *Oh, dear God!* Was it possible Charles had come by to check on the house? And if so, he would surely come upstairs and find the door to his sister's bedchamber open.

Considering her options, Patience glanced about the room for a place to hide. The best place was under the bed. There simply wasn't time to go anywhere else.

First, she had to get the candle and extinguish it, then hide and pray she'd not be discovered. Grateful the room had a large Turkish carpet she tiptoed to the dressing table. With each step she listened for creaks in the floorboards that might echo downstairs.

Still holding the contents from Anne's secret drawer, she balanced the candlestick in one hand and returned to the bed—opting for the side farthest away from the door. Forcing back nausea, she blew out the candle and slowly lowered herself to the floor.

Inch by inch, Patience maneuvered her body under the bed, holding fast to the items with one hand and the dripping candlestick in the other.

Remaining still as possible, she closed her eyes and waited. Either she would be discovered and handed over to the magistrate, or she would safely leave the house after the gentlemen departed.

Footsteps sounded in the hall. They were coming.

"Ho, what's this? Anne's bedchamber door is open." Charles Melville's voice seemed to echo like a cannon blast.

His companion murmured an expletive.

Suddenly, she knew they stood at the threshold.

"For a moment, I thought…"

"I know," replied a masculine voice she'd not heard in years. "Perhaps she was here. Is anything missing?"

Patience blinked back tears, aware her heart had somehow leapt to her throat. For the second time since arriving back in London, the threat of discovery by Tristan St. Ives, Viscount Leighton, threatened.

After all she'd said and done to him, the man would waste no time exacting revenge and sealing her fate in Bedlam. Yet the tears rising from the depths of her soul were not caused by fear, but by the certain knowledge the one person she loved most in the world hated her.

With a hush of movement, a man entered the room—presumably Charles Melville. Though only able to see his boots, Patience watched as he walked about the room, pausing every so often. "No, nothing looks disturbed—nothing at all."

Leighton entered. "Do you smell something?"

"Just the wax from my candle," Anne's brother replied.

"No, there's a scent I have not encountered in…" Leighton's voice trailed off, not completing his remark. Gruffly, he cleared his throat. Slow, steady steps crossed to the dressing table. "Perhaps it is a perfume your sister used."

Patience heard what sounded like both men examining the French and Venetian glass objects on the dressing table, obviously looking for an item that matched the scent.

"This is ridiculous. I don't smell anything, and I cannot stand being in this room. If my scandalous, spoiled sister decided to pay her room a visit in secret, I no longer care. The house is secure; 'tis all that matters to me."

"Did you hear what he said?"

Patience almost screamed as she turned her head quickly and saw the ghostly figure of Anne Melville beside her under the bed. Thankfully, the men had already left the room. Conversing about horses and going to Tattersall's, their voices became nothing more than faint masculine murmurings. Shortly thereafter, they left the house altogether. Only then did Patience come out from her hiding place. Whether her trembling had been caused by fear of discovery in the Melville home or coming face-to-face with her lost love, she did not know.

Setting the items and candlestick on a nearby table, Patience sat on the bed. Cradling her head in her hands, she tried to stop shaking and think. She then pinned Anne with a stern look. "Do you realize what might have happened if they had found me here? Where did you go? You cannot leave me like that. If you want me to help you, you must help me in return. Do you understand?"

With a sheepish expression, Anne nodded.

"Good."

"But did you hear what my brother said about me?"

Standing, refusing to be bated to lose her temper, Patience gathered the glove and letters she'd found, as well as the candlestick, and walked over to the doorway. "Yes, I heard what he said."

"Well, I find his behavior abominably cruel. After all, even if he thinks I have run away with no intention of ever returning, one still wants to be missed by one's family. And it is even more distressing because…well…I'm dead."

"Charles does not know you're dead, Anne. I am sure he misses you, even though he may be angry with you for running away."

"Well, I certainly hope so."

Practically hugging the wall in the dark, Patience descended the staircase. "Let us please concentrate on getting out of here without any more surprises. All I want right now is to be back at Carlyle House."

Once downstairs, Patience hesitated at the front door. "On second thought, perhaps we should take the servants entrance out." Glancing at Anne, she found her twirling around as if dancing with an invisible partner.

Patience cleared her throat to gain the easily distracted spirit's attention. "Anne, do remember to lock the door after I leave."

Chapter 5

The last thing Patience expected to find departing the Melville town house was dense fog blanketing London and, in particular, Mayfair. To be certain, it helped obscure her from being seen by other residents—or anyone out and about at such an ungodly hour of the night. Unfortunately, the thick mist also made it difficult to find Auntie Catherine's carriage waiting on a nearby street…that is, unless it had been chased off by a constable.

Adjusting the full hood of her woolen cloak, she tried to get her bearings once more, but panic had a foothold on her heart.

"Might I be of assistance?"

Hearing the disembodied voice of the enquiring gentleman, Patience struggled for breath. Indeed, it seemed every bit of air inside her lungs had been seized. An instinct for self-preservation enabled her to remain standing until precious air returned. Still, she kept her back to the man, regardless how rude her behavior must seem to Viscount Leighton.

What was *he* doing walking the streets of Mayfair?

For that matter, was Charles Melville still with him?

She took a few steps away, needing to create a greater distance then turned to face Leighton. He stood alone. She also realized if the fog prevented her from seeing his face, neither could he identify her.

"I cannot find my carriage." She tried to disguise her voice.

"Little wonder at that," he answered with a low chuckle. "I take it you do not live in Mayfair?"

"No, I was visiting a friend's house."

"Your carriage was not waiting when you departed?" He took a couple steps toward her.

"No." She took two steps backward. "I—I, that is to say, my driver must have misunderstood my instructions."

"Then you must permit me to escort you home. I know where my carriage is and…Good God, is that a *wolf*?"

Patience spun around to see a large, four-legged creature galloping toward her in the fog and now misting rain. She knew of only one animal with that powerful yet graceful gait. "No, not a wolf," she said with a sigh of relief. "My dog."

"*That* is your dog?"

"Yes", she replied distractedly, narrowing her gaze to identify someone else in the distance. A man, bobbing lantern in hand, appeared to be chasing after Henrietta.

"Come back 'ere, ye filthy beast or I'll make a rug outta ya!"

"And *there* is my driver," she said, unable to suppress a soft laugh as an uncultured accent roared through the privileged serenity of Mayfair. Glancing back at Leighton, she noted he now stood with hands resting on his hips, reminding her of a temperamental sea captain on the bridge of a lost ship.

Henrietta slid to a clumsy stop by Patience's side, and she lovingly petted her faithful friend. "It appears my rescue is at hand, but I do thank you for offering to assist me. Good evening."

He said nothing in response.

Realizing her lantern-carrying driver would soon be upon them, providing enough light for Leighton to see her face, Patience turned away and swiftly walked toward the driver.

"Is that ye, miss?" Ben Owens asked, clearly winded from giving chase to her dog.

"Yes, Ben." She spoke in a whisper, and motioned for the driver to turn around. "We must depart quickly, before that man discovers who I am."

Leighton watched the retreating trio until the night and fog enveloped them like a forgotten dream. And yet, sometimes dreams like distant, painful memories return to haunt a person.

The scent he'd noticed in Anne Melville's room had provoked his memory, so much so that he'd decided to clear his head by taking a walk alone in the fog. Now, breathing fast and hard, he questioned his sanity. Indeed, it took several moments to recover from whirling thoughts and his strange encounter with a woman all but obscured by fog and a deeply hooded cloak. Even when the racing of his heart and the clenching of his gut subsided, he could not quell his confusion and anger.

He hadn't recognized her, not at first, not until he'd heard her soft laugh. Unwelcome emotions surfaced, along with a question he wanted answered with keen desperation.

What the blazes is Patience Sinclair doing back in London?

Chapter 6

Carlyle House, London

Alone, seated at the highly polished mahogany table in the dining room of Carlyle House, tears blurred Patience's vision as she finished reading the bundle of letters taken from the secret drawer of Anne Melville's French wardrobe. A shaky hand pressed against quivering lips attempted to silence uncontrollable sobs.

The depth of cruelty Anne possessed pierced her heart again. This time she didn't think she'd recover…or be able to forgive.

Nine letters addressed to her from Leighton had somehow been intercepted by Anne Melville. Opened and read by the very girl she now tried to help. Not only had Anne taken the letters, she'd hoarded them away.

Letters where Leighton beseeched Patience to help him understand what happened, what *he* had done to deserve her scorn and contempt. Letters where he said he loved her still, and cared not what others thought…not if she loved him in return. All he asked for was to understand.

For three years she'd thought he had abandoned her, like her family and everyone else. The pain of those lost years consumed her now, as well as the knowledge that no response to his beautiful, thoughtful letters must have hurt him even more than her words that fateful day. Indeed, his last two letters were filled with anger, claiming her continued silence revealed how unworthy she'd ever been of his affection.

If only I received one of the letters…just one.

She'd always suspected Anne fancied Leighton, but never knew to what degree. Now, she understood. Anne wanted the viscount for herself, and took steps to ensure victory. Not only did the fair Miss Melville betray their friendship, she'd set a trap for a romantic rival that resulted in public ridicule and ruin for Patience.

With a shuddering breath, Patience wiped her face dry with a handkerchief. She then picked up the riding glove, yet saw no vision of its owner. It bore no identifiable initials, but a number and symbol of two overlapping circles were embroidered inside the cuff. Judging from the size of the item, it might belong to Leighton.

A sudden thought prompted Patience to drop the glove. She stared at the items on the table anew. Was Leighton the man Anne ran away to meet? Did he kill her?

No, it couldn't be.

The man she loved would not harm a woman. Besides which, Anne showed no reaction to Leighton's presence tonight.

Then again, if she doesn't remember what happened, she might not react to the identity of her killer…especially at first sight.

Much as Patience hated to admit it, the only clue about the man Anne had run away with pointed to Leighton.

An ensuing argument between her heart and head made Patience realize she had to find out the truth, one way or another.

Gathering the letters together, she refastened the gold ribbon about them. She'd not seen Anne since being inside the Melville home hours ago, a blessing really since she didn't want to see or speak with the spiteful ghost right now. The pain of Anne's treachery was too raw. In truth, were the ghost of her tormentor to appear now, she'd be sorely tempted to tell Anne to expect no more assistance from her.

Instead, Auntie Catherine's beautiful Ormolu twin branch crystal candelabra captured her attention. The steady flame from four candles, each staggered in height, reflected in the polished surface of the table. Feather-shaped prisms dangled from diamond-cut crystal pan bases. She lightly stroked the prisms, creating a soft tinkling sound, delicate and beautiful. With the crystal's movement, candlelight briefly danced about the shadows of the room.

In many ways, candlelight dancing through shadows symbolized life. People failed to realize how quickly, often without warning, life's light could be extinguished. Even now, she remembered all the faces of spirits she'd helped since childhood, from children to elderly people, commoners to nobility, all lost souls caught between two worlds. Yet never before had the compassion to help someone lost been challenged by such a strong desire to walk away.

Why should I help Anne, knowing the lengths she took to destroy me and my relationship with Leighton?

"Miss Sinclair?"

Patience looked up to see Whaley standing beside her, his white gloved hands clasped together. Judging from his concerned expression, no doubt she looked a fright with puffy, red-rimmed eyes.

“Yes, Whaley.”

“Is there anything I can do for you, Miss? It is very late; perhaps you should get some rest now.”

“Yes, ‘tis very late,” she said. “It may be far too late.”

Not wanting to alarm Auntie Catherine’s butler any more than she had already—especially with her late night excursion to Mayfair—she tried to smile. “Thank you for your concern, Whaley. I *am* very tired.” She picked up the bundle of letters and glove. “Has there been any word when Lady Carlyle will return?”

“No, Miss, but I am sure she will be here as soon as possible.”

“Yes, yes, I’m sure she will.” Wanting nothing more than to go to bed, she crossed the dining room. At the threshold, she looked back at the butler. “Goodnight, Whaley.”

“Goodnight, Miss,” he replied softly.

Patience started to ascend the elegant staircase of Carlyle House when an otherworldly freezing breeze swept about her, one usually associated with an angry ghost. With a shudder, she noticed her breath lifted into the suddenly icy air on a small cloud. Expecting to see Anne, she looked over her shoulder. The entry hall with its white and black marble floor appeared empty.

Still, she sensed a spirit hovered nearby. One strong enough to break through the protective barrier she’d created with her mind then placed about the house. The notion worried her. She needed Carlyle House to be shielded. Otherwise, any ghost or malevolent spirit could enter to disturb her privacy and peace of mind. Not to mention the fear and mischief they could cause Auntie Catherine and the household staff.

She continued up the stairs, but her gaze returned with a will of its own to search the walls and dark corners. Another thought came to mind; one she hadn’t considered before.

What if Carlyle House has a ghost of its own? One clever and powerful enough to remain quiet and hidden until now?

Emotionally and physically exhausted, Patience directed her thoughts toward nothing more than rest as she prepared for bed. She all but collapsed into the comfort of lavender scented fine linen sheets and silk-embroidered covers, the bundle of Leighton's letters once more clutched in her hands.

It did not take long before she slipped into a deep yet fretful sleep.

Cruel laughter and angry voices surrounded her. A thousand memories, stirred by an angry tempest, returned like thunderous waves upon an unforgiving, rocky shoreline.

Again and again, she protested against harsh accusations, still so fresh and real in her dreams that she spoke aloud in sleep.

I am not mad, she moaned.

Her judge and jury loomed before her in memory as he had three years ago in life. A black eye patch enhanced Lord Henley's stern countenance. Both arms folded across his broad chest, her stepfather resembled a one-eyed pirate about to tell a member of his crew to walk the plank. To crown and country he was a respected hero of the Royal Navy, but not to her.

From the moment he'd first entered her life, two years to the day after the death of her father, Henley had been a heartless monster with never a word of kindness. For as far back as she remembered he'd always looked upon her in a cold, disapproving manner. An attitude neither time nor distance would amend.

He'd always resented how close Patience had been to her mother. In harsh tones he'd often accused her of being an over-indulged, most *peculiar* child, and wasted no time proclaiming his theory to others. Whereas her mother had smiled and loved to hear stories about the special friends her little daughter had found—friends no one else saw or heard—Henley found it unseemly and vastly annoying.

Time and again he ordered her mother not to indulge such fantasies. "Do you not see your actions serve only to give the child permission to lie and deceive?"

Relentless, he repeated his judgmental viewpoint until her mother agreed and became more distant from her firstborn child.

Fearful of losing her mother's love and desperate to find approval in her stepfather's eyes, Patience tried to adapt to her family's expectations. But as her tenuous control and ability to communicate with ghosts increased, there were times when concealing her reaction to their sudden presence proved impossible.

Matters worsened when her mother and Henley focused on their own family—a son and three daughters incapable of doing anything wrong in their father's eyes.

"You do not understand," Patience cried out in sleep, returned in memory to the time when Lord Henley issued his threatening proclamation then severed her ties to the family. "It wasn't my fault. You must listen to me."

He glared at Patience with nothing but loathing then looked to her mother with an '*I told you this would happen*' look. The expression on her mother's face conveyed there would be no plea for mercy on her behalf. No softly spoken words to appease Lord Henley's temper.

"You have embarrassed us for the last time," Henley bit out. "Your behavior has not only scandalized my family, but the man who—for whatever reason—considered you might be worthy of marriage. No more, I say! You will leave this house and not return. Do you understand? I want you out of our lives."

"Where am I to go?"

"Your grandmother bequeathed a property to you in Scotland, such as it is in the wilds of that heathen land. You will stay there until such time as *I* decide you may return to England...if ever."

"You are banishing me?"

"Indeed I am. Have I not warned you for years to stop this propensity for drama and attention? Each time you make a fool of yourself in public this family suffers the consequences. Half the *Beau Monde* believed you mad, as I have long suspected. This latest debacle, in a churchyard no less, has now caused *everyone* to see the truth."

"Mother, surely you do not agree with this?" She tried to stem the tears pooling in her eyes, but to no avail. "Do you also want to send me a-away?"

Lady Henley looked down, unable or unwilling to respond.

"Do not seek intervention from your mother!" Lord Henley bellowed. "Not even a mother's love can save you. Our concern now is for the reputation of this family, and the future of your siblings."

"But you do not understand," Patience cried. "I have tried. I have tried so very hard."

"Balderdash!" he shouted. "Your outlandish, absurd behavior has worsened since coming to town, dashing our hope you might redeem yourself, and one day secure an advantageous alliance. The only measure that can turn the tide for this family's future is for you to go far away until such time as this ugly scandal has been forgotten...if ever."

"How long must I be exiled?"

"Until I see fit to allow your return," he said with a curled lip. "Living a solitary existence will teach you the importance of decorum, if not duty to one's family and reputation. I have great aspirations for my family and you will not destroy them."

"Please, allow me to explain what happened."

"You will leave immediately for Scotland," he continued, dismissing her plea. "Do not correspond with anyone in this family. Neither will they communicate with you. From this day forth, consider yourself a prisoner of Scotland by your own doing. Under no circumstance are you to return to England without my permission. Disobey me and I will see you tossed into Bedlam for the remainder of your life."

Patience woke with a start, her face wet with tears. Over and over in her mind she heard the words, '*tossed into Bedlam for the remainder of your life*'.

The threat echoed, reverberating to the depths of her soul.

She sat upright in bed, immediately looking about the large, darkened bedchamber at Carlyle House for Henrietta, but her pup wasn't there.

Alone and friendless, she questioned the sanity of returning to England and the vow to help Anne Melville. What would happen if her family learned of her escape?

The longer it took for Lady Carlyle to return, the greater the risk of discovery. As kind and helpful as Auntie Catherine's servants had been, Patience remained wary about them, and what they must think of her odd behavior.

"I have no one," she whispered.

"Nae, caileag," said a familiar voice. "Ye have me."

From the shadows on the far side of the room, the tall, ghostly figure of Sam MacGregor walked toward her. He stopped beside the bed, arms folded across his chest, and shook his head. "Here less than a fortnight and already the Sassenachs have ye in tears."

Her throat closed tight with emotion, touched beyond measure that Sam had come to England. "You were the ghost I sensed on the stairs?" she managed to ask.

"Aye."

Wiping the halting tears away with her hands, she sniffled. "What made you change your mind?"

"Hearin' ye weep, and the thought of ye bein' outnumbered. I may nae be able tae protect ye much against mortals but should any foul Sassenach spirits try tae harm ye, them I can dispatch."

Patience nodded, and studied the Scotsman thoughtfully. Even as a ghost, Sam had such a vibrant aura. A strong, shimmering sapphire and white light outlined his body and face like a halo. Without question he must have been a handsome man in life—tall and strong as an oak with somewhat long, dark, wavy hair. His eyes were brown, heavily lashed, and expressive.

What had he been like when alive? Had he always been so serious, stubborn and willful? A warrior who loved his clan and Scotland more than life or death. Did he ever fall in love, or had death intervened?

In many respects, Sam had become her dearest friend and almost a guardian angel. How would she ever be able to thank him for the years he'd kept her sane in Scotland? Though often gruff and moody, especially when she'd first arrived at *Ceòthar Innis*, he'd been the only person—living or dead—who'd remained constantly by her side during the darkest moments of her despair.

She smiled through misty eyes. "Well then, perhaps you can keep an eye on Miss Melville. She keeps disappearing on me. I fear she may be weaker than I thought and disappear altogether before this task is finished."

"She lingers…in her fashion," he replied. "Are ye wantin' tae speak tae her now?"

"No," she said, somewhat heatedly. "I cannot bear to look at her, let alone speak with her."

"Aye." He nodded with a grim expression. "Death never changes a person's soul, caileag. The way they were in life is what ye find in the spirit that remains behind…be they good, kind, cruel, bad, or jest selfish, deceitful, and spoiled."

"I daresay I have only now come to realize how truly selfish and spoiled Miss Melville was in life. Had I known the lengths she took to destroy my reputation and happiness, I do not think I could have agreed to help her or return to England."

"Then let us leave this place." He spoke with urgency, sitting down upon the edge of her bed, his large hands clasped together. "Mayhap 'tis her fate tae wander the netherworld, or become a *droch dubhar*?"

"Sam, I cannot wish *that* fate upon anyone, not even Anne Melville."

"Then what will ye have me do? How can I help?"

"Stay close," she answered. "So far I've been able to block foul spirits from approaching me or entering this house, but I need you to follow or watch Miss Melville. I cannot help but doubt her honesty now. Part of me believes she is sincere and truly needs my help. She may also be playing me false, wanting to destroy me in death as she tried to in life."

Chapter 7

He had been watching the raven-haired creature from the moment she arrived. Spoiled, selfish and beautiful, the young woman pouted prettily in the midst of eager admirers.

The so-called Dandies all vied for her attention, beside themselves with lust as she pouted seductively and made each one think she wanted him.

Judging from the way she glanced about the room, more than once pausing overlong to return his admittedly intrigued gaze, the lady calculated what men in attendance might be worthy candidates for her affections. The criteria required three things: an impressive title, wealth, and suitable properties.

She looked at him again, a rather brazen, lingering gaze.

Did she really think him just another besotted male, admiring her beauty? Basking in the unspoken promise of breathless, passionate surrender and flirtatious gestures she'd obviously practiced to wield so skillfully?

It never ceased to amaze him how greedy and ambitious some ladies were these days.

He'd observed this one for weeks now, not the least surprised to find her here tonight. Despite the confidence of her smiles and the female charm she affected so well, she was clearly not content—nor would she ever be. He knew her kind too well.

She recognized the power she had and would stop at nothing to get what she wanted for her future. As such, she turned her greedy mind toward whatever specimen caught her eye. Some poor fool who would embody everything she wanted in life—at least for the moment.

Pity, with so many dashing soldiers off to War, the number of eager young men available to secure the beauty's interest proved rather limited. No matter. For whatever the reason, he'd definitely captured her attention tonight.

He'd been careful to keep a distance, aware a cloud of mystery and danger surrounded him—not to mention a certain amount of rumor, most of which proved salacious. Most women, no matter the age, found those qualities intoxicating and very seductive.

On the one hand, he was considered young and handsome, connected to a magnificent world that most only dreamt about. On the other hand, within that world, he simply didn't exist. Even should society deem to see him in their midst, he was someone whose very presence had always been ignored.

Much like one might forget to notice a dog sleeping nearby, half cast in shadow. Little did they know how very much this sleeping dog—when wakened—liked to hunt, bite, and kill.

His prey watched him now, breathless, captivated by what she thought she saw in his returning gaze, even from across the room.

Not yet, he thought to himself. My overtures have only begun. There were still a great many preparations to be made. Then, like the other foolish girl, this delicious morsel would eagerly come to him, only to discover the fate of spoiled, selfish beauties who flirted with the devil's spawn.

With a courtly bow, he smiled, his gaze never leaving hers. Her answering blush was all the reply he needed…for now.

Chapter 8

Hoping to not attract attention, Patience adjusted the hood of her cloak and departed the shop on St. James, the stalwart presence of Sam by her side. As she'd feared, the glove found in Anne's hidden drawer belonged to Viscount Leighton.

Strange her second sight had not seen Leighton when holding his glove. A soft breeze stirred the air as she folded the pliant leather article and placed it inside her reticule.

She looked up to find Anne Melville across the street, standing outside a tobacconist's shop and flirting in vain with every mortal man.

"Ach, will ye look at the foolish English miss bein' a bluidy nuisance, and on a public thoroughfare. I dinnae ken why ye chose to help that one."

"I ask myself the same thing most every day," Patience whispered under her breath. No sooner had she finished speaking than Anne met her gaze then floated across the street on an unseen current.

"There you are," Anne said with a giddy smile. "I have been looking all over for you. I must say, there is no shortage of attractive men frequenting their clubs today. One walked right through me!"

Still angry over Anne's theft of Leighton's letters, Patience bit her tongue, not wanting to lash out in public at a spirit no one else saw.

Glancing about, Patience saw several gentlemen had taken note of her presence. Little wonder; after all, she was a young lady unaccompanied on a street with no less than three gentlemen's clubs. For heaven's sake, the bow window of White's was a stone's throw away.

Chin lowered, she looked inside her reticule, pretending to search for something. "I cannot speak with you now. Return to Carlyle House and await me there."

"Are you following me, Miss Sinclair?"

Startled out of her wits, Patience spun around to see Viscount Leighton glaring down at her. His heavily lashed eyes were as green as she remembered. Tall, several inches over six feet, he looked handsome as ever. The perfect symmetry of his face and form could well be found on a Grecian statue. With broad shoulders, a slender waist, and long limbs, she tried not to drink in the sight of him. How often she had dreamt about him in Scotland, of seeing his dimpled smile and the twinkle that so often came to his eyes. Now, however, his gaze was hard and cold.

Remembering her manners, she curtsied slightly. "Good day, Lord Leighton." Her voice trembled slightly. "I do not understand what you mean. Following you?"

His gaze narrowed; his jaw visibly clenched. "You know exactly what I mean." His voice lowered and sounded tense with controlled rage.

Whereas Sam studied Leighton with a suspicious expression, for some strange reason Anne Melville decided to take that moment to stand beside the viscount and make silly faces as if mocking the man. Her behavior was most odd, not to mention distracting.

"I am waiting for an answer, Miss Sinclair."

Returning her attention to Leighton, Patience softly cleared her throat. "I—I had some errands to run this morning. One of them brought me to St. James Street."

"And what errand brought you to Mayfair last night?" He removed a box from the pocket of his waistcoat.

"Mayfair? Why ever would I be in Mayfair?"

Sam threw up his hands with obvious exasperation, shaking his head at her lame attempt to lie. Grumbling under his breath, her guardian ghost walked away to lean against a storefront. Her other distraction, the amused-with-herself Miss Anne Melville continued to imitate Leighton in an absurd, silly schoolgirl manner.

As for his lordship, rather than pinch off a bit of snuff, Leighton paused then targeted Patience with a hard stare. "I suspect you followed me there, but how you got inside the Melville town house before me remains a mystery."

Patience tried to think of something clever to say when she noticed Anne Melville had stopped her antics and looked positively terrified. Even more alarming, she seemed to be motioning for Patience not to speak further with Leighton.

"Noooo," Anne cried in a panicked whisper. "Get away. Get away. Get away!"

"What in God's name are you looking at?" Leighton snapped, glancing over his left shoulder.

Instinctively, Patience heeded Anne's dramatic warning and stepped away from the viscount. She looked at Sam, noting his posture had also become tense, his hands clenched in fists at his sides. Well aware the mischief Sam caused when provoked, she frantically looked for some means of escape. She then noticed Sam stood before a bakery with a large glass-front window.

"Cakes," she all but shouted. "I—I love cakes, you see. Not that I am a pig about it, mind you. Um, that is to say, I just remembered I need cakes…for tea. This particular shop has an excellent reputation and a delightful assortment. Pray excuse me, Lord Leighton."

With that, she all but ran to the bakery shop. Once inside she scurried to stand by the window where she could best spy on Leighton. He remained standing where she'd left him, his gaze narrowed suspiciously at the shop.

Unbeknownst to Leighton, however, the ghost of Sam MacGregor also stood beside him, arms folded across his chest as he scrutinized the tall mortal up close and personal.

"Can I help you, my lady?"

Not wanting to take her gaze away from Leighton, she nodded. "I wish to buy some cakes."

"What kind, my lady?"

"It doesn't matter…give me what you have there." She waved distractedly at the display in the window.

"What? All of them? The bread and biscuits, too?"

"Yes, yes, fine…all of them."

"Right away, my lady," the clerk replied with marked enthusiasm. "You must be expecting a great deal of company."

"I hope not," she muttered under her breath then sighed with relief to see Leighton walk away shaking his head, oblivious to the kilt-wearing ghost following him.

"He's gone," Anne Melville said, now standing beside her.

"Yes." Patience glanced about the shop, and saw no other customers. The clerk was busy humming and boxing her purchases. She distanced herself and whispered to Anne. "Is he the one?"

"The one, what?"

"The man you ran away to meet? The man who killed you?"

"Who? Lord Leighton?"

"Yes."

Anne started to laugh. "Me? Run away with boorish Leighton? What an absurd notion. Oh, perhaps I fancied him once, but, well…no."

She fancied him *once*? Patience clenched her gloved fists and spoke in a heated whisper. "Is that all you have to say on the matter? After everything you did?"

"What are you talking about, Patience?"

"The letters, Anne. The letters Lord Leighton wrote to *me*. How did you get them? And why did you keep them?"

"Oh, those." Anne waved her hand dismissively. "That was years ago, Patience."

"Maybe for you, but it seems like yesterday to me." She blinked away angry tears. "Oh, never mind, we will discuss the letters later. If he isn't the man you ran away to be with, then why were you acting so frightened outside?"

"I don't know." Anne's brow furrowed in concentration. A moment later, she gasped. "The snuffbox!"

"What about it? Do you mean to say the man who hurt you had a snuffbox like that?"

"Yes, exactly like the one Lord Leighton held." Her gaze lifted to Patience with a wide-eyed expression. "Oh, my, perhaps he *is* the one? Perhaps he found out about the letters I kept and all the things I did to you…and he…he *killed* me."

Patience shook her head. "No, he would never do such a thing. Besides which, many men must have snuffboxes like that."

"No," Anne said. "The one I remember is different, rare even, and has special meaning…" Her voice drifted on and her gaze took on a faraway look.

"Yes?" Patience prompted.

Anne looked about the shop as if embarrassed then back at Patience. "There is a secret compartment under the lid with a most…*unseemly* image. I—I don't want to think about it now." With that, Anne's form shimmered and disappeared.

"What the devil?" Startled, Marcus Hawthorne, Earl of Hawthorne, crooked a brow and studied Leighton after the obviously angry viscount stormed into the library of his residence off St. James Park, slamming the door in his wake. "Where did you run off to?"

"Yes, by jove," added Adam Aldrich, Viscount Hunter, his manner curious yet distracted. Sorting playing cards, he slapped each one down onto the surface of an inlaid gaming table with almost artistic flair. "One moment you were with us and the next you'd vanished. I trust you don't mind we opted to wait at your humble abode."

Leighton poured himself a brandy, and downed the drink as if it were water. "I don't want to talk about it."

"Very well then," Hawthorne murmured with an indifferent shrug. "So, Hunter, have you decided to accompany me to Tattersalls next week? I'm of a mind to add several thoroughbreds to my stables."

"Need you ask?" Hunter smiled, his attention still fixed on the playing cards. "Tattersalls is heaven on earth to me. I believe Melville also plans to join us."

"If you *must* know, I saw Patience Sinclair!" Leighton all but shouted at his two friends. He tried to rein in his temper, but their dumbfounded expressions served only to aggravate him all the more. Did they doubt him?

"Indeed, my friends, you heard me correctly." He poured himself another drink. "Here. In London. And it wasn't the first time I have seen her either."

Hawthorne and Hunter continued to stare at Leighton with their mouths agape. Their lack of vocal response encouraged Leighton to continue. "I might add, not only has the black-hearted wench returned from the wilds of Scotland, it appears she has been following me about town."

"Why would Miss Sinclair be in London?" Hawthorne asked with an infuriating smirk. "The chit was banished years ago by her family."

"Never to set foot in England again," added Hunter.

Earl Hawthorne shot a reproving glance at Hunter for having interrupted him. "As I was saying, even if she were in England, why would she conceive to follow you? The woman made it quite clear how she felt about you before being expelled by her family."

"Zounds." Hunter resumed sorting cards. "All England heard how she felt about you. As I recall, she screamed it like a banshee."

Then, using the most absurd falsetto voice, Hunter added, *"You horrid, vile beast. Can you not see how much I loathe and despise you? The very sight of you sickens and repulses me. What must I do for you to understand that I never, ever, want you to come near me or speak to me again? Do you hear me? I said NEVER!"*

"I remember her comments quite well, thank you," Leighton growled. "Lest you forgot, I *was* the object of her contempt that day."

"And with half the *Ton* there to bear witness, not to mention a few Royals," Hunter added with a nod. "All there to attend the nuptials of Lord Westerbrook, wasn't it?"

Leighton crossed to the semi-circular bank of windows in his library, pulling back a portion of plum colored drapery. All was quiet. Not a carriage or person in sight.

Maybe Hawthorne was right.

He had to look at this situation logically. Just because the blasted woman was in England did not mean she happened to be following him. In point of fact, she hated him. It must be coincidence their paths had crossed. He must have imagined her scent inside the Melville home as well.

Like hell I did.

Still, why would she return to England, let alone London? If that wretched stepfather of hers learned she'd put one toe out of Scotland, he would make good his threat to place her in the asylum. Then again, Patience Sinclair might not realize the danger she could be in...and not only from her stepfather. An innocent young woman roaming about town unescorted...

As if on cue, an unbidden memory returned of Miss Patience Sinclair and the first time he'd seen her. No young woman had ever compared to her. She had a radiant almost otherworldly beauty that seemed lit from within. Innocent and young at the time, sixteen as he recalled, yet he'd seen remarkable insight and wisdom behind eyes that belied her tender years. Shy, quiet, somewhat guarded around others, she'd always made him laugh with her astute, often unpredictable observations about so many things.

He'd loved to listen to her talk with a lilting voice that reflected a slight Scottish accent, especially whenever using the letter '*r*'. It rolled about on her tongue in a rather tantalizing manner. In point of fact, what first caught his attention had been overhearing her soft voice and the subtle rolling of the '*r*' as she talked to herself at a garden party.

Young ladies simply did not hide behind fronds of large, potted ferns let alone speak to themselves in public. Such was how he'd first encountered the auburn-haired young woman.

She'd been arguing softly with herself, all about how she knew what to do, and how to behave. Ultimately, she'd promised with steadfast determination that she'd not allow anyone to intimidate her. Then, quite hilariously, she categorized every guest by name, age, and what she knew about their pompous, judgmental families.

As the eldest of ten, with six of his siblings being female, he'd heard more than his fair share of gossip. However, the observations of Patience Sinclair were not mean-spirited or intended for others to hear. They seemed more a way to remind herself she had every right to be there, and that no one was perfect. Whereas some people might be impressed by the arrogant, privileged, superficial graces among the impressive guest list, she was not.

And they had *that* in common.

Grandson of a duke, son and heir to an earl, and a viscount himself, he'd been targeted for matrimony by some of the most conniving families since birth. By the time he'd first met Patience Sinclair most ladies who'd recently made their debut, or were preparing to do so, bored him to near death. Everything about them seemed false. They saw him as a prize, nothing more.

Miss Patience Sinclair, who'd not yet been presented at Court, was different. Hiding at what must have been her first informal but important social engagement with her family, she'd intrigued him. A rare flower no one else had taken time to notice, she'd captivated his heart, body, and soul from the start.

In very little time he'd spoken with his family—including his grandfather the Duke of Windermere. They tried to dissuade his interest in Miss Patience Sinclair, citing differences in backgrounds. Young and determined, he'd remained firm in his resolve and even vowed to *never* marry if they did not accept his choice. Let one of his younger brothers inherit the title. With or without their approval, he intended to marry Miss Patience Sinclair. To their credit, his family knew he meant every word.

Of course, the lady was very young—so was he then—but he'd intended to broach the subject with her at the Westerbrook wedding. He also planned to introduce her to his family. They were all in attendance, his parents, his brothers and sisters…even his grandfather.

Yet toward the end of the wedding ceremony, Patience had become exceedingly pale, distracted, and agitated. Attributing her behavior to nervousness in the presence of his family, he'd tried to calm her fears. Then, without warning, in a state of sheer panic, she'd bolted from the church.

He'd found her in the churchyard pacing in a circle, gloved hands cupped over her ears, making senseless singsong noises. When she saw him, she bade him to leave her alone. Her voice shook with emotion. Her eyes filled with tears glistening in the sunlight. He'd tried to approach, to calm her, but she became all the more hysterical.

Nothing helped. If anything, trying to talk to her made matters worse. Still, he had to find out what had caused her affection to twist into such foul contempt. He didn't realize until it was too late that the wedding had ended and everyone had come outside to witness the spectacle.

Only the sound of her stepfather's bellowing voice silenced Patience Sinclair that day.

"What have I done?" Leighton said in a near whisper, recalling the exact words Patience said after coming to her senses, blinking wide-eyed at the sight of him, their families, and all the wedding guests. Each person stared at the scandalous scene with horrified expressions.

"I don't know," murmured Hawthorne. "What *have* you done?"

Turning with a start, Leighton noted his closest childhood friend had come to stand beside him, a grave look of concern in Hawthorne's eyes.

"Do not do this, Saint." Hawthorne spoke in a firm but quiet voice, using the nickname reminiscent of their years at Eton. "I'll not let you go down a path of despair and self-destruction again. Forget her."

"Do you not think I have tried, Thorne?"

"Then what is this about?"

"I just...never mind," Leighton said. "You're right. Miss Sinclair's return is of no consequence to me. Best to forget she exists. I only hope I never see her again."

Chapter 9

"I must be mad."

Patience stood in a steady, drizzling rain and looked at the darkened residence of Viscount Leighton. "Are you quite certain he isn't home?"

"Aye." Sam said with a disgruntled tone. "Dinnae I tell ye the man is playin' cards and talkin' politics at his club?"

"Yes." She nibbled on her thumbnail. "What about servants…the cook, housekeeper, butler…"

"The house is empty. Stop dallyin' and get out of the rain."

With an exasperated sigh, Anne folded her arms across her chest and glared at Sam. "I must say, this entire excursion is *common.* You could have made things easier for everyone had you simply removed the snuffbox from his house rather than hide it."

"Common? Listen tae me ye foolish twit. Ghosts dinnae steal, only misplace. Och, but then since yer *English,* takin' what dinnae belong tae ye is more yer nature. Letters, gloves, snuffboxes…nae difference, eh?"

"Beast." Anne stomped her ghostly foot. "If you spoke proper English, I might listen to you."

"Stop it, the two of you. This is neither the time nor place to argue." Patience directed her attention to Anne. "You would be wise to learn from Sam, not challenge him."

Without another word, Sam boldly walked up the steps to the house then disappeared behind the front door in a mist. Anne Melville followed. A moment later, the door to Leighton's home opened and Patience scurried inside.

The moment she entered Leighton's residence, the distinctive, expensive scent of wood treated by French polishing prompted Patience to inhale deeply. After lighting a candle, not surprisingly, she stood in a stately entrance hall surrounded by wood. An intricate parquet floor lay beneath her feet. Four beautiful, carved, tree-size mahogany columns reached up to the next floor whilst rich dark paneling covered all the walls.

Never before had she been in the home of a bachelor. Indeed, it seemed such a bastion of masculinity she suspected no woman had ever been permitted to enter. Were there any doubt in her mind, the sight of an enormous marble statue on guard duty told her otherwise.

Resembling a mythical god from Rome or Mount Olympus, the near naked man stared down at her with stern, lifeless eyes. She studied the folds of a marble sheet barely draped about his hips, curious but thankful not to see what it hid from view. Instead she focused on what the statue held in its upraised hand. Ready to strike her dead for trespassing, the statue aimed a threatening lightning bolt at her heart.

Feeling strangely intoxicated, she wanted to visit every room of the residence belonging to the man she would always love. Dark, mysterious, provocative, and wholly personifying Tristan St. Ives with every detail, even the large vase of cut flowers on a round inlaid table could not alter the impression this was *his* home.

"Come, caileag," Sam said gently. "I hid the snuffbox in his library."

With a nod, she started to follow Sam but hesitated, noting Anne had vanished once again and, of course, at a time when her presence was necessary.

"Sam", she called in a loud whisper. "Anne has wandered off again."

The Scotsman turned and grumbled under his breath. "If I were nae already dead, that female would be the death of me."

"Find her, please. She needs to identify the snuffbox."

"Aye."

"Where did you hide it?" she asked then realized Sam had already left to find Anne.

The first thing Patience did in the library was set her candle upon a large desk then closed the heavy drapes. Her heart raced with trepidation. Stirrings of nausea burned the back of her throat. Without even the warmth or light from a lit hearth, she stood in a room filled with walls of bookcases, various pieces of furniture, a table set with a chess game in play, and all manner of masculine decorative accoutrements.

Where do I begin to look? It could be anywhere.

Nibbling on her thumb nail, she eyed the desk. "Too obvious." And likely the first place Leighton would have searched before quitting the house for his club.

Then again, sometimes the most obvious place is the best hiding place.

She examined the top of the desk, taking pains to not disturb how items had been situated. Proceeding to the desk drawers, she gently searched through papers and ledgers without leaving a telltale sign anything had been touched. Seeing a droplet of rain water from her cloak glistening on the desk, she inhaled sharply. As she wiped it away, she felt another then another. Frantic, she swiped at them all with the dry sleeve of her gown.

"I cannae find the blasted twit!" Sam bellowed like a clap of thunder.

Unable to stop a cry of distress from leaving her throat, Patience held a hand to her racing heart. "Never yell like that again. You almost scared the life out of me. Show me where you hid the snuffbox so we can leave."

Sam shook his head and walked over to a chair before the hearth. Next to the chair, a small side table held a book, its opened pages faced down. She quickly joined him there, watching as he lifted the book to reveal the snuffbox.

Picking the item up, she examined it. Made of gold framed tortoise shell, the cover had a gold rectangle in its center, chased with scrolling foliage. A narrow gold border around the lid also had the same foliage design, as did the slightly raised thumb piece.

She opened the cover, revealing a gleaming gold interior. A tiny gold hinge released a plate behind which rested a small amount of mint-scented pulverized tobacco. Mindful not to upset the contents, she tried to find a secret compartment within the lid.

A moment later, her heart sank.

She pressed gently against the bottom left corner of the lid; the cover separated. Like Anne described, there was a hidden compartment. Whether or not it held a miniature painting remained to be seen.

"I ought to wring your reckless little neck."

Knowing well all color had drained from her face, Patience looked up to see the imposing, angry figure of Viscount Leighton standing in the doorway.

Chapter 10

Trembling with cold, Patience stood in a room where the temperature had dramatically dropped. It seemed as if the library had been suddenly transported to a vast wasteland of snow and ice. A surreptitious glance at Sam explained why. His ghostly form now shimmered with a green aura as he glared at Leighton, ready to stand between her and the viscount if the man moved toward her.

"Mind your temper. Don't do anything foolish."

"I daresay it is too late to mind my temper." Leighton's right brow arched toward the ceiling as he removed white evening gloves. "And when it comes to doing something foolish your *uninvited* presence into my home wins the prize."

Patience tried to calm her breathing. If she told him her words had been meant for an angry Scottish ghost, Leighton would see her put in Bedlam himself.

"I can explain."

"Indeed." Leighton approached with a slow, determined stride, walking through the biting cold, invisible barrier Sam created to protect her. As he did so, Leighton paused and looked over his shoulder. A moment later, his expression truculent, he turned again toward her, hand outstretched for the small object she held.

More than anything, she wanted to look inside the secret compartment before returning the snuffbox to its owner. Difficult as it might be to believe Leighton capable of cruelty and murder, she wanted…nay, needed, proof.

Despite the animosity Leighton directed at her, her love for him had remained constant. In point of fact, the brief moments she'd spent in his company years ago had provided the only happy memories that warmed her during cold years of exile.

Apart from her father and grandmother, both of whom died when she was very young, Tristan St. Ives, Viscount Leighton, had been the first living person she trusted—and the only one who seemed to not only enjoy her company but had sought it out.

Whenever she'd contemplated her fate in Scotland, the remembrance of Leighton never abandoned her. The way he listened to whatever she had to say with interest. The way he used to look at her with tenderness and love. The way he would grin and wink then squeeze her hand gently, a reassuring gesture.

On those rare occasions when they had a brief but cherished moment alone together, there were sweet words of affection, shared dreams about the future, and the ever so romantic yet chaste kiss from his lips upon the curve of her cheek as he bid her farewell.

Three years ago. They were both so young then. She'd been a girl of sixteen and Leighton but four years older. Though more muscular now, his face was still as handsome. In truth, his almost chiseled bone structure, striking green eyes, and dark brown hair had always made her breathless. However, the cold, hard man who stood before her now bore little resemblance to the Tristan St. Ives she remembered.

Had she hurt him so badly he'd lost all the joy in his soul?

The notion proved heartbreaking.

More frightening, had his barely controlled rage and obvious hatred for her altered his disposition in other ways? In truth, she knew nothing about the man he was now.

Was he capable of murder?

I must know. If the box does not contain the picture Anne spoke of, he must be innocent.

The sound of Leighton gruffly clearing his throat distracted her. She'd been staring at the snuffbox in her hand. Raising her gaze to meet his, the burnished brilliant emerald eyes that once looked upon her with affection were now narrowed with contempt.

Tears threatened. Forcing back the tight ache of emotion closing her throat, she placed the snuffbox into his open palm. She noticed his jaw pulsed as he studied her in silence. Then, without a word or removing his gaze, he pocketed the box.

Unable to bear the coldness in his expression, she looked away. Sam stood by the fireplace, arms folded across his chest. "I'm here, caileag," he assured.

"I'm waiting, Miss Sinclair."

Her gaze shot back to Leighton, noting the firm, unrelenting line of his lips.

"You did say you could explain," he continued. "Explain."

Although it seemed Leighton's initial rage upon discovering her in his library had subsided a bit, she had no idea what he might do next.

The situation might become explosive, especially remembering the words he'd said in the doorway.

Would he listen and let her leave? Would a wrong word spoken find her placed under arrest? Would he summon her stepfather? Or, would his large hands encircle her little neck and crush the life out of her? The same fate Anne Melville had found.

No, I will not believe him a murderer.

"I—I am trying to help someone who is lost; a friend from childhood." Her words lingered in the air for several moments.

What Leighton thought of her explanation she had no idea. Between the clenched pulse point in his jaw, the heavy sound of his breathing, and the rapid rise and fall of his chest, it seemed control of his temper remained tenuous. He continued to study her, almost as if he were comparing the woman standing before him to the one he remembered. She'd not fault him for that; she had done the same thing a moment ago.

Patience remained silent, watchful, as his gaze left her face and proceeded to scrutinize her appearance. She fought the urge to pull up the deep hood of her crimson cloak, now situated about her shoulders. She could well imagine what her unruly long curls must look like from the damp, night air and rain.

His gaze soon settled on her worn, leather half boots. His lips curled into a slight smirk of disapproval. Though wounded, she understood his reaction. By comparison to his stylish evening clothes and polished Hessians, she must look a fright.

"Do go on." His tone was hard, abrasive.

He crossed to his desk. Placing his white evening gloves on the wood surface, he casually looked over the piece of furniture, even the closed drawers—obviously considering whether she might have stolen anything.

"I have taken nothing," she impulsively volunteered.

Leighton clenched his back teeth, the infuriating woman's words ringing in his ears. She had taken nothing? Nothing? What about his heart and soul?

Needing a moment to gather his wits, he walked over to stand before the window, opening the heavy drapes once more—his first indication upon returning home that something was amiss.

He stared out into the night. His thoughts could not get beyond the fact *she* was here—inside his house. Instead of simply haunting his dreams, Patience Sinclair had returned to *his* world. Not a recurring dream, flight of fancy, or apparition, she was real.

By God, I'll not let it happen again.

Leighton fisted one hand in the other. He'd not be swayed by traitorous longings. He would hold onto the fiery anger and annoyance that rushed forward upon finding her in his library. He would show her nothing but contempt; it was his due. Unfortunately, he'd made the mistake of looking into her eyes, and recognized the danger having done so now presented.

Patience Sinclair is my Achilles' heel.

Even in garb better suited for a peasant, she looked lovely as ever. Then again, the room was filled with shadows. Perhaps his memory and the woman before him no longer resembled one another. Their encounter on St. James had been tense, brief. His perception blurred by anger. Then, she'd worn the same cloak, the hood of which had covered her hair, and she'd avoided looking at him.

Now, in his home, he wondered…

Was her hair, when dry, still the color of polished chestnuts? Her eyes the dazzling color of the cerulean sea on a sunlit day? They'd seemed darker a moment ago although still framed by thick lashes. Did her pale skin still have a slight dusting of freckles on the bridge of a petite nose?

Of one thing he was certain. In her expression, he saw more than the enchanting innocent face he'd once imagined had been kissed by faerie folk.

She was pale, guarded, and ill at ease in his presence.

Yet like the first time they'd met, something about her struck a chord deep inside him, touching his heart, soul, and body in a way no other woman ever had.

It was still there, that mysterious connection. He'd embraced it years ago. Certain sure he'd found the love of a lifetime—the only woman meant for him.

Then, after she left England, he'd tried to purge the acute pain, along with all memory of Patience Sinclair. Taking refuge in drink and reckless behavior had almost killed him. He'd survived somehow, with the grace of God and help from Thorne.

Now, when he'd thought that almost fatal wound had healed, she had the audacity to return and rip it open again and—by her very presence—the strange link between their souls.

Try as he might to deny it, they were still connected. He'd also seen enough in her gaze to know, despite her words about helping a friend, Patience Sinclair was fragile, frightened, and alone.

Enough, he told himself. *I'll not become involved. I want nothing more to do with her. She will explain herself, leave this house and understand the sooner she returns to Scotland, the better it will be for everyone concerned.*

He turned to face her—anxious to put an end to her unwanted presence. Shaking her head at the fireplace surround, she made a hushing gesture with both hands. The image brought back far too many memories of similarly peculiar behavior she'd often displayed. Little things he'd chosen to ignore out of tender affection.

Perhaps she was mad after all.

"Miss Sinclair, if you are trying to help a friend, why do you find it necessary to follow me about town and break into my home? Or, are *you* the mysterious friend and your presence in my home an excuse to see me or… steal from me?"

"No," she said. "I would never steal from you or anyone."

"Then tell me the complete truth or I shall have no choice but to contact your family."

She paled at his words. Indeed, for a moment he feared she might faint. So fragile, she trembled at his threat. Of course, he would never do such a thing, hating Lord Henley as much as he did, but she didn't know that. Still, he had to impress upon her the dire circumstances of her situation.

At once, an icy wind swelled about him. "Why is it so blasted cold in here?" He looked about a usually cozy room that now felt like an icehouse. The windows were closed. The rain had stopped. It was spring, for God's sake.

He went to the hearth, absently noticing her walk away, creating a greater distance between them. After he'd started a fire, he watched as she moved again, this time to stand before the bookcases, gripping her cloak tightly about her small, shivering frame.

"Come and sit before the fire. Warm yourself."

She nodded and sat in one of two chairs facing the fireplace. He remained standing, baffled why a steady, icy current of air seemed to be circling him. It made no sense at all. Returning his attention to the woman in his home, he folded his arms across his chest.

"Now then, Miss Sinclair, explain your presence."

"The truth is I *am* trying to help someone who is lost. I have returned to England to do so."

"Knowing what will happen if Lord Henley learns of your presence?"

"Yes."

"You intend to do this alone?"

"I am not alone."

"Are you not?" He glanced about the room, gesturing that the library was empty but for them. "It isn't wise for a young lady to wander about town unaccompanied. Anything might happen."

"I am never alone."

"With whom are you staying in town?"

"I have an aunt at whose residence I am welcome. She has vowed to help me."

"What aunt?" When she didn't answer, he laughed. "By the saints, you do not mean Lady Carlyle?" As if affronted by his tone, she lifted her chin and frowned at him. He shook his head, and sighed. "Do not misunderstand me, Miss Sinclair, the woman is rich as sin and has, shall we say, *influential* friends. Still, she is hardly the proper ally for a young, unmarried lady—even if she is old enough to be your grandmother."

"Whatever you think of the countess does not matter to me, Lord Leighton. I am myself familiar with how hurtful malicious gossip can be…and how wrong one can be to unfairly judge another."

He felt the urge to grin, but swallowed it. "Very well, then Lady Carlyle is aware of your nocturnal visit here?"

"She has not interfered," Patience replied with a direct gaze.

Since the room seemed to feel somewhat warmer, he decided to sit in the chair next to her. Stretching his long limbs toward the hearth, he crossed his booted feet. Elbows situated on the arms of the chair, he laced his fingers together and rested them on his stomach. "So, you put your freedom at risk to find someone lost? Why? Who is this person to you?"

"As I said, she was a childhood friend."

"Was?"

"We…grew apart."

He studied her in profile. "Then why help her?"

She appeared startled by the question, her expression marked with confusion then somber regard. Her gaze returned to the hearth and it seemed she would not answer.

"I have no choice." Her soft voice fringed with a slight Scottish accent lifted into the room. "There are many roads to redemption."

Redemption? He pondered her odd choice of words, and the endearing rolling of the *'r'* when she spoke.

For several moments they sat in silence, both staring at the firelight flickering in the hearth. He rubbed his chin thoughtfully. "What has your helping this friend have to do with me? Why did you find it necessary to break into my home this evening?"

"I had to examine your snuffbox." She turned in her chair to face him. "You see, she ran away to meet a man who, in turn, prevented her from going back home. All I know of him is he had a snuffbox identical to yours."

Her words made him bolt from the chair. "What the devil! You think that I…that she ran away to meet *me*? That's why you have been following me?"

"No, I do not think you are the man, but I had to come here tonight because…well, you have a snuffbox like his and I had to be sure. You see, I must find this man..."

Highly insulted by her suspicions, aware his heartbeat raced and pounded in his chest like thunder, Leighton realized if his expression fit his mood, it might explain why she hadn't finished her statement. Struggling to remain calm, he rubbed his mouth, wishing he had a drink in hand.

"Go on," he said, his voice raspy, his throat tight. "You best tell me everything."

She nibbled briefly on her bottom lip then nodded. "I believe this man held her prisoner. That he treated her most foul and forever made it impossible for her to return to her family…or be found."

"Then I suggest you inform her family and let them handle it."

"I cannot," she said. "They would not believe me, and I must find her without delay. Regrettably, the only clue I have to her whereabouts is a snuffbox like yours."

He removed his box from the pocket of his waistcoat. "You say this man's snuffbox resembles mine?"

"Yes, and she told me it has a secret compartment."

Keeping his gaze steady upon her, he nimbly clicked open the secret compartment of his box and crooked a brow. "And you are fairly certain I am not this man?"

"Yes," she whispered. Her eyes glistened in the firelight. "In truth, I believe you could never be this man."

"But you want proof, is that it?"

She bowed her head, silent, hands clasped together in her lap.

He knelt before her, snuffbox in hand. "What did your friend tell you about this secret compartment?"

Lifting her gaze to meet his, she said, "Only that it contained a most unseemly painting upon which she would not elaborate."

Leighton directed the opened lid of the secret compartment at her.

Inhaling sharply, Patience covered her mouth with a delicate hand. Tears resembling liquid crystal gathered and slowly fell upon her pale cheeks.

"I had it made years ago." Determined to not be affected by her feminine distress, he snapped the box closed, stood then gruffly cleared his throat. "Now then, since I have satisfied your curiosity, I suggest you leave. Pray, do not contact me again, Miss Sinclair. Know this; whatever I once felt for you has long since died. Indeed, there is nothing for you here in England. I suggest you forget this quest and return to Scotland without delay."

His gut wrenched and somewhere deep inside his chest he felt an odd stabbing pain. Still, he stood firm and watched her walk in silence toward the library doors. She paused halfway then crossed back to him, chin held high. He tensed as she removed something from a pocket inside her cloak. To his surprise and great relief, it was not a pistol.

"The reason I was on St. James the other day was to find the owner of this glove." She placed it in his hand. "I was told it belongs to you."

He turned over the article in his hand. It was indeed one of his riding gloves. "I don't understand. How did you get this?"

"I found it in Anne Melville's bedchamber"

"Then you *were* there."

"Yes," she said. "If you must know, the young lady I am trying to help is Anne Melville. Forgive my intrusion upon your privacy. I shan't bother you again." Turning away, she quickly walked toward the library doors.

He was at her side in three steps, taking hold of her arm to make her face him. "You're trying to help Anne Melville? Tell me everything you know." At once, an unseen force pushed him bodily away. "What in God's name…"

"Why do you want to know everything?" she asked.

"Because…" He paused, distracted by what had just happened to him. Indeed, it took a moment to remember her question. "Miss Melville's family has been distraught over her absence. They are sick at heart. If the poor girl is being held against her will somewhere, they must know immediately. Action must be taken."

"They will not believe anything I have to say."

"Then tell me," he stressed. "I will believe you."

"Will you?" Her eyes glistened. "What if I told you Anne Melville is dead? That her ghost came to me in Scotland, pleading for my help?"

He instinctively stepped away. "What?"

"You want the truth? The truth is I see ghosts. I have since childhood. All those times when people thought I was talking to myself, I wasn't. Ghosts talk to me. They seek me out. They want my help. Sometimes they have even hurt me. I tried to ignore them. At times, I tried to run from them. Strange, but now when I think of it, they were the only *true* friends I have ever had. So, tell me, Lord Leighton, do you believe me?"

He rubbed the back of his neck, trying to make sense of what she'd said. A sudden thought came to mind, and in the deep recesses of his heart, he felt a sharp, burning pain. There could be only one explanation for the revelation she'd made.

Patience Sinclair was delusional, indeed mad.

"No doubt you believe this, but more likely you have imagined this or perhaps were… confused."

"Like you imagined the cold, winter wind blowing around you in this room? Or, the unseen hand that pushed you away when you grabbed my arm a moment ago?"

"Are you saying that was the ghost of Anne Melville?"

A faint smile curved her lips. "No, 'twas the ghost of a strong Scotsman named Sam. He is a member of my grandmother's clan who feels it his duty to protect me. He also opened the door to your home for me this evening."

"I see." But he didn't see; reason battled against the impracticality of her words. Still, he had felt a cold, persistent current in the library. An icy gust of wind had seemed to follow him wherever he walked. Something strong *did* push him bodily away from her. Then there was the fact she'd gained admittance into his locked home, and the Melville residence as well.

Much as he liked to consider himself a student of science and logic, he also believed a realm of the unknown existed beyond science. A realm where strange things happened, and where mystifying events occurred that contradicted all logic and reason.

The sound of movement distracted him. He turned to see Patience had left the library.

He ran to the entrance hall. "Wait."

She stopped at the front door and turned to face him.

"You must realize what you've told me comes as a surprise. At least permit me the opportunity to think upon the matter. I am not saying I believe you nor am I saying I do *not* believe you. You needed to see my snuffbox to chase away doubts about me. If what you say is true, I need some proof that I might believe in you again."

She nodded and released a shuddering breath. "When I was in Miss Melville's bedroom I not only found your glove but a bundle of letters—letters you wrote to me. How she came to be in possession of them, I do not know. But I never knew of their existence…not until I found them here in London."

"She kept the letters?"

"Yes."

He narrowed his gaze at the disclosure. "I don't understand. Why would she do such a thing? She promised the letters would reach you. That they *had* reached you, and that you both wrote to each other."

"No," Patience replied with a humorless laugh. "No one ever wrote me, not even my mother. Do you not understand? She lied. Miss Melville wanted you for herself."

He began to pace, his thoughts whirling. "But I never encouraged her. I never thought of her as anything more than Melville's rather annoying sister. There was nothing between us."

He looked back at Patience, unable to forget the pain she'd caused him—or the silence from her that had tormented him for years. "Very well, so she took my letters because of some absurd infatuation. Her actions do not explain why *you* never wrote to *me.*"

"After everything that happened?" She shook her head. "My reputation was shattered. My own family disowned and abandoned me. Everyone believed me mad. They still do. What was I to say? That I wasn't speaking to you that day, but a malevolent ghost that had been tormenting me for weeks? That I wasn't looking at you, but at him? You do not believe me now. You would not have believed me then."

"Miss Sinclair, in all honesty I do not know what to think."

"Please,"—she wiped away gathering tears— "I must go. I *want* to go."

"I will take you home."

"No." She held up a shaky hand to stop him. "I have a carriage."

"Very well, but we must talk again soon. May I call upon you at Carlyle House tomorrow?"

"If you wish," she said and sniffled. "I ask only that you do not let my family, or anyone who knows them, become aware that I am in town."

"Of course," he acknowledged. "Let me walk you to your carriage." He stepped forward but a swift, cold gust of air blasted him in the face. "Then again, it seems you already have an escort."

Chapter 11

Unable to sleep, Leighton returned to his library, poured himself a brandy then sat before the fire. His gaze frequently drifted to the other chair, now empty, remembering how right it had seemed to sit with Patience again and talk. That is, until she admitted suspecting he might be a lecher who'd abducted and harmed some young woman.

No, not *some* young woman, but Anne Melville.

Resting his drink on a nearby table, he rubbed his brow and tried to piece together everything Patience said to him.

First, she hadn't returned to England for him, but to help a ghost. He certainly didn't know what to make of it. Considering all the pain and havoc she'd unleashed on his life years ago, it would have been satisfying to think she still bore him some affection—as well as remorse for her past behavior—rather than suspect him of possible murder.

Retrieving the object that brought them together again, he opened the secret lid, recalling the emotional reaction she had upon seeing it contained a portrait of her.

Having never met Miss Patience Sinclair, it had taken Richard Cosway months to get the image right. The only description he'd been able to provide the prestigious artist was for Cosway to think of the face from Botticelli's Venus, only more ethereal with vibrant chestnut colored hair and striking cerulean eyes. He'd contracted the piece in secret, a young fool tormented by the thought he'd lost the only woman he would ever love.

Three years ago, he'd been certain spiteful gossip had caused Patience Sinclair—who'd never said an unkind word to anyone—to lash out in public at him. Indeed, he'd been so certain—and so defensive of her character—that even ridicule and embarrassment before half the *Ton* hadn't mattered, much to the amazement of his family and closest friends.

Unfortunately, he never had an opportunity to speak with Patience afterwards. Thus, like a wounded animal, he'd retreated from society with their awkward, piteous glances and wagging tongues. Feeling as though his soul had been brutally ripped from his body, he'd refused social engagements, the company of well-meaning friends, and even his concerned family, preferring to stay in town alone.

Day after day, night after night, he sat in this very room, staring at a miniature painting in the hidden compartment of a damn snuffbox. On those occasions when he ventured out, it was to ride like the devil in the early morning mist along Rotten Row, or walk alone in the rain, fog, and even snow.

As time passed, there followed a period of rage and self-loathing. He'd been foolish to love her, to want her, or even think her worthy of his affection. He hated her then, often tempted to smash the small portrait into pieces. But he'd always stayed his hand.

And now, when he'd all but forgotten the miniature of Patience Sinclair existed…she'd returned.

"What would have happened had you received my letters?" he asked the delicate portrait. "Could we have found a way back to each other? Shared our lives together?"

"The truth is I see ghosts." Her words echoed in his thoughts.

A distant memory flashed before his mind's eye. Knowing how much Patience disliked crowds, he'd surprised her with an outing on the Thames. The sky had been clear, blue. Sunshine glistened like floating diamonds on the gently rippling water. The morning had been filled with light, laughter, and the golden promise of a love that would never grow old.

Then, she'd noticeably paled. Shuddering, she'd shifted in her seat, her face turned away. He'd looked over his shoulder to see what might have upset her. He'd even tried to enquire what was wrong, to console Patience. Nothing would ease her turmoil.

"Turn the boat around," she'd pleaded in a small voice. *"This is a very bad place."*

As recollection served, they'd been nearing the southern gatehouse of London Bridge. Had she seen a ghost? Some spirit standing on the bridge? Had it waved to her? He shook his head at the absurd notion.

Standing, Leighton placed the snuffbox on the table and stretched with a loud yawn. No ghost would be on the bridge, especially in bright daylight. Besides which, if Patience grew up seeing ghosts as she claimed, why would one terrify her so much that day?

The small hairs on the back of his neck lifted as another thought came to mind.

Before the hearth, he rested his palms on the Italian marble mantle, staring down into the firelight. If everything Patience said was true, what must it have been like to see ghosts and all manner of terrors, and not be able to tell anyone?

"They seek me out", she'd said.

The mist of memory cleared to remember the day she'd fled from the Westerbrook wedding. He'd found her exceedingly upset in the churchyard, pacing frantically whilst unleashing a verbal tirade at him that seemed impossible to contain if she'd tried.

Leighton's breath came fast and hard. He raked his fingers through his hair. Could it be true? Had she been frightened that day with the same type terror she'd experienced while boating on the Thames?

Her panicked, irrational behavior in the churchyard that fateful day now made sense. That is, if he gave credence to the strange ability Patience Sinclair claimed to possess.

Instinct told him Patience would never lie about such a thing. Then again, if she were indeed mentally ill, would not she believe these delusions of her mind to be real? Although instinct deep inside his soul argued Patience Sinclair was sane, reason dictated the best way to determine the truth was to be in her company.

A thousand questions raced through his brain.

Damn the hour. This time I will not wait for the answer.

Patience heard a persistent, heavy pounding as if an enemy had come laying siege to the medieval tower of her ancestral home in the highlands. However, the frantic barking of Henrietta not only told her it wasn't a dream, but reminded Patience she was not in Scotland anymore.

Sitting upright in bed, she listened as doors were being flown open with great force, accompanied by a clearly appalled protest from Whaley.

Her stepfather must have learned of her whereabouts.

Had he come to take her by force to Bedlam?

"Go no further, my lord!" Whaley shouted.

The clip of swift boot steps advanced toward her chamber door, accompanied by Whaley and Henrietta, each barking loudly according to their fashion.

Patience leapt from her bed. Determined to not be taken without a fight, she looked about for a weapon. Frantic, she raced over to the writing desk. Picking up a heavy glass ink bottle from an ebony and brass desk piece, she considered its merit. It took less than a heartbeat to decide the wood and brass spyglass resting on a wooden base made a better weapon—and far less messy than wielding ink across the room.

She raised the spyglass above her head, ready to strike, but its brass sections retracted inside the wooden shaft holding the lens. She shook the instrument, frustrated it would not obey her wish to remain locked and fully extended.

The door to her bedchamber burst open.

She blinked wide-eyed at the man in the doorway.

Leighton, still in his evening clothes, crossed the threshold into her chamber. For what seemed an eternity neither spoke.

"I—I thought you were calling in the morning," she offered inanely, holding the raised spyglass in what must surely be the bizarre pose of a truly insane woman.

"It *is* morning…somewhat. We need to talk."

"Now?"

"Yes." He glanced dismissively at the small army of Lady Carlyle's devoted servants behind him and they reluctantly retreated. Then, with a look that could summon storm clouds, he directed his attention back to her. "And tell that blustery Scots ghost to keep his distance, too."

Chapter 12

Pensive, Leighton stood before one of two floor-to-ceiling windows, framed between a pair of indigo silk brocade drapes. Light blue paint covered the walls.

White plasterwork garlands—specifically framing paintings—reminded him of clouds. Combined with the ornate plasterwork of the ceiling and a white marble fireplace surround, the room gave one the soothing feeling of a heavenly sky and a promising day—no matter what weather might be waiting outside.

The décor was lovely, but its serenity conflicted with his thoughts. True, a new day had begun. Unfortunately, as sunlight slowly illuminated subdued hues of early dawn, his day was not off to a promising start.

Not only had he demanded entrance into Carlyle House, but he'd searched the private residence with a bevy of confused servants—still in bedclothes—following him. To say he'd upset the household was an understatement. However, as the light of day increased, quiet introspection helped him understand the reason for his impulsive behavior.

Put simply, what happened three years ago returned in a heartbeat. Then, he'd taken another pre-dawn ride, desperate to see and speak with Patience. Then, a strange disquiet in his soul had urged him forward regardless of the hour. Then, he'd been too late.

No one would tell him how to find her—especially Lord Henley, whose indignation knew no bounds. Fearful for her welfare, he'd tried to find her on his own, and even hired a Bow Street Runner. But wherever in Scotland she'd been exiled might as well have been on another world. If Patience Sinclair still lived, she'd been concealed inside a dense mist that would never abate.

What remained for him afterwards had been a prevailing sense of insurmountable loss no one understood. The powerful, almost magical link he'd felt with Patience had been severed—no less painful than if a limb had been hacked from his body. For days, weeks, and months, he'd been desperate to be whole again. Perhaps that explained why he'd chosen to believe Anne Melville when she vowed Patience would receive his letters. He should have known the cloying brat lied.

But he'd needed to believe.

He'd wanted to hope.

This morning, another impulsive need to see and speak with Patience Sinclair possessed his thoughts and emotions, causing him to experience the anguish he'd felt years ago. What if she disappeared again? What if Lord Henley had already found her?

A tremendous relief cascaded over him upon finding her at Carlyle House. And in that moment, he recognized all too well a grave danger.

The danger that comes from loving someone.

And the painful death in one's soul when love is lost.

It almost destroyed him once before.

This time, I will not let it happen.

Of two things he was certain. Lady Carlyle was not in residence which meant Patience was very much alone in town. If discovered by Lord Henley, her fate would be sealed.

Too, if she spoke the truth about Anne Melville's murder, and was trying to help his friend's sister, Patience could find herself face-to-face with a threat even greater than Bedlam.

Each clue, each step she took on this quest to help Anne Melville could bring her closer to a murderer.

Someone I might even know.

The sound of a throat being cleared turned him about.

Lady Carlyle's now properly attired, bewigged butler stood in the doorway. "My lord, forgive me, but your visit this morning is most unseemly. Miss Sinclair is a relation and guest of Lady Carlyle. As such, it is my duty to ensure Miss Sinclair is treated with all due respect and civility."

Although he admired the butler's devotion to duty, Leighton wasn't about to turn back now. "Be assured, I have Miss Sinclair's best interests in mind. Still, I apologize for the upset caused the household by my ill-timed visit."

"But…" the butler sputtered.

"I am here, Whaley." Patience spoke softly upon entering the room. "His lordship did say he was coming to speak with me this morning. I am certain he meant no disrespect."

"Very well, Miss Sinclair." Whaley bowed. "I shall ask cook to have a proper breakfast prepared."

After the butler quit the room, an uncomfortable silence ensued. For his part, Leighton drank in the sight of Miss Patience Sinclair.

Now wearing a simple morning gown of slightly faded periwinkle color, it was the first time he'd actually seen her without a blanket of fog obscuring her facial features. Or, in a room of shadows where too little candlelight, a rush of unwanted emotion, and an unseen icy wind cloaked their encounter with confusion.

The majority of her auburn hair had been gathered and pinned up, her luxurious natural ringlets confined, most likely with some skilled assistance from a ladies' maid. Still, a few rebellious curls had escaped to form soft wisps about her pale face.

The enchanting, guileless sixteen-year-old girl who laughed sweetly and conversed so engagingly years ago now stood before him as a young woman of almost twenty. Her face and form were just as lovely, but it pained him to notice her eyes held a great sadness; her demeanor…uncertainty.

He glanced about the room. "Is that Scottish protector of yours about?"

"No, we are alone."

He scratched his jaw, debating how best to proceed, and felt the shadowed growth of whiskers budding upon his chin. "I must apologize for my intrusion this morning. I was unable to sleep after you left. I kept thinking about what you told me. I confess, my thoughts became muddled by many unanswered questions and far too many memories."

She walked further into the room and sat upon one of two matching sofas. He noticed the indigo, azure, and pale yellow striped upholstery complimented her gown. In the past, he might have smiled or commented upon it. He refrained from doing so now.

"What questions do you want answered?" Her expression remained wary.

"What did you see on London Bridge?"

She blinked at the question. "London Bridge?"

"That day we went boating…" He paused, noting by her expression the precise moment she remembered the outing. "What did you see that day?"

She hesitated, as if uncertain whether or not she wanted to answer. She rubbed her hands together rather nervously then released a sigh of apparent resignation. "I saw men tossing severed heads about in sport. And there were other heads in various stages of decay…impaled on…"

She shivered. "I call them *droch tannasg* or phantom spirits—ghosts from the past that appear without warning. I might see Roman Soldiers marching into a wall, unaware that life, death, and time has passed them by. More often than not, I see horrid violence—murders, hangings, beheadings, people being beaten, tortured, or burned at the stake. Sometimes, I get a warning before I see it, usually anguished cries or screams."

Numbed by the heinous images her words conjured, Leighton lowered his weary body into a chair. "Why do they appear? Do they want something from you?"

She shook her head. "They are not aware of my presence or that I see them. They are trapped on an invisible wheel that keeps turning, repeating a moment from their life. It could be their punishment. I do not know."

"Sounds more like punishment to you." He gruffly cleared his throat. "Last night you said you were not speaking to me in the churchyard after the Westerbrook wedding."

"No," she replied in a soft whisper.

"Who was it?"

"A ghost—one that refused to leave me alone. It may be difficult to understand, but some spirits are very angry, even cruel at times. They can be strong and quite powerful. I am usually able to block them, to keep them from bothering me. Still, London is a constant challenge, or whenever I am in a crowd. This particular ghost had been following me for weeks. He looked for any opportunity when my guard was down. At the Westerbrook wedding, I was distracted, happy, and… well…he found me."

"It sounds so implausible," Leighton murmured.

"You do not believe me?"

"I didn't say that." He leaned forward, clasping his hands together as he studied her. "I am willing to keep an open mind. If, as you claim, Miss Melville is dead, we will work together to prove it. However, I want your promise you will not do anything or go anywhere without me. Clearly, Lady Carlyle is not in residence."

"Lady Carlyle *is* expected, and has promised to protect me from my stepfather."

"That may well be true, but she isn't here now. I need not remind you that Henley does not make idle threats."

"But if I can prove I am not mad…" Patience stood and crossed to the window. "Oh, I suppose it wouldn't matter to him. I realized in Scotland my stepfather intended to keep me there forever. There is no hope of reconciliation with my family. For that matter, I do not think there is anything I can do that will change what others think of me."

She turned about and faced him, purpose and determination in her expression. "But I still want to be free, to have a chance for happiness. 'Tisn't fair or right to condemn me because of some unwanted *ability* I have."

Contrary to the strength of her words, Patience returned with gentle grace to her seat on the sofa. “I deserve to have a life, Lord Leighton. And I feel ‘tis past time for me to embrace *who* I am, and *what* I am—even if others do not.”

Leighton could only nod. His throat ached, tight with emotions he didn’t want to consider. Words he didn’t want to voice. Rather, he’d best keep on the subject at hand.

“When Miss Melville’s ghost came to you in Scotland, what did she say?”

“She was frightened and wanted my help. She told me she ran away to meet a man, believing herself in love. She does not remember his name or what happened to her, only that he had a snuffbox identical to the one you own.”

“Except for the miniature painting,” he reminded then realized he didn’t want to explain how or why he’d had a miniature portrait of her made. “Why is she a ghost?”

“When a person dies suddenly or violently, they often do not realize what happened to them. Sometimes the spirit refuses to leave; sometimes they cannot. Often there is something they must do before they can find peace. I believe the latter is true for Miss Melville.”

“Why didn’t she try to communicate with her family?”

“She did, but they could not see her or hear her. Many ghosts do not realize they are dead, and fewer more among the living believe spirits roam the earth. Miss Melville felt her family ignored her deliberately—angry and unwilling to forgive her for running away. When other people treated her the same way, she became very frightened. All Miss Melville knew was that she needed to find someone who could help her.”

“How did she know to find you?”

“When we were children, I confided to her that I saw people no one else could see. People lost and alone who needed my help. Somehow, after her death, she remembered that.”

“But how do you know she was murdered? Is it not possible she met with an accident, or even took her own life?”

“The marks around her neck would indicate otherwise. I believe someone strangled her.”

“I see,” he murmured. Unable to remain seated, Leighton stood and paced before the fireplace. “She doesn’t remember this man’s name? Only that bit about the snuffbox?”

“No, and I also do not know when she ran away… or died.”

“She ran away last August. I helped Melville try to find her.” Arms folded across his chest, he turned to face Patience. “We need to tell her family. At the very least, her brother must know.”

"How would you explain knowing she is dead?" Patience asked. "If you tell them what I've told you, what would they say? How would they react?"

"I have no idea, but Melville might be able to help us. She was his only sister. If nothing else, he could tell us names of her admirers."

She nodded "We must tell him about the snuffbox as well."

"A snuffbox proves nothing, Miss Sinclair." He closed his eyes and pinched the bridge of his nose, sighing heavily. "Still, I will look into it on my own."

Patience felt a sense of unease. Was Leighton keeping information from her? Whenever she broached the subject of the snuffbox he became agitated.

Then again, he might only be distraught by everything she'd told him. Charles Melville was a close friend, and Leighton had tried to help the family when Anne ran away. To tell them their loved one was dead, possibly murdered, wasn't news anyone would want to convey to a family they cared about.

Would Leighton's personal regard for the Melville family complicate matters? Trying to prevent the family further pain, he might keep important information from them.

"I think it best I continue alone." She tried to sound confident, but her voice emerged from her throat with a tremulous quality.

"So, you admit you are doing this alone, eh?" He smiled faintly. "Much as I admire your determination to pursue this quest, a young woman alone in town—especially someone not supposed to be in England—may prove difficult on many fronts."

He sat down in the chair once more, arms folded across his chest. "Apart from the fact you are looking for the body of a murdered girl, a task which might place your life in danger with her murderer, England is rather preoccupied with War; lots of military and maneuverings of regiments about. Not to mention our Prince Regent is trying to convince the population—and likely himself—that everything is under control. Unfortunately, all anyone can gossip about at the moment is his recent, somewhat macabre examination of two dead kings in St. George's Chapel."

"What dead kings?" she asked.

"Whilst trying to make room for the recently departed Dowager Duchess of Brunswick's coffin, workmen damaged a wall in St. George's Chapel. A wall behind which the coffins of Henry VIII, Jane Seymour, and two others rested—one for an infant, the other an adult. No one has ever been able to locate the burial spot of King Charles I after his execution by Cromwell. And since the Stuart king has long been a favorite monarch of the Prince Regent, he wanted to personally determine if the unknown adult coffin belonged to the beheaded king. Positive identification was made, confirming the remains of King Charles I."

"The Prince Regent did that? He looked at the skeleton?" Hearing admiration in her voice, Patience attempted a more somber expression. "That is to say, is it not a good thing to find the remains of a lost king? To learn the truth about his fate?"

He crooked a brow at her. "Are you thinking perchance we should ask the Prince Regent to join us? He might at that, if you could convince Miss Melville to haunt him."

"Let us hope that will not be necessary," she murmured. "So, Lord Leighton, how do we proceed?"

"You need to press Miss Melville for information. The only facts I have is she feigned being ill rather than attend a ball with her parents. The family returned to find her gone. She left no note. We later learned she hired a hackney and met another carriage in Hyde Park. The hackney driver said she was very happy and went willingly."

"He did not see who she met?"

"No, most likely she left London that very night for heaven knows where." He narrowed his gaze at every corner of the room. "I don't suppose she is here so we might ask questions."

"Not at present," Patience replied. "In truth, she is rarely about, which complicates matters. I have no idea how much time there will be to help her. I have repeatedly told her we must make haste, but she is impulsive, easily distracted, and exceedingly unreliable."

"You forgot spoiled, and a liar."

Patience felt a cold breeze quickly sweep by a mere heartbeat before Anne Melville materialized, hovering mid-air over Leighton's right shoulder.

"How dare you?" Anne's face shimmered with indignation. "Of all the boorish, pig-headed beasts!"

"Um…" Patience began.

"No need," Leighton said. "Not the violent icy gale I felt from the Scotsman, but I detect a definite change in the room's temperature."

Chapter 13

"What is *he* doing here?" Anne asked in a haughty manner. "How dare he call me a liar!"

"Is she talking to you?" Leighton asked.

"Yes," Patience replied. "She doesn't like that you called her a liar. Indeed, she is rather indignant about it."

"Then perhaps you should enlighten her as to why I said it."

Patience observed Leighton standing well over six feet in height with his arms folded across his chest, and Anne's shimmering image with her arms folded in the same manner, glaring at him.

"Go ahead, tell her." Leighton encouraged.

"Anne, I believe Lord Leighton's remark has to do with your promise to deliver his letters to me."

"Most definitely," he grumbled.

"Again with the letters?" Anne whined then floated over to stand before Patience, her expression sad and pitiful. "I said I was sorry for the things I did when I asked for your help. Besides which, I couldn't very well deliver the letters when I had no idea where you were. I'm not the Royal Mail you know."

"But you told him you would deliver them, yes?"

"More than that," Leighton contributed. "She told me you received them."

Anne sneered at Leighton. "Oh, why don't you just go away? We have no need or want of you."

"Anne, Lord Leighton cannot hear you, so losing your temper serves no purpose. However, you should know, he graciously volunteered to help me find you."

"He did?" Anne's attitude changed. Her chin quivered. "He is going to help you find my body?"

"Yes, Anne."

"Well, I—I did lie to him, Patience. I wanted him to like me. I always wanted him to like me, to look at me the way he looked at you. I fancied myself in love with him the first time he came home from school with Charles to visit. I was twelve years old at the time. And it made me so angry that after all the years I adored him, he fell in love with someone like *you*."

"Excuse me?" Patience blinked at the insult. Just when she felt her heart softening toward Anne Melville, the fair-haired ghost slipped in some snide comment. "What do you mean someone like me?"

"You know," Anne whispered loudly, her eyes narrowed with hidden meaning. "He's the grandson of a duke and you, well, you're...*Scottish*."

Unable to hide her surprise, Patience raised a hand to her brow and quickly tried to hide her reaction. Of all the reasons Anne might have given for her being unsuitable for Leighton's affections, being Scottish never came to mind.

"Are you crying or laughing?" Leighton asked.

Patience lowered her hand and wiped away the moisture from her eyes. She noted Leighton had crossed the room to stand before her, his concern evident. "Laughing."

"Why? What did she say?"

"Don't you dare tell him what I said to you, Patience Sinclair!"

Pressing her lips together to stave off another round of giggles, Patience shook her head. "She apologized, in her fashion, for lying, and then said the fact I am Scottish prevented me from being acceptable amongst English society."

"What does that have to do with anything?"

"I do not want to venture a guess," Patience said with another small giggle. "But I am glad she didn't say it in front of my Scots protector."

"I need coffee," Leighton murmured. He turned about and started walking toward the door. "Where the devil is the dining room?"

Leighton leaned back in his chair at the dining table and studied Patience Sinclair. Now that he'd had some breakfast and three cups of coffee, he felt less vulnerable emotionally and more thoughtful mentally.

Having been interested in science and religious philosophy most all his life, if what Patience said was true—and gut instinct told him it was—her ability proved fascinating.

"I always considered ghost stories simple flights of fancy, the product of overactive imaginations. Now, you claim there is an invisible world surrounding the living, one layered with spirits that have varied and different functioning capabilities. Is that correct?"

"Very much so." She paused to sip some tea. "Some ghosts try to interact with the living, whilst others cannot. Some are merely images, terrifying at times. Some are lost, unaware they are dead. Or, they do not know how to move on. Those I can help."

She paused a moment. Then, with a wary expression, she continued. "Then there are those who wander, eternally lost in the netherworld. The *droch dubhar*—shadow figures. They are the most frightening. I do not know how or why they become like that, 'tis as if everything about them has been swallowed up by an all-encompassing darkness. They do not communicate. They have no strength, no body, or any resemblance to ever having been human."

"Damnation, perhaps?" Leighton pondered the matter. "Some form of limbo or punishment? To paraphrase Shakespeare, *'There are more things in heaven and earth than are dreamt of'*...or, I suppose, understood by mortal men."

"Man still has free will," she replied. "All of us will be held accountable for the choices we make in our lives and perhaps even at the moment of our death. Still, I believe many souls remain behind by choice. Sam vowed to protect his clan forever. He has very much been like a guardian angel to me. I don't have all the answers, but I can tell you redemption does exist. My faith has not faltered. There *is* a heavenly realm...or whatever you want to call it...and most of us will find it the moment we die."

"I must say, lovers talking about death and redemption at breakfast does not bode well for what happened between you both last night."

Startled, Leighton looked toward the doorway to see the famous Lady Carlyle enter the dining room. Elegant, vibrant, regal as a queen, she wore a dove gray ensemble with a white fox fur draped about her slender arms and shoulders.

A pair of yapping, small brown and white dogs raced into the room, chased by the barking black behemoth otherwise recognized as Patience's dog.

Utter chaos was afoot—in more ways than one. Thankfully, the butler quickly entered and shooed the beasts out of the room, closing the doors behind him.

Leighton looked at Patience, and judged by her pale, apprehensive expression she'd not be able to speak if her life depended upon it. Somehow he had to diffuse the situation. He certainly did not want—or need—Lady Carlyle assuming he and Patience were lovers.

The older woman—considered by men particularly of his grandfather's generation to be the epitome of grace and beauty—walked up to him with an enigmatic, rather intimidating expression on her face.

"Lady Carlyle." He made a polite bow.

"Lord Leighton, you look rather…" She paused to scrutinize his shadowed jaw and somewhat disheveled evening attire from the night before. "Topsy-turvy."

"Permit me to explain, Lady Carlyle…"

"No need." Lady Carlyle waved a bejeweled, gloved hand dismissively. "Whaley told me you arrived this morning." She paused and arched an elegant brow at him. "At dawn, I believe?"

"Yes." He gruffly cleared his throat.

Without another word or apparently any interest in whatever else he might want to say, Lady Carlyle walked over to where Patience stood. The manner in which the elegant countess looked at her relation conveyed nothing but pride and abiding affection, giving him no small amount of relief in return.

"Dearest Patience," Lady Carlyle said with a dimpled smile. "I am so happy to see you here. So *very* happy."

Chapter 14

As Patience walked about the walled courtyard at Carlyle House, quietly watching a portly gardener named Timmons meticulously tend flowerbeds, she considered how much her life had changed, especially in the past twenty-four hours.

She still could not believe Leighton had promised to help her. Then there had been the almost miraculous revelation. He believed in ghosts, and her ability to communicate with them.

A small smile came to her lips remembering his frustration at being unable to hear what Anne Melville said in the morning room.

To be certain, he no longer looked upon her with the tender, romantic affection that once left her breathless, but she found comfort he no longer appeared to hate her. Neither did he seem to judge her which, in itself, felt like a reprieve from heaven.

With her aunt's arrival, and after what must have been a tiring night, Leighton departed Carlyle House. His demeanor had been subdued when he said goodbye, yet he remained firm in his resolve to help. However, he had insisted Charles Melville be apprised of the situation, and intended to do so at first opportunity.

The thought of anyone else knowing about her ability unnerved Patience. She'd made a large gamble telling Leighton. How would Charles Melville react? Would he focus on the nasty rumors about her being mad? Argue against any claim the ghost of his sister spoke to her? For that matter, would he be trustworthy and secretive about her presence in England—at least for the time being?

She sat on a wooden bench, and closed her eyes, listening to the soothing sound of water trickling from a nearby fountain. The thought of going back to bed—just for a brief nap—seemed appealing. But 'twould be rude to sleep so soon after Auntie Catherine's homecoming. Still, for a few moments in the quiet of the garden, perhaps she could rest her eyes a bit.

A delicate Chinese porcelain cup of tea in hand, Lady Carlyle stood at the window in her bedchamber and watched her beloved sister's granddaughter in the garden. "The girl is clearly exhausted."

"Aye, that she is."

Never removing her gaze from the auburn-haired young lady, she asked, "What do you think of Leighton? Is he good enough for our Patience?"

"Bah."

Tilting the angle of her head slightly, she studied Sam MacGregor's scowl, and how both his tree-trunk sized arms were folded across his broad chest. "I take it you don't like him."

"'Tisn't that I dinnae like him, 'tis that I dinnae trust him."

"Time will tell." She savored another sip of tea. "I believe he cares deeply for Patience, reticent though he may be to do anything about it. Still, he has promised to help her, which will prove a great tactical advantage."

"What do ye intend tae do about that tyrant Henley?" Sam asked.

She rested her cup and saucer on a table. "Trust me, old friend, I have just begun to sharpen my claws."

Turning to face the Scotsman, she shook her head. "Seasons change, years pass, but you never change, Sam MacGregor. You shall be eternally handsome and protective whilst I age and wither away. Might I add, your presence in London is most telling. Our little lass means a great deal to you, doesn't she?"

They both looked back at Patience nodding off in the garden. "Aye," he said. "Reminds me of our dear Margaret. I want her happy, Catherine. She deserves tae be happy, nae caged like a bird."

"Yes, she does. In the meantime, let us see if we can get her to sleep in a bed. Tell her I am weary from traveling and will visit with her later this afternoon."

A heartbeat later, the countess watched Sam materialize and converse with Patience. With a wary look to the gardener nearby, her only living relation stood and slowly returned to the house, a tall Scottish ghost by her side.

"Well done," Lady Carlyle murmured then sighed. "Oh, Sam, I wonder if you will ever tell Patience the truth about who you are, and why we are… the way we are."

Chapter 15

Later that afternoon, after a restful nap, Patience joined Lady Carlyle, as requested. Having never been in her great aunt's private rooms before, it took a moment to catch her breath.

She tried not to stare at the elegant furnishings in the mint green and cream room, but it proved impossible. As the countess sat penning letters at a desk, Patience's gaze lifted to an exquisite crystal chandelier hanging from an exotic mosaic ceiling. When next she looked at Lady Carlyle, Patience found the countess observing her.

"I did not mean to disturb you, Auntie Catherine."

"You are not disturbing me, dear," Lady Carlyle replied with a gentle smile. "I have been responding to invitations, which reminds me…I would like to plan a lovely reception for you."

"But I am here in secret," Patience managed to sputter out.

"You are not here to hide, Patience. You are here to take control of your life."

"Auntie Catherine, I do not think a reception is wise. Besides which, I have no friends or acquaintances. No one will come. The truth is everyone thinks me mad. In actual fact, there is something important I must tell you."

Lady Carlyle rose from her desk and seemed to glide across the room to a gilded arm chair, its seat and back upholstered with a pastoral scene embroidered on cream silk. She gestured for Patience to be seated at a matching settee.

"Now then, whatever are you talking about?" Her expression grew pensive. "Oh, dear me, we need to go shopping. Your clothes might have been practical for a cloistered life in Scotland, but this is London."

"Yes, well, that would be lovely, but back to the reception. You see, there is a secret about me you should know." Patience looked down at her hands, realizing she'd been twisting them nervously in her lap.

"Go on, dear."

"Well..." Looking up, Patience swallowed a gasp. Sam had materialized and stood directly behind the countess, arms folded across his chest.

Sheer panic robbed Patience of breath for several moments. *God in heaven, what if he does something? Says something?* She tried not to look at him, to focus her attention on her aunt, but the blasted, brown-eyed Scot shook his head and smirked at her.

"Do ye expect me tae tell her?"

Patience bit her tongue, and tried to offer some semblance of a relaxed smile to her aunt. "Um...I do not quite know how to say this."

"Och, put the lass out of her misery."

The countess laughed softly. "That will be enough, Sam."

"Sam?" Patience looked back and forth between her aunt and Sam, a whirlwind of emotions rising from the depths of her soul. "Auntie Catherine, you can hear him? Can you see him, too?"

"Well, I *am* a MacGregor."

Never in her life had Patience imagined anyone else might have the same ability she possessed. The realization she was not alone with her otherworldly dilemma unleashed a sudden flood of tears she could not contain.

"Now, now, no need for tears." Lady Carlyle moved to sit beside Patience. "The truth is you inherited a family trait. Some might consider it a curse, others a gift—but a trait nonetheless."

"I—I don't understand."

"Legend has it we are descended from faerie folk, going back eons to some High King of Ireland—long before our ancestors settled in the highlands. In truth, our clan has often been referred to as '*children of the mist'*. Granted, some might attribute that name to the unfortunate outlawing of Clan MacGregor back in 1604. Nevertheless, I find the magical connotation more appropriate. Mind you, not every MacGregor has the gift, but it seems persistent in our particular line."

"Why did no one tell me?"

"Your grandmother suspected you inherited the trait, but you were so young when your mother remarried, it was impossible for Margaret to know for sure. On those occasions when you spent time with her in Scotland, you were always quiet and never demonstrated any tendencies."

"I was afraid to..." Patience smiled through her tears when her aunt extended a monogrammed handkerchief. "My mother told me never to speak about my imaginary friends."

"Good heavens, is *that* what they were called?" Lady Carlyle glanced at Sam, listening intently to their every word. She patted Patience's hand then squeezed it gently. "I am sorry, dear. I daresay had you remained in Scotland, closer to your grandmother, she would have been able to help you, guide you. She did make me promise to keep an eye on you. Speaking of which…"

Patience watched as Lady Carlyle rose once more and crossed to her writing desk. There she removed an object from a familiar velvet bag—the brooch containing the porcelain miniature of the young ladies' eye.

"This is yours." She extended the piece to Patience.

"I've been meaning to ask, who is the lady?"

"Why, 'tis you, my dear."

"But I never…I don't understand."

"Your grandmother was quite special. As you know, we were twins and very close. We both inherited the gift, hers to a much stronger degree. We also had special abilities individually. For me it was a sense, if you will, to perceive deception from truth. It proved quite helpful in determining if something might be a prosperous venture or a dangerous gamble. One might say, 'tis an ability that has helped me become financially secure and independent. Your grandmother was able to see visions. One of those was the image of you in years to come. The miniature is how she saw you as a grown woman. A very close likeness, don't you think?"

"I—I don't know what to say. I wish I'd known her better. I was so little when she died. My memories of her are precious few."

"Och, stop yer weepin', caileag."

Upon hearing Sam's gruff command, Patience and the countess laughed.

"Yes, no more tears," Lady Carlyle seconded. "We have much work to do. First, you must tell me about this other houseguest. I daresay Sam has not spoken well of her. And I want to hear about these late night excursions you have taken during my absence. He also told me about your twilight adventure at Lord Leighton's town house. You must promise not to go into anyone's home without their knowledge. Is that understood?"

"Yes."

"Good. Now then, I have important facts to impress upon you, so listen carefully. You are descended from two strong Scottish families, the Sinclairs and the MacGregors. Your father's mother, my sister, was a MacGregor, and his father a Sinclair. For now, we will focus on the MacGregor side. No doubt, doing so will make Sam exceedingly happy."

Patience could not help but smile to see Sam nodding his head approvingly.

"There are two facts about being a MacGregor you must remember. Firstly, MacGregors are fighters. Freedom is as important to us as our life's blood. There have been times when others maligned us, persecuted us, took our lands, and tried to destroy us. Many of your ancestors were killed or forced to hide—even assume other names, simply as a means of survival. Such was the MacGregor fate for one hundred and seventy-four years. Now, like the MacGregor clan in the past, your time of being persecuted and hiding has come to an end."

"Aye," Sam contributed.

"I understand." Patience said, an indescribable strength of purpose rising within her spirit. "What was the second thing you wanted to tell me?"

"Oh, that." Lady Carlyle grinned mischievously. "Remember, if people do not talk about you, you are not interesting. And, my darling Patience, MacGregors are never boring."

Chapter 16

"Leighton, much as I enjoy any opportunity to win a game of chess, I almost feel guilty tonight." Contrary to his words, a calculating gleam sparked in Charles Melville's eyes as he captured his opponent's queen. "Mind you, I said *almost*."

The knots twisting in Leighton's stomach tightened. He tried to offer a smile or some semblance of good humor at his friend's comment, but bile slithered up his throat. If his face showed any indication how he felt inside, he must look like he'd sucked on a lemon.

Seated in the library of his town house, Leighton considered how best to tell his friend why he'd invited him over tonight. Like some fool stage actor, he'd even practiced the words to use. Nothing sounded right. And yet, he'd dallied long enough.

"Do you believe in ghosts, Melville?"

Melville studied the board before answering. "What, rattling chains and disembodied heads floating about at midnight?"

"Regardless how they might appear to the living, do you believe they exist?"

Leaning back in his chair, Melville crossed his arms and clearly struggled against laughter. "It seems rather obvious you do."

"Just answer the damn question."

"Very well, I suppose it is possible they exist. Does that make you feel better?"

"Yes, you see, I have something important to tell you and I need you to be objective. I also want this conversation to remain between us—at least for the time being."

"Of course, if that is your wish."

"What if I were to tell you someone has seen Anne?"

"Who? Where?"

"Miss Sinclair…in Scotland."

"Why the blazes would Anne visit her?"

"Because Miss Sinclair has a gift, a remarkable gift—one that has been misunderstood for years."

"A gift? Odin presenting the hammer *Mjölnir* to Thor was a gift. Miss Sinclair is mad. Everyone knows that."

"She is not mad. She has never been mad."

"How can you, of all people, say that? We are speaking about the same screaming, clearly out-of-her wits female that ridiculed you in public. Accused you of all manner of foul depravity, and made you the object of heinous gossip before your family and half the *Ton*."

Frustrated, on the verge of losing his temper, Leighton crossed to the window. His fists clenched. The muscles of his stomach contracted. Still, he made every effort to remain calm. "I am very much aware our acquaintance ended badly."

"My, my, time does distort reality, or one's perspective of it. Some might say the same about Anne Boleyn and Henry VIII, or the misunderstanding that cost King Charles I his head."

"I hardly lost my head because of Miss Sinclair."

"No, you lost your heart." Melville's voice grew quiet.

Leighton turned about to face his friend. "Very well, it was hell. However, I have since learned facts explaining her behavior. Facts that now involve helping your sister."

"Zounds," Melville exclaimed. "I don't mind telling you this conversation is not only confusing but disturbing. Whatever that little Scottish witch told you, is a lie. I can say with all confidence that my sister would never have anything to do with Miss Sinclair. Not in this lifetime."

"I agree with you…but I speak the truth." Leighton rubbed his mouth, absently aware a fine mist of perspiration had surfaced upon his upper lip.

He cleared his throat for good measure. "Implausible as what I am about to say may sound, Miss Sinclair has the ability to see and speak with ghosts. Please trust I would never come to you with such a declaration unless I felt it necessary."

Melville snorted with derision. In the ensuing silence, however, his sardonic smile of doubt vanished. He slowly came to his feet.

"Are you trying to tell me Anne is *dead*?"

Leighton nodded. "She does not remember what happened to her. According to Miss Sinclair, Anne must do so as soon as possible. There is some question as to the fate of her soul."

Melville suddenly stepped back, as if he'd been struck. "Do you hear what you're saying? My sister is dead and appears to Miss Sinclair? The very woman whose irrational, perhaps dangerous, behavior Anne exposed to everyone? And that unless this deranged young woman now helps my sister, Anne's soul is forever damned? By all that is holy, Leighton, she speaks madness."

Anne's brother circled the library, grumbling under his breath. "To suggest such a fate is beyond cruel. Why would you give this twisted story any credence?"

"Because I believe it is the truth, my friend. Even if you do not, should you dismiss the possibility so easily?"

"My sister is *not* dead. No, I shan't believe it. She cannot be dead." He crossed to the fireplace. Both palms gripped the mantle's edge.

Leighton walked over to Melville and noted the tense, labored rise and fall of his friend's shoulders. He waited in silence, unable to find any words of comfort.

"I want to speak with Miss Sinclair." Melville faced Leighton, his voice stern, his emotional state marked by ragged breathing. "I trust you, Saint. If you, of all people, believe Miss Sinclair, I shan't argue. My sister has been gone almost a year. Perhaps she is dead. God knows we've had no success learning where she went. You say her ghost converses with Miss Sinclair. Very well, I want to pose a few questions to this woman. Questions only Anne can answer."

"I understand. I will arrange a meeting."

"Give me a day or two. I must tend to some business first, and then we can depart for Scotland."

"There is no need to travel any distance. Miss Sinclair is in town. At great risk to her personal freedom, I might add…and only because she promised to help find Anne."

"Find her? What do you mean find her? Oh, dear God. You mean, find Anne's *body?*"

"I'm so sorry, my friend, but Miss Sinclair believes your sister was murdered."

Chapter 17

Why is it always the last place you look?

Patience sighed with relief. She had at long last located Anne, with precious little time to spare. Receiving word Leighton would arrive shortly with Charles Melville, she'd been frantically searching Carlyle House for the unpredictable, elusive spirit.

It had been three days since Leighton had been at Carlyle House. And three days since Anne's ghost had last been seen. Whether Anne's absence had been caused by weakening of her ability to manifest or—as Patience suspected—an inclination to brood and sulk, Miss Melville had to be present today.

Not knowing what Charles Melville's reaction had been to Leighton's news about her ability to communicate with ghosts, Patience feared the worse.

Anne's brother might be judgmental, even hostile. It seemed obvious he'd agreed to the meeting to prove his suspicion and doubt about her. After all, according to Leighton's brief missive, Charles had questions only his sister could answer. As such, 'twas imperative Anne not fade away.

Chilled, Patience looked toward the window of her storm darkened bedchamber. Amidst a cacophony of thunder and heavy rain, the eternally young Miss Melville's vaporous image stared out the window, periodically illuminated by lightning.

Patience crossed to stand beside Anne. The fair-haired ghost seemed not to notice her presence. Had the storm triggered a distant memory?

"They should be here any time now, Anne."

Anne nodded absently.

They continued to stand side-by-side, not speaking, listening to the rumble and quake of thunder. Heavy rain and high winds pounded against fragile buds and blossoms unprotected outside, as well as the secure barrier of thick glazed window glass.

"What if I want to stay?"

"Stay?" Patience looked at Anne, not quite sure she'd heard correctly.

"To remain here. To always be a ghost."

"This isn't where you belong."

"Why not?" Anne pouted like a petulant child. "Other ghosts stay. Sam stayed."

"He made a vow—a declaration—before he died."

Anne's expression hardened. Her lips thinned, her eyes appeared hollow, empty sockets enveloped by darkness. "Well, forgive me, but no one told me the rules before I was *murdered*."

Taking care to not fuel the ghost's temper, Patience gentled her voice. "Why do you want to stay, Anne?"

"I want to, that's all."

The now icy current conjured by Anne's temper prompted Patience to shiver. She went to her wardrobe, removed an ivory colored soft woolen shawl, and draped it about her shoulders. She then closed the wardrobe and turned about, startled to find Anne a hairsbreadth from her face.

"Where will I go?" Anne demanded, obviously thinking Patience had all the answers about the afterlife. "We both know I've done and said hurtful things. God knows I could have been kinder, a more respectful, obedient daughter…and a better sister. I know what you are thinking, Patience Sinclair. This is what I deserve…"

With a startled gasp, Anne raised a spectral hand to her lips. If it were possible for a vaporous spirit to seem paler, Anne Melville appeared so at that moment.

"What is it? Do you remember something?"

"Yes," Anne whispered. "I said that…those exact words."

"Where?"

"I was running…trying to get away."

"Do you remember a house? Any type of structure?"

"No."

"Try to visualize it, Anne. You mustn't fear the memory. It cannot hurt you now. Tell me what you see…what you hear."

Anne's mist-white hand touched the right side of her head. "It was night. I was running in the rain. The ground was uneven, slippery. I fell once…twice. I hit my head on a low tree branch. I remember the pain. Blood mixed with rain down the side of my face. But I dare not stop. He was coming."

"Go on," Patience prompted.

"He said, '*I hear you breathing, my pet*'." Anne's haunted whisper gave voice to fragmented images. "His voice was menacing, yet amused. I remember thinking how was it possible he discovered my absence so soon? It wasn't fair. It should have been hours. Then again, time ceased to have meaning for me."

Patience tried to remain calm, to control the increased racing of her heart and the fear Anne's memory conjured.

"I don't know how long I'd been running,"—Anne's voice grew stronger— "or how far I had traveled in the woods. Yes, woods…thick and heavy…they surrounded me. The branches thwarted any attempt for moonlight to illuminate a path to freedom."

Hands clutched together and pressed against her lips, Patience envisioned everything Anne told her. She understood the terror that had seized the young woman as she fled for her life. Combined with the violence of the storm outside and the otherworldly voice of the ghost before her, part of Patience wished not to hear another word. But this was what they had been waiting for—a memory that would help them on their quest.

"Hadn't I paid the price for my reckless behavior?" Anne's voice vibrated with rising emotion. "Endured the pain and humiliation of his unquenchable thirst for my flesh? Suffered lurid, unspeakable atrocities upon my person by a man I not only trusted but foolishly believed I loved?"

Anne looked at Patience then, her once more pale eyes brilliant with a sense of defiance. "One thought sustained me. Escape. Yet when that moment arrived…" She paused, sobbing hard, covering her face with her hands.

Patience blinked away tears awash in her own eyes, wishing she were able to touch Anne, to somehow comfort the young woman for all that happened to her. It seemed obvious Anne remembered more, perhaps the moment of her death. For that reason, however painful or cruel it might be, Patience had to press on and retrieve that memory.

"What happened next, Anne?" She tried to keep her voice as soothing as possible. "You are in the woods. 'Tis raining and he is coming for you."

"He said, *'Your fear excites me, Anne.'* His voice sounded close, a breath away in the darkness. He toyed with me, strong and sure what the outcome of his hunt would be. Leaving no doubt which of us was prey. I struggled to steady the trembling of my body, to slow the cadence of my breathing." Anne turned toward the window, as if seeing another time and place.

"I stood in a pile of pungent, wet leaves," she continued. "My back pressed against the rough trunk of a large tree. I tried to ignore how it felt against my wet gown, and the throbbing of the wound on my head. Blood continued to stream down the side of my face. I wanted to wipe it away."

She looked down at her mist-like hands. "I held something in my hands. Something that belonged to him. Something that would expose him."

"The snuffbox?" Patience asked.

Anne did not respond. Instead, she stared at sheets of rain pounding against the window glass. "He said there was no escape, that I belonged to him. So close. I did not know if he stood before me or not. Between the rain and dense shadows of the woods, I saw nothing. Perhaps he lay coiled at my feet, slithering about in the leaves like a venomous snake ready to strike a final, fatal time. Perhaps he does not know where I am. Perhaps, if I remained quiet and still, he would walk away. Search elsewhere. I dared to hope. I would make my way to the nearest village. Someone would help me. Believe me."

Patience tightened her grip about the ends of her shawl and brought them to her chin. Her rapid, warm breath escaped her parted lips, and she feared she might scream with terror as Anne drew closer to the memory of her murder.

"And then I thought what if they don't believe me?" Anne's eyes glistened with tears when she looked at Patience again. "What if my parents didn't want me back, especially after everything I had done? For that matter, would anyone good and decent speak to me again? Hadn't I seen firsthand what happened to women shunned by society? At that moment, the memory of you washed over me like an icy wave—and with good reason. I was the one who started the poisonous, malicious gossip about you being mad, Patience. I lied. I said you practiced witchery, that you were evil and dangerous. Then I watched smugly when others ostracized you most foul. And when you were banished by your family, I rejoiced in my heart. Don't you see? I was the evil one. I realized it that night in the woods. That was when I whispered, 'this is what I deserve'. He heard me. A twig snapped. Suddenly he was upon me, restraining me. I felt his breath upon my face. He laughed and said, '*Perhaps it is at that'*."

Patience shuddered, desperate to not release the magnitude of emotions she felt. She'd been battling tears since Anne started remembering. But the fact Anne had finally acknowledged and regretted the wrong she'd done during the final, terrifying moments of her life not only proved Anne had a conscience but shattered any reservations Patience might have felt about helping her once childhood friend's soul move on.

Anne Melville raised her hands to caress the eternal strangulation marks on her vaporous neck, clearly remembering the moment of her murder.

"Oh, Anne," Patience whispered, unable to hold back the rush of tears from her eyes.

The sound of someone knocking loudly on the chamber door startled them both. Barely audible above the whining of the wind and echo of rain, the voice of Lady Carlyle's butler spoke. "Lord Leighton and his guest have arrived, Miss Sinclair."

Patience wiped her face with her shawl, needing a moment to compose herself before speaking. "Thank you, Whaley."

Directing her attention back to Anne, she found the tragic spirit sobbing uncontrollably and shimmering.

The ghost of Anne Melville had every right at that moment to fade, to not endure questions or confrontation with anyone. However, she must attend the meeting. A threshold had been crossed, but they still needed to find her remains…and her murderer.

"Anne, you cannot fade. I need you to remain strong, to focus and be present at this meeting. You must do this for Charles…for your brother. We need his help. Do you understand?"

Chapter 18

Leighton could almost read Melville's thoughts as his friend stared back at him. Neither of them had expected the legendary Lady Carlyle to remain present during the meeting.

Did the woman intend to chaperone her niece now?

After Patience Sinclair had been wandering unescorted about town at all hours of the day and night? Not to mention breaking into private homes? He hoped once Patience joined them, Lady Carlyle would find a reason to quit the room. If not, by God, he would ask her to leave. At the very least, her departure would put an end to the lecture on Greek mythology.

"And so you see,"—Lady Carlyle paused to pour tea— "Zeus was not only king of the Greek Gods, but God of thunder and lightning. Well, the entire sky as it were."

As fate would have it, a violent clap of thunder chose that moment to sound with such force the crystals on the chandelier shook. Blessedly, Patience also arrived and appeared, much to his relief, not the least bit nervous about their meeting. If anything she seemed ready for battle, so much so that when he and Melville stood in greeting, she nodded distractedly and motioned for them to be seated.

"We must be quick about this." She spoke in a hurried manner. "Anne is weak."

"What the devil..." Charles Melville blurted then paused, somewhat flushed, obviously recollecting the presence of the very rich and powerful lady of the house.

Leighton tugged absently at his cravat, almost preferring to be out in the now roaring tempest, soaked to the skin, and a prime target for one of Zeus' lightning bolts.

"Miss Sinclair, perhaps it would be best if we spoke in private?" Turning to Lady Carlyle, he continued. "It is a rather delicate matter, countess, involving Mr. Melville's sister."

With a delicately arched eyebrow, Lady Carlyle sipped her tea, paused then sipped again. Indeed, she seemed intent on savoring the brew and not setting the cup down until the contents were empty. For a moment he did not think the woman heard him. He soon realized she had a flair for the dramatic.

"I feel I must be candid with you, Lord Leighton." Lady Carlyle's voice was cultured, elegant as the lady herself. "Let me see…how do I put this? Ah! As Sophocles said to Antigone, '*No one loves the messenger who brings bad news'*."

"I beg your pardon," Leighton remarked.

"In other words, I shall stay in the best interest of my niece."

"I can assure you…"

She stopped Leighton from further comment with an enigmatic yet effective *'be silent'* look he'd only seen coming from his grandfather the duke. Then, with a smile as demure and sweet as her advanced years might warrant, she continued.

"Although I appreciate the distress Mr. Melville might feel during this meeting, I wish to remind you both that my niece had nothing to do with the death of his sister. Quite the contrary, she has shown great compassion by helping Miss Melville at a most precarious time when the fate of her very soul is at stake."

Leighton turned to Patience. "You told her?"

"What goes on here, Leighton?" Charles Melville stood, his dark expression darting from Leighton to Patience, to Lady Carlyle and then back at his friend. "I'll not be made a fool of by anyone."

"Melville, I assumed our meeting would be private."

"Stop being an idiot, Charles!"

Leighton realized his jaw had dropped open. Judging by the stunned silence in the room, he imagined Melville and even Lady Carlyle might have had a similar reaction.

With an expression of exasperation, Patience Sinclair, hands braced on her hips, appeared not the least bit remorseful about what she'd said to one of his closest friends. Except for that day in the churchyard at the Westerbrook wedding, he'd never heard the young woman raise her voice to anyone.

His thoughts whirled at the disastrous effect this display of temper would have on his efforts to convince Melville she wasn't mad. Unable to hide his disappointment, Leighton released a heavy sigh and shook his head at Patience.

Regret and embarrassment colored her cheeks.

"Actually, um, Anne told me to tell you that, Mr. Melville," Patience said, looking at a still red-faced Charles Melville. "For my part, I beg your pardon. But, as I said, Anne is very weak at present. I cannot anticipate how long she will be able to remain for this meeting. Therefore, I suggest whatever questions you wish to ask her, you do so quickly."

Melville folded his arms across his chest, and seemed intent on staring a hole through Lady Carlyle's Aubusson carpet. A heavy silence enveloped the room wherein Leighton believed his quick-tempered friend would stalk out of the house altogether. To his great relief, however, Melville inhaled deeply then narrowed his gaze at Miss Sinclair.

"You claim my sister's ghost is here in this room now?" Melville questioned.

"Yes." Patience replied, and sat upon the matching sofa facing the countess.

"Why did she run away that night?" Melville asked. "Why did she not have the courtesy to leave a note for our parents? Does she have any idea how deeply she hurt them, especially our mother?"

Leighton watched with interest as Patience looked at something—he assumed to be the ghost of Anne Melville—just to the right of his friend. A heartbeat later her gaze slowly drifted toward the pianoforte, whereupon her expression became concerned. Indeed, he noted a slight glimmer of tears in her eyes.

"I understand your frustration, Mr. Melville." Patience spoke softly, her attention still directed near the pianoforte a moment longer before looking at Melville again. "However, it serves no purpose to point out decisions Anne made that fateful night or what happened afterwards."

"A convenient response, Miss Sinclair." Melville snorted with derision. "So, you claim my sister is a ghost. That she was murdered and needs your help—of all people. Yet you cannot tell me why she ran away, with whom, where she went…nothing. I am to believe instead her soul is in jeopardy and *you* are some type of avenging angel. You are, I am told, intent upon finding not only her body but, I presume, catch the killer. My, my, how diligent of you."

Patience glanced toward the pianoforte again. "Mr. Melville, you do not know what happens to a lost soul. As such, I will forgive your sarcasm and ignorance in the matter. If you do not believe me, it changes nothing. I shall continue to help your sister. I shall see that her earthly remains are found and given a proper burial. As for her killer, he deserves to be found…and punished. If I should learn his identity and obtain proof of what he did, so much the better. But make no mistake, sir, my concern is for your sister's soul. Whatever regrettable decisions she made in life, or whomever she might have hurt, no longer matters. One cannot change the past."

"I do not understand any of this." Melville paced hurriedly in front of the fireplace.

"Has Miss Melville told you nothing new?" Leighton asked.

"Before we came to the drawing room, she remembered trying to get away from her killer." Patience paused, glancing at Charles Melville. "She was in a wood, perhaps a park or on a large estate. And it was dark and raining."

"That's it?" Melville made a cynical laugh. "She was running at night in the woods and it was raining?"

"She remembered being murdered." Patience narrowed her gaze in obvious disapproval at Melville's response. To Leighton's relief, although she looked as if she wanted to chastise Anne's obstinate brother, Miss Sinclair remained calm.

"Mr. Melville, you must realize this is the first memory Anne has been able to recover. Even so, the identity of her killer remains shrouded. I realize this is difficult for you, but details such as a wooded area, hitting her head on a tree branch and wanting to stop but knowing she had to keep running…the things he said to her before she died, and, of course, her memory of the snuffbox—"

"Snuffbox?" Melville glanced quickly at Leighton then Patience Sinclair. "What's this about a snuffbox?"

Leighton swore under his breath. No doubt Patience could see by his expression that he was displeased she brought up the item. This wasn't the way he wanted to broach the subject. In truth, he'd wanted time to investigate the matter on his own—privately—and with discretion. He looked at Lady Carlyle. For her part, the poised woman remained silent and attentive, interested but not judgmental.

Leighton cleared his throat then faced his friend. "Miss Sinclair told me your sister remembered a snuffbox. She felt it might be a clue as to the identity of the killer."

"Why didn't you tell me this before?" Melville asked.

Removing the object of discussion from his waistcoat pocket, Leighton sighed. "Because you and I both have one just like it."

Chapter 19

For as long as she lived, Patience did not think she would ever forget the terrified look on Anne Melville's face. The pale spirit appeared more frightened than when speaking of her final mortal moments on earth.

Anne soared to where her brother stood. "How could you have one, Charles?" Anne's voice shrieked, imbued with dire panic.

Melville, unable to hear his sister, stared hard at Leighton.

A moment later, Anne raced to Patience, conjuring a cold current of air in her wake. "Why does my brother have one? Why do they *both* have one like it?"

"I do not know," Patience replied in a half whisper. However, judging by the reaction of the two men, she suspected they were not the only ones who possessed such an item.

Their temperament certainly explained Leighton's attitude whenever she'd mentioned the box, as well as his adamant declaration he would investigate the matter.

A heartbeat later, the room exploded with shouting.

"What treachery are you hiding from me?" Melville's eyes flashed with outrage. "You intentionally kept this information from me."

"It could mean nothing." Leighton spoke in a firm, controlled manner. "Just a meaningless memory."

"And it could mean *everything*!"

Breathing hard and fast, Melville stalked over to stand before one of the arched windows. The violence of the storm seemed to escalate in unison with the tempest inside the young man.

"Someone tell me what they are talking about!" Anne screamed as she circled mid-air. The icy chill caused by her temperament and movement caused Leighton and Melville to pause and look about the room.

"Miss Melville, do stop screeching and flying about," Lady Carlyle commanded. "Calm yourself at once."

Patience witnessed the surprise and dawn of understanding as Leighton and Melville ceased arguing and stared at Lady Carlyle. Not only had the woman's reprimand caused the cold wind to dissipate, they now realized an important truth.

Lady Carlyle had announced to all present that she possessed the same gift as her niece.

Pride and a sense of belonging swelled within the heart of Patience. For the moment she could only smile, allowing her lips to form a silent *thank you.*

Lady Carlyle reciprocated by blowing Patience a kiss then turned her attention to their guests. "Now then, since Miss Melville is stronger and more attentive, I suggest we gain control of our emotions and be seated. We must strive to remain calm and objective if we are to help Mr. Melville's sister."

Standing behind the sofa where Patience sat, Anne whispered. "She can see me, too?"

"She can indeed," Patience looked over her shoulder at the spirit. Anne's visage had indeed become stronger; her attention more alert and focused. "Come, sit beside me."

Anne glanced at the others gathered in the room. Everyone was not only seated but looking in her direction. "Very well," she said. "Will you tell them what I say?"

"Yes," Patience murmured.

Once beside Patience, Anne fluttered with the skirt of her gown, clearly nervous. Then, with a sheepish expression, her gaunt eyes slowly drifted up to look at her brother.

"I left no note because I was excited, embarking on what I believed to be a great romantic adventure. I didn't want to be stopped or forced to come home. To be lectured or treated like a child. Besides which, I thought I was to be married, not murdered."

Patience repeated Anne's words, noting how Charles Melville swallowed hard, trying with obvious difficulty to not display further upset or emotion.

"I have tried to remember what happened to me. Where I went. Where he took me. The more I try, the more difficult it is. Sometimes I go to my room, and sit beside the window. Sometimes I wander about town, seeking familiar faces. No one sees me. No one hears me. No one misses me. And I know why. I was not a good person."

"That is not true," Melville said.

"Tell him to be honest," Anne said to Patience. "I went out of my way to cause mischief and blame others. All I cared about was my happiness. What I wanted. *Who* I wanted. Never a care for how it might hurt someone. Make no mistake, my actions were deliberate. I knew what I was doing. I must be honest with myself...especially now. Nothing and no one mattered as much to me as *me.* Would I have changed had I lived? I do not know. Even in death I haven't changed, not really. Oh, there is sadness and regret, but 'tis more for fear of the judgment awaiting me. And *that* does not a good person make."

The room grew quiet. In truth, what could one say? The brutal honesty of Anne's words lingered in the air and conjured a heaviness of heart.

Patience looked at the others, each one thoughtful. In particular, Leighton and Melville appeared to be contemplating their actions and deeds. Regrettable choices they might have made with no regard how it affected others.

Patience considered her own life. One lesson her ability had taught her long ago was the time to change and become a better person could only happen in the present—whilst we take those fragile steps, brisk walks, or exciting runs and leaps of faith.

She'd heard confessions like Anne's from other spirits whose mortal journey ended abruptly. Face-to-face with a lifetime of choices, they could no longer ignore the stark reality of wrong turns and bad decisions. The living rarely take time to consider we are all headed toward the same last door in the distance.

Death does not alter life; it defines it.

Patience glanced at Anne, still seated beside her. "You did well, Anne. Is there anything more you wish to say?"

The now weakening, fragile spirit lifted her gaze to look at her brother once more. "I would like Charles to help find me. And I want him to tell our parents I love them and...um...also to tell mother I am sorry I took her emerald and diamond necklace without permission. I wanted to be married in it."

No sooner had Patience spoken Anne's words than Melville stood abruptly. He crossed the short distance to where she sat and stared at the space next to her on the sofa. "It *is* her," he said in a ragged voice. "No one knew she took the necklace but me and my parents. They wanted it kept private."

"Anne knew." Patience looked at Anne then noticed how closely their hands rested on the seat of the sofa. She wished she could take hold of Anne's ghostly hand at that moment, but all she could do was smile at the fading apparition.

A heartbeat later Anne vanished, sadly when her overwrought brother had begun to accept the fact his sister was dead and a ghost. He continued to stare at the sofa, his eyes awash with tears. The sight of a grown man so distraught, and in such turmoil, proved difficult to behold.

Patience's throat burned, constricted with pain. Somehow she found the ability to speak. "She is gone, Mr. Melville."

"Gone? You mean she shan't come back?" He knelt before Patience. "Please, ask my sister to come back. There is more I must say to her."

Patience glanced over Melville's head and saw Leighton, stoic and silent, although clearly moved by his friend's anguish.

Returning her attention to Anne's brother, she spoke softly. "I cannot be certain, but I believe Anne will remain earthbound until we find her body. If possible, she will speak with you again."

He nodded, wiped his red-rimmed eyes and tear-stained face with his bare hands then stood. As if embarrassed, not wanting his friend or her aunt to see his distress, Melville kept his back to them.

Patience considered how to alleviate Melville's discomfort. Although she had sensed mistrust and dislike from him upon entering the room for their meeting, the pain he now felt was heart-wrenching to witness.

Mr. Melville may still harbor ill feelings toward her as a person, despite the fact he now believed she could see and speak with ghosts. Regardless, 'twould be impossible for her to ignore anyone wounded—physically or emotionally.

Not knowing what else to do, and however improper it might be, Patience touched one of Melville's hands. "Do not be embarrassed," she whispered low. "Your grief and sorrow shows the pain of loss and depth of affection you have for your sister. There is no one in this room who does not understand."

Patience watched the workings of Melville's throat as he swallowed hard. With a slight nod, he said, "Thank you, and thank you for helping my sister. I will do whatever I can to assist you."

As Anne's brother crossed to stand beside the pianoforte, clearly needing more time to compose himself, Patience looked toward Leighton.

He stood before the hearth, both hands clasped behind his back. Their gazes held. Her heart fluttered in her chest; her breath quivered upon release.

What was he thinking?

His expression gave no indication, not like before when she'd mentioned the snuffbox. His acute displeasure still puzzled her. Were they alone she would ask why he kept knowledge of other identical snuffboxes from her.

Catching herself staring too long at the man, she glanced once more at Melville, still with his back to everyone else. Whatever secret knowledge the two gentlemen shared about a snuffbox that Anne's killer also owned, she hoped Leighton would reveal to her sooner…rather than later.

Chapter 20

Leighton's Town House, London

"We should ask everyone outright."

Leighton studied Melville's agitation. No matter how hard he'd tried to convince Miss Melville's brother of the need for discretion, and had cautioned him not to leap to judgments that could destroy reputations and lives, his friend refused to listen.

Ever since they were boys together, Melville had a fiery temper. A tendency to act without thinking, usually when upset. One of the reasons they'd nicknamed him *Dragon* in private. Well, that and the fact his full name was Charles Arthur Pendragon Melville.

Now, since learning the ghost of his sister remembered a snuffbox identical to one they each secretly possessed, Melville more resembled a smoldering volcano, ready to spew ash and molten lava at anyone who crossed his path.

Glancing at the long case clock, Leighton noted the hour. Seven o'clock. Any moment the other friends in their secret society would arrive for dinner, unaware and unprepared for what could very well turn into an inquisition.

"Do you honestly believe one of our friends is a murderer?"

"Yes, and because of that blasted snuffbox." Melville's face reddened with temper.

Leighton crossed to the windows, making every attempt to remain calm. He'd not engage in a shouting match.

"I'll not assume the worst," he said, opting for diplomacy.

Turning about to face Melville, Leighton continued. "We've known one another most all our lives. There must be a logical explanation, one that has nothing to do with any of our set."

Melville raked a hand through his thick, ginger colored hair. "I simply do not know how to proceed. Try as I want to be objective, we're talking about my sister. I cannot be sure of my composure, or that I won't do or say something regrettable. It may have been better for me to not be here at all."

"Let me bring up the subject," Leighton assured. "Under the circumstances, perhaps it would be best you remain quiet. Gauge everyone's reactions as it were. Together, we will find out what happened. I promise you that much."

No sooner had Leighton spoken the words than the sound of guests arriving distracted both friends. A moment later amidst ribald laughter the other members of the *Legion of Mithras* arrived.

They'd met as boys at school and almost immediately became close as brothers. They'd even created their secret alliance involving blood oaths. Strong, often defiant, sometimes reckless, they considered themselves soldiers on life's journey. Friends who would not only protect and defend one another amidst any adversary, but keep one another's darkest secrets.

As members of the *Legion,* they each had survived a life-threatening event. In truth, they were closer to one another than they were to their families and siblings. Because of what happened to them, and the danger it would pose their loved ones if revealed, they trusted no one but each other.

Ever vigilant in the secret they guarded, from childhood through impulsive adolescence—and now as young men in their early twenties—Leighton knew each member of the *Legion* as well as he did himself. For that reason, he could not believe one of them might be capable of murder.

Marcus Hawthorne, Earl of Hawthorne, was first to enter the room. Called simply *Thorne* in private, he stood an imposing height of six foot four. His coal black hair appeared slightly windblown; his piercing brown eyes alight with amusement.

Adam Aldrich, Viscount Hunter, crossed the threshold next. Also fairly windblown, it would seem he and Hawthorne had arrived by horseback. Most likely racing at Hunter's suggestion. Standing two inches under Hawthorne, Hunter had the most gregarious, generous personality within their group. His favorite amusements were women and adventure, particularly any form of racing. Among those who did not know him well, Hunter was viewed as a true Corinthian who practiced a life of overindulgence amidst lavish luxury.

Peter Cavendish Knightly entered after Hunter. He stood three inches over six feet, and arrived in a far more dignified manner, as was his usual disposition—not surprising considering his family surname and chivalrous nature. At present, Knightly combed a hand through Nordic-looking golden hair whilst his blue eyes quickly surveyed the room.

Last to enter the drawing room was *Lyon*, officially known as Mr. Edward F.W. Lyon Courtenay. The initials stood for FitzWilliam, a name he resented for it brought unwanted attention to a very private man. Whatever personal family issues he had regarding his birthright, Courtenay was the one member of the *Legion* upon whom Leighton depended for sound judgment, advice, and assistance. The fact he had come to dinner tonight, leaving his beloved residence, was rare indeed, especially considering his precarious health. No doubt, he sensed something serious afoot for members of the *Legion* to be assembled on such short notice.

Those newly arrived conversed in good spirit, commenting how long it had been for them all to be together again. Leighton glanced at Melville. He gave every appearance of trying to remain calm, and even forced a faint smile at Hunter.

Crossing the room, Leighton closed and secured the doors then turned to face the group. He said nothing for several moments, studying his friends and their demeanors in silence.

Hawthorne was first to look at him. His eyes narrowed slightly and a slight smirk curved his mouth. "You look altogether too serious, *Saint.* I do hope you intend to feed us before we learn why we've been summoned tonight."

Leighton ignored Hawthorne's good humored emphasis on his nickname. Granted, no one knew the reason why they were gathered, but everyone needed to settle down for a serious conversation. Besides which, although adapted from his given name of Tristan St. Ives, the nickname had been bestowed because his friends believed his tendency for mischief destined him least likely for sainthood. Tonight, he neither needed nor wanted reminder of that truth.

"All in good time, *Thorne,*" he answered with equal emphasis on the earl's nickname.

"You wish to start the meeting now?" Courtenay asked.

"Perhaps it would be best." Leighton waited while every guest except Melville took a seat. Instead, Miss Melville's brother poured himself a drink then walked over to stand before the hearth. There, Leighton joined his bereaved friend.

Rubbing his jaw, Leighton considered how best to begin. After all, these were his closest friends. He didn't want to accuse. He didn't want to insult. However, a quick glance to his right—noting the tension evident in Melville's face—made him realize he'd best begin immediately…and with the truth.

"Years ago when the *Legion of Mithras* was established, we were boys. I shan't discuss the events of that distant day, but over time we came to realize the importance of our group being united. More than bonds of friendship have been forged. We are brothers who—in this often false and chaotic world—can depend upon one another. We vowed to protect and defend each other. To guard our most private secrets and scars. I pray those bonds of trust and friendship have not changed." Leighton paused, dreading the words he must speak next.

"As brothers of the *Legion,* we've been through a great deal together. From the mischief of disobedient boys who delighted in challenging authority at school, to dangerous escapades that threatened our very lives. But, to my knowledge, none of us has broken the most sacred vow we made. To never engage in evil or deadly violence."

"Good God." Hunter leaned forward, elbows resting upon his knees and both hands clasped together. His brow furrowed with concern. "What has happened?"

"It has come to my knowledge that a young woman has died, allegedly at the hands of someone who could be a member of the *Legion*." Leighton studied the reaction of his friends. To the last, not one displayed anything by demeanor or expression except shock and perhaps confusion.

"No." Hawthorne broke the silence. "I don't believe it."

"I agree," Courtenay's dignified voice conveyed its usual calm. "How could this supposed murderer be a member of the *Legion*? No one here would break that vow, and no one else knows the *Legion* exists."

"Are we sure of that?" Knightly stood and walked over to the cellaret. He paused in the midst of pouring himself a drink and raised his eyes to the group. "Mind you, I'm not saying any of us has revealed its existence, but who's to say someone—perhaps an enemy—has not found out?"

"Do you think that possible?" Melville quickly walked over to stand beside Knightly. "Or, do you suggest the possibility because of guilt?"

Knightly stared hard at his accuser then directed his gaze to Leighton. "Is that what this is about? You called us together to bait and accuse one of us of killing someone?" He snorted with derision then downed his drink. "Well, I, for one, would like to know who it is I am supposed to have killed."

Leighton walked over and rested a hand of support upon the shoulder of Melville, hoping to also convey in silence the need to remain calm. "No one is accusing anyone in this room. Isn't that right, Dragon?"

"I hope to God you're right." Melville spoke in a tight voice, clearly trying to rein in his temper. However, the task proved a losing battle when he turned and pitched his drink into the hearth. Glass shattered amidst a burst of flames.

"Oh, I see what this is about now," Hunter said. "It's his sister then? The dead girl?"

Leighton nodded, noting Melville's breathing had become more agitated, and his jaw visibly clenched. "As you can well imagine, our brother is distraught. And so, I must put before you all a question. Answer on your sacred oath as members of the *Legion.*"

A somber heaviness permeated the room.

"Has any of you ever had a romantic or intimate relationship with Miss Anne Melville?"

"No, but not for lack of trying on her part," Hawthorne said. Noting the volatile reaction of Melville, the earl shrugged. "Sorry, Dragon, but your sister flirted with every man she met. In truth, I often suspected she'd rather pursue the life of a courtesan and follow in the footsteps of Harriette Wilson than any docile path which led to matrimony."

"Damn you, Hawthorne!" Melville bellowed. "How dare you speak of her like that?"

"I said I was sorry," Hawthorne quickly responded. "Look here, you're my friend. I care for you like a brother, but what I said is true. She craved attention from men, and pursued it."

Leighton noticed the other men in the room were clearly uncomfortable with the topic of discussion. "Very well, since we all need to be truthful, Miss Melville also took a fancy to me. She even plotted to sabotage my affections for someone else." He turned to Melville. "I swear to you, I neither knew about it at the time, nor did I ever have any romantic interest in her."

"Bloody hell," Melville murmured. "That's two of you." He gestured like an exasperated maestro. "Please, gentlemen, do step forward and tell me if my sister attempted to seduce you as well." When he saw the lowered eyes and sheepish expressions of his other friends, Melville paled and shook his head.

Knightly walked over to Melville, handing him a new drink. "She was your sister, Dragon. For that reason, no matter how beautiful or fetching she might have been, none of us would have dallied with her or harmed her in any way."

Turning to face Leighton, Knightly sighed heavily. "Please tell me you do not believe one of us could have killed Miss Melville."

"No," Leighton replied. "But just to be sure, I need to see everyone's snuffbox."

"For pity's sake, is *that* the connection to the *Legion?*" With a derisive snort, Hawthorne reached into his coat pocket and removed the object, tossing it at Leighton, who caught it easily. "I stopped counting how often at the club, theatre, or races various gentlemen admired mine and commented they wanted to have one made like it."

Leighton flipped open the secret compartment of Hawthorne's box and saw the painting of a woman bathing beside a stream.

"I agree such a possibility exists," Leighton said. "But there are differences between originals and copies. Details only the original contains. For example, this box has a well concealed secret compartment, so obscure that unless someone knew it existed, it might never be discovered."

He closed the secret compartment lid then secured the entire box before handing it back to the Earl of Hawthorne.

"Hidden compartments are not exclusive to our snuffboxes," Knightly commented.

Leighton accepted the box Knightly extended. Upon checking the secret compartment, he found the painting of a beautiful nude odalisque reclining invitingly in what appeared to be a harem. A gold hookah rested at her side, whilst an Ottoman slave stood nearby fanning her.

Knowing how well traveled Knightly was—and that his family's extraordinary wealth came from shipping and spice trade ventures in India and Morocco—the exotic nature of the painting did not surprise him.

"True, but our boxes also contain symbols that would mean nothing to others." He returned Knightly's snuffbox to him. "Apart from an identifying mark for each of us, our boxes feature a secret insignia for the *Legion* on the back of the hidden compartment's lid."

Knightly looked down at his box. "I remember when we decided upon it...all of us drawing it out in various ways. We agreed upon engraving the letter '*M*' for *Mithras*—representing the ancient Roman temple that inspired our name whilst visiting Hadrian's Wall in northern England..."

"Yes." Courtenay looked at his now open box. "And how a descending line of that letter should extend to the left then turn down with a flourish to form the letter '*L*' for *Legion*." He extended his box toward Leighton.

"An unusual insignia—with meaning only to us." Leighton looked down at an exquisite, detailed painting of his friend's famous country residence concealed within the secret compartment's lid. He could not help but smile and handed the box back to its owner.

"Do you never tire of that place?"

"Never," Courtenay grinned, pocketing his box.

Next, the secret compartment in Hunter's snuffbox revealed a painting of his prized racehorse, Bad Boy.

Leighton could not suppress a soft laugh. "Good God, Hunter. Have you no imagination? Not even a painting of your mistress?"

"Bad Boy is dearer to me than Evangeline Bailey," Hunter replied with the utmost sincerity. "He is irreplaceable, not to mention the income from his stud fees has lined my pockets rather nicely. Best investment I've ever made."

"A fact, no doubt, Miss Bailey appreciates," Hawthorne remarked sarcastically. "Take care, Hunter. Many a lover has been cast aside for failing to meet her demanding, somewhat greedy appetite for expensive trinkets and baubles. You best hope Bad Boy's endurance holds out."

"Why?" Hunter queried. "Have you heard something?"

Hawthorne shrugged. "You know the woman's history as well as anyone."

Hunter shot Hawthorne a suspicious, rather stormy look.

"Back to the matter at hand," Courtenay said with perfect timing. "Saint, do you believe the killer has a box with our insignia?"

"I do not believe so, but the killer's box does contain a secret painting that would be *unseemly* to ladies. Indeed, the implication made when that particular word was used would indicate the painting is beyond licentious...one might say even evil."

"Well, as you can see, our boxes hardly qualify." Hawthorne folded his arms across his chest and arched an ebony brow. "By the by, we've not seen your box."

Before Leighton could react, Hawthorne walked up to him and removed the snuffbox Leighton always kept in his waistcoat pocket. The earl then opened the compartment lid and shook his head at the image. "I might have known."

"What is it?" Hunter asked.

"The portrait of a lost love, hardly licentious." Hawthorne placed the closed box back into Leighton's pocket. Then, leaning forward, he whispered, "But, in my opinion, definitely evil."

"Saint, please tell us how you came to know about this matter?" Knightly asked.

"Yes, I vow I am curious as well," Courtenay contributed. "Clearly, you invited us here based on information you believed strongly enough to consider us suspect."

Leighton glanced at Melville, uncertain how much should be revealed at this moment, particularly with regard to the involvement of Miss Patience Sinclair.

Granted, none of their friends had a snuffbox featuring a painting that would have been frightening or vastly offensive to any female, especially Anne Melville. But he'd also wanted to make sure the boxes were not duplicates. He doubted any of his friends would have parted with their box short of death. Not only was it a symbol of their friendship but of the *Legion.* A fact that caused a gnawing fear in the pit of his stomach, especially with regard to tonight's meeting.

Since learning Anne's ghost had been terrified about the snuffbox she remembered, he realized it had to be a connection to her killer. Another possibility had also kept him awake at night.

What if Anne had taken and hidden the box on her body, unbeknownst to the killer? If the killer had been one of his friends, surely he would have discovered the box missing. Fearing exposure, he might have had a duplicate made.

Consequently, what his friends did not realize while he made a show of examining their individual snuffbox, was that he'd also checked to make sure each person had an original box.

As the man who'd designed and gifted each *Legion* member with the item, there was another hidden detail only he knew about. Apart from the *Legion*'s insignia—and a symbol in gold raised relief on the lid that each person had requested to signify their identity—the boxes also had a special hieroglyphic-type mark and letter made at Leighton's request.

Concealed within the jeweler's mark, this secret code allowed Leighton to determine if each member had replicated their snuffbox or still had the original. To his relief, the secret compartment paintings did not meet the criteria Miss Melville's ghost stipulated. In addition, each member still had their original box.

Suspicion removed from the *Legion* members, the small pond that might have contained the murder suspect had now become a river as long and deep as the Thames—with limitless possibilities as to the killer's identity.

Leighton recollected Hawthorne's comment that many among his acquaintance had admired the box and desired one like it. Knightly also proposed the possibility someone wanted a box made to resemble theirs for a more nefarious reason.

God knows they'd each had rivals and enemies—especially whilst at school—but who would bear such an evil grudge. Much as he detested the thought, one such person could have plotted and committed a crime hoping to implicate one of them.

Who could it be?

How many years was he to go back to glean the truth?

How am I supposed to find the killer now?

Another thought froze his blood. Patience Sinclair's determination to help the ghost of Anne Melville meant finding the dead girl's body. Where might such a search take her? Since she'd repeatedly said time was of the essence, Miss Sinclair had no intention to delay in her quest.

Somehow he had to devise a plan to learn the identity of the killer whilst protecting Miss Sinclair. And the best way to do that was for no one, not even his closest friends, to know of her involvement as yet.

"Well?" Hawthorne prompted.

Leighton looked at Anne's brother, hoping Melville would understand and keep his promise to help Miss Sinclair.

"Anne Melville spoke to me…as a ghost. Her memory has been impaired. Indeed, she remembers nothing about her killer except he had a snuffbox like ours. And before you question the state of my mind—or how much I'd been drinking at the time—I swear it is the truth."

Stunned silence ensued for several moments.

Almost instinctively everyone looked at Charles Melville. He inhaled deeply and nodded. "My sister…Anne's ghost spoke to me as well. We have no proof of her death, not even her body. Mind you, no one else knows about this. As such, without actual evidence, I intend to keep this information quiet…even from my parents."

"You *both* spoke with this ghost?" Hawthorne asked with a decidedly dubious tone.

"Yes," Leighton and Melville answered at the same time.

"And Miss Melville's ghost said she was murdered by a man with a snuffbox like ours?" Hawthorne continued, one of his habitually unruly ebony eyebrows arched rather imperiously.

"For God's sake!" Melville exclaimed. "Anne never saw my snuffbox. She never even knew it existed. Do you think we are making this up?"

"No", answered Courtenay. "Of course you wouldn't."

"Well, I must say this situation is both alarming and intriguing," Knightly remarked, his visage pensive. "The fact you *both* claim to have seen and spoken with a ghost lends credibility to the—for lack of a better word—haunting. Miss Melville has been missing for quite some time."

Knightly returned to the cellaret, poured another brandy then walked back to his chair. "But since you don't have a body or witness to the crime," he continued. "Let alone any clue as to the identity of the killer, how can you possibly hope to prove it?"

"I was hoping the *Legion* could work together. Dragon's sister has been murdered." Leighton studied his friends, all of whom were clearly appalled and sympathetic. "Since this killer is not one of us, we need to find out who he is without delay. What if this fiend seeks to kill another of our loved ones? As Knightly pointed out earlier, an unknown enemy may seek revenge and implicate one of us in the crime."

"I will ask once more," Hawthorne said, his voice somber. "Do you both swear by all that is holy that Miss Melville is really a ghost?

You are sure this is not some cruel trick someone has played upon you?"

"I swear," Leighton said.

"There is no doubt in my mind whatsoever," Melville added.

Hawthorne rubbed his jaw distractedly then shrugged. "Well, I agree with Knightly. I don't know how you intend to find this killer, but I will do what I can to help…under one condition."

"What condition?" Leighton asked.

"That we, please, have the dinner you promised."

Courtenay nodded. "I must admit, I am half-starved." When he noticed Leighton waiting for his answer, he added, "Oh, yes, I will also help. We are, after all, brothers of the *Legion.*"

"That we are," Knightly agreed as he stood.

Seated with his hands still clasped together, Hunter stared at the flames in the hearth.

"Hunter?" Leighton asked.

"Huh?" Hunter's rather disturbed expression soothed fairly quickly. "Oh, help you find proof about what happened to Melville's sister?"

"That *has* been the topic of discussion," chided Hawthorne.

Hunter stood and nodded. "Of course I will."

Leighton opened the doors to the drawing room. "Then let us feed our bellies and try to determine how best to proceed." He watched his friends move toward the dining room, noting Hunter lingered behind, rather distracted.

"Is something wrong?" Leighton asked.

Hunter paused at the drawing room doors, his gaze drifting to Hawthorne walking beside Courtenay on their way to dinner. "You don't think Evangeline has set her sights on another man, do you?"

"I hardly know the woman, my friend."

"Yes, of course," Hunter murmured. "Still, I don't think Thorne would have made that comment unless he'd heard some rumor on the wind."

"Then perhaps you best ask him."

Hunter nodded then exited the drawing room, muttering under his breath. "Not an honest one among the lot. All women are false. They care only about money, and what they can get from a man."

Chapter 21

I must have misunderstood, Patience thought to herself.

There could be no other explanation. Whaley had said the countess wanted to speak with her in Lady Carlyle's bedchamber.

Had the butler meant now, or later in the day?

For at least a quarter hour, Auntie Catherine had not said a word. Still, the woman had bid her to enter and be seated, albeit in a rather distracted manner.

Patience instinctively nibbled on her bottom lip, caught herself and stopped lest the countess noticed. Then, beneath the skirt of her gown, Patience's right leg started to bounce in a most unladylike, restless manner. Embarrassed, Patience discreetly smoothed the fabric over her knee and gently squeezed the unruly appendage, thereby distracting the impertinence of her limb.

No question about it, despite the meaning of her name, Patience Sinclair found her limit of being able to sit still and remain quiet sorely tested.

With nothing else to do, she focused her attention once more on the woman who had volunteered to assist in her escape from exile. She seemed such a dignified, fine-boned, and delicate silver-haired lady of advanced years. Good intentions are admirable, but did the countess have the power to prevail against Lord Henley?

At present, Lady Carlyle seemed more concerned with inspecting and organizing an impressive assortment of matching jewel boxes. Each velvet lined case held a queen's treasure with drawers and hidden compartments that opened like wings on the various mahogany veneered chests.

Patience had never seen so many rings, bracelets, brooches and necklaces made with diamonds of various color and size, as well as emeralds, sapphires, and rubies. There were also three diamond tiaras, each one resting within their own private box that had been opened for inspection.

How does one person possess so many jewels?

Patience recollected Leighton's somewhat rude reaction upon learning Lady Carlyle was the relation helping her. What did he know about her?

Apparently, more than I do.

Even Anne Melville knew more about her grandmother's twin sister, especially with regard to the woman's social connections.

Observing the lady before her, Patience wanted to know everything she could about Lady Carlyle—well, apart from the fact the countess had the same ability to see and speak with ghosts.

Most important of all, she must know what the countess intended to do with regard to Lord Henley. Her stepfather had a cruel sense of power, and he did not make idle threats.

What if he'd already learned of her flight from Scotland? Surely, the countess had a planned course of action to take.

"Did you hear me, Patience?"

Patience blinked. "No, Auntie Catherine, I was…thinking."

The regal countess studied Patience with a decidedly mischievous expression. "No doubt, you were thinking I have too many jewels."

Warmth could be felt rising upon Patience's cheeks. Could her aunt read minds, too? "They are very beautiful." She softly cleared her throat. "They must have special meaning to you."

"Some." Lady Carlyle directed her attention toward closing each jewel box, a rather secretive smile about her lips. "I promise none of the Crown Jewels are missing." The countess looked at Patience then winked. "Not as far as they know anyway."

A frisson of apprehension seized Patience's breath.

Lady Carlyle's laughter lifted into the room, and she patted Patience's hand. "Now then, back to what I asked you a few moments ago when you were *thinking*. What do you do to protect yourself from unwanted contact?"

"Unwanted contact?"

"From spirits," Lady Carlyle clarified. "Heavens, I hope unwanted contact from a mortal is not a problem. Dear me, has that devilishly handsome Lord Leighton made advances toward you?"

"No," Patience answered quickly.

"Pity." Lady Carlyle sighed "He would be a good match."

"Lord Leighton?"

"Well, 'tis obvious you care much for him. I also recall a history of sorts together. A budding relationship that encountered a most unfortunate early frost."

Not comfortable in the least discussing Leighton or her feelings toward him, Patience stood and walked about the room. She made a pretense of looking at its décor and contents.

"I think of bubbles."

"I beg your pardon," Lady Carlyle commented.

Patience paused to study a beautiful framed watercolor of Scotland's Jedburgh Abbey as viewed from the river. She looked closer at the artist's signature and noted his name, Thomas Girtin.

"You asked how I block unwanted contact," she continued. "I think of a white bubble filled with light. The bubble surrounds me with light and the power of angels."

She turned toward her aunt. "It works well. I used it here when first I arrived. I did not sense any spirits in the house, but the only ones who could enter after my protective shield had to be spirits I welcomed...like Anne."

"And Sam," Lady Carlyle said in a quiet voice. "You say this bubble is filled with light and the power of angels. What do you mean?"

"I have always felt as if angels surround me, even when I was quite small." Feeling awkward beneath her aunt's steady gaze, Patience turned back toward the painting. "So, I say a prayer and ask my angels to surround me with light. The bubble is like armor for me."

"How long have you used this method?"

Patience shrugged. "I first used it when I was about eight. I had a dream where Grandmother came to me. In the dream, she told me to trust the angels."

She walked over to one of the windows of her aunt's private bedchamber and watched the orange and pink fading rays of sunset through the trees. "How do you block spirits, Auntie Catherine?"

Hearing no reply, Patience glanced over her shoulder and saw the older woman dabbing at her eyes with a handkerchief.

"It doesn't matter," the countess replied. "I like your method better." With a delicate sniffle, Lady Carlyle stood and joined Patience at the window.

"The reason I wanted to know about your technique is because we shall take a trip tomorrow."

"But I must stay here and help Anne."

"I cannot leave you here alone, and Anne cannot come with us. Not at first. Sam will remain and keep watch over Miss Melville."

"Where are we going?"

"Hampton Court. I have an apartment—actually, a suite of rooms bestowed upon me years ago by His Majesty with certain obligations. There are residents I am required to visit. Their welfare is most important, you see."

"My presence has inconvenienced you from this obligation?"

"No," Lady Carlyle assured. She brushed back a strand of Patience's curly hair that had fallen loose from the confines of pins.

"Quite the contrary," the countess continued. "It seems providence you are here now. Your welfare is also my concern, and that is why I believe we must travel together to Hampton Court without delay."

"Miss Melville needs—"

"I understand you want to help Miss Melville," Lady Carlyle interrupted. "However, you lived in an isolated area for some time, and I worry about your ability to protect yourself. I also did not anticipate that when you came to me, you would be looking for the body of a dead girl and the identity of her killer."

"I promised to find Anne's body and help her move on."

"I know," she answered with a soft smile. "Please try to understand, my dear. You are impulsive about Miss Melville, yet for three years have remained hidden away from the living and avoided the dead. Everything now depends upon how best I can teach you to protect yourself. Ultimately, it is my responsibility—and my duty to your grandmother—to keep you safe."

"Lord Leighton and Mr. Melville will also help."

"Yes, well…" Lady Carlyle sighed and focused her attention outside the window. "Life is uncertain, Patience. Involving Leighton and Miss Melville's brother may well invite more danger."

"But—"

"No, Patience." Lady Carlyle clasped her hands together and returned to her dressing table. "You must trust me. We go to Hampton Court tomorrow. Once there, I want you to tell me what you think and feel. If you feel comfortable there, we shall remain and Miss Melville can join us. Lord Leighton and Mr. Melville may do their part in town."

"And if I do not feel comfortable there?"

"If you do not like Hampton Court, or feel overwhelmed, we will return to town."

"Overwhelmed?" Patience crossed to stand before her aunt, understanding the full measure of the woman's somber words. "There must be a great many ghosts at Hampton Court."

"Yes, there are many ghosts. However, I feel it will be a better setting for you—a more contained and manageable situation than what you would experience here in town."

Much as Patience did not welcome the notion of leaving London where she believed Anne's fate would be realized, her heart warmed by the concern Lady Carlyle had for her welfare.

I do possess a tendency to act without considering the consequences, she reminded herself.

Leighton had even warned against her impulsiveness.

"I understand, Auntie Catherine. Is it a long journey?"

"It will take some time. We shall travel by boat...far more enjoyable."

Boat? Patience swallowed hard, determined not to reveal her fear of water—or the terrors often encountered in or near water.

Lady Carlyle secured her many jewel boxes. "We shall bring along a lovely luncheon basket. And I defy any spring showers to dampen our day."

After placing the key to her jewel boxes inside a large, beautifully etched gold locket on a chain about her neck, Lady Carlyle returned her attention to Patience.

"Oh, 'tis ever so relaxing to travel by boat. There is nothing like approaching Hampton Court from that perspective."

Patience tried to smile, to remember Lady Carlyle was her only loving and supportive relation. The countess cared about her. What choice did she have but to trust the older, wiser woman's judgment?

"Now run along. Instruct your maid to pack those lovely new gowns my modiste delivered for you. Tell Gates we will be gone no longer than a fortnight. She will know what to pack."

Not trusting her throat to work properly, Patience nodded and walked in silence down the long hallway toward her bedchamber. Why did she have this sense of foreboding? They were going to a palace, not a prison.

A fortnight, she reminded herself. *And if I don't like it there, we will return to London.*

Try as she might, Patience could not muster any semblance of enthusiasm for the journey to Hampton Court in the morning. She tried to understand what disturbed her the most.

It wasn't so much the fact they would travel by boat, although that aspect did make her anxious. Neither did it upset her that Lady Carlyle had obvious doubts with regard to her ability to help Anne and protect herself from an abundance of bothersome spirits.

What caused an almost crippling ache in her heart was the thought of being taken to another place, away from Leighton. Not that she had hope of a future with the viscount.

In truth, she cared too much for him to sentence the man to a life with someone like her. Besides which, now that he knew her ability was an inherited trait, no man would want their children so cursed.

He should love and marry a woman of grace and beauty, a lady who'd bring honor to him and his family. Not someone who would bring him shame, embarrassment, and no end of gossip.

Someone of good family.

Someone who would fit perfectly in his world.

Someone like him.

What does it matter? He doesn't love me.

He made it quite clear any affection he once felt had long since died. He only wished to help her now because of Anne's brother.

Patience paused in the doorway of her bedchamber, hugging her waist. Across the room she noted dusk had settled outside the window. Any remnant of the day's sunlight had vanished. Soon a blanket of bleak darkness would be cast over the city.

Come morning, she would be gone from London.

Somehow I must tell Leighton where I am going... and why.

She crossed to the bell pull in her room and summoned her maid. After instructing the petite Gates to do as Lady Carlyle bid, Patience sat down at her writing desk.

Chapter 22

Leighton's Town House, London

"Then we are agreed?" Leighton and his friends were still seated in the dining room as the midnight hour tolled. Even after the cloth had been removed following their meal, they'd remained seated at the polished table to speak over brandy. "You each know what to do," he continued, "and will contact me immediately with your findings."

Everyone reaffirmed their commitment to the cause.

As they all stood, preparing to depart, a degree of weighty concern lifted from Leighton's shoulders. He'd had doubts about how they would work together and decide upon a course of action, especially after a rather heated conversation at dinner—which included reminiscing about the past and any possible enemies they might have. Now, he felt optimistic. No matter what challenges might face them; the *Legion* would stand together and solve the mystery of Anne Melville's murder.

"It has been a long evening," Melville said.

"Yes, it has…but productive, I think." Leighton watched as Anne's brother said farewell to the other members of the *Legion.*

It did not surprise him that Melville, pale and obviously weary to the core, was first to depart for home. He could well imagine the turmoil engulfing his friend, and his gnawing desperation to find and punish the man responsible for his sister's death.

At the same time, a sense of guilt disturbed Leighton. Much as he wanted to help his friend, the lion's share of his reason for undertaking the search had been because of Patience Sinclair.

To be sure, he felt great sadness for Miss Melville, for what had happened to her and the plight of her soul, but his primary focus was to make sure nothing happened to Miss Sinclair. If that meant taking charge of the investigation to find Miss Melville's body and her murderer, so be it.

He'd even lied to his friends to protect Miss Sinclair from their scrutiny. Doing so forced him to acknowledge a startling truth—one he would admit to no one.

Leighton glanced toward Hawthorne, talking amiably with Knightly and Courtenay. His gut clenched when Thorne made that snide comment about Patience being evil. He knew evil better than anyone, and such a foul darkness could not be more removed from the mind, body, and soul of Miss Sinclair.

With restraint he'd managed to rein in his temper and reason away the earl's contempt. His friend's prejudice existed only because of what happened in the past. For that reason, if Hawthorne knew the truth—that Patience Sinclair had been the one who'd communicated with Anne Melville's ghost—the man's reaction would have been explosive.

"Well, I'm off." Courtenay walked across the foyer to leave. "That is, if my host here in town is ready to depart."

Knightly nodded at his houseguest whilst Hunter leaned toward Hawthorne to tell him something in hushed tones. Leighton watched their interaction with interest and assumed whatever Hunter said concerned possible gossip about his mistress. The amusement in Hawthorne's expression left no other explanation.

Hunter then departed, followed by Knightly and Courtenay. Leighton studied his remaining guest, the friend he'd known since they were both six years of age.

"Well," Hawthorne said with the crook of a brow. "I must say this was an ever so enlightening evening. You might have prepared me. I know a gypsy woman who might have been of some assistance."

"You don't believe me?"

Hawthorne chuckled and shook his head. "About the fact you spoke with a ghost? You forget, my friend. I know all about you and nothing surprises me."

"I appreciate the vote of confidence."

Opening the front door, Hawthorne donned his black leather riding gloves and glanced toward Leighton's stableboy patiently holding the reins to his mount. Looking up at the velvet sky, the earl grinned. "Nothing like a midnight ride on a cool evening"

"Be safe, Thorne."

"How many times must I tell you, there is no fun being safe?"

Leighton remained standing outside his residence, watching as Hawthorne rode away, waiting until the rhythmic sound of a single rider's horse faded into the distance. Still, he lingered and inhaled deeply of the night air.

A gust of wind whispered and circled, caressing his hair, soothing his face. He glanced about, wondering if some unseen spirit might this very moment be observing him. Closing his eyes, he listened for possible murmurings of ghosts. Nothing, not even the song of a nightingale. The corners of his mouth lifted into a faint grin.

He returned to his residence, ready at long last to retire and sleep, if only for a few hours. Yet as he prepared to enter his home, a hurried rustling sound distracted Leighton. Suddenly, a strong, icy current of air pushed his body slightly forward and to the right.

Swearing under his breath, he turned to face the spot where he presumed the ghost of that damn Scotsman stood. In truth, he hadn't expected to actually see the ghost Patience called Sam. Still, some type of explanation was warranted as to why the obnoxious spirit felt it necessary to haunt his residence at midnight and physically start an argument...of sorts.

It was then he saw it. A letter dangling in the air on an unseen current...waving at him. Not knowing how to respond or what else to do, he extended his hand to take the letter. After a sharp tug of resistance, the infuriating ghost released the mail.

Leighton turned the sealed correspondence over in his hand, and saw the letter was indeed addressed to him.

Sensing the ghost of the Scotsman had departed, Leighton entered his home and slid the bolt. To make sure no unseen spirit had entered his home, he extended his right hand to sweep the air about him. Detecting no unusual change in temperature, he walked across the hall toward his library.

Once seated, he stared at the missive.

She'd finally written him a letter.

A sense of dread as to its contents gave him pause.

Shrugging off his anxiety, Leighton broke the seal and unfolded the fine linen parchment. He glanced down to make sure the letter was from Patience Sinclair, not her aunt, and sighed with relief.

Reading aloud, he said, '*L - Lady Carlyle is taking me to Hampton Court in the morning. She has an apartment there. She has suggested it might be safer for me to be there. We are going alone...by boat...which as you know is something I do not favor. Please contact me at Hampton Court with any information you may learn to help Miss M. Your friend, Miss S'*.

"Your friend?" He pondered the possible inference on the two words. Is that how she thought of him? A friend, nothing more? The possibility left a sour taste in his mouth. Yet more important was why had Lady Carlyle—whom Patience said had vowed to help her claim freedom from the banishment her stepfather imposed—now decided to take her niece to what might very well be a prison of another sort.

He had half a mind to ride over to Carlyle House and find out the real reason for Lady Carlyle's decision. If not satisfied her actions were in the best interest of her niece, he would physically remove Patience and install her at his home.

Leighton blinked wide-eyed.

No, that would definitely not work. Instead, he thought upon an alternative that would allow him to keep a close eye on Patience and still maintain a discreet distance.

"What the devil are you doing here at this hour?" Knightly awkwardly adjusted a wine-colored blanket around his naked shoulders. In the darkness of the man's house, the blanket more resembled a long makeshift cape, especially when Knightly turned around.

Leighton bit back a laugh. From his big, bare feet to the total disarray of his golden blonde hair, Knightly looked like a disgruntled medieval Viking.

"I do apologize, Knightly." Leighton tactfully cleared his throat. "However, I need to speak with Lyon."

Knightly frowned and rubbed his right eye rather harshly. It seemed to work; one azure eye opened to glare at Leighton. "For God's sake, couldn't it have waited until morning? We just left your house. What time is it, anyway?"

"Half past two," Leighton murmured. "Again, I apologize, but I must speak with him before he departs for home. I didn't expect you to answer the door. Where are your servants?"

Knightly made no comment. He simply closed his eyes, giving the impression he might easily fall asleep standing upright. Then, with a start, he opened his eyes extremely wide, as if forcing his body and mind to remain awake. "What did you say?"

"I asked about your servants."

"Obviously, they are not about. My butler is having a blasted holiday, and the cook and maids do not stay here at night. I am a bachelor, man. If you must know, I prefer privacy in my home, especially at half past two!" Disgruntled, but duly embarrassed for his outburst, he sighed. "I beg your pardon, I am exceedingly tired, Saint."

"Yes, I can see that."

Inhaling deeply, the master of the house clutched at the unorthodox garment slipping from his shoulders. "You'll find him upstairs. I'm going back to my bed."

Leighton followed Knightly, finding it difficult to not laugh as his friend tried to maneuver stairs wearing a long blanket. Tripping more than once, Knightly swore under his breath. Thinking it might be best to not trail behind the man, Leighton paused.

After what seemed a suitable interval, Leighton started up the stairs only to stop short at the sound of someone pounding on a closed door.

"Wake up!" Knightly yelled. "Saint wants to speak with you."

By the time Leighton reached the top of the stairs, Courtenay had not only opened his door but met Leighton halfway down the hallway, more appropriately wearing a pair of trousers and unfastened shirt. "Is something wrong?"

"I need to accompany you back to Hampton Court and stay with you for a few days."

"You're more than welcome, of course, but I thought you intended to start questioning jewelers."

"I did, but Knightly can do it for both of us." Leighton glanced at the closed door where their friend had blessedly quieted. He then returned his attention to the man he came to see. "I need to speak with you in confidence."

Courtenay motioned Leighton toward his guest chamber. Selecting one of two chairs situated near the fireplace, Leighton noticed a fire burned low in the hearth, barely giving off any light to the quiet room. A glance to the bed showed he had indeed awakened another friend from restful slumber. Stirrings of guilt surfaced again.

After closing the door to the chamber, Courtenay sat down opposite Leighton, his naturally pale skin even more pronounced against dark hair and eyes. He said nothing, but studied Leighton with a bemused expression.

"Lyon, do you remember Miss Patience Sinclair?"

Chapter 23

North Bank ~ River Thames,
Middlesex County

Lady Carlyle's boatman steered his passengers effortlessly across the River Thames. However, since departing Westminster for Hampton Court, Patience found it increasingly difficult to push aside her fear of the ancient river.

Although she trusted her aunt, almost immediately upon boarding the boat Patience said her special prayer and created a shield of angelic light for protection. It proved rather exhausting to sustain the defense as they traveled, but seemed to be working. She'd seen no spirits thus far, especially those that might rise from the depths of the dark gray water. Still, how much longer would it be until they reached their destination?

Time moved too slowly…as if it would stop altogether.

I may fall asleep if we don't get there soon.

Glancing at her aunt, Patience noted Lady Carlyle showed no sign of weariness. On the contrary, the older woman looked vibrant and cheerful as she continued her history lesson.

"The grapes are black and sweet," Lady Carlyle said with a wistful smile. "In 1807 the Vine Keeper harvested over 2,000 bunches of the delectable fruit."

Despite her aunt's enthusiasm for a half century old thriving grape vine, Patience looked back at the water. Her thoughts drifted without direction…without substance.

The calm water rippling against the black hull of the boat, the soft breeze caressing her face, and the gentle voice of Lady Carlyle all seemed part of a distant dream, working together to wrap about her like a comforting cocoon. She wanted to sleep, to simply drift like the water…and the wind.

Looking toward the shore, ducks nestled securely among wet meadow grass. Tall trees nodded in the wind, obscuring any view of pastureland, village, or estates. One could hardly tell where they were at this point. The river kept twisting and winding.

After a while, trees became fewer. The land opened to reveal a great expanse of emerald carpet.

And then she saw it.

Hampton Court.

Her first view of the palace was the south facade which, according to her aunt, had been designed by Sir Christopher Wren. Sunlight cast a golden glow against the vermilion and white baroque exterior. Without question the structure was beautiful, conveying both the formal grace and stately beauty one expected of a royal palace. At the same time, it seemed lonely as if waiting for someone to return and fill its rooms with light and laughter.

"Stunning, is it not?" Lady Carlyle asked.

"Most assuredly, 'tis not what I expected. Other than a feeling of sadness, I am not picking up on anything."

"You will."

Expecting the boatman to steer toward the shore, Patience noted he did not alter their course. Instead, the boat continued to pull steadily through the river, following a curve and current that seemed to somehow affect even the weather.

Had a cloud drifted to hide the sun?

Patience looked up. Gnarled branches from tall elms and wraith-like tendrils of weeping willows by the shoreline blocked sunlight. Reaching out toward the water, they seemed determined to pull free from their ancient roots.

From one heartbeat to the next, a powerful chill rippled down her spine. She soon knew the reason why.

Dark and foreboding, a cluster of narrow towers came into view. Chimneys, too many to count, reached up like stone fingers against the sky. Soon, high pitched gables, turrets, and towers could be seen. A peculiar heaviness in the air stilted her breathing, and the wind off the water now caused her to shiver.

How many others from long ago had followed this same route to Hampton Court? Excited or wary as to what fate awaited them once inside its palace walls?

In truth, the only thing that kept Patience from thinking she had actually journeyed to another time was an increasingly numb sensation sweeping through her body. As it had with Anne, and countless other spirits before her, Patience sensed the triggering of her powers. The lightning-type current channeled through her body, picking up on all the spectral beings aware of her arrival.

She closed her eyes, and focused on other techniques to block the spirits from surging toward her at once. They were obviously ready to pounce soon as the boat docked.

Vise-like pressure—a thousand times worse than what she'd experienced with Anne's presence in Scotland—wrapped about her brain, causing it to throb mercilessly as if each individual spirit demanded personal attention.

"Breathe, Patience." The soothing voice of Lady Carlyle beckoned.

Biting back a cry of pain, Patience raised both hands to cradle her head. "It is too much. There are too many."

A gentle circular motion stroked her back, as if her aunt were drawing circles or patterns with a delicate finger. "They are curious about you, nothing more. Focus on breathing slowly…in and out. You are in your bubble of light, dear Patience. No one can enter it or approach you without your permission."

Patience nodded, and soon her breathing relaxed. The piercing pain in her head dissipated. Only then did she open her eyes and see the boat had docked. The servants they'd brought from Carlyle House had already exited and stood silent, watching her.

"It is alright." Lady Carlyle assured. "I told you, my servants are very loyal. They will protect your privacy and keep you safe."

"Yes, but what must they think of me?"

"According to Whaley, the entire household thinks you are sweet as a lamb."

"Do they know?"

"About our gift?" the countess asked.

"Yes."

Lady Carlyle glanced at the servants then spoke in a near whisper. "With the exception of your little maid, yes. They will not tell her anything. It shall be up to you to tell Gates what you want her to know. I suggest you come up with something quickly. She looks a bit bewildered."

Patience saw her young maid, frowning and nibbling somewhat frantically on her thumbnail. She stood next to Kelly, a plump ladies maid to her aunt. Not knowing if Gates was afraid or concerned for the welfare of her new mistress, Patience tried to smile.

"I am fine, Gates. I daresay I am not a good traveler by water."

"A rest is what you need, Miss Patience," Gates said in her sweet, childlike voice. "I'll see to it straight away." The little voice and confident enthusiasm of Gates prompted Patience to laugh softly.

"You see," Lady Carlyle said. "Gates knows what to do now."

A few moments later they climbed the steps from the dock and entered the palace gates. Patience tried to put on a brave face despite the fact her heart raced like a frightened horse freed from a cart that had just overturned.

She glanced every so often to her aunt for guidance. Regal as a queen, Lady Carlyle spoke softly with the man Patience realized was both trusted friend and butler to her aunt. Whaley had left his duties overseeing Carlyle House to accompany them to Hampton Court. His nephew and head footman, Nicholas, had been left in charge of the London residence during their absence.

Looking about the beautifully manicured grounds, Patience barely noticed the flowers and fauna. She saw nothing but ghosts milling about everywhere. Most all of them wore extravagant jewels and elegant garments. The colors of their clothing shimmered with a fine white mist. Still, she could well imagine how sumptuous they must have been when their owner lived.

She tried not to stare, but had never seen men wearing such rich attire. Handsomely embroidered doublets had slits cut into the fabric to reveal silk lining that puffed out slightly to show another color. Full sleeves and a ruffed collar surrounded their necks. Beneath the doublet they wore hose and codpieces. Atop their heads were hats that looked to be made of velvet or silk, each with a feather and jeweled brooch fastened to stylishly pin up one side.

As interesting as the men appeared, the ladies' attire seemed nothing less than a work of art. Most assuredly, a hoop of some sort was worn beneath the gown, creating a cumbersome width to the skirt whilst not adding any volume to the front or back. Like a man's doublet, cuts were made into wing-type sleeves—but in the shape of diamonds and stars—through which the lining fabric—also of another color—had been pulled to show its quality. The ladies also wore ruffs, pleated and decorated with lace.

It seemed odd their clothing looked so impeccable—not frayed or damaged in any way—especially considering they had been dead for centuries.

Did the palace possess some kind of magic that caused this effect? Surely they had not all died in full dress with jewels.

At first she thought them phantom spirits, but when they paused and smiled at her, it became obvious they could interact. In truth, they did more than smile. The men made a chivalrous bow and the ladies curtseyed—far more formally than was required for common courtesy.

"Who are all these ghosts?" she asked. "They can see us. Interact. And their clothing and jewels…"

Lady Carlyle nodded graciously at the ghosts strolling about the gardens. "They do not accept they are dead."

"After all this time?" Patience paused to look back at the ghosts. They were smiling and chatting happily with one another. "They should have moved on. Why haven't they? Could you not help them?"

Walking ahead, Lady Carlyle laughed. "Why should they move on? They were here first. Are they not content?"

Patience quickened her pace to walk beside her aunt. "How can they not know they are dead after all this time?"

Her aunt paused and looked at her with a rather amused, indulgent expression. "I said, they do not *accept* they are dead. Neither are they ready to leave. They do no harm and keep to themselves. Some are most amusing and rather pleasant."

"Auntie Catherine, I have never known ghosts who remained behind and sought not to frighten or push the living away. For certain, they never want to share their home with anyone, well, except Sam. Surely, the presence of so many spirits must bother the living people who reside here. Those who have apartments like you."

Lady Carlyle laughed, the whimsical sound drifting to where a white-haired old gentlemen sat reading a book. He looked up and grimaced at them.

Patience blinked. There had been so many ghosts in the gardens she hadn't noticed the mortal man. With chagrin, she wondered how much of their conversation he'd overheard.

An arm slipped around her waist as the countess encouraged her to keep walking. "Dearest Patience, I daresay you are more a disturbance at present. Think of Hampton Court like a village unto itself. Some residents are living and some are…"

Refusing to take another step, Patience pulled away. "Are you telling me this palace is a contained city filled with mortal and spectral residents? That these ghosts interact with the living?"

"Only if the living can see them," Lady Carlyle replied.

Anger simmered to a quick boil in Patience's veins. She did not want this. She had far more pressing things to do than spend her time blocking contact from every ghost that wanted to talk or interact with her on a daily basis.

She needed to find Anne's body. To help her move on. Tempted to return to the boat, Patience bit her tongue.

"Do you not understand why I brought you here?"

"Not really. It seems a waste of my time."

"Does it?" Lady Carlyle sighed. "In town, you insulated yourself at Carlyle House which, by the by, was already left protected by me. You were also fortunate to block unwanted spirits when, on occasion and very briefly, you left the house. In addition, you had Sam to chase off the unwanted. My dear, if you are going to truly help Miss Melville, and navigate your way through life, you need to learn how to rely only upon yourself."

Patience looked toward the dark, original structure of Hampton Court, yawning before her like an ominous ghost in its own right. Everywhere she looked, from the gardens, courtyards and walls, the palace retained all it had experienced—births and deaths, laughter and tears. The joy of celebrations as well as the suffering and horrible cruelty the palace witnessed. Everything remained imprinted.

Even if one were to remove the ghosts who dwelled here—the memories of Hampton Court resonated in every brick, stone, window, and room.

"This is your training ground, Patience. There is good and evil in this place, a sampling of all you will encounter wherever you go for the rest of your life. The time has come to embrace who and what you are. Most important of all, you must strengthen your skills of protection."

Chapter 24

"Observe how she feigns interest in their words, yet speaketh not to us."

"Aye, whilst we, in good faith, wait a fair word or gesture."

"Mayhap she cannot hear us?"

"Nay, she both sees and hears."

"This will not do. She must cease ignoring us anon."

"Aye, else deadly harm befalls her."

Patience clenched her teeth, determined to ignore the ghostly conversation all but being shouted above the din of polite conversation at the elegant dining table.

Alone, she would have put an end to their antics when first they started. However, she must not react in any manner that might prove embarrassing—especially since Lady Carlyle had not so much as blinked an eye at some of the outrageous things the ghosts said in their rather demanding efforts to gain attention.

Absently rubbing her right temple, Patience wished the gripping pain in her head would go away—the reason, as it were, that her protective shield had faltered. A sense of inadequacy and failure swelled within her. How naïve and confident she'd been in her ability to block unwanted spirits.

Here less than a day and I cannot keep a few ghosts from disturbing my supper.

The last time her gaze drifted in their direction, there had been nine—all male from the time of the Tudors. There were more voices now. If she knew how many were gathered, she might not feel so bad about losing the battle to block them. With her right hand still poised at her temple, Patience peeked.

At least thirty ghosts were gathered by the enormous bay window of what had been King Henry's Great Watching Chamber. Many stood or were seated. Far more hovered mid-air at various heights before the tall stained glass window. One even had the audacity to wiggle his fingers at her and make cooing noises.

Despite their threat of harm, they didn't look dangerous.

If she weren't so tired, their behavior might have been laughable. But all she wanted to do right now was find her bed and go to sleep.

The journey to Hampton Court had been tedious, stressful. Upon arrival she barely had time to adjust to a battering ram of ghostly activity before summoned for dinner. The light repast she expected in the private dining room of her aunt's apartments had been replaced by a surprise supper hosted by a group of *still breathing* tenants to welcome Lady Carlyle back to Hampton Court.

Under the circumstances, it would have been impolite to not attend.

Their hosts consisted of eight former Ladies-In-Waiting, all elderly with silver or white hair. Despite their advanced age, they smiled engagingly and spoke softly. Clearly anxious to hear about the goings on in town, and Lady Carlyle's recent travels to Prussia, her aunt indulged their curiosity with stylish flair and grace.

Of the eight ancient men at table, two looked particularly frail and pale, as if not long for this world. Without question they all appeared most dignified, with still keen minds and eyes that conveyed a certain melancholy she could not dismiss.

It did not escape her attention they listened with serious expressions as matters of grave importance regarding the fate of the country were discussed. At times they would nod, comment about their past travels to other lands in service or duty, or enquire about certain individuals by name.

Patience had studied them during supper—all seemingly intelligent albeit elderly people who had, at one time, played important roles of service to their majesties, King George and Queen Charlotte. Sadly, despite the fact they still had much insight and wisdom to give, they were here…

Alive, yet cut adrift from life.

Unwanted.

She thought of her isolation in Scotland.

Weariness and empathy stirred her emotions.

Tears welled in her eyes; she quickly blinked them away.

Unable to endure another moment, Patience stood. "Please excuse me," she managed to say. "It has been lovely to meet all of you, but I—I…"

"No explanations are necessary, my dear," Lady Carlyle said. "It has been a long day, and a lovely evening with good friends. Still, I daresay 'tis past time for all of us to say goodnight."

Everyone stood, still chatting amiably, obviously reticent to depart. Patience glanced toward the watching ghosts. She found something unsettling about the way they now looked at her. Their expressions and postures were tense, as if they waited to pounce on her like a wild beast.

She looked back at her aunt, still smiling, saying her farewells.

What is taking her so long?

Patience trembled. Nausea that had been churning in her belly rose to her throat. Uncertain why she suddenly felt so ill, Patience recognized a desperate need to leave the ancient room where Henry VIII had once dined.

Hoping to withdraw like a proper young lady, she quietly exited then proceeded through a small portrait gallery—the first of which she recalled having taken earlier.

She noted a definite chill in the air, and a shiver ominously rippled down her spine. A quick glance at a fireplace—cold and untended at this late hour—offered a logical explanation for the change in temperature. Still, as her footsteps echoed on the floor, they announced to any spectral being intent on mischief that she walked alone.

She next crossed a threshold through a pair of opened doors and into a longer gallery that, as she remembered, would turn to the right. Unfortunately, as she turned the corner, the hairs on the back of her neck lifted. A thousand tiny needles pricked her skin.

Glancing over her shoulder, Patience debated whether she should turn back and find her aunt. For a moment she did nothing. Then, like someone forced against their will, she slowly walked forward—one step then another until, for some reason, she could go no farther. Paused outside the Chapel Royal, something instinctively held her back.

A forceful blast of frigid air.

The icy breeze did not surprise her. She'd been expecting some type of contact. But there was something different about the dramatic plummeting temperature, just as there was a difference in the way spirits affected her at Hampton Court.

Apart from the pressure pain in her head, stilted breathing, and the tingling sensation spiraling inside her body, she now experienced waves of nausea and a weakness unlike anything she'd ever known.

Compared to unexpected, random sensations of danger or dread she experienced in London—especially going to different parts of the city—Hampton Court was different. Here, she felt a constant, almost desperate desire to flee.

Her sensitivity to smell also seemed more pronounced at the palace. Most were fragrant, pleasant smells of the living world combined with the haunting scent of ancient perfumes or spices that lingered from another time. Yet something else—very faint but cloying and repugnant made her skin crawl.

And that foul odor was here…now.

Hesitant to proceed, Patience could hardly believe what she saw. The shadows of the gallery—its paintings and furniture, even the walls themselves—lengthened before her.

Closing her eyes, she attempted to summon enough strength of will, mind, and spirit to create her invisible barrier. However, oppressive weariness combined with uncertainty as to which direction to follow prevented her ability to focus. Vulnerable without her blocking technique, she opened her eyes and studied the dimly lit gallery again.

Don't panic.

She tried to assure herself the direction followed had been the one taken to dinner. Rubbing her hands together, she cupped them about her mouth. She blew warm air into her palms. Air cloaked with invisible ice surrounded her. Interlocking her fingers as if in prayer, she held them against her lips, and waited for whatever was about to happen.

The gallery enveloped in darkness.

The cadence of her breathing quickened with the beat of her heart. Of one thing she was certain. She must not show fear to any spirit. Not now. Not ever.

She heard the sound first. Footsteps tapping in quick rhythm against the floor. Someone ran toward her from the far end of the gallery. A heartbeat later, a small glimmer of vaporous celeste-white light appeared, twisting, billowing in shape and size as it neared. Soon, the shape of a young woman manifested. Dressed in rich clothing of the Tudor period, the ghost frantically looked over her shoulder as if being chased.

Unsure if the spirit could see her or not, and realizing she stood in the direct path of the distressed ghost, Patience stepped aside. She pressed her back against a darkened wall.

Still running with desperation to reach the holy chapel, the young woman looked over her shoulder again and screamed with terror. Patience looked in the same direction.

The heavy steps of others approached.

Suddenly, as if witnessing a portal opening into another time, the gallery itself changed. Bright daylight replaced night. The walls transformed to a different color altogether. Even the body of the young woman solidified into a living being as she pummeled with both hands on the chapel doors.

"Henry!" the woman screamed repeatedly.

"Catherine Howard," Patience whispered. She swallowed the burning pain in her throat, remembering what her aunt had said about the ill-fated young queen of Henry VIII.

I don't want to see this.

Her emotions were already wound too tight. Whether or not the young woman had been innocent or guilty, the sight of anyone—desperate and frightened—begging for their life, was not something Patience could handle in her present state.

Her head pounded so hard it felt as if it would split asunder. Shaking uncontrollably, the freezing temperature made Patience's body feel packed in blocks of ice. At the same time, like one drugged into a helpless state, she had not the strength to look away.

Two guards appeared, armed with swords extended as they raced toward the young woman. As one stood ready to use his weapon, the other quickly sheathed his sword then pulled Catherine Howard away from the doors. She kicked and scratched his face, drawing blood and breaking free again. Returning to the heavy doors of the chapel, she struck them with all her might, her hysterical cries reverberating throughout the gallery.

Both guards grabbed hold of her a second time, twisting her arms without mercy. They pulled the terrified young woman away with such force she lost her footing and howled like an animal in pain. Then, standing on either side of her frail body, they dragged King Henry's young, soon-to-be-executed, queen away.

Patience covered her ears. The piercing sound of Catherine Howard's screams escalated in volume and pitch, echoing with such force they could never be silenced.

Ignoring her tirade, the guards forced the doomed queen's unwilling body and tumultuous spirit to accompany them. As they did so, the room shifted.

Darkness overtook the light.

The three Tudor spirits changed back into mist-like ghostly entities. By the time they'd returned to that distant spot from whence they first appeared, they were once again orbs that simply dissolved.

At the same time, whatever window that opened—allowing Patience to see vividly into the 16th century—had closed. She stood once more in the haunted gallery as it appeared in 1813.

Biting her bottom lip, Patience realized she'd been sobbing. Her face awash with tears, her body shuddered most violently. Unable to catch her breath, her heartbeat pulsed hard and fast within her chest, seemingly determined to leap free or explode. She gasped for air, struggling like one who'd almost succumbed to drowning, desperate to now remain conscious.

What was happening to her?

If this were to be the first of many experiences she'd have at Hampton Court, unless she could shield herself and maintain it, her health might be destroyed.

What she'd witnessed were not phantom spirits. The too real tableau and ghosts looked alive—not iridescent, mist-like, faded watercolor images imprisoned within a mortal world.

Considering Hampton Court's history, the entire palace could have places where such hauntings occurred.

"Patience…dear, are you alright?"

She blinked and looked toward the direction of the voice. Lady Carlyle, candle in hand, studied her with no small amount of concern in her eyes. How long had her aunt been there? How much had she seen?

"Yes," Patience managed to say, her voice weak, broken.

"Like hell you are."

The sound of Leighton's voice shot forth like a clap of thunder. Standing in the shadows behind her aunt, he stepped forward—accompanied by a slender, dark-haired man.

Patience braced her back against the wall. She tried to hide the quaking of her body, or the fact she could hardly breathe let alone stand. But as a swirling mist blurred her vision, she could do nothing but embrace it.

Chapter 25

"A tisane is what the child needs. Lavender, butterbur, and blessed thistle with barley water will set her to rights."

"God's teeth, Sybil, she has naught the plague. Pear or quince custard will do greater good... and so much more delicious."

"A tisane."

"Custard."

Patience opened her eyes. Two old women stood beside her bed. Dressed as Tudor servants, they glared at one another. However, the moment they noticed she'd awakened—and could see them—they gasped and vanished.

Although the pain inside her skull throbbed without mercy, Patience felt relieved to be back in her aunt's apartment, comfortably situated in the bedchamber assigned to her. Unfortunately, two other voices that also awakened her were still present. Judging by the expressions on their faces—neither Leighton nor Lady Carlyle wanted to be challenged on what they considered her best interest.

"I appreciate your concern, Lord Leighton, but you have no say in the matter." Despite the fact Lady Carlyle spoke in a calm manner, her hands visibly trembled as she rinsed a cloth in a basin of water. "This is a family matter."

"A family matter?" Leighton stood in profile, arms crossed. "Countess, you saw what happened to her. She was pale as death. She requires a physician, not a handkerchief rinsed in rose water."

The dark-haired man Patience remembered seeing in the gallery with Leighton leaned against a far wall. Noting her gaze, he stepped forward.

"Calm yourself, Leighton," he said. "I daresay Lady Carlyle had no idea Miss Sinclair would be so affected. Besides which, the young lady is now awake."

Patience struggled to pull herself up to a seated position as all three individuals approached her bed. She brushed some loose strands of hair away from her face, and could well imagine how unattractive *pale as death* must look.

When Lady Carlyle tried to apply the damp cloth to her aching brow, Patience waved it away—earning a displeased frown from the countess. Much as it might ease her pain, Patience didn't want to look worse than she did to Leighton and his companion.

"What are you doing here, Lord Leighton?" She tried to sound composed, mildly curious. Unfortunately, raw tightening of her throat made it necessary to cough before being able to speak again. "That is to say, 'tis such a coincidence you should be here…now."

Leighton's lips twisted into something between a frown and a smirk that then changed into a rather annoying, placating smile. "Permit me to apprise you of what happened during your faint, Miss Sinclair. Lady Carlyle knows you wrote me of your travel plans."

"Oh?"

"Yes," Lady Carlyle said. "And as you can see, Lord Leighton, concerned for your welfare, accompanied his friend to Hampton Court without delay."

"A good thing, too," Leighton bit out. "I cannot stress enough that I find your decision impulsive and questionable, Lady Carlyle."

"Now, now," said the dark-haired man. "Perhaps we should direct our attention to Miss Sinclair and ascertain how she feels."

Patience studied Leighton's friend, comforted by the non-judgmental warmth of his smile and the sincere concern she saw in his dark brown eyes. But what she liked most about this stranger was his voice. Deep, quiet, soothing—like liquid velvet.

"I am better," she said.

"No, you are not," Leighton argued.

Startled by Leighton's somewhat hostile tone, Patience forced a smile and hoped to change the subject.

"Perhaps you should introduce me to your friend, Lord Leighton?"

"Yes, introduce us," the friend replied with a grin.

Leighton stared hard at her a moment longer then sighed. "Miss Sinclair, allow me to present Mr. Edward FitzWilliam Lyon Courtenay, a good friend who also resides at Hampton Court."

"You live here?" Patience asked.

"Yes, and have most all my life." Courtenay replied. "I am pleased to meet you, Miss Sinclair, though I regret we found you in such discomfort."

"Discomfort?" Leighton stared hard at his friend. "She was pale as death and cold as ice."

"Please stop saying that," Patience murmured.

"Saying what?" Leighton asked.

"That I was pale as death."

"Well…you were."

"How do you feel now?" Lady Carlyle asked.

"Do not think to say *better,*" Leighton contributed. "I can tell when you are not truthful, Patience."

"Patience?" Courtenay remarked with an amused expression.

"I meant, Miss Sinclair," Leighton corrected himself, his brow furrowed slightly.

Lady Carlyle sat on the edge of the bed. "You gave us quite a fright, my dear. What happened to you in the gallery?"

Even if she wanted to tell her aunt about the all-too-real experience, Patience had no intention of speaking in front of Leighton or his impeccably dressed friend.

For that matter, what had Leighton said to Mr. Courtenay about her? Unlike her first encounter with Charles Melville, she felt neither hostility nor reproach from this particular friend of Leighton. If anything, she saw only kindness in Courtenay's manner. Still…

"What did Lord Leighton tell you about me, Mr. Courtenay?"

The words came forth of their own volition, much to her embarrassment. She thought to clarify the question was not due to romantic curiosity, but the gentleman—having glanced briefly at Leighton—stepped closer to the bed.

"I shan't deceive you, Miss Sinclair. My friendship with Lord Leighton goes back many years. As such, I have known about you for some time. I always felt you were treated in a most unjust and cruel manner. I am pleased for your return."

"Thank you," she replied, surprised any of Leighton's friends might think favorably of her.

She nervously fidgeted with the bed covers until silenced by her aunt's stilling hand. Although the countess meant well, resentment stirred to have been silently reprimanded like a child.

Lady Carlyle glanced over her shoulder at the gentlemen. "I suspect my niece would like to know what Lord Leighton might have told Mr. Courtenay as to his reason for coming here."

"I know what she means." Leighton's gaze fixed on Patience. "She wants to know if I betrayed her confidence. Yes, Miss Sinclair, I told Lyon, or rather Mr. Courtenay, about your gift and my concern for your safety."

Patience struggled against tears. More than anything she wanted to prove she could live a normal life—especially to Leighton. Embracing her gift played a big part in taking control of her life, but she'd intended to keep it a guarded secret from the world. When and how she used it should be her choice, as well as who knows the secret.

Someone as respected and normal as Leighton could never understand how hard it has been for her to be accepted.

To be treated like everyone else.

Or, that this may be her last chance.

Patience looked steadily at Leighton, knowing he waited for her to respond. He had no idea how embarrassed she felt by his presence. Or, how much his controlling manner conveyed how little he believed in her.

If only he could hear her thoughts, he might know the depth of pain and disappointment spiraling through her body.

Not only had he broken his promise to keep her secret, but she realized by his display of temper and unyielding manner that even friendship with Leighton would be impossible. He saw her as someone ill, damaged. A frail damsel who would forever need someone to make decisions for her.

Anger stirred to a heated simmer in her veins.

Much as she didn't want people judging her, she didn't want people making decisions for her either. Not anymore.

How naïve she'd been. How trusting.

No one in this room believed her capable of taking care of herself. Neither did they respect her judgment. After betraying her trust, Leighton followed her to Hampton Court then presumed to argue he knew how she felt…and even the truthfulness of her words.

Most likely the kindness she'd seen in Courtenay's eyes had been pity. How could he not look upon her so, after seeing her wretched reaction to something he couldn't see or hear?

Even her aunt, whom she'd trusted to help secure her freedom, had brought her to Hampton Court as a testing ground. No thought given to her choice in the matter, or the fact she'd promised to help Anne. Even now, Anne could be weak to the point her soul might become doomed forever.

"Please leave," Patience said in a raw whisper.

Lady Carlyle turned toward Leighton. "Yes, I quite agree. We appreciate your assistance, but it would be best if you gentlemen leave."

"All of you," Patience clarified.

Clearly taken aback, Lady Carlyle turned toward Patience again, a curious expression upon her face. Not wanting to say anything more on the matter, especially in front of Leighton and the man he'd called Lyon, Patience returned her aunt's questioning stare with steady calm.

"Very well," Lady Carlyle said. "It has been a long, tiring day. If you need anything, I am in the next room."

As the countess and Mr. Courtenay walked toward the door, Leighton remained standing beside her bed.

"I did it for a reason," he said in a hushed voice.

"I am quite sure you did," she replied, noting Lady Carlyle and Courtenay talked in the doorway. "Just like my stepfather had his reasons."

"How can you compare me to Henley? I was concerned for your safety. I don't know why Lady Carlyle brought you here, but thought my friend could look out for you in my absence."

"I do not need or want anyone looking out for me."

"You don't?" He folded his arms across his chest. "Then shall I remind you how we found you in the gallery?"

"I was frightened." She glanced once more to where Lady Carlyle and Leighton's friend stood.

Leighton leaned down, his face inches away from her. "You were more than frightened."

"You do not understand. You could never understand."

"Understand what?"

"What 'tis like to *not* be normal."

He blanched and stepped back, staring at her with a stunned, slack-jawed expression.

Tears brimmed in her eyes. "Please go. I want only to sleep."

"You could always tell her," Courtenay said.

"Tell her what?" Leighton paced before the hearth.

"That you're not normal."

Leighton paused and noticed his friend trying not to laugh.

"I do not find this at all amusing, Lyon."

"I'm sure you don't, my friend." Leaning back in his chair, Courtenay stretched his arms over his head then crossed his booted feet.

Courtenay smiled wistfully. "Someone should tell her being normal can be limiting, rather like watching others run a race when you can barely walk. Everybody wants what they cannot have."

Taking a seat, Leighton studied his friend, remembering the years of chronic ill health that plagued Courtenay. "What do you think of her, really?"

"I like her." Courtenay replied. "Indeed, I find her refreshingly sweet, gentle, and genuine. I suspect she also has a will of iron as well."

"How could she compare me to her stepfather?"

"She wasn't comparing you. She was making a point." Courtenay leaned forward, hands clasped together. "Let me tell you what I saw that you did not. I saw an innocent, young lady who experienced something neither one of us can begin to describe. Something I also suspect she has not encountered before. She fainted then woke to the sound of you and Lady Carlyle arguing. Did you see how quickly she tried to show some semblance of composure in your presence? How she pushed aside the cool compress Lady Carlyle tried to apply? She was embarrassed—still feeling quite unwell—yet concerned with how much I knew about her ability."

"You're right," Leighton murmured.

"We all have secrets," Courtenay continued. "We all wear masks for one reason or another. One must trust someone very much to take off their mask. To show their true self, warts and all. Think of yourself. We have known each other since we were children. You confide in me because you trust me. She doesn't know me. I haven't earned her trust. For you to tell me her secret betrayed the trust she had in you."

"I had no choice. You know that."

"I'm not quite so sure. I do not doubt your concern for her welfare, and I can see there is reason for it. But I also think you told me because you wanted my reaction."

"No, I needed your help."

"Yes, but you also know my opinion on certain things, and my empathy for anyone maligned by gossip. You confided in me rather than Thorne or someone else, because you love her. And you know I understand the isolated, set apart life she has led. Who knows better what it is like to not be wanted than one also unwanted."

"Do you ever tire of being right, Lyon?"

Courtenay poured them both a glass of wine. "My vast intellect is my one saving grace."

Leighton studied the glass in his hand. "I do love her."

"Admitting it is half the battle…or so they say."

"I need to find a way to make her understand how frightened I am for her. She has no idea how much evil there is in the world. With each step she takes, I find myself so concerned for her safety I can barely think."

"You want my advice, Saint?"

Leighton downed his glass of wine then nodded.

"Take off your mask."

Chapter 26

Patience woke before dawn, wanting more than anything to take control of her life—if only for a short while before everyone else roused, anxious to question her about what happened in the gallery.

As she had done each day during her exile in Scotland, she dressed herself without the aid of a maid, and hastily fashioned her long auburn hair into a single plait down her back.

She wanted to clear her head. She needed fresh air.

Since leaving Scotland, she'd missed walking outside and breathing the crisp, fresh, highland air. Despite the loneliness of exile, it now seemed she'd had more personal freedom to do as she pleased in the highlands than since returning to England. Her stepfather would be sorely displeased to know that rather than make her more compliant, exile in Scotland had made her more unyielding—at least when it came to letting others tell her what to do.

Gathering a lightweight Kashmir shawl about her shoulders, she slipped out of her chamber and made her way toward the King's staircase, her footsteps echoing upon the stone steps.

The silence within the palace proved daunting, especially since she sensed the presence of spirits very near. For whatever reason, however, they lingered in the shadows—not attempting to contact her. For that, she was exceedingly grateful.

Although a better view of sunrise could best be seen from the East garden, Patience decided she would feel more comfortable in one of the smaller, walled gardens on the Tudor side, not far from where Cardinal Wolsey's rooms were located.

Cloaked in mist and lingering deep gray hues from the night, the fragrance of the garden prompted Patience to inhale deeply. Not sensing the presence of any wandering spirits, she smiled, closed her eyes. Needing to test her strength, she conjured her protective bubble.

After taking a leisurely promenade about the manicured hedgerows and knot-shaped flowerbeds, she sat upon a stone bench. Embracing the serenity of the garden, Patience considered the choices now facing her, not the least of which was whether to return to London or remain at Hampton Court a few more days.

In silence and solitude, Patience studied Hampton Court's gothic spires, parapets, and forest of twisted and carved chimneys. The brickwork looked different in the pre-dawn shading. An otherworldly magical serenity existed at the palace, especially now when the souls within its walls were peaceful and the palace slept.

Lady Carlyle's reasons for bringing her to Hampton Court could not be ignored.

The palace was indeed a contained village, inhabited by the living and ghosts of the past. Neither could she ignore it held only a small ripple of what she would experience in the great expanse of London—or anywhere else she might visit.

If she wanted to be free, she needed to learn how to protect herself from the multitude of spirits who roamed the earth. To be able to navigate life among mortals with ease and grace—like Lady Carlyle had learned to master.

Much as she thought she had the strength to do so, what happened in the gallery proved otherwise. Seeing ghosts trapped in a pivotal moment of their life was one thing. To feel physically transported into that time—to lose strength in the mortal world in which she lived—had been terrifying.

What if it happened again?

What if she found herself trapped in that other time?

The call of a songbird distracted Patience.

Inhaling deeply, trying to chase away her fears, the remaining shadows of dawn slowly faded with the new day's lengthening light. She could not help but wonder if, as she witnessed the brief blending of night and day in the garden, it might prove an omen. Hampton Court had shown her there were times when the worlds of the living and the dead shared the same space.

To the north, where the kitchens were located, smoke drifted from a cluster of chimneys into the cool morning sky.

She needed to return to her aunt's apartments, but did not know what to say to Lady Carlyle—or Leighton, for that matter. Instead, she wanted to remain in the garden.

Dew glistened like diamonds upon emerald turf. An ethereal white mist continued to hover above shrubs and flowerbeds like a magical, warm blanket conjured by faeries during the night.

A smile curved her lips as she listened to a soft breeze drifting hither and yon. Ever so delicate, it comforted her like a loving embrace.

At once, something caught her eye—a slight movement to her left.

She looked quickly and saw what appeared to be the shimmering ghost of a very small child. It looked briefly at her then turned and darted into an arched opening formed between two dense Yew trees. Beyond the arch, she could see the top half of the Banqueting House—a small brick building set apart from the palace.

Perhaps the young ghost dwelled there.

If there was something she could not block out—nor, indeed, did she ever want to— 'twas ghost children. Nothing took precedence over helping those innocent little ones find the peace and paradise they deserved.

Standing, Patience quickly walked toward the arch, noting how mist on the finely crushed gravel path drifted away with her movement. Pausing before the green arch the wee ghost had entered, she glanced back toward the rest of the garden. A few of the same spirits she'd seen upon arrival were now in the far distance, once more floating about and conversing. They seemed not to notice her which meant her shield was working.

Her confidence—all but torn to shreds yesterday—seemed to grow with each beat of her heart. At the same time, Patience reminded herself this was one garden. Hundreds of spirits resided within the palace walls—perhaps even thousands. Thus, after what happened to her in the haunted gallery last night, she needed to be diligent and focused at all times.

She looked at the cool, dark opening under the arch and saw a narrow path—one the ghost child must have followed. Did it lead to a private entrance to the Banqueting House or perhaps another garden? Stepping cautiously inside, it did not take long to realize the path ended at a high brick wall that appeared to surround the Banqueting House. She had no recollection what might be on the other side of the pavilion.

Had the child disappeared behind the wall and into the Banqueting House? Perhaps it turned to the right or left—both paths narrow and almost hidden by overgrown foliage that allowed very little sunlight to penetrate.

"Are you here, *leanaban*?" Staring at the ancient brick and mortar barrier before her, Patience rested her palm against the wall and tried to sense the small spirit. There was nothing.

Sadness swept over her. With all the spirits at Hampton Court, she hadn't thought there might be a young child amongst them.

She turned about, resting her back against the wall. At once, her breath caught in her throat. From where she now stood, the dark green natural arch formed by the Yew trees resembled a keyhole into another world. A small glimpse of the pond garden could be seen. Vibrant with sunlight, color, fragrance, and life—it beckoned.

More than ever, she realized what it must be like to be a ghost. To not know where you belong. Standing back, forever hidden in the shadows, taunted by reminders of life in all its glory. Clinging to what you know and desperate to be part of it again.

'*Why should they move on?*', Lady Carlyle had said yesterday. '*They were here first.*'

Confusion and guilt ripped through her. Rather than put up walls between herself and ghosts, what would happen if she treated them the way she wanted to be treated? Rather than assume they wanted to bother or torment her, perhaps she was meant to speak with them. To listen to what, if anything, they had to say. Not everyone may want to move on. They may only want to be accepted.

Like me.

Her blocking technique had done its job, so much so that a wee child spirit had been unable to communicate with her.

Walking back inside the serene pond garden, she remembered the ghosts at supper last evening. Perhaps they wanted to warn her about harm she might encounter in the haunted gallery?

Had I listened to them, I might have been better prepared. Or, been able to avoid the pain and illness that overcame me.

After exiting the garden, she proceeded to Clock Court and paused to study the wall of arched mullioned windows for the Great Hall. The exterior stone casing of the two-story high, stained glass window gave her pause.

Were the Tudor ghosts still there?

Were they watching her at this very moment—frustrated by her refusal to speak with them?

Realizing she needed to fight her fears and truly embrace her gift, Patience lowered her head. Keeping her gaze on the cobblestone pavement of the courtyard, she slowly exhaled and released the protective bubble she'd conjured about herself. At once, the all-too-familiar pins and needles sensation pierced her body, alarm bells that struck every fiber of her being and warned a multitude of spirits were near.

I can do this.

Chin held high, she gathered her shawl tighter about her shoulders and entered the palace. If someone wanted to speak to her, she would be cordial and polite.

Who's to say fear of the unknown had not been her greatest weakness?

Fear of what people thought of her.

Fear of opening herself to spirits who wanted to talk with her.

After all, Patience had only to look at her Aunt Catherine to realize she could also live a happy, normal life…without being constantly on guard or exhausting her physical strength.

There is a way to filter the good from the bad.

And I will find it.

"You should not be here."

The disembodied voice had a slight foreign accent and sounded gruff, almost hoarse…as if the person speaking were ill or had not used their voice to speak in a very long time.

Standing in the center of the massive marble foyer leading to the base of the King's staircase, Patience looked about. She saw no one, alive or dead. Regardless, an icy chill surrounded her—and she sensed an angry spirit's presence.

With trepidation, she slowly ascended the great staircase, each step made of Irish stone. The fingertips of her right hand lightly trailed the wood and ironwork railing—ready to turn back and flee at a moment's notice. As she steadily climbed the massive wide steps, the cold intensified. Reminded of her frightening encounter in the gallery by the Chapel Royal, she paused.

Shivering, her gaze swept to the top of the staircase and to who or what might be waiting for her there.

"Did you not hear what I said, foolish girl? Leave this place!"

With stilted breathing, she carefully studied the various monochromatic painted panels depicting emblems and trophies of war. An elaborately detailed mural of Romanesque and Grecian splendor also lined the winding wall of King William's Great Staircase.

Sensing the entity's voice came from that direction, she scrutinized the fresco with its frolicking Nymphs, Satyrs, Cupids, and Zephyrs. Fame blew its trumpet whilst Pan played his flute. Gods and Goddesses, including Apollo, Hercules, Mercury, and Diana were immortalized in glorious attire of various hues and color—forever frozen in an idyllic columned domain amongst the clouds.

In one such cloud she saw the vaporous image of a ghost staring down at her with contemptuous, narrowed eyes. Like a storm cloud brewing at sea, his resentment—or ill temper—at her presence caused its gray-white aura to undulate and increase in size, moment by moment, almost like the rapid breathing of an angry mortal. The ghost's eyes—large, dark, and piercing seemed to bore into her very soul.

Her body tensed, watching, waiting to see if the spirit would leave its lofty perch and lash out violently at her. He did not move, but continued to glare with great hostility.

She could not help but note the billowing mist that surrounded the ghost—blending as it were with the clouds of the painting—made it difficult to see his body in any detail. The thought occurred he hoped to frighten her by showing only his head.

Keeping her gaze fixed on the ghost, Patience moistened her lips and contemplated what she might say to engage the spirit in conversation rather than stoke its fiery temper.

"You should not be here."

The sound of another voice—louder, closer in proximity, and using the same words spoken by the enraged mural ghost—startled Patience so badly she screamed and lost her footing on the ancient steps.

It happened so fast.

She desperately tried to regain her balance. Both arms flailed like the sails of a windmill as she teetered on a slick precipice, to no avail. In the next heartbeat, as her body toppled backwards, Patience could do nothing more than squeeze her eyes shut in anticipation of certain death.

Chapter 27

Cursing himself for a fool, Leighton watched with horror as Patience fell backwards from King William's Great Staircase.

Not caring who might see, he extended his right arm, palm facing down, fingers spread wide. At once, bursts of white light shot forth from his fingertips, one after another like shooting stars. They merged together to form a half-circle protective arc behind Patience's body.

With focused determination, Leighton held the position of his arm steady as the light bands cradled Patience mid-air, and guided her body down to where he stood. Once safely within reach of his arms, the light vanished.

Leighton tensed as the dazed woman in his arms opened her eyes, blinked at him, and then looked toward the tall, winding staircase.

"What just happened?" she whispered.

"You fell."

"And you caught me?"

"In a manner of speaking." Leighton gruffly cleared his throat, well aware the heat pulsating through his body, all but boiling his blood, had more to do with desire for Patience than any residual effect from the powers that saved her life.

"I don't understand. Where were you standing?"

"Does it matter?" he asked. "You fell. I caught you."

"But 'twas so strange. I was falling. Then it seemed as if time stood still and I was floating."

He opted to remain silent. After all, what could he say in response? Besides which, he held Miss Patience Sinclair in his arms. Considering how thankful he was she'd not been harmed, all he wanted to do was kiss her soundly. Unfortunately, the fright she'd suffered, and the wary expression in her eyes, made him more guarded.

"Yes, well, I daresay I should apologize for startling you. I didn't realize how preoccupied you were studying Verrio's mural when I spoke."

"Verrio?" She looked again at the high point on the staircase where she'd been standing.

It didn't take much effort on his part to know what she thought. Namely, how had she fallen backwards down the King's staircase from that point, landing at the base of the stairs in his arms?

"As I said, you shouldn't be here," he repeated in a somewhat stern tone. "There is evil in this place."

Patience's gaze returned to meet his. Her eyes sparkled like radiant jewels. Perhaps she did not believe him, or wanted further explanation. Then again, as a young woman who saw ghosts—and after what had happened to her in the gallery—she might already be aware of the evil energy at Hampton Court.

He waited expectantly for her to say something. To ask something. However, the ensuing silence as they stared at one another generated an altogether different energy, one that conjured, at least for him, fires of passion he'd been determined to control.

A sudden blush blossomed on her cheeks. He desperately wanted to know if the heightened color had been triggered by earnest affection or—far less encouraging—simple embarrassment.

Does she feel the same current racing through her body? The same exhilarating, almost overpowering quickening that makes my heart thunder in my chest?

"I—I cannot thank you enough for coming to my rescue, Lord Leighton." Her voice had a breathless quality. "I shouldn't have wanted to die in such a stupid fashion."

"I shouldn't want you to die at all!" The impulsive words shot forth from his suddenly constricted throat before he could hold them back.

A faint smile curled the corners of her mouth. "Alas, I fear that end is inevitable, but I thank you for the thought."

Realizing he still held her in his arms and anyone could come upon them, Leighton gently placed Patience back on her feet. Not prepared for the strange emptiness he then felt, he clasped his hands together behind his back.

"Lord Leighton, might I ask why you think there is evil in this place? That is to say, why do you speak of evil with such certainty?" Her gaze swept up the staircase again before returning to study him more thoughtfully.

Clearly, her intelligent, curious mind would not rest without an explanation. At once, the words of his friend repeated in his thoughts. The time had come to take off his mask.

Somehow he sensed Patience, above anyone else, would understand. Her ability to see and communicate with ghosts had been a closely guarded secret, one she'd been desperate to hide. Ironically, he could not help but recognize the powers that made them so different—abilities kept private even from one another—now explained the intense emotional, physical, and even spiritual connection he'd experienced with Patience from the moment they met.

Years ago, he hadn't known about her unique power—only that when she came into his world he'd suddenly felt alive and whole for the first time.

Losing her then had almost destroyed him. And there was no denying that since her return, he'd been fighting another losing battle—trying to protect his heart and deny the desire and depth of emotion he had for her.

It proved an impossible task.

Each beat of his heart echoed a constant warning.

You cannot lose her again.

She is the one you have been waiting for.

No one could ever understand the unrelenting magnitude of his emotions. God knows he dreaded the reaction of his friends. Thorne would smirk with disgust and consider him a love-struck fool.

But as he studied the upturned face of Patience Sinclair, so lovely and innocent, curious yet wary, what others thought no longer concerned him. There was only one thing that mattered at the moment. Her.

A hush settled within him.

A strange knowing lifted from the depths of his being.

If love and trust are meant to walk hand-in-hand through life, now is the time to begin that journey.

Leighton swallowed the lump of raw emotion stuck in his throat. "Miss Sinclair, there is something important I need to tell you…now…without delay." He glanced about the hall. "But not here. Someplace more private."

"If you'd like." She looked down and fiddled somewhat with her shawl. In actual fact, her attention focused more on situating it about her shoulders than their conversation.

"Have you seen the Banqueting House?" he asked.

She looked at him quickly, eyes widened with obvious surprise.

"I know where it is," she answered.

"It would offer us privacy. You see, I am staying there. It is the residence of my friend, Lyon…Mr. Courtenay. You met him last night."

"I remember."

"He will, of course, not be there when we speak…unless you are not comfortable being alone with me. However, I must insist your aunt not be present."

A delicate eyebrow arched in response. Leighton couldn't help but find a small measure of amusement in the way she contemplated his words. Or, the possible reason he had for speaking with her in private without a proper chaperone.

No matter how hard she tried, Miss Patience Sinclair would never be able to presume or predict what he intended to tell her.

"Do you trust me?" he asked, determined to hide the ache in his heart if she did not.

"Lord Leighton, you saved my life. I trust you implicitly."

He bowed at the waist. "I thank you for the compliment."

"However, I do have one request. I have been walking about in the garden since dawn and not yet had breakfast. So that I may be more attentive to what you wish to say, it may be best if I return to my aunt's apartment, have something to eat, and come to the Banqueting House afterwards."

The thought of Patience returning to her aunt's apartments concerned him. Lady Carlyle might detain her niece, or insist upon being present during their private conversation. He wanted neither to happen, especially since he wasn't sure he trusted Lady Carlyle. Most definitely, he questioned her plans for Patience, and her ability to keep her niece safe.

"No need for that," he answered. "My friend has an excellent, most amiable cook. Since I am always hungry, no doubt he can conjure something up for us both in a wink."

"Well, at the very least, I should send word to my aunt and let her know—"

"I prefer you do not."

She studied him thoughtfully. "I must say your attitude toward Lady Carlyle is very telling. Is it that you do not like her, or that you know she would not approve of my meeting with you at the Banqueting House?"

"What I have to say is a private matter. Indeed, it is something I must ask you to not discuss. If you cannot do so, tell me now."

"Does this have anything to do with the snuffbox and Anne?"

Leighton tried to hide his disappointment at her question. Still, he should have known she would think he wished to speak with her about helping Anne's ghost.

"I do have information to discuss with you about that," he said with a slight nod. "But what I have to tell you is in reference to the remark you made to me last night."

"My remark?"

"The remark that I do not know what it is like to not be normal," he reminded. "You see, Miss Patience Sinclair, nothing could be further from the truth."

Chapter 28

Patience observed Leighton as he paced before the fireplace in the Banqueting House. The steady, masculine movement of his body reminded her of a restless racehorse. His hands, clasped together behind his back, only seemed to accentuate the width of his broad shoulders.

Every so often he paused, looked at her as if about to speak, then would shake his head and pace again. His behavior proved exceedingly odd. She didn't know what to think, but the notion he intended to lecture her seemed a distinct possibility.

Not wanting to interrupt his thoughts, she glanced about the room. In particular, she studied the ornate ceiling and wall murals that appeared to have been painted by the same artist who did the King's staircase. However, one could stare only so long at frescoes of cherubs and naked people without feeling rather awkward—especially in mixed company.

With a sigh, she shifted in her chair. Noting a crease in the skirt of her morning dress, she smoothed it. Realizing her shawl had slipped about her shoulders, she adjusted it.

Embarrassed she had not taken time to fashion her hair or wear a bonnet, Patience silently vowed never to leave her chamber again without taking greater pains with her appearance. Self-consciously, she pulled forward her single plait of long hair from behind her back to drape it—in what she hoped might look more fetching—over one shoulder.

As for Leighton, he looked immaculately attired—from his polished black boots to form-fitting buff trousers. Beneath a black superfine and meticulously tailored coat, he wore a gray, black, and white diamond-patterned waistcoat. A snowy white shirt could be glimpsed beneath his handsomely fashioned cravat.

The disparity between their contrasting attire served to remind Patience—as Anne Melville had so boldly stated—that Leighton was the grandson of a duke and she was...*Scottish.*

In truth, there were far more alarming discrepancies about their lives that made it impossible for her to be anything more than a friend to Viscount Leighton.

Suddenly, she heard a soft chuckle and looked toward the open doorway where Leighton's friend, Mr. Courtenay, stood in obvious amusement.

"Good God, Leighton," he said. "You have been pacing for the past twenty minutes."

"I was not," Leighton responded with a decidedly peevish expression.

"I beg to differ." Courtenay entered. Arms folded across his chest, he proceeded to stand in the center of the room and observe them both. "Tell me, Miss Sinclair, has he spoken at all in the past twenty minutes?"

"I do not know if it has been twenty minutes, but…no, he has not spoken."

Mirroring his friend's posture, Leighton crooked a brow. "If you must know, I have been thinking of the best way to broach the subject."

"Of course you were," replied Courtenay. "Well, my friend, not that I want to rush you, but you best speak your mind before Lady Carlyle dispatches servants to find her niece."

Leighton and his friend stared at one another, communicating something with their eyes that Patience could in no way imagine. One thing was certain. Much as she enjoyed being in Leighton's company—if only to watch him pace—she desperately wanted to know what the man had intended to tell her. And Mr. Courtenay had given her a clever idea how to go about it.

"Perhaps it would be best if we discussed the matter another time." She stood and smiled at the two men. "I daresay Lady Carlyle is looking for me at this moment. I should not want to distress her further by my absence."

In response, Courtenay arched an eyebrow at Leighton.

Leighton, on the other hand, shook his head and gestured for her to be seated again. After she had done so, he rubbed the back of his neck then moved a chair from a gaming table, setting it in front of her. When he sat, they faced one another close enough to whisper.

She looked steadily into his eyes, waiting for him to speak, desperately fighting the desire to nibble on her bottom lip.

"Last night," he began, "when you said I would never know what it is like to not be normal, the words pierced me like an arrow. You see, contrary to what you might think of me, I do know. Like you, I have kept a carefully guarded secret all my life. You think you are not normal because you see and speak with ghosts? Well, I am proof there are other people who have abilities so frightening they have no choice but to hide them."

Her gaze drifted to his friend, now standing behind Leighton with a somber expression. She sensed whatever Leighton had to tell her was not only the truth, but very difficult, perhaps painful, for him to confess.

Returning her attention to Leighton, Patience felt such overwhelming concern for him she instinctively cupped the side of his face. "Whatever it is, I believe in your goodness, Leighton. I will tell no one."

A slight glimmer shined in his eyes, making them seem more aquamarine in color, but he quickly blinked it away. Then, taking her hand from his face, he kissed the palm before releasing it.

Courtenay rested a hand on Leighton's shoulder. "I will leave you two now."

"Thank you, my friend," Leighton said.

After Leighton's friend had quit the room, closing the doors behind him, Patience clasped her hands together in her lap and tried to offer Leighton an encouraging smile. He did smile in return then rubbed his jaw in a thoughtful manner.

"What is this ability you have, Tristan?"

His eyes widened upon hearing her call him by his given name. "I have often wondered if you would ever call me by that name, again."

"We are friends, are we not?"

"Yes…friends." Standing, he returned his chair to its place at the gaming table. With his hands resting on the back of the chair, he looked toward a window that overlooked the garden. "The ability I have is something that has been passed down to the men in my family. In another time, another age, we were believed to be everything from the mortal children of angels or gods, to descendants of magical beings or sorcerers. There is a name for us, one often misinterpreted."

He looked at her again. "Lightbearer."

"I have never heard of it before."

"I am not surprised. In any event, we have the ability to conjure and control radiant light. This light emanates from our body and can be manipulated in a very powerful, protective, or even deadly manner. We also have the ability to perceive evil. That is why I said you should not be here at Hampton Court."

She stood and crossed to him, an overwhelming warmth sweeping from her heart into every part of her body. "You used this power to save me this morning."

"Yes."

"Then I *was* truly floating."

"Yes."

Patience clasped her hands together and pressed them against her mouth, unable to suppress a giggle. "I think this power you have is wonderful. For certain, I would have been seriously injured or died had you not been there to help me."

"Yes, you likely would have...but you also would not have fallen had I not surprised you. And this power is not as wonderful as it might seem, especially when one is a frightened child and has not learned how to control it."

"Something happened to you as a boy," she said, sensing from Leighton's expression he spoke about himself.

He nodded. "I was a boy of eleven, away at school. We had been studying ancient Rome and visited Hadrian's Wall. Full of mischief, I went with a group of friends off to do some exploring on our own. We found a cave. It contained the ruins of an ancient temple. There was an altar, and a stone circle on the floor with various symbols etched into its surface. Inside this circle were large statues of Roman gods. My friends were excited at what we'd found, but I had sensed evil from the moment we entered the cave."

"Oh, my," Patience whispered.

"My friends were laughing, eager to play. They climbed onto the bases of the statues and pretended to be a Roman god. I stood in the center of the circle. I told them we should leave. That we must return to our school group. But they were too caught up in their game, and did not listen. I turned toward my other friend, the more scholarly one in our group. He was inspecting the altar, several feet away outside the circle."

Leighton slowly walked over to stand before the window, and although he appeared to be looking down at the gardens it seemed obvious to Patience he saw that cave from his boyhood again.

She joined him at the window. "What happened?"

"The evil I sensed began to grow, almost as if our presence in the cave fed it, or strengthened it. It began to move, ever so slowly, from the shadows. I was frozen, terrified. I knew only that I had to protect us. So, I did."

He looked down, his brow furrowed with a great sadness. "Something went terribly wrong. To this day, I don't quite understand what happened. I only know I am responsible."

He turned to face Patience. "I summoned every bit of power I possessed. Something I had been warned by my grandfather could be deadly. But I didn't know what else to do. Too focused upon what I needed to do, I didn't realize the power I wielded. I was later told, from my friend who'd been standing on the altar, that the entire cave began to quake, and a strange wind came out of nowhere. The water in an underground lake first steamed then bubbled like boiling black oil. My body was enclosed is a circle of blinding light that magnified and emanated outward like a giant wave, striking each one of my friends in the circle."

"The boys playing on the statues?"

"Yes," he replied in a near whisper.

"Did they…did they die?"

"Die? No, blessedly they didn't die. But impossible as it sounds, my power somehow triggered some great magical force in that cave. What I did altered the very core of their beings. Each boy in the circle came out of that cave with the legendary power of the Roman god whose statue upon which they stood. They didn't understand what had happened to them. Neither did I. In truth, we were fortunate to get out of the cave at all. It was completely destroyed."

"What happened afterwards to these boys?"

"We were good friends before, but after sharing an experience no one else could ever imagine we became close as brothers. Our lives were irreparably changed by what happened in that cave. Even my power, which was unusually strong for a boy, increased threefold. As you can well imagine, dealing with the aftermath—the manifestation of powers and changes to our bodies as we matured—proved dangerous and frightening. As a result, apart from my father and grandfather—and now you—no one but those who were in that cave knows what happened."

"What about the families of your friends?"

"No," Leighton said with a sad sigh. "We realized what happened had to be kept secret from even them. The revelation that a group of boys possessed supernatural powers could easily have targeted us and our families for persecution, trial, or imprisonment—perhaps all three. My family, with its legacy as Lightbearers, has long accepted that society is not so civilized. They will seek to destroy what they do not understand."

"Or, say someone is mad and put them in an asylum against their will." Patience lightly touched Leighton's forearm. "Like the threats of my stepfather."

He cupped his hand over hers. "Threats should never be taken lightly, but Lord Henley will have to deal with me first."

Patience felt herself blush beneath Leighton steady gaze. "So, you and your friends have protected one another's secret since childhood?"

"Yes, and with the help of my father and grandfather, we learned how to control our abilities. We also formed a secret group—or rather an allegiance—called the *Legion of Mithras*. We vowed to protect one another, to guard the truth about our powers, and use them only in life or death situations, always careful not to be observed. Most of all, we vowed never to harm or injure anyone."

A movement outside the window drew their attention. Leighton's friend sat in his private garden reading a book. "Which one is he?" Patience asked.

"The boy on the altar, the one outside the circle. He didn't receive any powers. Truth be told, he became gravely ill in the weeks and months after the incident. He'd always been a frail, sickly child, but his health deteriorated so much we feared he would die. Because the school felt him contagious to others, he was sent home where he spent most of his youth. Still, the bonds of our friendship were unbreakable. He is not only a member of the *Legion*, but its rock foundation. If not for him, I know not what might have happened to the rest of us…or our friendships."

"You called him Lyon," she said. "I somehow think it has another meaning rather than its reference to a family name."

"True. In my opinion, his courage knows no bounds. He is loyal to a fault, wise beyond his years, and always the voice of calm and reason."

"Leighton, I cannot help but feel there is a reason you told me about the *Legion of Mithras*."

"You are too perceptive, Miss Sinclair," he said with a gentle smile. "But yes, there is something I need to tell you. Something that concerns the murder of Miss Melville."

She tensed as Leighton removed his snuffbox from the pocket of his waistcoat.

"The snuffbox," Patience said in a near whisper.

"Years ago, I had identical boxes made as a gift for each member of the *Legion*."

Patience inhaled sharply. "Then Charles Melville is also a member of the *Legion*. That is why he became so angry when he heard Anne remembered her killer had an identical box."

"Yes," Leighton replied. "Set your mind at ease. I met with all the members of the group and inspected their boxes. Not one had the painting Miss Melville mentioned. I also made sure to verify that each box was an original, not a copy."

"But how could someone else have an identical snuffbox?"

"That is what the *Legion* is trying to find out. We suspect someone had a replica made, which means the killer could be anyone."

"The other members are looking?"

He nodded. "Melville and I told them his sister is dead; indeed, that she has been murdered by someone with a box like ours. To protect you, I said she appeared to us as a ghost."

"You told them that? And they believed you?"

"The fact Melville substantiated my story helped. Still, it was the first time I have ever lied to my friends. I do not rest easy with that knowledge. But I hope, now that you know about *us*, that you and I can tell them the truth. That we can all work together to solve this murder."

Patience recognized a strange disquiet in her soul. She trusted Leighton, but was she ready to blindly trust his friends in the *Legion*? She could understand Leighton's reasoning. As he said, the killer could be anyone.

All things considered, her heart urged her to trust Leighton's judgment. Having the *Legion* working with her and Leighton seemed the best way to find Anne's murderer, and to stop him before he killed again.

"If only Anne could remember his identity." She released a heavy sigh. "For all I know, she may have remembered something. This morning I considered staying here—as Lady Carlyle wants—to learn how to strengthen my ability to protect myself. I cannot waste time, however, and must return to London."

"Wrong." Leighton held both of her hands in his. "*We* must return. Furthermore, I believe I know how to stop Lady Carlyle from interfering and also remove that vile threat from your stepfather."

"How?" asked Patience.

"The solution is simple. I intend to marry you."

Chapter 29

Between the frantic beating of Patience's heart and a sudden sensation she could not breathe, she could do little more than stare at Leighton.

He intends to marry...me?

The thought proved at first exhilarating then frightening. She studied Leighton's somber expression, void of any emotion. Looking down at her small hands confined rather helplessly in his powerful grasp, she realized a painful truth.

His decision to marry her had been based on chivalrous concern, not love. Like a noble knight, he saw her as a helpless, fragile, young woman.

She could not condemn him for it. Had he not seen her cowering in fear, physically affected by what she'd witnessed in the haunted gallery? Was he not aware of the threat her stepfather had made? For that matter, her own mother had shunned and abandoned her, refusing to listen to any explanation that might justify her daughter's often odd behavior.

In truth, Leighton could protect her.

She'd always felt safe with him and now, knowing the truth about his supernatural powers, she recognized there was no one alive who could be a warrior for her like Tristan St. Ives, Viscount Leighton. The man could even sense evil.

And yet, she'd seen how strong-willed Leighton could be. Although a good man, she could not help but think marriage to him would become another type of prison. The independence and freedom she so desperately wanted—to be herself, without others telling her what to do and how to live—would be forfeited.

Because she loved him, she might be able to endure the loss of freedom, especially at first. But seeing him every day, knowing he did not love her, and constantly aware he made this great sacrifice because he felt sorry for her...would become unbearable.

Much as she'd always dreamed they might one day marry, to do so now—under these conditions—would be altogether too selfish of her to consider.

"You are truly my good friend," Patience said, her voice faint, emerging from a throat taut with emotion. "But I could never be the wife you deserve."

His grip on her hands softened, although he did not pull away.

"What kind of marriage can replace finding true love?" she continued, struggling not to let him see the torment in her heart.

"You care for me," he replied. "Not every marriage has a guarantee of love."

Patience squeezed his hands for emphasis, knowing she had to make him understand. "Please know I am honored, and would marry you, but not at the price of your happiness."

Much to her amazement, a slow, almost mischievous grin came upon his face and his eyes twinkled. "You must not fear for my happiness. I know exactly what I am doing."

Not so easily convinced, Patience withdrew her hands from his grasp. "Do you? Marriage is…forever."

Needing space to think, she crossed to stand before the fireplace. "I appreciate your willingness to help and protect me, especially from my stepfather, but to gamble with your future is a wager not to be taken lightly."

"I would never gamble with your future…or mine."

"But it *is* a gamble." She turned to face him, exasperated by his stubborn refusal to understand her meaning. "All my life, I have wanted to be loved and accepted for myself. To not be forced to hide or made to feel I am unworthy or unwanted. You, on the other hand, were raised with love and understanding. Mayhap 'tis difficult for you to understand what it feels like to have neither. Or, how important it becomes to want both."

Unable to look at his bewildered face, Patience turned to face the hearth again. "I know you care about me, but however noble your intentions, or how right it seems to you at this moment, I feel it wrong to compromise one's hopes or expectations for marriage."

"One must always hope for love," he said, coming to her side. "I understand you have doubts. That you may not feel ready to embrace the idea of marriage to me. However, ask yourself who would understand you as I do. Now that you know about me, you must see the logic. There may be no two people so well suited."

"So, you feel we should marry because of our abilities?"

"Not *because* of them, but with each other we have no need to hide what the world is not ready to understand. With me, you can always be you—not what someone expects you to be. I cannot help but feel fate, or whatever you wish to call it, has brought us together for a reason."

"Fate is determined upon one's choices," she replied.

"You know what will happen if Lord Henley learns you have left Scotland. The man would like nothing better than to see you completely destroyed. You are not of age. He has the authority to deal with you as he sees fit. As for Lady Carlyle, however sincere her motives, she has made decisions for you that I do not think you wanted but simply obeyed. Why else did you write me the letter about leaving for Hampton Court? You did not want to come here."

"No, I wanted to stay in town to help Anne and—"

"And prove you are *not* mad? Yes, I heard you say those words the morning I first came to Carlyle House." He shook his head. "You are not mad, Patience. You have nothing to prove…to anyone."

Patience struggled against tears. "What about your grandfather the duke, and your entire family—"

"My family will support my decision, and understand how special you are—particularly my grandfather and my parents."

"You make it sound so easy. Acceptance. Protection. Yet you have said nothing about what you gain from this marriage—or anything about…well…intimacy."

He cleared his throat softly, as if broaching the subject of physical relations with her was not a discussion he wanted to explore. She also noticed the cadence of his breathing quickened. The thought occurred he did not know what to say without offending her. No doubt, he already had a beautiful mistress, someone who knew far more about pleasing a man than she could ever imagine.

An awkward silence lengthened, adding to her dismal view that she would be a wife in name only.

"I should not have said anything," she murmured.

"No, you ask a practical question," he replied at long last. "I know my proposal of marriage is sudden. It will take time for us *both* to adjust as husband and wife. All I can say is, despite the fact I feel we should wed without delay—and at least make a *public* pretense ours is a true marriage—I have no intention of demanding husbandly rights. I will never expect you to do anything you do not want."

A wave of embarrassment swept over Patience.

She stepped away and made a pretense of straightening her shawl.

'Twas worse than she imagined.

She had thought he might want to consummate their union if, for no other reason, but to *not* have its validity questioned. She also considered he would want children to carry on his family name.

However, not only did Leighton want a marriage in name only, they were to pretend otherwise.

She needed no other acknowledgement that the man she loved harbored not an inkling of desire for her. Then again, the very fact of his proposal said he truly cared about her as a friend, and was concerned for her future.

Perhaps she expected too much far too soon.

He may grow to love me in time.

In the past, before secrets and the machinations of others had separated them, Leighton had shown her tenderness and affection, albeit chaste kisses and gentle embraces.

She then recalled his words that one must always hope for love. Such hope conjured a spark deep in her soul, one that ignited into a fiery challenge to win his abiding love and desire for intimacy with her.

"Perhaps in time I *could* be his true wife," she whispered to herself, realizing all too late that in the stillness of the room Leighton might have overheard. She quickly looked over her shoulder to gauge a possible reaction.

Leighton stood with his muscular arms folded across his chest, a contemplative pose, whilst looking down at his boots with a quirked brow.

She nibbled nervously on her bottom lip, hoping he had not heard her wistful remark but merely spotted a speck of dirt on his Hessians. After clearing her throat to gain his attention, Leighton looked at her with an expression which neither indicated what he thought or felt.

"Leighton, if you should change your mind…"

"I will not change my mind. In point of fact, I have never been so sure of anything in my life."

He closed the distance between them. His thumb and forefinger nudged her chin to look up at him. "Trust me, as your *good* friend—one who cares for your happiness very much."

Patience gazed up at the man she had never stopped loving—and thought would never see again—ever aware of the almost breathless effect he had on her and the warm, fluttering sensation that coursed through her body whenever he came near.

"I do trust you," she said.

"Do you agree to marry me?"

The intensity of Leighton's expression and the rhythm of his low breathing—almost in tandem with her own—combined with the hairsbreadth-from-an-embrace closeness of their bodies had an almost hypnotic effect on Patience.

More than anything she wanted to marry Leighton.

To never be parted from him.

Now, it seemed the once fragile dream—all but torn to shreds three years ago—could become a reality.

If only she could cast aside her insecurity and doubts about making him happy. Of not being an obligation and burden he would soon regret.

"You could have anyone," she whispered.

"So could you," he said with a wink and dimpled smile.

Tears blurred her vision. His wink and smile touched her heart and roused a precious memory. Sweeping her back in time to when they'd first met. He would do that exact thing whenever he noticed she seemed afraid or uncomfortable—especially in public.

Removing a handkerchief from his coat pocket, Leighton dabbed at her eyes ever so gently, making a tsking sound with his tongue.

"Enough tears and chitchat to dissuade me from my course, Miss Sinclair. I will have your answer now."

She sniffled and grabbed his handkerchief, properly blotting her eyes and cheeks. "Oh, very well then, yes. I will marry you and do my best to be a good and loving wife. But do not blame me if you live to regret it."

Once the words were spoken, she tried to hand him back the embroidered piece of white linen and found him staring at her with a somewhat stunned expression.

"What did you say?" he asked.

"I said that I will marry you."

"No, after that," he prompted.

"You mean about not blaming me if you live to regret it."

"No,"—he made a backwards circular motion with his fingertip—"before that."

Patience had to pause for a moment then blanched upon recalling what she had said without thinking. "Um…" She swallowed the knot of horrid embarrassment lodged in her throat.

Leighton's dramatically arched right eyebrow and expectant expression made matters worse.

"I said I will do my best to be a good and…loving…wife."

"Yes, that was it." The color of his eyes deepened. "Are you saying you *want* to be a loving wife to me?"

His breathing sounded increasingly labored as he stared with great intensity at her. Clearly, he did not appreciate her disregarding the terms already set forth for their marriage.

"There is no need for upset," she said. "I—I only meant that I would do as you wish in public and make others believe—"

"As *I* wish?" he interrupted.

"Yes, *that* is what you said."

After studying her a moment longer with an enigmatic expression, Leighton nodded. He then crooked a finger behind the knot on his cravat, and tugged slightly.

"Forgive me, I mistook your meaning." He turned his back and walked over to stand before the window. There, with arms folded across his chest, the man shook his head and laughed.

To see him first so panicked at the notion of making love to her—and now obviously relieved to be pardoned from such a grueling sentence—he could not have hurt Patience more had he shot her in the heart.

Did he think she had no feelings at all?

No sense of womanly pride?

Granted, she was young and inexperienced when it came to many things, especially men, their desires, or any discussions of relations between men and women. But his callous behavior was both insulting and cruel.

"I cannot do this," Patience managed to say then had to firmly press her lips together to keep them from quivering. A torrent of tears rose swiftly. She tried to brush them aside as fast as they fell.

"Do what?" he asked, with his back to her…still chuckling.

"Marry you, or anyone who does not love me," she answered then fled from the room.

Chapter 30

Patience had no idea where she was going—only that she wanted to be far away from the gardens, the palace, and Leighton. Hearing him call her name, she quickened her pace.

I must be mad to have considered marrying him.

How foolish a notion to give up one's hopes and dreams to be loved, only to become so much baggage for the rest of her life.

After leaving the Banqueting House, she considered going down to the dock, thinking there might be a boat to take her back to London. To Carlyle House. To Henrietta, and Sam. In truth, they were the only ones she could trust unconditionally. The only ones who truly loved her. Despite the fact Sam could often be a blustering, moody Scots ghost and dear Henrietta, a gangling and sweet-natured puppy, both had never failed to support and protect her.

No longer hearing Leighton's voice, Patience altered her pace to an unhurried walk. Hugging her waist, she thought about the viscount and his oh-so-charitable proposal.

She'd been willing to marry him. Mutual friendship could provide a good foundation for love and marriage. Yet when she'd seen his reaction to the thought she wanted to be a loving wife, and then heard him laugh...everything changed.

"He thinks I am in danger," she muttered under her breath.

The man had no idea the danger he posed to her heart.

"Well, I don't want his pity. I don't want anyone's pity."

Thunder rumbled. A chilly breeze circled. Regretting she had not worn her cloak, Patience pulled her shawl close against her body. She looked up at the sky.

Befitting her mood, the soft, wispy white clouds against a lovely blue sky she'd seen earlier that morning were now gone. In their place, dense, angry storm clouds blanketed the sky, so swollen with rain they could burst any moment. In point of fact, as she studied the sky, two large drops of rain splattered upon her face, warning to seek shelter or become thoroughly drenched.

Unfortunately, finding immediate shelter presented a problem. Her hasty exit from the Banqueting House, followed by sprints of half-running and half-walking—turning this way and that to avoid people and find the perfect private place to tend her wounded spirit—now found her in an area of the palace grounds she'd never been before. Surprised by how far she'd walked, Patience could not help but wonder how much time had passed since she'd left Leighton's company.

Patience studied her surroundings more carefully.

Gray smoke drifted upwards from a cluster of red-brick Tudor chimneys, so close now she could see every detail of their unique design and skilled masonry. She inhaled deeply, savoring the enticing aroma of bread baking and roasting meat.

For a moment she could do nothing more than stare at the ancient palace of Henry VIII and, in particular, the vast kitchens he had built. Hampton Court—especially now with storm clouds casting their shadows—had a powerful, strangely mystical quality, especially the original medieval buildings.

Against a rumbling, stormy skyline and the glistening effect of light rain, the brickwork appeared almost purple in color. Mullioned windows, from which once royal residents gazed out at their privileged world, still remained intact long after the bones of kings and queens had become dust.

But beyond the opulence and magnificence of the palace, she understood too well that strange, eternal ties had tethered spirits to the palace. She might be able to help some move on; others perhaps were doomed to haunt forever.

At once, lightning flashed and thunder rumbled. Rain descended with relentless fury, so fast and hard, Patience used her shawl to cover her head.

Seeking shelter had become a priority.

The thought of a hot cup of tea and some warm bread with sweet butter—or perhaps some jam—proved irresistible.

Using her view of the windows on the north side of the Great Hall as a compass, Patience soon found herself in a small courtyard. A dark, narrow passageway between brick walls extended to the left, but she chose to continue straight ahead where a door stood closed. Upon finding the door locked, she turned around.

Careful not to slip on slick stones, she ran back and entered the narrow close. On either side were doors to various storerooms or chambers. Each door she tried was also locked.

Unexpectedly, a sweeping breeze rose from the ancient stones beneath her feet, spiraling like a zephyr, and pulling her away from where she stood.

Toward the end of the narrow lane—beneath a white stone gothic arch—a door slowly opened.

Prickly needles stung her body with familiar warning. She raced toward the threshold, and wondered who beckoned her beyond the door.

Within moments, she entered one of the kitchens and immediately looked for the ghost who had come to her aid. She saw no one. Yet the sound of voices and activity drew her cautiously forward. Several people, clearly employed at the palace in some capacity or other, stood with their backs to her. Apart from one or two curious glances in her direction, they paid her no mind.

Odd, she thought.

One would think a stranger entering the private kitchens at Hampton Court, especially a young woman wet from the rain and lost, might warrant some manner of enquiry.

"They will not speak to you."

Patience all but jumped when a voice spoke close to her ear. The ghost of a woman in white stood beside her, holding a spectral candlestick complete with its own glowing aura where a true flame should be.

The lady appeared to be wearing a richly embroidered gown, perhaps a sleeping garment. Long, billowing sleeves with fine lace cuffs were gathered at her wrists with what appeared to be a dark silk ribbon. Her long light brown hair had been parted into two sections. Each section had been fastened, several inches from the ends, with the same type dark ribbon. Both sections had been brought forward over her shoulders to rest against the small bodice of her loose, yet elegant frock.

A quick glance back to the people in the kitchen proved the woman's statement true. Not only were they ignoring Patience, they were going about their work in a state of frenzy.

Looking back to the ghost, she was about to speak when the woman held up a hand to silence her. Then, the spirit motioned for Patience to follow.

Shivering from her damp clothing and shoes, Patience wondered if the ghost intended to lead her back outside into the deluge. Instead, the ghost led her into a small room that contained, of all things, a secret passageway.

Narrow stone steps took them up to another corridor outside the Great Hall. Patience peeked to see if anyone might be about, dreading the notion her aunt—or someone else—might see her in such a bedraggled state.

She looked back at the ghost. "Who are you?"

"I am Jane."

"Thank you for helping me, Jane."

The ghost nodded, but her dark eyes then narrowed with intensity. "You must be careful. You must not wander about the palace alone. He watches."

Patience stepped toward her. "Who watches?"

"I cannot say his name."

"But he watches *me*?" Patience asked.

"He watches everyone."

"Where is he now?"

Jane lifted her chin and turned her head slightly, as if listening to some secret sound. "I do not know," she said in a chilling whisper. "I only know you cannot leave Hampton Court."

Patience impulsively stepped away. "I must leave. There is someone who needs me."

"There are many who need you." The fear in Jane's voice could not be mistaken.

"Why? Does this man threaten you…or others like you?"

"How can I make you understand?" An expression of frustration worried Jane's brow. "He watches. He waits. We cannot stop him. You must."

Apprehension rippled down Patience's spine.

Whomever Jane spoke of must be threatening the ghosts of Hampton Court. Did he keep them captive in some way? Prevent them from moving on? Was that why there were so many ghosts still remaining at Hampton Court?

Ghosts she had not seen, but whose presence she felt.

The words of the man on the King's Great Staircase held new meaning. Had he been frightened, not angry with her? Was that why he hid among the clouds in the mural, trying to warn her?

Were the courtly ghosts who tried to speak with her in the Great Watching Chamber also trying to warn her? Even Leighton said there was evil at Hampton Court.

It seemed a fair assumption the controlling, cruel ghost of whom Jane spoke must be the same evil Leighton sensed at the palace. In truth, although Patience could not detect evil, she had felt something almost physically overpowering from the moment she arrived at Hampton Court. Such an evil could also have prompted the multitude of ghosts to attempt to seize her attention.

Remorse pricked at her conscience. Not only had she ignored them, she'd used a protective shield to deny contact. Now, they sent Jane, a chosen representative, to ask for assistance.

But what can I do?

Granted, Patience had encountered evil spirits before, but used every means of defense she could to protect herself. Even so, there had been times when angry, vicious spirits had pursued her. In unguarded moments, some inflicted physical pain upon her.

The thought of encountering a spirit so powerful it could inflict fear upon ghosts was not something she wanted to consider. For certain, she had no idea how to rid Hampton Court of such a menace.

Unfortunately, she'd seen a great fear in Jane's eyes, and heard the terror in the spirit's voice. How could she walk away, knowing some horrid ghost might harm a spirit so concerned about others? Or, brutally terrorize other good spirits at Hampton Court?

No. I must first keep my promise to Anne. I should not even be here. Not now.

She looked again at the vaporous face of the medieval ghost staring back at her, and a wellspring of emotion pierced Patience's heart.

"Why do you think *I* can stop him?"

"Because you see what others do not," Jane answered. "You are the key, the only one who can see between the shadows of your world and ours."

Patience contemplated Jane's words as the sweet-faced ghost turned and walked away. The lady in white paused before a brick wall then looked over her shoulder at Patience, her expression wrought with great sadness. "There is one thing more you must know."

"What is it?"

"The evil which threatens our world also dwells in yours."

Jane's image started to fade, her form changing from an almost solid fog-type vapor into a fine white mist.

"Wait!" An overpowering sense of urgency prompted Patience to step toward Jane. "Can you not tell me anything more?"

"The answers you seek are here. Others will try to help you if they can. Watch for their signs."

Jane's spectral image vanished. Yet from that unknown, mystic place where earthbound spirits went to rest, a final mournful plea lingered in the air.

"Do not forsake us, I beg you."

Chapter 31

"Where could she have gone?"

Leighton tossed his damp waistcoat and cravat onto the carpet where his wet coat already rested. He yanked his shirt hem out from the waist of his trousers, and proceeded to peel that garment from his body as well. "I looked all about the grounds. What if she is outdoors in this weather?"

Courtenay signaled for a valet to retrieve the wet garments from the floor. "Lady Carlyle said she would send word when Miss Sinclair returns. The young woman wanted to be alone, nothing more. Can't say I blame her after the mess you made of your proposal."

Hands on his hips, Leighton stared hard at his friend. "I did not make a mess of it. I told you she *agreed* to marry me."

"Then recanted her decision." Courtenay handed Leighton a glass of brandy.

"It was a misunderstanding…on both our parts. After I find her, I will better explain myself."

"Take your bath and put on some dry clothes." Courtenay walked to the door then paused at the threshold. "She may still not want to do your bidding, my friend."

Leighton shot him an exasperated look. "I leave Hampton Court in the morning and, by God, she is coming with me. I'll hear no arguments about it either. She promised to marry me, and that, as they say, is that."

"Indeed," his friend replied with a sardonic grin. "I suggest when you do find Miss Sinclair, you try being more romantic and less logical. Not that Thorne would ever agree with me, but it does not make a man weak to admit he is in love…only human."

As Courtenay turned to leave, a servant arrived and handed him a letter. However, before he could read it, Leighton crossed the room and grabbed the sealed missive out of his hands.

Tearing open the correspondence, Leighton read aloud, "Miss Sinclair has returned."

"I am not surprised," Courtenay replied. "I doubted the young woman might be lost."

"Not lost perhaps, but not safe either." Leighton glanced at the copper tub situated before the hearth, its contents warm and inviting. Unfortunately, he couldn't take time to enjoy it now. He went to an elaborate mirrored wardrobe, from which he claimed a clean, dry shirt.

"What are you doing? Take your bath, man, before you catch your death. You'll be no good to Miss Sinclair if you become sick."

"Lady Carlyle wishes to speak with us as soon as it is convenient." Leighton pulled the white shirt on over his head then crooked a brow at his friend. "In my opinion, *convenient* means now. Something happened."

"Did Lady Carlyle say that in her letter?"

"She didn't have to, Lyon. I can feel it."

Chapter 32

A short while later, Leighton and Courtenay entered the drawing room of Lady Carlyle's suite, only to find the countess alone. At first glance, she looked quite regal seated on a gold leaf sofa upholstered in mint green and gold silk. However, Leighton noticed the woman kept twisting an embroidered handkerchief.

"Where is Miss Sinclair?" he asked.

"Resting." Lady Carlyle gestured to two arm chairs. "Please sit down, gentlemen."

Courtenay politely complied.

Too wary and restless to be seated, Leighton ignored Lady Carlyle's request, and stood before the crackling hearth and an elaborately carved marble fireplace surround. Arms folded across his chest, he studied the older woman's uncharacteristic discomfiture.

Trouble weighed heavy on Lady Carlyle's mind; no doubt another incident that concerned and frightened her. The thought came as no surprise to him. He'd known all along the countess never should have brought her niece to Hampton Court. Most likely, Lady Carlyle realized the truth now as well.

"What happened?" His question garnered a startled reaction from Lady Carlyle. When the countess did not respond, his body tensed. "Is she ill or hurt?"

"No, no, she is not ill, but something did happen." Lady Carlyle looked at Leighton. "I had no idea about the strength of her abilities, or how sensitive she is to the spirits. She wants so much to live like everyone else. I thought it would be best to teach her how to protect herself at Hampton Court first, rather than in town." She choked the handkerchief in her hands again. "Now, I know not what to do."

"Countess," Courtenay said in his usual, gentle manner. "Perhaps if you told us what happened, we might better understand."

Lady Carlyle nodded, and pressed both her hands against her chest as if willing her heart to be calm. "I have only just learned that the night of our arrival—the night we found her so ill in the chapel gallery—she experienced a transition haunting."

"What is that?" Leighton asked, unable to quell his sense of foreboding.

"It is when someone has the power to cross the veil."

"The veil?" Courtenay questioned.

"Yes, the veil." Lady Carlyle said with a nod. "The threshold, if you will, which separates the present from the past. A dream from reality. It is also the boundary between the realms of life and death. In other words, my niece saw something in that gallery. She believed it an imprinted haunting of an incident that happened long ago. However, rather than see it as a ghostly, non-threatening image, the magnitude of her power somehow pulled her into the actual event."

"Forgive me, countess," Courtenay said. "But I do not understand what you mean."

"She became part of both worlds," the countess continued. "I believe the reason she became so weak and ill is because she instinctively fought to remain in our world."

"Are you saying, she was pulled into the past?" Leighton paused to calm his breathing and racing heart. "Or, that she was being pulled into the spirit world and might have been trapped there?"

"I do not know." Lady Carlyle wept in earnest then struggled for composure. "I only know I cannot help her. She is more powerful than I am. More powerful than my sister or anyone that has been in our family."

"What do you mean you do not know?" Unmoved by the woman's distress, Leighton stepped toward Lady Carlyle. Desperate for answers, he struggled against a tempest of indignation to remain calm. "Clearly you have some knowledge about this type haunting."

"Only stories I heard as a child," she replied. "Those gifted with this power lived in ancient times. They were called *visionaries*. Stories about them were the stuff of legend. Fanciful, magical, very much like tales of faeries or giants."

The countess then seemed to remember something and started to weep again, muttering almost incoherently into her handkerchief about faeries and children of the mist.

Frustrated, Leighton's temper flared. He needed facts, not tears. The thought Patience might become trapped in another time or the spirit world terrified him.

Not knowing how to question the countess in her present distress, he looked to his friend for assistance.

With an understanding nod, Courtenay moved to sit beside the countess on the sofa. "Lady Carlyle, did another of these transition hauntings happen today?"

She blotted her face, her gaze distant for a moment. Then she looked at Courtenay. "No, something else happened today. A lady in white appeared to Patience, and asked my niece to help her and the other spirits at Hampton Court."

"Is that not common for ghosts to seek her help?" Courtenay asked in a reassuring manner. "As for the incident in the gallery, perhaps it will not happen again."

Lady Carlyle looked at Leighton. "You were right. I never should have brought her here. Please, help me take her away. Patience said this lady warned of danger—of an evil spirit threatening the other ghosts. A spirit that moves between both worlds. Do you not see? Such a spirit could use a transition haunting to trap Patience."

Fury unlike anything he'd ever known swept through Leighton. Nothing evil would trap or harm Patience. Not as long as he lived. As his heart raced. Radiant power surged with each rapid breath, so much so his Lightbearer aura became visible, rimming his body in a pure white nimbus.

Seated on the sofa facing him, Courtenay quickly shook his head, warning Leighton to control his emotions. Unfortunately, Lady Carlyle also chose that moment to look toward Leighton.

In the mere seconds before he could rein in his power, the countess saw the white light emanating from his body.

Lady Carlyle inhaled sharply, resting a hand against her throat. "What...what are you?"

"I beg your pardon, Lady Carlyle?" Leighton noticed Courtenay wore one of his chastising frowns.

"You were...glowing," the countess said in a half-whisper.

"Glowing? I daresay you are overwrought, countess." Leighton spoke in a calm voice, hoping to convince the older woman she had imagined what she'd seen. "Little wonder from what you've told us. Rest assured, I have every intention of taking Miss Sinclair away from Hampton Court in the morning. In fact, she has agreed to marry me."

"Marry?" Lady Carlyle blinked wide-eyed.

Well, if nothing else, the announcement distracted the woman from further questions about information she must not know.

"Yes," he continued. "I intend to leave in the morning with your niece and obtain a Special License. We will wed without delay. I daresay there is no one, living or dead, who will harm her or dare take her from me again."

Lady Carlyle stood and crossed to him, her countenance transformed from worry and fear that plagued her a moment ago into one of joy and relief.

"I did agree to marry you, Lord Leighton, but rest assured I have no intention of leaving Hampton Court in the morning."

Everyone turned toward the direction of the voice.

Patience stood in the open doorway, a vision of loveliness in a white embroidered cotton muslin gown with a pale blue sash. Her hair had been styled most fashionably, and she looked not only rested but rather defiant.

More than anything Leighton wanted to cross the room and hold her in his arms. However, he also saw sadness in her luminescent eyes, and recognized a dire need for them to speak alone.

"Lady Carlyle," Courtenay with a smile. "I suggest we permit Lord Leighton and Miss Sinclair some privacy to discuss their forthcoming nuptials."

The countess hesitated, looking with speculative curiosity at both her niece and Leighton. "Mr. Courtenay, I do believe you are right. Let us withdraw to my writing closet."

As they walked arm in arm toward another door, Lady Carlyle glanced over her shoulder. "They do make a most attractive couple, do they not?"

"To say the least," Courtenay replied.

After his friend and Lady Carlyle quit the room, and the door had been closed behind them, Leighton gave his full attention to Patience. She still lingered in the doorway from which she had entered the drawing room.

"Will you not come and speak with me?"

She made no reply, but slowly entered the room and sat upon one of the chairs. Leighton hesitated then crossed the room to close the still open door to her bedchamber. He wanted no eavesdropping to their conversation, especially from servants.

He returned to where Patience sat. Her posture conveyed a great deal about her thoughts. Her back, straight as an arrow, a rigid indication of tension or temper—he knew not which. The exquisite nape of her neck—more exposed as she looked down at her hands clasped together in her lap—proved so alluring he paused and considered what she might do if he pressed a gentle kiss upon so delicious a spot.

She'd obviously noted he'd stopped walking and stood behind her chair a long moment. A blush rose on the arch of her cheeks, complimenting her sweet profile.

Somehow he found his way to the chair opposite Patience. When she still would not look at him, he crossed his booted feet and rested his elbows on the chair's arms. After what seemed a long moment, not knowing where or how best to begin, he spoke the only words that came to mind.

"How could you possibly think I do not love you?"

She looked up, clearly surprised. Her lips parted slightly, and he could see by the décolletage of her gown that she was breathing quickly. He watched the workings of her ivory throat as she swallowed, all the while staring at him in a cautious manner. So fascinated was he by her reaction it took a moment to realize she had spoken a response.

"I beg your pardon?"

"Why are you saying this now? Is it because Lady Carlyle told you she fears for my safety?"

"No, though her words have strengthened my resolve to protect you."

"Protect." She released a heavy sigh and turned her face away. She proceeded to stare at the fire in the hearth, her manner distant and somewhat agitated.

"Why is it so wrong I want to protect you? It is not intended as an insult, but an expression of my concern for your welfare."

"I have no doubt you are concerned for my welfare, Leighton." She looked once more at him. "But do not attach stronger emotion to it as a means to appease me."

"Appease you?" He stood, hoping by so doing the sudden knot in the pit of his belly would subside. Unfortunately, his temper had been riled. Neither did it escape his thinking there were any number of women who would be ecstatic if he showed them the least amount of interest, let alone offered marriage. In truth, after what happened between him and Patience years ago, wagers were still being made at all the clubs speculating he would *never* marry.

He struggled to remember his friend's sage advice. Much as he appreciated the suggestion to be more romantic, at present he only wanted to impress upon Miss Patience Sinclair that she'd insulted him beyond reason.

For that matter, why would he, as a man, consider professing love to her when she'd never been forthcoming in her feelings toward him? Well, other than friendship.

Arms folded across his chest, he narrowed his gaze at her. "Permit me to point out I am not so desperate for female companionship I would contemplate marriage to someone for whom I had no personal regard. Neither would I profess love as a means to *appease* you. And, I might add, the reason I want to protect you is because I *do* love you."

"You do?" She appeared astonished by his confession. "But you said any feelings you had toward me died long ago. You told me I should return to Scotland for there was nothing for me in England anymore."

"When did I say that?"

"The night you found me in your library." She nibbled on her bottom lip—a certain sign she was nervous, if not distraught.

He raked a hand through his hair in frustration. "I was angry. For God's sake, you disappeared for three years. I never heard a word from you, or any explanation for the things you said. Then, I found you in my home. Not there to see me, mind you, but to determine if I was a murderer. How did you expect me to react?"

"I thought you hated me. When you came to Carlyle House and said you would help me, I thought you felt sorry for me. I even told myself that since I was trying to help Anne, and she was the sister of your good friend, you wanted to learn the truth about her fate for him. I never…"

"You read my letters." He knelt before her. "The letters Anne had stolen. You knew how I felt."

"How you felt in the past—years ago."

"I never stopped loving you. I thought to prove my love now by helping you and keeping you safe. I soon realized the best way to do that was for us to marry. How foolish we both were. We misunderstood one another."

"You misunderstood *me*?" she asked.

"When I proposed this morning, you said one must marry for love. That you could never be the wife I deserve. I believed you said those words because you didn't love me. Indeed, you made it quite clear you think of me only as a friend. Still, I thought in time you would come to love me."

She reached out and touched his hand. "I called you my friend because I dared not hope for anything more." A single tear descended her cheek. "I have never stopped loving you either."

Raw emotion all but choked Leighton as he saw the undisguised love Patience felt for him shining in her eyes. For a moment, he could not speak. Instead, he raised her hand resting upon his, and solemnly kissed her palm.

Swiftly rising joy and the overwhelming need to adore her lips and hold her in his arms could not be denied a moment more. He stood, and gently guided her to stand with him.

He tried to be somber and romantic, but the happiness in his heart could not be contained. "Now that we have both confessed undying love, will you keep your promise to marry me?"

She smiled. "I shall be honored."

They held hands, looking into one another's eyes. With their bodies standing so close in proximity, the soft rhythm of their breathing escalated in tempo. The thought occurred to Leighton he might expire unless he kissed her.

Slowly, he leaned down until a breath away from her mouth. He paused, a heartbeat, no more, and then pressed a kiss of promise upon her soft, willing lips.

A spark rekindled. Memories returned anew of a past that had long since haunted him. Of being with Patience on sunlit walks in fragrant gardens, whispered conversations, unspoken desires, and secret smiles.

The kiss deepened almost immediately after contact. She returned his ardor and sighed with pleasure. He pulled her deeper within his embrace, yet in the back of his mind he recognized the need for restraint and respect.

Breathing hard and fast, Leighton forced himself to end the kiss. Still, he could not relinquish Patience from his arms. He held her close, savoring the way her head rested against his chest, knowing well she heard the frantic rhythm of his heart.

Soon, he told himself. *Soon, we will be married and nothing will take her from me ever again.*

Chapter 33

Patience rested her head against Leighton's chest, closed her eyes and listened to his heart. She smiled with the realization it beat in time with her own. Nothing had ever seemed so right as this moment.

The moment his lips touched hers, the physical sensations she'd always felt in Leighton's presence soared. The power and towering physique of his body, the dizzying finesse of his kiss—quite different from those brief chaste ones she'd cherished in the past—all served to create a memory she would never forget.

Even now, as he gently stroked her back, quivers of desire and anticipation rose anew. Having become so accustomed to hiding the truth of her feelings, she found it hard to believe all that had happened.

He loved and wanted her.

She no longer had to fear staring at him, struggling to disguise her feelings. Concerned she would embarrass herself by becoming lost in his dark-lashed green eyes and handsome, chiseled features.

No need to worry he might catch one of the surreptitious glances she took to watch the way he walked, or the way he often stood with his hands clasped behind his back.

She inhaled slowly, deeply, the scent uniquely his own—a perfect blending of citrus, spice, and sandalwood. Keeping her distance from Tristan St. Ives, Viscount Leighton, especially when they were alone together, had been her best defense against revealing her heart, as well as the effect his presence had on her.

Now, standing within his embrace, she could think of nothing and no one but him, and the life they would have together. The man had only to wink and smile at her, and she would be powerless. Without doubt, she would never be able to win an argument if he kissed her. The thought made her giggle softly, although she tried to muffle the sound against his chest. He must have heard, for he pulled back to study her with an enquiring grin.

"I have never felt so…happy," she sighed.

The dimples in his cheeks became more prominent as his smile deepened. "We will always be happy together. And I daresay we will both enjoy you being a loving wife."

Patience experienced a great wave of breathlessness as the object of his seductive scrutiny. She tried to think of an amusing retort, but her future husband's happy smile slowly faded before her eyes. In its place, a shadow fell across his face.

"You cannot stay here, Patience," he said. "When I leave in the morning, I want you with me. There are several things I must do, not the least of which is obtain a Special License so we can marry without delay. There is also a private dinner I must attend for a *Legion* member. The others will be there as well. Since I intend to inform them we are to be married, I would like you to attend the dinner with me. I also want to tell them the truth—that you are the one who saw Anne Melville's ghost."

"Do you not think it better to tell your friends without my presence?" Patience appreciated the way he always listened to her opinion on matters; a rare trait in a man.

"Besides which," she continued. "You draw much attention to yourself because of your title and family. My stepfather could learn I am in town. Hating me so much, he would likely interfere with our plans."

"Hear me well," he said. "I intend to confront Henley as soon as possible regarding my intentions. The man would be a fool to challenge me or our marriage."

She nodded absently then nibbled on her bottom lip.

"What is it?" he asked with a crooked brow. "Much as I adore your habit of biting that delicious bottom lip, when you do I know something is amiss."

"I would like to stay here at Hampton Court—"

"No", he interrupted.

"I am not afraid. If anything, what I learned today may well be the reason I am here at all, a far more important one than Lady Carlyle intended."

"I told you, there is evil here."

"There is evil everywhere, Tristan." She smiled, hoping to ease his concern by using his true name. "What if I promise to never go anywhere alone? Mr. Courtenay could accompany me. You trust him."

Leighton's frown deepened.

"You have much to do," she said. "Traveling with me could cause delays. You can go to town, see your friends, continue to make arrangements for our marriage, and then return for me."

"Courtenay could guard you in my absence, of that I have no doubt. Still, his strength is somewhat limited. Without knowing what you both might encounter in pursuit of this threatening ghost…" He scratched his jaw in a thoughtful manner. "What if that Scottish ghost came here? Could you summon him?"

"I could, but he cannot leave Anne alone in town. Sam is watching over her for me. And she cannot come here, especially when there is this threat to the ghosts of Hampton Court. I do not want to think what might happen to her here."

"What about what might happen to you? Lady Carlyle is afraid for you. In point of fact, your ability to see that so-called transition haunting terrified the countess. And let us not forget this evil spirit menacing other ghosts. No, I do not like it."

"Trust me, please. I can do this. For the first time in my life, I understand why I have this ability. How can I move forward with our life and be happy, knowing I ignored their pleas for help? They are frightened and alone. I know what that is like."

"You are not alone," he said. "Not anymore."

"Yes, but I will never forget what it felt like when I was."

He pulled her into his arms, and remained silent for several moments. Then, with a heavy sigh, he pulled back enough to look into her eyes.

"If you promise you will not go anywhere without Mr. Courtenay, I will not force you to come with me in the morning. But there is one other condition I insist upon…for my own peace of mind."

"What is it?"

"I am going to send word to my grandfather and ask him to come to Hampton Court. Hear me well, Patience, if the duke believes it necessary for you to leave—whether you help these ghosts or not—you must obey him."

"But…"

He pressed a finger against her lips. "No argument. Either I take you with me, kicking and screaming in the morning…or you agree."

Patience tensed. Far too many times in her life had she been ordered to obey—and threatened if she did not. She had to remind herself Leighton was not like her stepfather.

Leighton was good and loving.

He only wants me safe from harm.

The knowledge warmed her heart. Still, now that she had come to embrace the ability she had, to understand the good she could do, she could not live like a bird in a gilded cage, denied the freedom to be itself.

Somehow, I will help him understand.

But not now. She had seen something in Leighton's eyes that almost stilled her heart. He would have no peace in his travels unless she agreed to the terms.

There would be time enough to prove to him she was not so fragile and helpless as he thought. In truth, she needed to prove it to herself as well.

She thought about his grandfather, the Duke of Windermere. Leighton said his grandfather helped teach the members of the *Legion* how to cope with and use their powers.

If only she had someone to guide her, too.

It would be a lie to say she did not have concerns about the evil ghost she'd encounter in her efforts to help Jane and the other Hampton Court spirits.

To learn Auntie Catherine's abilities were not as powerful as she'd previously thought had been disturbing. When she'd told her aunt about what really happened in the gallery, it seemed the woman aged before her eyes.

Patience had seen the tall, distinguished Duke of Windermere only once—at the Westerbrook wedding years ago. He had not looked unkindly upon her then—not before the wedding or afterwards when she made a spectacle of herself in the churchyard.

Indeed, when she saw the duke observing her from his towering height over others, the man's expression had been calm, contemplative. Now, after learning about the magical hereditary powers in Leighton's family, perhaps the duke had sensed something about her that fateful day?

Something that told him she was not insane.

Something that assured him she had no evil in her heart toward his grandson or anyone.

What if the wizened, powerful patriarch and elder Lightbearer of the St. Ives family could help her as he helped the members of the *Legion*? The thought held promise.

"I agree." She smiled at Leighton. "I will do as His Grace advises."

Chapter 34

Knightly Town House, London

"You cannot be serious." Hawthorne growled. "You intend to marry that… for want of a better word…*girl*?

Leighton glanced at the other members of the *Legion*, all except the absent Lyon. They'd gathered at Knightly's town house for a private dinner honoring Hunter.

He did not want to ruin the evening before other invited guests arrived, but had to tell his friends about his imminent nuptials before they found out after the fact. He also needed to learn if they'd discovered anything about the copied snuffbox.

"This is madness," Hawthorne continued. "A fortnight ago you were irate she returned to England. Now, you want to *marry* her?"

"I daresay, I agree with Thorne." Knightly stood before the hearth with an elbow resting leisurely upon the mantelpiece.

Leighton smiled. "I love her."

"Bloody hell," Hawthorne muttered under his breath. "You love her? We are speaking about the same girl who humiliated you at the Westerbrook wedding? The girl belongs in Bedlam."

"She was not speaking to me then." Leighton looked toward Melville, hoping Anne's brother would soon voice support.

"Not speaking to you?" Hawthorne threw up his hands with obvious frustration, stalked across the room then returned quickly to stand before Leighton. "She was looking directly at you. You stood a few feet apart. We all saw it. We all heard her."

"Not everything is as it seems." Leighton crossed his arms, his temper rising. "After what happened to us in that blasted cave, we know better than most that some secrets are best left concealed. Whether out of necessity or fear of exposure, it takes time to trust someone enough to speak the truth."

Hawthorne snorted with derision. "Yes, well, in my opinion lust has clouded your thinking. What is this power Miss Sinclair has over you? None of us has seen you about town. Indeed, now that I think upon it, you've been behaving oddly since her return."

Turning about, the earl looked at the other members of the *Legion.* "Well, speak up, brothers. Or, am I to assume by your silence that you do not agree with me."

"Perhaps we should postpone this discussion," Knightly volunteered. "Other guests will be arriving. We can meet tomorrow."

"No." Leighton stared at Hawthorne, disappointed his friend could not see beyond prejudice toward Patience. "My apologies, but I cannot stay. There are things I must do without delay."

Hawthorne also folded his arms across his chest, his posture ever defiant. "In other words, you came here tonight to tell us you plan to marry Miss Sinclair, but refuse to explain why there is such need for haste? You speak of secrets and truths? Here is my truth. I do not like or trust Miss Sinclair. I never have. Long before what happened in that churchyard, I found her manner odd, if not bizarre. Yet from the moment you met her, she cast a spell on you. Mayhap she's a witch. There have been rumors."

"Careful, old friend," Leighton warned.

Hawthorne smiled in a caustic manner. "Did you not imply she trusted you with a secret? That she wasn't talking to you that day in the churchyard? Who, then? What possible, logical reason did she provide to explain her behavior?"

"She saw a ghost," Melville interjected.

Hawthorne snickered and looked at Melville. His amusement quickly vanished to see the remark had not been said in jest. Returning his attention to Leighton, he narrowed his dark eyes. "Tell me this does not have anything to do with the ghost you and Melville claimed to have seen. The ghost of his murdered sister who, by the by, was quite vocal and not the least bit shy about her intense dislike for Miss Sinclair."

Leighton expelled a heavy sigh, anticipating the reaction his next words would cause. "Neither Melville nor I saw the ghost. Miss Sinclair did."

"What the devil?" Knightly pulled away from his stance by the fireplace and moved to stand beside Hawthorne, facing Leighton. "You lied to us?" He glanced over his shoulder at Melville. "You both lied to us?"

"I do not believe this." Hunter rubbed his forehead as if in pain. "You mean to say we have been looking for a snuffbox like ours because Miss Sinclair told you the killer had one like it. And you both believed her?"

"Yes," Leighton replied. "We both believed her."

"Did it not occur to you she might have an ulterior motive for this concocted story?" Hawthorne all but demanded. "That she created this absurd fantasy to gain sympathy and further her goal to marry into your family? Then again, perhaps she returned to finish what she started three years ago, and destroy your life forever."

Leighton clenched his jaw. One more insinuation by Hawthorne and they would come to blows. "Thorne, I have tried with increasing difficulty to be understanding and make excuses for your contemptuous words against Miss Sinclair, but I will hear no more. Do you understand me? You have no knowledge of what she is like, or what she has been through. You certainly do not realize the depths of feelings we have for one another."

For several moments a heavy silence enveloped the room. Leighton could not recall any time in their past where he felt so at odds with his friends. In particular, Hawthorne glared at him with ill-disguised hostility as he breathed hard and fast.

Judging by their appearance, Knightly and Hunter looked as if they were in agreement with Hawthorne.

Leighton directed his gaze to Melville. When would Anne's brother speak up in defense of Patience? Realizing no such acknowledgement was forthcoming, he shook his head in disgust.

"You were there," he reminded Melville. "You know what the ghost of your sister said to Miss Sinclair—facts not known to anyone but you and your parents. How can you remain silent now?"

Still unwilling to respond, Melville looked down.

"Very well," Leighton said with an abrupt nod. "If I do not have anyone's support or understanding, so be it." Crossing to a nearby table where he'd previously deposited his hat and gloves—since he had not planned to remain for the dinner—he retrieved the items.

No one spoke as Leighton walked toward the drawing room doors. Pausing at the threshold, he turned once more to face his friends. He considered one final argument for reason, but the sound of another guest arriving distracted him.

Hunter's raven-haired mistress had arrived, haughty as a queen. A servant assisted with the removal of her cloak, beneath which she wore a provocative black evening gown clearly designed to display her wares.

Dripping in gold and precious stones, Evangeline Bailey stopped fussing with her appearance long enough to see him standing outside the drawing room. She smiled like a siren—no doubt assuming he'd been looking at her with admiration and desire.

In truth, the sight of her disgusted him.

The irony this woman had been invited as a welcomed guest by his friends galled him. Vain and immoral, her sense of loyalty and affection depended upon how much she could get from a man, and never from any sense of womanly virtue, let alone kindness or love.

"Good evening, Lord Leighton." She slowly walked toward him. "Have you just arrived as well?"

"I'm leaving."

She pouted, stroking the heavy jewels about her throat like a lover. "Pity, I should very much like us to become better, if not intimately, acquainted."

The brazenness of the wench appalled him. "I'd rather be a monk."

Curious if the others heard their exchange, he glanced over his shoulder. Apparently, they had.

Knightly approached, forcing a gracious smile as the evening's host. Behind him, Hunter and Melville followed, eager to greet the much sought after reigning queen among London's mistresses. Hawthorne, however, remained standing where he'd been, arms still crossed against his chest.

Not wanting to remain a moment longer, Leighton donned his hat. As he prepared to step away from the drawing room doorway, Melville raced forward. Pushing everyone aside, he seized the wrist of Hunter's mistress, twisting her arm upward in the process.

"Where the bloody hell did you get that necklace?" Melville shouted.

Evangeline Bailey inhaled sharply, trying to pull free. "Unhand me, Mr. Melville."

"Tell me where you got it!" Melville commanded.

Leighton observed, rather stunned, as Hunter and Knightly tried to remove the vise-like grip their friend had on the woman. Ordinarily, Leighton would have interceded as well, but Melville's reaction directed his attention to the object about the throat of Hunter's mistress—a stunning gold necklace set with huge emeralds and diamonds.

At once, he understood.

Miss Melville had the same necklace the night she ran away. As Leighton contemplated how Hunter's mistress came into possession of the item, Knightly managed to break the hold Melville had on the woman and pulled her safely aside.

This action prompted Melville and Hunter to shove one another then assume a fighting stance, fists clenched. Rather absurd behavior, to say the least. No good would come of a physical brawl, especially since both men had supernatural strength and an almost impervious reaction to pain.

Leighton tossed his hat aside and stepped between them. "Stop this. For God's sake, what is happening to us?" Both men appeared ready to kill one another. "Hunter, listen to me. Melville is upset because your mistress is wearing a necklace that belongs to his family."

Hunter shot a quick glance at Leighton. "What the devil are you talking about?"

"She's wearing the necklace my sister took with her the night she disappeared." Melville tried to reach around Leighton to engage Hunter in battle. "You did it, didn't you? You killed Anne."

"Are you out of your mind?" Hunter argued.

"Enough!" Knightly's voice echoed as he re-entered the hall. Pointing to the drawing room, he added, "Go back in there and try to be civilized." He then looked at a pair of bewigged footmen standing in the hallway. "When the other guests arrive, direct them to the library and give them a drink."

Turning back to his friends, their host physically shoved both Hunter and Melville toward the drawing room. Knightly glanced back at Leighton. "Well, are you going or staying?"

"Sir," a voice said to Leighton's right. He turned to see one of the servants had picked his hat up off the floor and extended it toward him. Leighton studied the still opened doors to the drawing room wherein loud voices continued to argue. Although he accepted the black silk item in hand, Leighton rejoined his friends.

Upon re-entering the drawing room, Leighton secured the doors for privacy. He turned to see Hunter seated beside his mistress on the sofa, gently stroking her swollen, already bruising wrist—pausing long enough to glare at Melville. "Touch her again and I'll kill you."

"Not if I kill you first," Melville replied with a sneer.

Stunned by the contemptible tension and behavior among a room of good friends, Leighton instinctively studied each *Legion* member.

Hawthorne now stood in the shadows on the far side of the room, and appeared to be watching him, no one else.

Hands on his hips, Knightly stood in the center of the room, his expression wholly exasperated. "I daresay your arrival has caused a problem, Miss Bailey."

"Ask her about the necklace," Melville bit out.

"Very well," Knightly replied. "Miss Bailey, where did you get the necklace?"

"It was gift," she answered, an annoyed, sharp-edged tone to her voice. "I most certainly did not steal it."

"A gift from whom?" Knightly asked.

She looked at Hunter and smiled. "I wore it tonight, as you requested. It is the most beautiful piece of jewelry ever given to me."

"What the blazes are you talking about, Evangeline?" Hunter quickly pivoted on the sofa and looked at his friends. "You don't think I gave it to her?"

"Of course, you gave it to me," his mistress contradicted. "Why deny it?"

Melville stepped forward, body tensed, but Leighton quickly grabbed hold of his left elbow and restrained him.

"I swear I don't know what she's talking about," Hunter protested. In the ensuing silence, he stood. "By thunder, I have never seen that necklace before in my life!"

"Liar," Melville accused.

"Miss Bailey, how do you know who gifted you with this item?" Leighton asked, keeping a firm grip on Melville. He then noticed Hawthorne smirking as he casually circled the perimeter of the room, observing them all as if they were insects under glass. "What the devil are you doing, Hawthorne?"

"Listening," Hawthorne replied with a slight shrug. "Do go on. This is proving to be a most enlightening evening. I must say the bonds of friendship and trust you once claimed were forged years ago have obviously corroded."

Frowning at the earl's observation, unwilling to consider any validity to such a statement, Leighton directed his attention to the woman seated on the sofa. "When did you receive this necklace, Miss Bailey?"

"I should like to leave," Miss Bailey replied.

"Not before you explain." Leighton released his hold on Melville, noting the man appeared somewhat calmer.

Miss Bailey huffed indignantly. "It arrived several days ago by special messenger."

"Lord Hunter did not give it to you personally?" Leighton asked.

"No." She frowned at her wrist. "Look at the ugly mark you made on my wrist, Mr. Melville."

"I could have done much worse," Melville retorted. "It might be said I demonstrated tremendous restraint. That necklace is a family heirloom. Gifted to an ancestor by Queen Elizabeth. There is not another like it." He stepped closer to the sofa. "So, do tell us again how you came to have it in your possession, madam."

Evangeline Bailey finally realized her predicament, and hastily removed the heirloom from about her throat. "Take it." She threw the treasured item at Melville, who caught the necklace easily in his right hand.

"I repeat, Miss Bailey,"—Leighton stared down at the woman—"why did you think Lord Hunter gave it to you? You mentioned being requested to wear it tonight. Was there a card or letter?"

She sighed with obvious impatience. "A box was delivered to my home, and brought to me by one of my servants. Inside the box, I found the necklace with an accompanying note asking me to wear it tonight. The note was unsigned. I assumed it came from Lord Hunter." She directed an icy stare at her lover. "If not you, who else?"

"Who else, indeed," Melville muttered.

"This is the last time I will say it, Melville," Hunter said, his voice low and threatening. "I have never seen or touched that necklace before." He then returned his attention to his mistress. "However, knowing the lady's proclivities for rich men, I can only suspect it came from another admirer."

"True, I am never at a loss for admirers," Miss Bailey said with a cat-like smile. "Indeed, I believe the time has come for me to bestow my company upon someone else. Indeed, there is an earl quite persistent in his desire to claim my affections. He is willing to do so at any cost. I think I will send for him tonight."

"You conniving witch," Hunter countered. "He can have you. God knows I have spent a fortune on you, including that gown you wear and the plush burgundy colored coach and four fine horses that brought you here tonight."

Miss Evangeline Bailey arched a delicate brow in response, clearly amused to have prompted such a virulent reaction in Hunter. "Knowing you as I do, sir, your upset has more to do about losing those fine horses than my attentions."

Standing, she crossed the room to leave. Hawthorne, now standing by the doors, moved forward to open one for her. She stared a long moment at him. "Thank you, Earl Hawthorne. Breeding always shows itself in one's manners."

Hawthorne turned away. "I need a drink."

Facing everyone in the drawing room a final time, the voluptuous woman lifted her chin and smiled as if looking upon peasants. "Gentlemen, I cannot help but notice one of your set is missing this evening." She tapped her lips with a gloved finger. "Ah, yes, Mr. Courtenay. A strikingly handsome man, albeit a trifle pale. Well spoken, but…alas…on a severely limited income."

"What are you implying?" Hunter snapped.

"Only that the box was delivered by a waterman; one of those men that ply the Thames between here and other places. I didn't pay much notice to it at the time, assuming Lord Hunter had purchased the necklace for me whilst away from town. However, since he obviously did not send it, I recall Mr. Courtenay lives at Hampton Court."

She exited the room but paused somewhat dramatically, glancing over her shoulder with a sardonic smile. "It's on the river, is it not?"

The implication of Evangeline Bailey's words stunned her audience. Leighton could not help but notice the dark, brooding expressions on the faces of his friends.

"Lyon," Melville grumbled.

"No," Leighton replied. "Not Lyon."

"How do you know?" Melville asked, with no small degree of irritation. "What makes him above suspicion? He isn't here, is he?"

"He's never here," Hunter contributed with a scowl.

"What is that supposed to mean?" Leighton asked.

"It means he isn't like us." Hawthorne finished the last of his blood red wine from a gold-rimmed crystal goblet. He continued speaking as he filled the glass again. "It wouldn't surprise me if he still harbored resentment toward us."

Leighton raked a hand through his hair. "For God's sake, why bring that up now? Those were dark days of confusion and physical suffering. Lyon was gravely ill. For him to see our already healthy bodies increasing with strength and other powers whilst he struggled daily against death would make anyone resentful. As I recall, fear and uncertainty about what was happening to our bodies—and the struggles we went through to control our abilities—made all of us often say things we didn't mean."

"Not Lyon," Hawthorne said with a quirked brow. "He just watched."

"What else could he do?" Leighton argued. "He was never healthy before we went into that cave. Afterwards, when illness forced him to leave school, he had no friends about him. It was to be expected when we visited, he seemed quiet. He almost died, for God's sake. Surely you remember what we all went through, especially him?"

"Right you are." Hawthorne set his glass on an octagon-shaped table. "I remember everything. Things you've clearly forgotten."

Hawthorne's expression and tone sparked Leighton's memory and kindled his temper anew. For inasmuch as the earl appeared to be referring to their childhood, and what happened in the cave, the man also addressed an incident the others knew nothing about. Namely, that during his dire depression after losing Patience Sinclair, Hawthorne had stopped Leighton from taking his own life.

Leighton returned Hawthorne's stare, hearing Knightly mumble under his breath. A moment later their host stood in front of Leighton, separating him from the earl.

"Saint," Knightly said in a quiet manner. "Is it not possible you defend Lyon so staunchly because you still feel guilty that what you caused to happen did not include him? We all know you blamed yourself when the wasting illness came upon him at school. We all feared he would not survive. But, as you said, he'd always been sick; cursed with a weak heart and poor lungs before we met him. Such suffering might take a toll on someone's way of thinking."

Leighton clenched his jaw. "I defend Lyon because I *know* him. Yes, he was resentful at first, but not for the reasons you think. He worried we would no longer want to be friends with someone so frail. In truth, he has always been braver and stronger than any of us. In my opinion, he still is."

Noting the somber expressions of his friends, Leighton continued. "When we struggled for control, his encouragement, compassion, and wisdom helped us remember our humanity."

How could they speak so ill against their *Legion* brother, the physically weakest of their group? Much as he hated to admit it, Leighton had seen darkness in each of them. Still, never before had suspicion of each other occurred. What would happen if they went their separate ways?

At once, a startling thought occurred.

"For what it's worth," Leighton continued. "It seems quite apparent to me someone is trying to turn us against one another, to destroy us from within."

For several moments no one spoke.

Leighton released a weary sigh. "What better way to pull us apart than implicate one of us? First the snuffbox; now the necklace delivered to Hunter's mistress."

Melville all but collapsed into a chair. "That would mean poor Anne's death is part of some vengeful plot against us."

"When I told everyone the killer had a snuffbox like ours," Leighton continued, "Knightly suggested the possibility of an enemy bent on vengeance. Such must be the case. And the last thing we should do now is doubt one another."

"Here, here," Hunter said with a nod.

"Miss Melville *is* dead," Leighton said. "Murdered by some fiend who, it would seem, wants to destroy us and has no qualms about using our loved ones to do so."

"By God," Hunter said in a raw whisper. "The killer could strike again. Target another member of our families."

"I doubt Miss Melville was chosen by accident," Leighton replied. "Had she been a random victim, why show her a copy of our snuffbox? Think upon it, my friends. No one, but us—and Miss Sinclair—knows Miss Melville is dead. We have no proof, not even her body. And now, the Melville necklace—the one piece of jewelry Anne Melville had in her possession—turns up as a gift to Hunter's mistress? Delivered no less by a waterman with an anonymous note it be worn tonight at a private dinner. A dinner where Miss Melville's brother would not only be present, but recognize it. What happened this evening was a carefully orchestrated plot to bait us. The killer wants to cause division amongst our group by creating suspicion and doubt. The necklace alone implicated two members—Hunter and Lyon."

"I agree," Knightly contributed. "This villain knows us and seems quite the strategist. Our families could be expendable pawns to him."

"Who hates us enough to do so foul a deed as murder?" Melville asked.

"That is what we need to find out," Leighton replied. "Before he strikes again."

"How are we to find him?" Hunter contributed. "He could be anyone."

Leighton rubbed his jaw. He then went to the cellaret and imbibed a quaff of brandy. He studied the empty glass in his hand. "The truth is, our best hope for identifying and stopping the killer is by working together—and with the assistance of Miss Sinclair."

When Hawthorne sniggered, Leighton shot him a reproving stare. "You must trust me. She has a remarkable power to see and speak with ghosts. And since our one witness to the killer's identity happens to be a ghost, Miss Sinclair is the only person who can help us. If this villain discovers Miss Sinclair is helping us—or learns of her ability—he will likely target her. Rest assured, I will not let that happen. Miss Sinclair's life is no less precious to me than my own family."

With a sheepish expression, Melville cleared his throat. "I should not want anything to happen to your Miss Sinclair, Saint." He looked at the other men in the room. "He's right. We must work together to find and stop this murderer."

Knightly rang for a servant. "First, we must cancel tonight's festivities."

"Most assuredly," Hunter agreed, seconded by Melville.

"You're nearest the window, Saint," Knightly continued. "Mind taking a look to see if any coaches have arrived or are waiting in queue?"

With a nod, Leighton stepped to the window and pulled back the sapphire colored velvet drape. "One," he said with a knowing look directed at Hunter.

Joining him at the window, Hunter grimaced. "What the devil is she up to now?"

"I take it Miss Bailey's coach has not departed," Knightly commented as he waited by the drawing room doors for a servant to answer his summons.

"She's likely waiting for me to chase after her," Hunter glowered then closed the drape.

"Will you?" Leighton donned his gloves and hat then adjusted his black evening cape with its gray silk lining about his shoulders.

"Never again," Hunter replied.

All things considered, severing ties with Miss Bailey tonight was the best thing that could have happened to Hunter.

"Gentlemen," Knightly said. "I suggest we take precautions for the safety of our loved ones."

A wave of icy terror swept over Leighton. His gut tightened, and he sensed all color had leached from his face.

"What is it?" Melville asked, standing near him.

"I was thinking," Leighton began, "there was a reason why he chose your sister as his first victim, and there must be a reason why her body has not been found."

He turned and paced before the hearth. "We know nothing about this villain, correct? But what if he has been watching our movements? Has seen us questioning jewelers about a duplicate snuffbox? We might have made him reveal his hand sooner than he wanted."

"Go on," Knightly's eyes narrowed thoughtfully.

"Would he not wonder how we came to know about a duplicate snuffbox?" Leighton questioned aloud. "When I learned about the item, I suspected it would be found with Miss Melville's body. At a time and place of the killer's design. One of us would then be implicated as her killer. However, we learned about the box from the ghost of the lady he murdered."

"I gather your meaning," Knightly said with a speculative gleam in his eyes. "If we have proof someone else had a replica made, the killer would be named suspect."

"We must consider," Leighton continued. "Everything he does is orchestrated to deceive us. To implicate us, destroy us, and conceal his identity. We have to assume he watches every move we make. That could mean he sent the necklace to make us suspicious of one another, and also gloat he is one step ahead of us."

"It's a game to him." Hunter drew back the curtain, obviously checking to see if Miss Bailey's coach had departed. "So, does that mean he sent the necklace to Evangeline and instructed her to wear it tonight as a test of some sort?"

Knightly nodded. "Possibly, if the killer suspects we've learned about Miss Melville's murder. Especially since her body has not been located. No doubt, he would want to know how we found out, and how much we know about him. I agree with Saint. The necklace could be his way of confirming suspicions—or make us turn against one another. And that, my friends, almost worked."

"God in heaven," Leighton whispered. "What if he is aware of the time I have spent with Miss Sinclair? He might even have heard rumors about her ability—which puts her life in immediate danger."

"How could he know about her ability to see ghosts?" Hunter asked. "Except for you and Melville, none of us knew about it until tonight."

"A servant at Carlyle House might have talked out of hand," Melville contributed.

Leighton shook his head. "From what I have learned of Lady Carlyle's household, I doubt it. Her people are extremely loyal. Still, we cannot be sure of anything, or anyone."

"I played right into his hands." Melville rubbed the back of his neck. "My reaction will tell him we know. But how could he learn about it? Unless…do you think he might be a guest tonight?"

Leighton's thoughts whirled with the significance of Melville's suggestion. A shaky breath escaped suddenly dry lips. His heart seemed to shudder to a stop. "Hunter's mistress heard you accuse him of killing your sister. If the killer is one of the guests this evening—and Miss Bailey tells him what happened—he will definitely know we are aware Miss Melville has been murdered."

"Didn't you say her coach was still outside?" Knightly's gaze shot toward the drawing room windows. "What if she was delayed by someone questioning her?"

"She's gone now," Hunter replied. "She might have waited to gossip with another guest, but I saw no other carriages arrive."

Leighton rubbed his brow. "The killer must be someone we know; someone who would have been here to judge our behavior."

A soft knock sounded. Knightly opened the drawing room door, but only slightly. As Leighton listened, their host calmly told the servant to tender his apologies and inform any guests that an unforeseen event has required him to cancel plans for the evening."

The momentary distraction over, Knightly faced his friends. "All things considered, I handled that very well."

Although he tried to appear nonchalant, Leighton saw in Knightly's expression an unsettling concern that one of his guests might indeed be the villain.

Who could they trust now?

"I am exceedingly worried for my family." Knightly crossed to a writing desk. "I suggest we not delay to ensure their safety."

Leighton must also warn his family, but could think of nothing else except returning to Hampton Court.

One fact eased his mind.

Lyon is there. He will watch over Patience until my return.

Besides which, a hastily written letter had by now been delivered by special messenger to his grandfather. Leighton had no doubt whatsoever the duke would immediately depart for Hampton Court.

In the meantime, he must ride to his family's town house and have a private talk with his father. He would take no chance a member of his family—especially his mother or one of his sisters—might be an intended victim. If his family quickly gathered at *Aldebaran*, their ancestral estate, they would be safe.

He paused, noting the sad expression on Melville's face. Everyone prepared to take steps to guard their loved ones. Anne's brother had no one to protect. His parents were safe at their estate in Ireland. His only sibling, dead, hidden away somewhere.

Their eyes met. "What can I do?" Melville asked.

Recognizing the restless need in Melville to be of help, Leighton rested a hand upon his bereaved friend's shoulder. "Ride to Hampton Court. Tell Lyon what happened here tonight."

"Consider it done," Melville answered.

"If only we had Knightly's talent for travel," Leighton said, noting the answering smirk from their host.

"A talent more trouble than it's worth," Knightly responded. "Still, with half my family in Derbyshire and the other half in Portsmouth, I have no choice. Heaven knows I don't relish terrifying them with facts they know nothing about. In truth, it's moments like this I wish I could manipulate time."

At the mention of controlling time, Leighton and the others turned to Hawthorne—the one man in the *Legion* with an almost mystical, uncanny ability to actually bend time to his will.

However, the Earl of Hawthorne was nowhere about. Had he used his power already and they only now realized it? One thing was certain. How, or when, he left their company was anyone's guess.

Chapter 35

Evangeline Bailey departed Knightly's residence in such a fit of temper she never noticed the change in her driver. Instead, she entered her luxurious coach without a word, rubbed her bruised wrist, and waited several minutes to see if Hunter would beg her forgiveness.

At long last, she signaled her coach to depart, expecting to be taken home without delay.

Unfortunately, *he* had other plans.

The night had turned rather cold, filled with shadows. Smoke gray clouds against an obsidian sky allowed the full moon fleeting moments to cast its illumination upon the earth.

He drove the four compliant horses skillfully, amused the lady had not called out in alarm, or ordered him to stop the coach. If nothing else, one might think she'd have become suspicious at how long it was taking to reach her home.

Foolish woman; she needed only to look out a window and see they were nowhere near where she lived. Not until the road turned rough did the uneven jostling of the coach capture her attention.

She called out then…twice.

The vehicle came to rest in a dark, ancient wooded area of Hampstead Heath. In seconds, he'd applied the brake, had jumped down from his seat, and then opened a door to the coach. He noted the initial interest upon her face to see him boldly enter without a word, and take the seat opposite her. Still, the vain woman showed no sign of alarm.

Quite the contrary, she seemed curiously intrigued, perhaps even pleased.

She began to deftly arrange herself in a rather alluring manner. The cloak draped about her shoulders was parted to best display the pale skin above the deep bodice of her gown. With a seductive smile, she raised her chin, and slowly moistened her lips with the tip of her pink tongue.

Much to his chagrin, his unruly primitive body stirred. A passing thought came to mind. Perhaps he might accept what she so willingly offered. He quickly cast aside such a notion. He had more important matters to attend.

He moved to sit beside her, content to let her think she had indeed enticed him whilst he, a master of deception, contemplated how much time he'd allow to pass before her desire turned to terror.

"So, it was you," she said.

"Me?" he questioned, almost disinterestedly, mindful to control his eagerness.

"You sent me the necklace."

He smiled in response.

She pivoted to look more squarely at him. "Why did you send it? And why did you ask me to wear it tonight? I must say, I have never been so insulted, or so rudely manhandled."

He continued to smile, saying nothing.

"Did you steal it?"

He chuckled softly. "No, I did not steal it." He traced the soft curve of her cheek with a finger then ever so slowly moved it downward to tease the area where the necklace had rested against her skin a short while ago.

Her breathing hitched, prompting him to gaze into her lapis lazuli eyes, now wide with desire. He leaned closer, as if he might kiss her. Instead he whispered, "You might say it was…left for me."

She frowned at his words. He noted the first sign of trepidation. Her gaze looked to the window behind him, and then the carriage door.

"You did well." He kept his voice low, soothing. "You were the perfect accomplice in tonight's masquerade." He stroked the hollow of her throat, relishing how she shuddered at his touch. Her breathing became shallow, somewhat stilted.

"You truly are quite fetching, my dear. Alas, I regret I cannot amuse myself further in your company this evening, but there are times when one must sacrifice desire to achieve a greater goal."

He moved closer. "You are part of that goal, Evangeline. Admittedly, I do find it interesting I had to woo and charm Miss Melville in order that she might aid me in my quest. Yet all I had to do for you to play your part was appeal to your vanity and greed."

"She's dead, isn't she?" Evangeline Bailey managed to ask.

"Dead, or murdered?" he replied with a quirked brow. "I do appreciate your interest, my dear, but I dislike discussing the past. Still, I suppose it is right you should know. Yes. I killed her. I had to, you see. She knew too much. She'd seen too much. I must say Miss

Melville suspected her fate long before you; in truth, she almost got away from me."

The harlot squirmed and made a pathetic mewling sound.

"I couldn't let that happen, now could I?" he continued with a playful tone. "Much as I found pleasure with Anne Melville, killing her proved far more necessary and intoxicating."

At this point, Evangeline Bailey managed to bolt from the seat and opened a carriage door. However, he easily pulled the woman back and restrained her with the brunt of his body. He used a strong hand to cover her mouth.

Her wide-eyed terror swiftly rose to a state of desperate panic. She struggled beneath him, trapped as much by the skirt of her gown and the fabric of her cloak as by the weight of his body pressed against hers.

"Shh," he whispered. "You must be quiet. Pay close attention. I am about to share a very important secret with you."

He paused a moment, increasing the pressure against her mouth after she tried to bite his palm. Tears spiked her lashes, but strangely, perhaps tragically, she seemed to accept her circumstances and nodded in compliance.

"Good," he responded, smiling gently although his tenuous control rapidly began to falter.

The dark abyss of centuries past that filled his every thought swelled within him. An ancient hunger awakened, sharp as a razor's edge—reminding him it had been too long since last he fed. And like before, in another darkened wood, no one was around to hear…or interfere.

Half-starved with need, his body trembled violently, preparing to embrace and savor the necessary addiction of what was about to happen. He released a guttural yell, arching his shoulders forward and back as if a fire-breathing dragon had spewed sulfur and molten ash inside his human belly.

The metamorphosis quickly revealed to his victim a shocking reality. She screamed with horror, over and over again. He was far too overcome by need and the freedom of his transformation to care how much noise she made now.

As she stared at him, a terrified witness to what no one had ever seen before and lived to tell, he rose above Evangeline Bailey a final moment before seizing her frail throat.

When it was over, when he had drained all life from his prey, he could not help but leer with satisfaction to see the result of his handiwork.

The courtesan would never sell her body to another. All the carefully employed tactics and wiles she once used to seduce wealthy, titled, powerful men had, in the end, brought her nothing but death and decay.

With one last look at the remains of his victim, he smiled and escaped silently into the night.

Chapter 36

Hampton Court Palace, England

Patience stared at the spot on a brick wall where the ghost she now believed to have been Jane Seymour had disappeared.

She could not understand why everywhere she went now, not one ghost tried to communicate with her. If what the spectral third wife of Henry VIII said was true, the Hampton Court ghosts desperately needed help. Yet although she sensed them about the palace and grounds, they kept their distance.

"You are a very curious young woman."

With a deflated sigh, Patience faced the slender man Leighton asked to serve as her protector until his return.

"Is curious your polite way of calling me strange, Mr. Courtenay?"

He chuckled, a pleasing sound that filled the brick and mortar hallway. Even after he'd gained control of his amusement, a gentle smile lingered. His warmth proved contagious.

Patience liked this man Leighton called Lyon. He had a calm demeanor and never seemed judgmental or prejudiced against her. Whether or not he believed in ghosts, she did not know. For now, it seemed enough Mr. Courtenay believed in her.

"To be honest, I see nothing wrong with being curious or strange." He looked at the spot where she'd been staring. "Curiosity is a desire to learn and understand. Knowledge—and the need to understand—is what life should be about. As for *strange,* it is simply a word used by those who lack imagination—or are unable to move beyond their own ignorance."

"Perhaps," Patience murmured, hugging her waist. Although she recognized the wisdom of his words, far too many painful memories rushed forward of being ridiculed by others and called names like *strange*, *mad*, and even *cursed.*

"Where to next, milady?"

Roused from painful recollections, she looked at Courtenay. "I do not understand why we have not encountered one spirit. We have walked all about the palace."

Turning to study the wall again, she rested a palm against the dark red bricks. Just as quickly, she pulled her hand away. "Cold as ice," she whispered. Without doubt, although she could not see the ghost of Jane, the gentle spirit was there...listening to them.

"Why won't you talk to me, Jane?"

Her impulsive question, spoken aloud to a brick wall, prompted Patience to glance over her shoulder. Silent, Courtenay studied the stone floor with a bemused expression, his lips pursed together thoughtfully.

For the first time since being alone in his company, Patience questioned her opinion of Leighton's friend. In this unguarded moment, when he did not realize she observed him, did she see wariness in the man's demeanor? Had he been trying to ease her mind, using false words to reassure or win her trust?

After all, he had promised Leighton to not allow her to go about the palace alone. As such, he might think it behooved him to speak to her in a kindly manner so that she would better accept his constant company. Even confide in him.

What did she really know about Courtenay? He might very well be a soft-spoken, considerate young man. Then again, what if he wasn't?

People often pretend to be something they are not. They speak gently, and behave sincerely. They pretend to be a friend—to win your trust—and then turn and betray you with a smile.

"How is it you have lived at Hampton Court all your life?" she asked, at once embarrassed by the suspicious, if not accusatory tone, in which she'd spoken.

He looked at her, his expression enigmatic. She could not tell if he was affronted by her insolent tone or by the question. He simply studied her in silence and it seemed he would not reply at all. Then, at long last, he spoke.

"You know nothing about me, then?"

Patience made a point to gentle her tone. "I know that you and Lord Leighton have been friends since childhood. That you became very ill after what happened in the cave, and that you did not receive any type of…"

"Power?" He expelled a heavy sigh, as if answering her question were an unavoidable, but necessary task. "I did say curiosity is a good thing. Yes, unlike the others, I have no powers. My health has been plagued since birth with a variety of illnesses. My condition worsened after the cave incident. As for why I have lived at Hampton Court all my life, the answer is simple. I am here because this is where my father placed me."

"Your father?"

A rueful smile curved his lips. "William, Duke of Clarence, is my father. He resides not far from here at Bushy House."

"But that means your grandfather is..."

"His Majesty, King George III." He spoke without any sign of emotion or pride.

Patience tried not to stare. Leighton's friend was grandson to the King of England, and nephew to the Prince Regent? She blinked in an owl-like manner, trying to understand the doings of nobility. Since his father had never married, Mr. Courtenay had obviously been born on the wrong side of the blanket.

Still, why did he not live at his father's house?

As ill-informed as she was about Royals and the peerage, 'twas well known the Duke of Clarence lived openly with his mistress and their brood of illegitimate children for many years.

Why isolate one child?

"I can almost read the questions spinning in your mind, Miss Sinclair." He folded his arms across his chest. "No, my mother is not Mrs. Jordan. I am, for lack of a better word, the result of an earlier dalliance. My mother died in childbirth. My father said he loved her dearly, and had me brought back to England. I almost died on the voyage. Even afterwards he feared I was not long for this world."

"You lived apart from your father here?"

"Mrs. Jordan did not want a sickly child around her babes. Thus, I was placed here—close enough that my father might visit on occasion. Two years ago, when the duke and Mrs. Jordan parted ways, my father told me the truth."

"What truth?"

"That Mrs. Jordan—much as he believed her a kindhearted woman—had told him she'd not have the child of another woman living underfoot—especially one who so resembled a lost love."

"How terrible," Patience gasped.

He shrugged his shoulders. "I am quite sure the fact I was a sickly child in need of constant medical attention was of greater importance to Mrs. Jordan. You see, I had a healthy older brother named William. When he wasn't at school, he lived in my father's house. He first went to sea in 1803. I never really knew him; he drowned in 1807 off Madagascar with the crew of the HMS Blenheim."

Not knowing what to do or say, overcome with a sense of guilt for prying into his past, Patience watched in silence as he walked toward the doors leading to the Great Hall.

Before he left, he paused and looked back at her. "So, you see, Miss Sinclair, I understand how you felt to be cast aside. Denied the company of blood relations, and exist as if you had no family at all."

She listened to Courtenay's retreating footsteps. Their echo sounded so lonely in the ancient tomb of a palace. The thought of a sickly little boy forced to live here whilst his father lived happily nearby with his mistress and healthy children made her want to weep.

A single tear slid down her cheek.

"Do not cry for him," a familiar voice said.

Patience turned quickly to see Jane Seymour's ghost standing before the wall through which she'd vanished at their last meeting.

"Why should I not cry?" Patience sniffled. "He was a sick, lonely little boy, brought to this wretched place when he might have had a real home with his father. If not for being sent away to school where he met Lord Leighton and the other boys, he might never have known friendship at all."

"You have a kind and gentle heart, Patience Sinclair." With a sad smile, Jane raised her vaporous hand to smooth the curve of Patience's cheek, as if the ghost wanted to wipe away her human tears. Instead, her otherworldly touch conjured a cool, strangely soothing comfort. "Then cry for the child, dear girl, but not the man."

Caught in a sense of wonder, Patience could not believe the ghost of a Tudor queen had touched her face—with such obvious concern for her sorrow. Then, curiosity for the meaning of Jane's words, prompted Patience to question the spectral lady.

"Why did you not answer when I called you?"

"Do you not remember what I told you?" Jane turned and floated gracefully toward that point in the corridor from whence the spirit had first brought Patience into this hallway.

"Yes, you told me to not wander about alone." Patience watched as Jane opened the secret doorway and entered the medieval stairwell.

Quickly following, Patience said, "As you saw and heard, I was not alone. I had someone to guard me."

Jane stopped her graceful, gliding descent down the staircase and flew back to where Patience stood halfway down the stairs.

"GUARD YOU?" Jane screamed, her face bristling with rage. "You think *he* can guard you?"

Turbulent icy air filled the small confines of the narrow staircase, making it feel more a mausoleum. The young queen's deep-set eyes glared. "You are not impervious to death, mortal girl. Best you remember that."

Jane's unexpected scream could only be described as an unsettling, screeching tone called a wail. Patience had often heard the wailing of ghosts.

Like the cry of the legendary *bean sith* or banshee, a ghostly wail could begin as a scream then quickly evolve into a blood-chilling, altogether piercing sound that she'd hated since childhood.

Experience had taught her ghost wails were a highly effective prolonged scream or howl, used by powerful ghosts to frighten mortals, or chase them away from where the spirit dwelled.

Spirits also sometimes emitted the horrific sound to convey intense anger, unending sorrow, or a terrifying physical pain that ghosts still felt somehow.

The lamentation took much energy to perform.

The fact Jane screamed so close in proximity to Patience's face showed how ancient and powerful she was as a spectral being. More importantly, though the wailing frightened Patience, she did not believe such had been Jane's intent.

Rather, she suspected it proved the malevolent being which threatened Jane and other spirits at Hampton Court was an evil that not only terrified the Tudor queen but warned could also take Patience's human life.

It took a moment for the ghost queen to calm herself. Patience saw immediately Jane regretted her outburst. Also apparent was the fact the energy she'd used had drained some of her ability to manifest.

She shimmered, weakened.

Jane's voice returned to its serene, soft tone when next she spoke. "If you are to help us and your friend, you must remember everything I tell you."

"I am trying to help you, Jane. And I am trying to understand. Yet if no one speaks to me, if everyone hides from me, there is nothing I can do."

"We do not hide from you." Intensity ignited Jane's luminescent eyes. "Listen carefully to me, Patience Sinclair. You have a gift to see beyond the boundary that separates the world of the living from the world of the dead. Verily, you also have the power to walk within those worlds. You stand upon a precipice. Danger and death are ever near. You must be on guard at all times. Both worlds are closing in upon you. Above all, you must not cloud your thoughts with pity for that which cannot be changed. Not everything or everyone is as they appear. No matter how much you wish otherwise."

Jane turned away and continued down the staircase, opening and entering an arched door which led to the small room adjoining the kitchens. When she magically opened the final door into the kitchen, a great light could be seen as if thousands of lanterns were lit.

Entering the kitchen, Patience saw a multitude of ghosts had gathered, far more than she'd ever seen at one time or place. Some were young, and some were old. All were wearing clothing from different times in the history of Hampton Court.

Amidst the vaporous images, she recognized the lavishly dressed, bejeweled spirits that usually lingered in the gardens. She also saw the courtly gentlemen who tried to talk with her in the Great Watching Chamber on the night of her arrival.

Even the angry old man from the painting on the Great Staircase was present.

They stared beseechingly at her—their expressions anxious, fearful, and desperate.

"You are the key," Jane said with the clarity of a bell. "The only one who can help us."

Jane's ethereal form stood surrounded by the blue-white glow radiating from the other Hampton Court ghosts. "Because you *can* see between the shadows of your world and ours, you must remember all I have said. Your life depends upon it."

Patience trembled, her breathing fast, unsteady.

"Repeat what I have told you thus far," Jane commanded.

"The evil that threatens your world also dwells in mine."

"Yes," Jane replied with a nod.

"You said he watches…and he waits."

"There is much more you need know." Jane continued in a chilling whisper. "He is both man and evil incarnate. He exists only to destroy, and grows stronger every day. A master of disguise, he deceives the living and wins their trust. He insinuates himself into their company only to bring about their doom. Make no mistake, he will destroy anything and anyone who tries to stop him, mortal or not. We are as much his prey as your world shall become…unless he is revealed and destroyed. And you, dear girl, are the only one who has the power to see through his many deceptions."

"I understand…I think." Patience's breath lifted into the room in a warm puff of air.

"Nay, you do not," Jane replied with a sad smile. "Alas, until you do, be wary. Guard yourself against people you do not know well. For that reason, we will not come and speak to you unless you are alone."

A sudden thought raced through Patience's mind.

There could be only one explanation why the spirits had not appeared to her when she searched for them after Leighton's departure.

"No, no, no," she repeated in a half whisper. "Please tell me this evil one is not Leighton's friend…not Mr. Courtenay."

"He has many names and many faces," Jane replied. "Even a coin has two sides."

Patience stood in the now freezing cold, hoping to ignore her body's quaking and make sense of what she'd been told. No doubt Jane spoke the truth, but how was it possible for Courtenay to traverse the world of the dead? According to Leighton, his friend had not received any powers in the ancient Roman temple.

Courtenay also said he'd always been a sickly child. How could she now tell Leighton his close friend terrorized ghosts and killed innocent people?

She inhaled sharply, remembering a comment Jane had said a few moments ago. Was it possible? Her throat constricted with a terrifying thought as she swallowed with difficulty.

"Jane, you said, '*if* you are to help me *and* my friend'. What friend do you speak of?"

With the hem of her iridescent gown hovering slightly above the stone flooring, Jane floated toward Patience, stopping halfway between the group of ghosts and where Patience stood. She seemed sad, reluctant to answer, wringing her hands nervously. She then glanced about the kitchen, as if listening for someone or perhaps fearful of a possible repercussion if she answered.

Patience's stomach twisted and churned. A strong suspicion gnawed at her insides. If true, the answer explained her sudden instinct to remain at Hampton Court rather than return to London.

"Where is Anne's body, Jane?"

Jane shook her head, her eyes wide with fear. "I dare only say 'tis near." The queen's expression conveyed her regret to not be more forthcoming.

Suddenly, the ghosts behind Jane became agitated, looking to one another, nodding with understanding and great urgency. Immediately, they started disappearing like puffs of white smoke.

"There is no more time to speak now," Jane whispered, drifting backwards with a mournful countenance.

"Wait, please. You must help me find my friend's body. Where do I look? How do I begin my search?"

Jane's expression became more anxious. "The only way to find your friend is to follow *him.*"

"Do you mean, Mr. Courtenay?" Patience moved forward as if she could chase and capture the ethereal spirit intent on departing.

Some of the female spirits began to cry fretfully then flee in dire panic. Their departure was soon followed by others, one after another.

Some male ghosts stood fast and shimmered, ready to dissipate at any moment.

Patience noted, with no small amount of discomfort, that a great darkness had started to cast its pall over the room. The menacing gloom reminded her of a shroud or cloth used to cover a coffin.

She quickly looked to the high windows, only to see the dark of night had fallen. It should not be possible. She'd only left Courtenay's company a short while ago and 'twas yet midday.

More and more Hampton Court ghosts disappeared, taking with them their iridescent aura. She would soon be alone in almost complete darkness, without a candle or lamp to light her way.

"What is happening?" Patience anxiously studied her surroundings anew. Since following Jane an icy cold had permeated the air. Now, an eerie darkness swelled around her.

The great fireplaces in the kitchen were dark and cold, as if extinguished for centuries. Patience had been so focused on Jane and all the ghosts gathered together she'd not noticed the room itself.

More troubling was the realization a strange weakness had seeped into her body. The slightest movement took great effort, as if her feet were buried in dense, wet sand. Even her breathing had become slow, labored.

She looked to Queen Jane. "What is happening to me?" Her voice held a panicked tone that could not be helped. "What have you done to me? Why is it so hard to move? Why does everything look and feel so different?"

Jane clasped her hands together and pressed them lightly against her lips a moment. "Forgive me, I thought you understood." She shook her head sadly.

"Understood what?" Patience demanded.

"That when you talk with me, you leave your world and enter mine. 'Tis how I can stay and speak with you for so long a time. How I can lead and take you places in this palace that do not exist in your time."

"What are you saying? This is the same palace. These are the same kitchens."

"The same yet not the same. Remember, you have the power to not only see but cross into our world. 'Tis the only way you can help us and find your friend…if you are brave enough."

Patience looked over her shoulder to the small room from whence they'd entered the kitchen, desperate to run back to her aunt's apartments and the Hampton Court Palace of her time. But the arched doorway was barely visible in the encroaching darkness.

"My queen, *he* comes!" shouted a Tudor ghost.

With a quick nod to her guard, Jane looked back at Patience. "There is no more time, dear Patience. You must find your own way back…as best you can. Find the door that leads outside. Or, if you truly want to find your friend, watch *him* and follow. Make no sound that might draw attention to you in this place. *He* does not know you suspect him, not yet."

"My queen, we must depart!" The guard urged again, a vaporous hand upon the hilt of his ghostly sword, ready to draw the weapon in defense against their evil adversary.

"Keep to the shadows," Jane stressed, her form fading. "I will try to guide your people to you…if I can."

Patience stood immobile, wishing she had a candle but understood the importance to not risk discovery. For now, not knowing what else to do, she summoned her will and strength to create an invisible barrier, hoping her protective shield would offer concealment from any power Courtenay might have to detect her.

Oddly enough, her blocking technique enabled her to move more easily, as if shackles of restraint had been lifted. With great caution, she moved toward the small doorway used to enter the kitchen with Jane. Feeling her way, she breathed a sigh of relief to touch the archway's cold stones. She felt the ancient wooden door still open.

However, before she entered the small room leading to the secret stairway, a sharp pain at the back of her head stopped her. She quickly applied pressure with her hand, massaging the area until the spasm subsided a bit. Still, the vise-like pressure continued—the intensity of which she'd never experienced.

The familiar pins and needles sensation stabbed from inside her body, confirming beyond any doubt that spirits were near, or some otherworldly essence so powerful her defensive technique provided little resistance.

She heard the echo of approaching footsteps. Slow. Steady. Despite the fact pain still gripped the back of her head, and her insides felt as if they were being repeatedly impaled, Patience quickly stepped away from the arched doorway.

Remembering Jane's warning to stay close to the shadows, she looked about the enormous room. Among several unlit fireplaces, large enough to stand in, and exceedingly dark, Patience made her way to the one nearest, a fairly safe distance from the door through which Anne Melville's killer would emerge. She entered a deep recessed stone alcove attached to the hearth, most likely used at one time to store firewood.

Pressing herself as far back into the darkened alcove as possible, Patience listened to the footsteps as they descended the secret staircase.

He seemed unhurried yet, in her mind's eye, she envisioned the pale, slender Courtenay—tired of his goodly pretense and now intent on her destruction.

Then again, Jane said he does not know I suspect him.

Her only hope was to not be heard or seen.

She pressed her terrified, tense body closer against the deepest corner of her hiding place. Blessedly, the pain at the back of her head finally faded.

Fear that her rapid breathing might be overheard prompted Patience to cup her hands loosely over her nose and lips. Her slender shoulders tensed as she tried to ignore the icy cold. She listened as his footsteps walked through the anteroom toward the kitchen. Despite the vast darkness, she tried to see the doorway, knowing any second he would cross its threshold.

A moment more, and he will be in this ghost kitchen...with me.

Chapter 37

As her eyesight adjusted to the darkness, Patience watched the doorway and saw the figure of a man enter the Great Kitchen. He appeared to be wearing what looked like a gentleman's black evening cloak or perhaps a tiered greatcoat, the folds of which lifted slightly as he turned to walk in the opposite direction from where she hid.

The shroud of darkness which had settled over the kitchen did not seem to hinder him in any fashion. Neither did he seem hurried. Perhaps he had the ability to see in the darkness, which made it all the more dangerous for her to be there. Or, it could simply be that he had walked this path so many times before its route had been committed to memory.

Her first thought was to remain hidden until he disappeared from sight and hearing. Only then would she attempt to find a way out. However, deep inside she recognized the importance of following the man, careful to remain at a safe distance.

She had to learn more about him in order that she might help those who needed her. And she must find Anne's body before it was too late. For all she knew, it might already be too late for the girl's spirit to cross into the eternal light.

Torn between self-preservation and an unexplainable sense of dire responsibility, Patience inched her way forward from the back of her hiding place. To linger behind any longer would make it impossible to follow him.

Patience glanced about the kitchen with its high ceiling. Numerous open areas would make it difficult should she need to hide again. Shivering, she walked in the direction Courtenay had taken, cautious to be silent, almost one with the shadows.

Dread made her hesitate. She gave a fleeting thought toward forgetting her plan and finding which door would bring her outside. But there were far too many to choose from.

Some doors were open, most likely leading to other kitchens and rooms that had been used for various aspects of preparing meals for kings and queens in ages past. Other doors were closed, their iron locks incapable of being opened by a living mortal in this dimension.

The Tudor kitchens were a labyrinth unto themselves, and she certainly had no knowledge which way to proceed in the ghostly shadowed world.

She stood frozen, unable to take the next step forward. Fragments of things Jane told her whispered in Patience's memory. '*...you stand upon a precipice ...danger and death are ever near.*'

What am I thinking? I cannot do this. I have no power or great strength.

Tears stung Patience's eyes. Her throat tightened. She tried to soothe it with gentle strokes, and remembered the ugly marks about Anne Melville's delicate throat.

She looked toward the direction Anne's killer had walked. He must be passing into another room. His footsteps could barely be heard upon the slate stone flooring.

Resolved to follow the man Jane called *evil incarnate,* Patience moved forward. With each tentative step, Patience remembered the Tudor queen's advice.

Try as she might to remain calm, her heart raced a frantic rhythm. Her body would not stop shaking with cold, and an ever-increasing fear rose from the depths of her soul.

From one room into another, she followed.

The fact he seemed oblivious to her presence instilled within Patience a wary confidence. Perhaps she could do this after all? She could follow in silence. Let him lead her to Anne's body. Then, somehow, she would find her way back to her aunt's apartments and send word to Leighton.

It seemed a good plan until, as he turned a corner into a corridor, he stopped. Still a safe distance, Patience pressed her body back against the brick wall that blessedly hid her from view. Believing she could not be seen, Patience waited, hoping he'd resume walking away from her. If, on the other hand, his footsteps came toward her, she would have no choice but to run as hard and fast as she could.

"Why are you following me?"

His voice sounded deceptively calm, and one she recognized as definitely belonging to Courtenay.

Patience pressed one hand over her mouth, certain sure he would otherwise hear her breathing.

"You have but one chance to tell me why you are following me."

She swallowed hard. Her mind raced with a possible answer. Should she say she had become lost while searching for the ghosts? That she thought to follow him to a familiar part of the palace? But then he might ask why she had not called out for assistance. Perhaps she should bolt from where she stood and run away, hoping she might escape?

She looked up toward the stone barrel-vaulted ceiling, praying anew for angels to protect her. To her surprise, she saw a faint yet luminous blue-white orb. Someone else had been following Anne Melville's killer.

"Come here. Now."

The orb descended, taking shape as it did in the form of a youth about sixteen years in age. His clothing appeared that of a Tudor household servant, a page perhaps. For a brief moment his eyes looked anxiously in her direction then quickly darted away. Clearly, the ghost knew of her presence.

Had the boy been following her, not Courtenay?

Although she could not peek around the corner from where she remained hidden, the bluish hue from the ghost's aura lit up one side of the brick wall—providing her with a view of shadows. Two figures faced one another; one a ghostly vaporous image, the other a mortal man.

"Speak." Courtenay spoke in a quiet, menacing manner.

"I—I came to warn ye," the Tudor youth said.

"Warn me?"

"Someone knows about ye."

Courtenay chuckled. "What is it this someone knows about me, boy? For that matter, what do *you* really know about me?"

Patience saw the ghost's shadow drift away slightly, his movement countered by Courtenay who stepped toward the spirit.

"I'm waiting," Courtenay said. "Answer the question."

"I—I know ye be a powerful master of darkness, and I want to serve ye."

"What makes you think for one moment I need someone as useless as you? You are nothing to me. Your very existence annoys me."

"I can help. I can spy for ye. I can tell ye about her."

"Her?" Courtenay stepped again toward the ghost.

"Yes, milord. She can destroy ye."

"You are more pathetic than I thought if you think any mortal can destroy me."

"But 'tis said she is the only one who can see who ye really are."

Too terrified to move, Patience watched as the shadow of Courtenay, arms folded across his chest, cocked his head slightly and studied the Tudor ghost.

"How intriguing," he said. "Do continue."

"She has the power to see and speak with all the ghosts here at the palace. And she knows about the girl ye killed. She searches for her body. 'Tis only a matter of time til she finds it in the burial vault 'neath the chapel. The others want to help her, but I am smart and wise. I want to serve ye."

"How do you know she can see my true identity?"

"Her…um…well, someone said she could," the youth replied nervously. "That is to say, 'tis what everyone says. 'Tis why they hide. Ye know, 'cause she's been walkin' about with ye and tryin' to talk to 'em."

"You make no sense, boy, and I grow weary of this conversation. Do you have any proof she can see me as I truly am? That she knows anything about me?" Courtenay paused a moment. "No answer, eh? In truth, I doubt you know anything at all."

"I know her name is Patience Sinclair," the Tudor page boasted.

Patience's spine stiffened. Deathly cold raked over her body. Standing with a hand still braced over her mouth, she stared at the shadows on the wall.

"She's not much older than me," the ghost continued. "When I died, that is. She can walk into our world. I know she be a relation to Lady Carlyle, too. The countess brought her here. But she has powers the countess don't have, that's for sure. All the other ghosts think she can destroy ye."

Courtenay laughed softly. "She has no power to destroy me, fool."

"I also saw the one called Leighton. He has a special power, too. I know 'cause he used it to save her already."

"Ah yes, the goodly Saint."

"Yes, milord, but his lordship 'tisn't here. If ye want, I can take ye to her now."

Patience swallowed a gasp and tightly closed her eyes, desperate to quell the panic seizing her body. Would this boy soar back toward her in a heartbeat? Would Courtenay follow?

No words were spoken for a few moments. Upon hearing footsteps, Patience looked with great effort to see the shadow of Courtenay walking a slow circle about the Tudor ghost.

"You are quite the little spy." He stopped in front of the ghost, arms still folded across his chest. "There is one small problem."

"Milord?" the ghost asked.

"You talk too much, which is why I do not trust spies."

Patience stared at the shadows on the wall as something strange began to happen. Courtenay raised one arm and, as he did so, the sound of cracking seemed to echo as if bones were breaking.

Her eyes widened, horrified, as his hand appeared to transform into an appendage that should belong on a beast. Long, talon-like claws hovered like a guillotine over the head of the page. Then, with one sudden downward strike, the claws sliced through the ghost's vaporous image.

Otherworldly shrieking unlike anything she'd ever heard emanated from the Tudor spy. The ghost writhed and wailed in great agony before dissolving into a black smoky mass that then disappeared.

The back of her head pressed hard against the cool bricks of the wall. She tried with feeble desperation to calm her racing heart. To ignore the sickening repulsion brewing in her belly.

At long last, she heard Courtenay's footsteps walking away, confident, steady, continuing on to whatever destination he had at the palace. She had no desire to find out where.

Instead, she thought of the Tudor ghost. Would she ever forget the torturous scream as the boy's spiritual essence was brutally mutilated? She couldn't help but feel pity for the foolish youth. To think he could betray his people here at the palace and bargain with someone who had been hurting them.

Little wonder the ghosts at Hampton Court hid from Courtenay. Or, why they were so afraid when she'd been roaming about the palace with the man. How many other ghosts at Hampton Court had met the same fate as the Tudor page?

He doesn't trust spies, she reminded herself.

Or, anyone who might reveal anything about him.

At once, his reason for destroying the ghosts at Hampton Court made sense. An earthbound spirit who could talk and communicate with mortals would be viewed as a threat. There were many ghosts at Hampton Court who could do that—even if it took tremendous effort to speak or manifest before someone not sensitive to their presence.

No wonder they were so happy I came to the palace.

There were others, however, that Courtenay would not view as a threat, namely spirits like Catherine Howard. They could not interact with, or even notice, the living. Ghosts like her were forever trapped in a moment from their lives.

Doomed to repeat it over and over again.

Always with the same outcome.

Possibly some form of punishment or a futile but eternal desire to return and change their fate.

Yet what she couldn't understand was how Courtenay's hand could change into something inhuman, something that had the power to harm a ghost.

No, not harm…eviscerate.

The page felt a torturous pain as if he were being murdered.

But how was that possible? He was already dead.

Just his spirit remained…and one's spirit was but another word for a person's soul.

Angels in heaven, did I really see Mr. Courtenay murder the soul of that ghost? No, it cannot be possible.

Souls cannot be destroyed. No man has the power to do that. Souls are God given. They continue on after death, an eternal energy force that returns to the light and finds peace. Or, they remained earthbound by choice or purpose.

Patience shuddered as she contemplated the magnitude of power Courtenay demonstrated. Her thoughts started to spin like a whirligig. To oscillate between the kind, intelligent, soft-spoken man befriended by Leighton—and the cold-hearted, arrogant, evil person she had witnessed savagely murder the soul of a Tudor ghost.

Two sides of the same coin.

He truly was a master of disguise and deception. Not only could he walk between both worlds like her, but the man had tormented and murdered Anne Melville—the only sister of a man who considered Courtenay a friend.

Courtenay had also kept secret the fact he, too, possessed a supernatural power—the extent of which she could not fully comprehend. All she knew was he could inflict a second death to still earthbound spirits by ripping apart their soul and, with it, the very essence of their once mortal self.

From where did such a power come?

The cave, Patience told herself. The cave where Leighton said supernatural powers had been given to the other members of the *Legion.* All except Courtenay.

Someone was not telling the truth.

And that someone could only be Courtenay.

Leighton would not protect a murderer, not the man she knew and loved.

She *had* to find Anne's body. Hidden with cold indifference by Mr. Edward FitzWilliam Lyon Courtenay in the underbelly of his palace home. Then she would reveal the truth about Courtenay to Leighton, Charles Melville, and the world.

A frisson of doubt pricked her conscience.

Why hadn't she seen through Courtenay's deception like Jane said she could? Not in all the time she'd spent in his company. The pale, thin young man had not demonstrated anything but kindness and understanding.

Besides which, he already knew everything about me before the Tudor page spoke to him. Well, everything except Jane's belief that I would be able to see through his deception.

Jane also warned about guarding her emotions.

Did I see what I wanted to see?

Patience thought again about Jane referencing two sides of the same coin. That everything or everyone is not as they seem.

After all the years of people pretending to be my friend and then hurting me, how could I be so trusting now?

The only logical explanation; Courtenay had been trying to learn as much as he could about what she knew. And, no doubt, what the ghosts at Hampton Court might tell her.

That was why the spirits stayed away.

Why they hid from him.

The time had come to focus on facts, without emotion.

Courtenay had been sent away from school as a boy after the cave incident due to a grave sickness. He'd also spent the majority of his life at Hampton Court.

Hampton Court, where she'd learned the body of Anne Melville would be found beneath the Chapel Royal, a place only someone who'd spent their life here would know about, as well as how to access secret rooms or hidden corridors.

Since Courtenay had also spent so much time away from Leighton and the other members of the *Legion*, he could easily have found a way to deceive them about having a power, especially one that manifested in such a monstrous manner.

For all she knew, the man had practiced his power here on the ghosts for years before venturing out to also kill mortals.

What if he could claim both the life and soul of mortals? If so, Anne had been fortunate to have only lost her physical life to the man.

What if the reason for Anne's spirit remaining earthbound was because her soul somehow managed to escape being destroyed by her killer?

What if, at the moment of her death, she vowed to tell someone the truth about Courtenay and stop him?

The time had come to get the proof Patience needed. She had to find Anne's body before Courtenay could move it. Locating the body was the best way to link him as the killer. Also, Anne must be present when her body is found.

Past experience had proven that when a ghost, who could not remember how they died, confronted their earthly remains, the memory of their death returned in a rush. She had every reason to believe the same would be true for Anne Melville.

Still, she'd need one or two respected people who could support her findings. She thought of her aunt as one such witness. At the very least, Lady Carlyle would also be able to hear and confirm the testimony of Anne.

As for the frightened ghosts of Hampton Court, she had not the power to protect them. Her best recourse would be to convince them to abandon the existence they loved at the haunted palace. They must seek the realm of the light.

Slowly, as if waking from a dream, Patience stepped away from where she stood. She started to walk back the way she came. By retracing her steps, she would eventually find a door leading outside.

As she walked, Patience absently noted the blanket of oppressive darkness that had permeated her surroundings seemed to be lifting. Then again, it could be her imagination. She'd become so accustomed to the darkness her vision was less hindered now.

In any event, she had much to do, quickly as possible. First, she must summon Sam and Anne Melville. Much as she hated the idea of either spirit being confronted by the monstrous Courtenay, she needed both of them now.

Somehow I will find a way to protect their souls.

Patience continued on her way in silence, contemplating all she'd learned. Suddenly, vise-like pressure twisted inside her head.

The air turned icy cold once more.

Each breath lifted in puffs of warm, white mist as she exhaled.

And what seemed like a thousand disembodied voices reached out from the ether, screaming again and again just one word.

RUN!

Chapter 38

Patience obeyed the urgent voices, although compelling curiosity prompted her to look over her shoulder.

The dark figure of a man followed—his pace unhurried, almost leisurely. By his posture and manner, even without seeing his features, she knew 'twas Courtenay.

He made no comment or threat. The steady sound of his footsteps carried with them unspoken confidence any attempt on her part to escape would prove futile.

She increased her pace and slipped, almost falling upon the slick stone flooring. Regaining a sense of balance, she ran again. Yet uncertainty which direction to follow hindered her progress.

At once, numerous candescent blue lights appeared high above her, one after another, blinking in the darkness. They beckoned to gain her attention then soared swiftly in a direction to follow.

She knew not what ghosts these orbs belonged to, but blessed them in her heart for appearing in a moment of such hopelessness. Like evening stars set in the heavens by the hand of God to guide a lost mariner at sea, they guided her.

Courtenay's footsteps increased in tempo.

She had no idea the distance separating them and could only assume 'twas not great. After all, he wasn't running after her. Rather, he continued to walk albeit somewhat more swiftly, as if no more than slightly frustrated by the intrusion of palace spirits attempting to help her.

She found herself entering the kitchens again and thought to race toward the small anteroom and secret staircase. The orbs, however, raced in another direction—toward a door that suddenly flew open wide.

Nearing the door's threshold, a soothing, warm breeze caressed her face. This door led outside.

Outside, away from the freezing confines of a ghostly domain.

Outside, into a living, breathing world.

Running faster, she followed orbs that seemed to now dance about in the night sky. Patience could not help but smile to feel the difference between the frightening ghost world she'd left behind and her world of life.

Indeed, such exuberance and relief swept through her that Patience paused to catch her breath and soothe the stitch in her right side. For the first time she realized how out of breath she'd become.

The sound of deep laughter caused her to quickly turn about.

He stood there plainly visible in the moonlight.

How could she have been so foolish to forget Jane's warning? Like her, he had the ability to walk in both the mortal and spirit worlds.

Mr. Courtenay, the man Leighton introduced as his good friend. The man she'd thought ever so kind, courteous and soft-spoken; a true gentleman. In reality, he was evil incarnate. A monstrous murderer of mortals and the destroyer of souls.

Now, when she had not the strength to run any further or knowledge how she might fight him, they stood a short distance apart. Facing one another like two duelists meeting at dawn.

He gloated as he looked at her. Though not the first time someone viewed her as beneath them, somehow she knew it would be the last. Even without him making a deadly move, she had no doubt he intended to kill her.

She'd not make it easy for him.

Patience glanced about to gauge their location. They stood beyond the Anne Boleyn Gate inside Clock Court. No bell tolled the hour of her imminent death. The irony did not escape her. The lines between her world and Queen Jane's ghostly realm were indeed blurred.

A short moment ago she'd felt so happy to be in the present, yet her death would take place in an area of the palace that existed in all three worlds. She stood where others walked in the past during Tudor times. Where spirits now dwelled in an unseen ghost world. And where mortal life and death existed in the present. All three realms preserved for centuries, connecting the past to the present.

Neither did it escape her thoughts that perhaps a thousand eyes were upon them now. However, there would be no further assistance from that quarter. The spirits were too frightened of this man.

Still, they might be visible to any mortal strolling about or perchance glancing out a window. Unfortunately, judging from the silence permeating the air, and the darkness of the evening sky, 'twas quite late and no one was looking.

"Lovely evening for a stroll," he said with a sardonic grin. "Although I do believe what you were doing constitutes a form of running."

She said nothing, preferring to steady her breathing, calm the frantic racing of her heart, and ponder her predicament. One thing was certain. She'd not show fear. She simply would not give him the satisfaction.

"Have you nothing to say for yourself? No explanation as to why you were running like a young woman gone mad?"

"You were chasing me," she said succinctly. "Why didn't you make your presence known? How was I to know it was you?"

"I see," he murmured. "And as a young lady alone, you feared for your safety. Understandable, if not warranted." He took a step toward her then arched an eyebrow, noting how she took one step away in return.

"I suppose had you known it was me, you would have stopped and chatted. After all, there is no reason why you would be afraid of me. We know each other, do we not?"

"I thought I knew you," she replied. "Before I saw you murder the soul of that ghost."

"Ah, well…" he shrugged.

"You destroyed a human soul. Do you not have any sense of remorse or conscience about what you have done?"

He rubbed his chin thoughtfully as he studied her. "Why would his fate concern you? He was no friend to you. Besides, he annoyed me."

"It doesn't matter if we were friends or not. And it doesn't matter if he annoyed you. Do you not see that you have become corrupt with power? What gives you the right to destroy like that?"

"Well, I *am* a god."

"What?"

He sighed heavily. "You really have no idea what you are doing, do you? This is all so very disappointing. I had such hopes for a fierce battle with you. Although I find myself impressed by your courage, especially for a female, this conversation has become tedious."

She slowly slid a foot back again, desperate to create more distance. He seemed not to notice. His intense gaze remained fixed on her face. Remembering how he'd studied the Tudor page before destroying him, Patience returned his stare and took another step back.

Suddenly, she felt as if her heart shuddered to a stop and all the blood in her veins had ceased to flow. Every muscle in her body became stiff, frozen in place.

A strange glow flickered in his eyes then flared stronger like a fire ignited. His eye color completely changed from dark brown to bright yellow-gold.

Instinctively, she knew.

This monster was *not* Courtenay.

"Who are you?"

"Who do I look like?" he countered. "Come now, Miss Sinclair, impress me with your power to see me as I truly am."

His words gave her pause. She looked steadily at him then almost gasped to notice his image began to waver and blur. If she blinked a few times in succession, the image of Courtenay returned, clear and exact. However, the longer she stared at the man's face, the more the likeness melted away.

Patience found herself reminded of a pastoral painting she'd once seen completed by an artist and left on an easel in bright sunlight. As she'd studied that painting, a man's face appeared beneath the pastoral scene. The fresh, wet paint melted in the heat of the sun, thus revealing a former image on the canvas. Unfortunately, the evil before her was not a painting, but alive, breathing, and stalking toward her.

"Very well," she said in a voice somewhat stilted. "*What* are you?"

"Ah, well, *that* is a better question but I am not sure I should tell you."

"Yet you intend to kill me?"

"Yes, please." He grinned as if she'd offered him a sweet.

Patience narrowed her gaze, her thoughts whirling. He was clearly very arrogant. Perhaps engaging him in conversation, getting him to talk about himself, might give her the time she needed to elude him. Or, bide more time for someone to come to her aid.

Feigning confidence she used whenever an angry ghost tried to bully, frighten, or hurt her, Patience raised her chin. "Well, I think I should like some questions answered first. Before you kill me. Unless you think I can escape from you."

He laughed. The harsh sound echoed in the courtyard. "You are a very curious young woman. Very well, ask your questions."

She cringed inside to hear him repeat the same words the real Mr. Courtenay had said when she'd been looking for Jane Seymour's ghost. The similarity between the two men in appearance and manner of speech proved most unsettling.

"Why do you look like Mr. Courtenay?"

"The answer to that is rather complicated. Let me simply say at one time we were *very* close. You might even say I wouldn't be here today if not for him. Next question."

"Did you kill Anne Melville?"

"Oh, come now. If you are going to ask inane questions that I know you already have the answer to, this charade is over. And I am becoming…restless."

"What is your name?"

"In what language?"

"I don't know; English, I suppose."

He grimaced as if he found the English language distasteful. "In your tongue, I would be called *Baltharach*." He said the name slowly, with a strange accent. "An ancient name, from another civilization far greater and more powerful than you or the Romans."

"The Romans?" A thought sparked. "Were you in that Roman cave?"

"Very good, yes, I *was* in the cave," he replied. "The Romans put me there; imprisoned by their idols. It took many of them to keep me restrained."

Patience eyed him carefully. If he'd been imprisoned in that cave by ancient Roman deities, how did he escape?

Her thoughts returned to what Leighton said about sensing a great evil in the cave. He'd felt it growing, emerging from the darkness. He then used his power to protect his friends. Therefore, there must be a connection between what happened in the cave and this evil incarnate who looked like Courtenay.

Patience carefully stepped away from Baltharach—one, two, three more steps. He did not notice. Rather, he mumbled under his breath, seemingly agitated remembering the cave.

Although frightened beyond words, part of her recognized that what Baltharach might reveal without thinking could be the key to his destruction, or at least imprisonment again.

She now understood what Jane meant about standing upon a precipice. Part of Patience wanted desperately to run away, to think only of saving her own life. Within her soul, however, she knew learning more about Baltharach would help save others.

Struggling to remain focused, Patience swallowed the sour bile rising from her churning stomach.

"Where do you come from?" She took a larger step away from him.

He inhaled deeply then answered in a strange language. "*Mayim b'thrach kai Alla Xul Baltharach ina Babylonia. Nisme, Nise Matati Kisitti Qatiya, Baltharach—Kima Telal—Elu Ana Harrani Sa Alaktasa La Tarat, Ina Shulim Eli Baltuti Ima' 'Idu Mituti.*"

His words offered no meaning to her, but the more Baltharach spoke, the greater his anger increased. He paced repeatedly in front of her. With each step, his breathing sounded strange, first labored then hissing and heavy.

She rubbed her forearms, feeling as if invisible bugs crawled on her flesh.

The sudden sound of bones cracking reminded her all too well of what had happened to his hand before he eviscerated the ghostly Tudor page. Whoever Baltharach was, his true form was not human.

Desperate to run, Patience could not seem to move. Instead, she stared in horror as Baltharach's body started to change, accompanied by the sound of flesh tearing and clothes ripping.

His body remained upright, although his height increased tremendously in size. His chest, shoulders, torso, and arms became massive, a suit of armor unto themselves.

Narrow, sharp wings slowly unfolded behind each shoulder to form three distinct ebony panels that glistened in the night. His limbs were as muscular as his upper body.

Both hands and feet changed into large scaled appendages, and his toes and fingers had sharp claws at their tips. But the changes to his body could little compare to what happened to his face.

Before her eyes, the pale, handsome, human face of Mr. Courtenay transformed into what looked like the elongated head of a dragon-type man with gleaming dark gray scales for skin and eyes now bright amber in color.

His false human head had been shed like an outer skin cast aside. Great horns erupted from the top of his skull, growing and twisting into three large upward spirals.

A snout glistened like wet, black leather, similar to that belonging on a beast.

He turned toward her then, threw back his head, and made a monstrous cry that reverberated into the night. What caught her eye most, however, were long, fang-shaped teeth dripping with black liquid.

Her throat burned, taut with a terror.

Would he devour her or kill her the way he murdered Anne Melville? Her eyes widened at the blades protruding threateningly from his fingers.

When he'd killed the Tudor ghost, he'd been standing close to the spirit with only his hand transformed. In the frantic whirlwind of her thoughts, Patience wondered if—in his repulsive cumbersome state—Baltharach would not be able to move quickly.

She could think of no better time to test her theory.

Yet the moment she decided to run, someone loomed before her.

A presence that filled her with the worse possible fear of her life.

Sam MacGregor materialized to stand between her and Baltharach. Her beloved ghost friend and protector must have sensed her danger. However, instead of the comfort his presence usually brought, seeing her dearest friend ready to face down such an evil beast—knowing

Sam's soul would be destroyed forever—conjured within Patience a fury and strength she did not know she possessed.

"NO", she screamed and lurched forward. "Get back, Sam. He can destroy your soul!" Then, to her astonishment, she physically pushed Sam far aside.

Sam looked at her—equally stunned she'd pushed him away with such force. He opened his mouth as if to argue with her, but his gaze narrowed on someone over her shoulder. He nodded as if given instruction.

"Follow me, lass. Now!"

She turned about. Two men ran toward them, one of whom was the real Courtenay. The other man she did not recognize. He appeared quite tall with white hair and seemed to be shouting at her. However, amidst the thunderous bellowing of the enraged creature behind her, she could not understand the man's words.

As she ran toward them, Courtenay veered off to the right, away from the older man she now recognized as Leighton's grandfather, the Duke of Windermere.

"Come to me, Patience," Courtenay yelled.

She stopped, hesitating, even though she knew he wasn't the foul monster behind her.

"Please," he urged. "You must trust me, Patience. Come here at once and get out of the way."

Patience glanced over her shoulder at Baltharach. For some strange reason, he'd stopped stalking her. Instead, he stood breathing heavy and glared at Windermere, who fearlessly moved toward him.

She realized then the duke had not been speaking to her.

The words he spoke were in another language.

One which sounded vaguely Celtic.

Regardless, his words were directed at Baltharach.

"Hurry!" Courtenay yelled.

With a quick nod, she ran toward Leighton's friend. He immediately pulled her into his embrace, cupped the back of her head and pressed her face against his chest. Then, with one smooth motion, he turned them both away.

Patience heard the duke's deep voice shouting into the night, repeating the same words over and over. The ferocity of his voice did not escape her. It seemed as if he recited an ancient prayer or mystical incantation.

She tried to move, to see what was happening, but Courtenay held her so tightly against his chest she could not move. Whatever the duke was doing, they were not supposed to witness.

Although he'd wanted a fierce battle with her, Baltharach was getting his wish with the Duke of Windermere. All she could do was pray that when it ended, the evil creature would be gone.

Chapter 39

Seated before the fireplace in the drawing room of Lady Carlyle's apartment, Patience could not stop shivering. Despite the soft woolen blanket clutched about her shoulders, the warmth and comfort she sought proved elusive.

The monstrous memory of Baltharach taunted her within the hearth's flickering flames. So very tired, she closed her eyes, hoping to forget the repulsive image of the creature's true form. Finding no escape, she opened her eyes again and struggled to think of anything else.

Her gaze lifted to a large portrait situated above the fireplace. A handsome young man with long dark hair, pale skin, a slender moustache, and dark eyes stared down at her. She focused on his face, and remembered what Lady Carlyle had said about the painting and its Royal subject.

Painted during his exile at The Hague, Charles Stuart, the future King Charles II, wore an armor breastplate and his Knight of the Garter sash. His expression, although strong and intelligent, held a rather defiant, enigmatic quality.

What had the Prince Royal been thinking when sitting for the portrait? Retribution against those who betrayed his family? His father, King Charles I, had been captured by Cromwell and the Roundheads, and imprisoned without his family at the very place where she now sat.

Such remained one bit of history about Hampton Court. A palace often occupied by Charles I and the Royal Family in happier times, it later became a place of forced isolation for the deposed king. Still, there would be even darker days ahead for the Stuart king, his family, and this firstborn prince—not the least of which would be the execution of Charles I.

Whatever the future Charles II had been thinking when the artist skillfully immortalized his image, he could not have imagined one day this very portrait would be situated in a place of honor at Hampton Court. Treasured by Lady Carlyle, a noblewoman of Scots blood.

Then again, in the spirit world, perhaps he did.

The longer Patience studied his expression, the more she decided the prince looked resolved to bide his time, wait for the moment to strike, and avenge his father.

And he would succeed.

Did she have strength to do what must be done in her life? Like the prince in the portrait, she'd been forced into exile, abandoned by those she trusted, sequestered from life, and denied freedom. She had bided her time, too. Yet after years of waiting for a reprieve, she rebelled against her constraints when the ghost of Anne Melville appeared seeking help.

Agreeing to help Anne had been a turning point in her life. She might have remained in Scotland, but her conscience could not ignore Anne's pleas. Now, more than ever, she understood the importance of helping Anne find peace.

At the same time, she found herself in terrifying danger.

Her encounter with Baltharach had proven she had no strength, no power whatsoever, to fight him.

If I come face-to-face with him again, what will I do?

Patience continued to study the portrait of Charles II, feeling an odd, otherworldly kinship to the man. Although she knew his spirit no longer walked the earth, if only he could advise her.

How had he found the unconquerable spirit and inner strength to conquer his circumstances?

With a start, she understood what must be done.

Having strength of purpose is important, but so is having an army to stand with you.

Distracted by the soft clattering of china and glassware behind her, Patience listened to murmured voices. The Duke of Windermere and Courtenay spoke in hushed tones with Lady Carlyle and a newly arrived Charles Melville.

"I was able to chase him away from the palace grounds," the duke said. "But there is no telling when he might try to return."

"Courtenay, you say at first he looked like you?" Melville asked.

"I thought I imagined what I saw," Courtenay commented. "One minute I saw myself, and then he turned into that monster."

"We must learn more about him," the duke said.

Somehow, Patience found the strength to stand. She tightened her hold on the blanket about her shoulders. "His name is Baltharach." Hardly recognizing the hoarse, weak voice as her own, Patience swallowed the pain in her sore throat, and turned to face the others.

The way they looked at her made Patience uncomfortable. Their expressions seemed torn between pity for her ordeal, concern for her health, and a keen curiosity about what she knew.

"He was in the cave." She cleared her aching throat, hoping her voice would sound stronger. "The Romans used their gods to imprison him there."

The Duke of Windermere tapped a long finger against his lips, his brow furrowed and his eyes narrowed slightly. He might have been considering her words, but she sensed a memory troubled him.

Despite the great weakness that had come upon her, and the almost numb sensation of her body, Patience approached the seated, intimidating duke.

"You knew about him, didn't you, Your Grace?"

His gaze lifted to meet hers. For a moment she did not think he would answer. "I thought I might be mistaken." He sighed heavily and looked at Courtenay. "You were a child."

"You suspected this?" Courtenay asked.

The duke leaned forward, elbows resting upon his knees, and interlocked his fingers together as he focused on Courtenay. "When my grandson told me what happened in the cave—that he'd sensed a great evil—I worried what he did to protect his friends might have caused a consequence other than four of the boys developing supernatural powers."

"What other consequence?" Courtenay asked.

The duke did not respond directly. Instead, he looked at Melville. "When it happened, I asked you and the other boys to describe the statues you played upon."

"I remember." Melville nodded, standing behind Courtenay's chair.

"They were powerful Roman gods," the duke continued. "Arranged in a protective circle. When Leighton used his power to repel the evil, his power joined with whatever ancient spell had been cast upon that circle. A cataclysm resulted. Somehow, the powers attributed to those gods transferred to you boys…except for one."

"We know all that," Melville said, confusion lining his brow.

Patience stood silent, observing a very pale Courtenay and frustrated Melville as they listened to the duke. How long would it take for the two men to understand the magnitude of what else happened in that cave?

"The ancient spell must have been used to restrain this creature Baltharach." The duke paused to study their reaction. "Thus, when the power of the circle changed, the restraint no longer existed."

"In other words," Courtenay said. "Leighton released this evil into the world."

"Unknowingly, yes," the duke replied.

In the ensuing silence, Patience could not help but consider how Leighton would cope with such knowledge. He already felt tremendous guilt the one he called Lyon had almost died in that cave. Learning Baltharach now existed because of him might prompt Leighton to do anything to make amends, even sacrifice his own life.

The need to protect and defend Leighton swelled within Patience. "Lord Leighton told me he'd never felt such evil that day. He also said the evil was growing, moving in the darkness. If it had been moving, is it not possible the magic of the circle had weakened over time? That its power to keep Baltharach prisoner had already diminished?"

"Most astute, Miss Sinclair," the duke replied.

Windermere studied her a moment in a thoughtful manner. "For certain, its power had weakened, as had the power of Baltharach. We can now surmise the creature had no strength to take physical form. Thus, with the cave being destroyed, he needed to find a way to escape. A living form his essence could use. He chose the person nearest, the one not in the circle."

Courtenay's dark eyes looked huge against his pale face, his expression one of horror. "This evil… this foul creature…became part of me?"

"Yes, but in a dormant state," the duke replied. "He needed strength and used your body over the years until he became strong enough to separate and manifest in mortal form. The fact you were such a sickly child obviously hindered his progress."

Courtenay stood and stared down at the seated duke. "If you suspected this…" He paused to clearly gain control of his emotions. Even so, his voice shook with anger when next he spoke. "Why didn't you do something?"

"What could I do? Kill you?" The duke shook his head. "I am no monster. There were times I thought I sensed a whisper of darkness, a faint thread. Yet in all the time I spent time with you…you had no evil whatsoever. You were a weak but very innocent, good boy. Dear to me as my own grandchildren."

"By the saints," Melville whispered. "This Baltharach slept inside him for years? Then found the strength to break away, copying the image of Courtenay?"

"He knows everything about you," Windermere stood, looking only at Courtenay. "What you know, he knows. Your emotions, fears, anything you might have felt, he felt. Whatever you learned or were told, he learned. In many ways, he is your twin."

"Well," Melville said with a snort of derision. "Now we know who wants revenge against the *Legion*. "We have been trying to think who hated us so much they would murder my sister, and then try to turn us against one another. For that matter, who even knew the *Legion* existed?"

"It isn't you he hates," the duke replied. "It is who you represent. Remember, the ancient power of those Roman gods kept him imprisoned for centuries. Thus, he now sees the *Legion* as a threat to his continued existence."

Patience studied Courtenay with increasing concern. Thin, pale, distraught by all he had learned, she could not imagine what he must be feeling now. As if he sensed her worry, he looked at her. He attempted a reassuring smile, but it only made her want to weep.

Courtenay walked a few steps away then paused. "If it took the combined power of *all* those Roman gods to restrain him in that cave..." He looked at Melville. "Individually, you likely pose little threat to him—which is why he plots to turn you against one another. One by one, he could destroy you. But together—all of you using your powers as one—"

"The *Legion* could destroy *him,*" Melville said.

"Theoretically," Courtenay replied.

Silence filled the room. They spoke of battle, of destroying a monster so evil an army of mortal soldiers could offer no resistance or defense. Courtenay was right. The only hope to imprison or kill Baltharach was by using the collective powers of the *Legion.*

Patience recognized another terrifying truth. She had been able to see through Baltharach's human disguise—an ability Jane said no one else could do. No doubt, he would seek to kill her again. She would indeed need a powerful army beside her when that happened.

Would the *Legion* stand with her?

Or, would she meet the same fate as Anne Melville?

She inhaled sharply, drawing the attention of the others. "I know where to find Miss Melville's body." She approached Anne's brother. "We must retrieve it before Baltharach comes back."

When Melville nodded, Patience started to walk toward the door. Her aunt intercepted her. She'd almost forgotten the woman was there, so silent had Lady Carlyle been.

"You cannot go anywhere." Lady Carlyle gently rested her hands upon Patience's shoulders. "You could have died this night. Tell them where she is, and they will find her."

"I have to be there," she said gently. "God willing, Anne will remember what happened to her. We might also learn information that will help the *Legion* fight this monster. And I would very much like him destroyed before he comes after me again."

Patience glanced toward the fireplace where Sam in his MacGregor tartan stood. He had not left her side since arriving in the courtyard. Despite the fact only Lady Carlyle could also see him, Patience addressed her ghost protector. "Go to Miss Melville, Sam. Stay with her until we find the body."

With a solemn nod, Sam disappeared. Patience then approached Courtenay. He looked a wee bit better, but still shaken by all he'd learned about his innocent part in Baltharach's return.

"We must go to the burial vault beneath the Chapel Royal," she said. "Can you take us there, or is there someone else with a key?"

"I can take you," he replied softly.

Melville crossed to the door and opened it. When Courtenay joined him there, Melville looked upon his friend with endearing compassion. "Lead the way, Lyon."

They walked in silence along the empty, ancient corridors of Hampton Court, each person holding a lit candle. At times, an unseen current swept by, making it necessary to cup one's hand slightly about the flame to prevent it being extinguished.

No one questioned from whence those cold breezes came.

For her part, Patience had too much burdening her thoughts to acknowledge the curious spirits who'd ventured from hiding places to watch the group of mortals. Besides, the ghosts understood the sad, solemn procession.

No one spoke, living or dead.

No one dared even whisper.

However, each time Lady Carlyle glanced at Patience, their eyes met. Patience saw the worry her aunt felt for her, as well as the woman's fears about the evening's revelations.

Without question, the countess appeared to have aged considerably this night. The happy, seemingly youthful energy Lady Carlyle possessed before they came to Hampton Court had weakened greatly in the face of terrifying events and supernatural powers she could not understand.

She wanted so much to help me. Now, she feels guilty she cannot.

The knowledge she had become a target for Baltharach prompted Patience to consider how best to protect her aunt. Perhaps she should run away, disappear into the night. Sever ties with anyone who might be hurt or killed because of her.

Even Sam would not be safe from Baltharach.

I will not put them in danger.

Her heart ached with the certain knowledge that by leaving Scotland with selfish hopes of being free and proving her right to live amongst people, her so-called gift had proven to be a curse. And unless the *Legion* could destroy Baltharach, her life—perhaps even her soul—would be forfeited.

They arrived at the Chapel Royal. However, before Courtenay could insert a large iron key into the door's lock, it opened of its own accord. The men looked about with wide-eyed confusion.

Patience nodded at the ghost who'd granted them access, the same Tudor guard who'd been so protective of Jane in the Great Kitchens.

The Duke of Windermere instructed Courtenay and Melville to light candles about the chapel. One by one, tapers illuminated, casting a soft, flickering glow to chase away the shadows.

Patience had never been inside the Chapel Royal before, and could not help but study its beauty. Ornate carvings of winged golden cherubs embellished the walls. The lingering scent of fine oak laced the air from the many pews and wall panels. She inhaled deeply its fragrance.

Her gaze continued upward, above mullioned windows. A breathtaking ceiling resembled an evening sky with heavenly stars set against a dark sapphire background.

The sound of a gate opening captured her attention again. About her height, the gate was heavy, gold and ornate, obviously placed to deny access to the altar for but a privileged few.

Having entered the most private, sacred part of the chapel, they stood upon the high altar then followed a somber Courtenay. He approached another door, almost hidden from view by what looked like the reliquary for a saint.

One by one they descended a stone staircase that opened into a vast burial vault beneath the floor of the Chapel Royal. They saw nothing but several untouched, sealed tombs of long forgotten dead.

They instinctively separated to investigate smaller, adjoining chambers situated off the main vault.

Patience looked about for which way to go, and noticed a faint blue glow emanating from a chamber to her left. She went in that direction.

There, behind a stone pillar, she came upon a heartbreakingly sad, mist-like image. Anne Melville stood several feet away from what could only be the earthly remains of her body.

"She's here," Patience called out.

Courtenay was first to join her. His ashen expression looked as horrified as she felt at that moment. The others joined a heartbeat later. Courtenay tried to hold Melville back, no doubt fearing the reaction of his friend. Anne's brother brushed the gesture aside and quickly knelt beside the remains of his sister.

Patience had never seen a dead body in such a condition. Although she expected decay, the remains of Anne Melville confused and frightened her.

"That is not normal, is it?" she asked, unable to steady the quivering of her voice.

The Duke of Windermere knelt beside the body, studying its position and condition. "No," he said in a hushed voice. He glanced at the young man next to him. "How long has your sister been missing?"

"Almost a year," Melville choked out. "Why does she look like that?"

"I suspect the method of her death is the reason," the duke replied. "Her body appears to be petrified, without enduring any manner of decomposition. I have never seen anything like this."

"Her clothing does not appear much changed," Lady Carlyle contributed. "Apart from some stains and a few tears, the fabric and color is still intact."

"Her placement in this cold burial vault might have helped preserve her clothing," the duke answered. He then looked up at Patience. "Is there anything you can tell us about how Miss Melville was killed?"

"I thought she'd been strangled," Patience said. "There were marks on either side of her neck."

"Her neck, eh?" Windermere murmured. "Show me exactly where you saw these marks. Point to the area; do not touch the remains."

Patience swallowed with difficulty. She didn't want to examine Anne's body, but knelt across from the duke and Melville. She tentatively leaned forward to study the neck area, but the gray discoloration and stone-like condition of the body made it difficult to see any marks.

She bit her bottom lip, and tried to focus on the neck area—ignoring the tightly closed eyes and open-mouthed scream of terror frozen on the petrified face of Anne Melville. Yet the brief glimpse of Anne's final moment of life made Patience want to weep.

"How terribly she must have suffered," she whispered to herself, blinking away tears, belatedly realizing her words had been overheard by Anne's brother. Their eyes met, and she saw he had tears in his eyes as well.

Returning her attention to the petrified body, she again looked for the ugly marks she'd seen on Anne's ghost. Leaning a bit closer, she gasped. "There."

Windermere and Melville moved nearer the body as well; Courtenay and the countess remained standing behind them, their eyes narrowed.

Patience pointed at the area. "Two, perhaps three, black slits. On her ghost, they more resembled bruising."

"We must learn how he kills," the duke commented. "There is a reason for these odd marks and the condition of the body."

"Shouldn't we call the authorities?" Melville asked.

"Yes, indeed we should." The duke stood and looked about the small room where the body had been placed. "The coroner will need to be summoned, but first we must notify a member of the Royal Family and the Lord Chancellor."

Windermere rested a hand on Courtenay's shoulder. "To avoid panic, the very nature of this situation requires utmost secrecy. Is your father in residence at Bushy House?"

"Yes," Courtenay replied.

"Good," Windermere nodded. "Go to him, but do not speak of the *Legion* or what happened in the cave years ago. Tell him only a body has been found in the palace. Ask him to meet me here. I will explain things in greater detail to him personally."

He then turned to Melville. "Charles, you must stay here with me, and keep watch over your sister's remains."

"I believe my niece and I should leave the palace," Lady Carlyle announced. "What if that creature returns?"

"I doubt he will tonight, not with me here," Windermere replied.

"You cannot be sure of that," the countess argued. "My niece has been through enough this night. When I look at that girl's body, all I can think about is..."

Lady Carlyle looked at Patience, a spark of temper in her green eyes. "I should take you back to Scotland immediately."

"You cannot do that! She promised to help me!"

Having all but forgotten Anne's presence, Patience and Lady Carlyle turned toward the ghost.

Sam now stood beside Anne and the differences in their manifestations proved startling. Sam's image remained steady, brilliant, and luminous with strength. However, the weakening mist of Anne's form said the girl's spirit had lost a great deal of strength to appear at all.

Not another moment could be wasted trying to determine how Anne died. Every bit of attention must be given to helping her soul move on.

"I will not leave before I help you, Anne."

"She's here?" Melville asked. "My sister's ghost is here?"

"Yes," Patience replied, keeping her voice calm. She extended her hand toward the willowy ghost. "Come here, Anne."

"Why? What are you all looking at?"

"Come and see," Patience answered.

"I don't want to." Anne's expression resembled that of a frightened child.

"You must."

A cold breeze swelled about those gathered as the spirit of the dead girl slowly approached, accompanied by Sam MacGregor. Lady Carlyle motioned for the duke and Courtenay to step away from the body. Melville did not move, but continued to stare in the direction where Patience looked.

"That's not me," Anne said.

"No, that is not you," Patience soothed. "That is an empty shell. You are still you, Anne."

Anne frowned all the same. "Why does it look like that?"

"We do not know," Patience replied. "Do you remember anything? How you came to be..." Patience stopped talking as she noticed Anne's gaze fixed upon Courtenay.

"Do you recognize Mr. Courtenay, Anne?"

"He is a friend of my brother," Anne answered, her voice a soft whisper.

"Yes, he is your brother's friend. We are all your friends. No one here would ever harm you. Do you believe that, Anne?"

"Yes." Anne's eyes glistened.

"I think you know the truth about what happened to you now," Patience said. "Please tell us. Help us to understand."

Anne looked down with a guilt-ridden, forlorn expression. Compelled to comfort the girl, Patience reached out and tilted the girl's chin up with her forefinger, absently hearing a gasp from her aunt standing off to the side.

How and why she was now able to touch ghosts, Patience did not understand. She only knew that she could.

"Anne, remember when I told you sometimes spirits remain behind because there is something important they must do?"

"Yes," Anne answered.

"I believe you found me so that what happened to you will not happen to someone else." She smiled reassuringly when Anne nodded in a childlike manner. "You know what killed you was not Mr. Courtenay, don't you?"

"Yes." Anne glanced at the young man standing next to the Duke of Windermere. "I thought it was him at first, and that he loved me." She looked up at the barrel-vaulted ceiling of the burial vault. "I took a hackney to meet him that night. He gave me some wine after I entered his carriage. The next thing I remembered I was in a boat. It was dark and cold, but I was not afraid."

Realizing she had to translate for those who could not hear Anne, Patience nodded. "So, you thought you were being courted and ran away to be with Mr. Courtenay. Were you here at Hampton Court all the time?"

"Yes, but not in this room," Anne replied. "He said we were far underground. That I could scream all I wanted, but no one would hear me or help."

"Did he say why he brought you here?" Lady Carlyle asked.

Anne studied the countess a moment then looked at her brother. "He was going to kill my brother and his friends for what they did to him. He showed me a snuffbox. He said it represented their evil, secret club. That they thought they were powerful and untouchable, but he would kill them one by one."

Suddenly, Anne became agitated, frantic. She looked again at Patience with an expression of horror. "He isn't human, Patience."

"How did you find out?" Patience asked.

"He kept me in a dungeon of sorts. I lost all sense of time. I told him I would escape and warn my brother. That was when he said the time had come to show me what he would do if I betrayed him."

Anne floated over to a far wall in the small room, perhaps not wanting to look at anyone. "He often left for long periods of time. I did not know where he went or what he did. But after I threatened to escape, he came back and had a woman with him. I don't know who she was or where she came from. She was…*not* a lady."

"What happened to this other woman?" Patience asked, shuddering as she spoke.

"He made me watch the woman do whatever he asked. I still thought he was Mr. Courtenay, and wanted to make me jealous, more cooperative. But then he did something that had never happened with me. He changed into this grotesque monster." Anne grasped either side of her head. "The woman screamed."

Lady Carlyle came to stand beside Patience, perhaps realizing how frightening Anne's words were for an innocent young woman to hear.

"How did he kill this other woman?" Lady Carlyle asked.

"I could not see. His body blocked the woman's body. I only saw his hands had turned into long scaled fingers with blade-like talons attached. He raised them to her neck; I saw that much. The woman kept screaming. Then she shuddered and died."

"Did her body look like this one?" Patience asked.

Anne glided toward the body on the floor. "Yes, like it had turned to stone. But he did more to it afterwards. He slashed at it with his hand. It turned to dust then disappeared. When he faced me again, he instantly changed back into Mr. Courtenay's image. I was so terrified I couldn't even scream."

"What is my sister saying?" Melville demanded. "How did he kill her? Who was this other woman?"

Patience noticed the pleading look from Anne's eyes. It served no point to tell Melville his sister had been seduced and defiled prior to her death.

"I will tell you about the other woman later," Patience said. "Your sister is very weak. We must help her spirit be at peace."

"No, detain her; she must not leave," Windermere ordered, his tone gruff.

"Her name is Miss Anne Melville," Patience said to the duke, finding his manner most callous under the circumstances.

Windermere bristled with indignation. "Need I remind you, Miss Sinclair, that the ghost of Melville's sister is our only clue to this creature? We must learn as much as we can before he strikes again. The next time, I might not be there to save *you*."

Anne drifted to stand beside Patience and whispered in her ear. "He did say he killed to keep up his strength, and that taking human form required many lives."

Patience repeated what Anne said to the duke.

"That means he has killed others before her," Courtenay said, clearly aghast.

"And more afterwards," Melville added.

Courtenay quickly combed a hand through his black hair. "Why has no one found their bodies? Especially in a condition like the remains of Miss Melville?"

"Because there are no bodies to find," Patience replied. "From what Miss Melville told me, Baltharach has the power to destroy the human body. When that happens, there are no remains."

"What happens to them?" Courtenay asked.

Patience conveyed what Anne told her about the unknown woman, much to the stunned expressions of those gathered.

"An important bit of information, Miss Sinclair," the duke commented in a chastising manner. "Persistence often bears results. We now know he must kill to maintain a human form, how he kills, and that he can do so without leaving proof of his victim."

"There is more information you should know, although it may be of no concern to you." Patience looked directly at Leighton's grandfather. "Apart from taking a human life for strength, he has the ability to destroy a human soul. This very night I saw him rake his transformed hand through a Tudor ghost. It screamed and writhed in torturous pain then dissolved into a black mist."

Lady Carlyle gasped. "How is that possible?"

"I do not know," Patience replied. "Neither do I know why he kept Miss Melville's body here when he could have destroyed it the way he did that unknown woman's remains. The decision must be important to his plot against the *Legion*. Or, perhaps Anne's spirit sought me out before he had a chance to destroy it?"

"Perhaps both," the duke acknowledged.

"Speaking on behalf of the other *Legion* members," Melville said, garnering everyone's attention. "We believe he wanted to use the body as evidence against one of us."

He turned toward Courtenay. "The reason I came to Hampton Court tonight is because the heirloom necklace my sister had when she ran away appeared about the neck of Miss Bailey when she arrived at Knightly's dinner for Hunter."

"The devil you say," Courtenay replied.

"That's not all of it," Melville continued. "There was quite a row afterwards, as well you can imagine. Hunter and I came close to blows. I suspected him as my sister's murderer. We might have killed one another if Leighton and Knightly hadn't intervened. We then learned the necklace had been delivered to Miss Bailey by a hired boatman. Our suspicions turned to you as the killer."

"Naturally," Courtenay replied.

"Leighton swore your innocence, and bade me come warn you."

"I see," Courtenay murmured. "Well, with her body hidden here at the palace, it does seem Baltharach wanted me blamed for her murder. Not only would he tear apart the *Legion's* unity by doing so, but imagine the scandal of a Royal bastard revealed as a monstrous murderer.

"No one is safe from him," the duke said. "If he needs to kill to keep up a human persona, we have no idea how many have died—or will die—at his hands."

"But his human disguise has been revealed," Lady Carlyle stated. "Should that not make it easier for the *Legion* to find him?"

"Yes," the duke agreed. "Knowing he looks like Courtenay should help us track him down."

"We might be able to learn his whereabouts from other ghosts," Lady Carlyle further speculated.

The duke shook his head. "Since he knows Miss Sinclair is able to speak with ghosts—as apparently do you, countess—I doubt he will now allow other souls to escape after he kills their mortal bodies. His death toll will comprise an ever-increasing list of missing people whose fate remains unknown."

As the men continued to talk about how to destroy Baltharach, Patience felt soothing warmth upon her face and turned toward it.

A glimmering light appeared below the ceiling. Increasing in size, its shape resembled an arched doorway. The interior appeared misty white, and stars within the mist sparkled like diamonds in the sun.

The outer edges were faceted with prisms of light, reaching outward with the most enchanting colors. Although it hovered slightly above their heads, none of the others seemed to notice—not even her aunt.

"Anne", Patience whispered. "Look."

Anne turned and sighed as the light beckoned. She quickly glanced back at Patience and then to her brother. "Is that for me?"

"Most assuredly," Patience said. "Are you ready to go to your true home?"

Anne looked at the portal. "I hear someone calling my name."

Patience glanced to her right as Melville came to stand beside her. Clearly, he'd heard her speaking to Anne.

"Before she leaves," he said, "can you tell her I love her, and that I am sorry I wasn't able to save her?"

"She heard you," Patience said.

Anne swept to her brother, newfound energy transforming her essence into a beautiful, strong, pure white aura. She kissed her brother's cheek. "You have always been a good brother to me, Charles. Please be safe and tell our parents I love you all."

Melville touched his cheek; his stunned expression showed he had not only felt his sister's kiss but heard her speak to him.

Anne then stood before Patience and took hold of her hands. "I was horrid to you, Patience. I am so sorry for all the pain I caused you. I shall never, ever, forget you and all you have done to save me. Make no mistake, I know *you* saved me. Thank you, my friend."

"You're welcome, Anne." Patience blinked away tears. Not only had Anne's apology healed a wound deep inside, but whenever a soul was able to move on into the light, joy for them never ceased to warm her heart. "I hope we see each other again someday."

"I know we will," Anne smiled.

Like a young girl about to make her grand debut at a ball, Anne's spirit moved toward the light. She paused and looked at Sam MacGregor. "What about you? Do you not want to go home?"

Standing beside Lady Carlyle, Sam employed his most boorish disposition. His muscular arms were folded across his chest as he grimaced. "Ye best leave before they change their minds, English."

Anne giggled. "Not English anymore. I am about to become an angel."

Sam rolled his eyes. "Och, there's a scary thought."

His comment earned a soft laugh from both Patience and her aunt. Together, the three of them stood before the portal to eternity, watching as Anne's spirit entered.

Almost immediately her worn, tattered dress transformed into a radiant gown of what looked like shimmering starlight. As befitting a glorious reunion, they smiled with heartfelt wonder to then see other transcended souls had gathered to embrace and welcome Anne.

"You can still go if you want," Patience whispered to Sam.

Sam looked down at her. A flicker of tenderness shined in his eyes. "And leave ye to this foul creature? Ye're a MacGregor, and 'tis my duty to keep ye safe from Sassenachs or…heathen devils."

Pulled from the joy she'd felt when Anne's spirit moved on into the eternal light, Patience shivered. Reality crashed upon her like an icy wave upon a sinking ship.

Standing in the cold burial vault with its stale air and lengthening shadows made her yearn for reassurance. She needed to know Baltharach could be destroyed.

She moved to listen and observe the other men in the room. They spoke in hushed voices, their backs to her, Lady Carlyle, and the petrified remains of Anne Melville.

"What do we tell them?" Melville asked.

"Only what we must, nothing more," the duke replied. "We must not reveal anything about the *Legion* or the powers you and the others possess. No one would understand, and what people do not understand, they destroy."

"What do we tell them about Baltharach?" Courtenay asked. "How can we possibly explain what he is?"

"We say nothing about him," the duke answered. "Nothing about what happened here tonight. The remains of a body were found in the palace. Based on the condition of the body, she has most likely been dead for centuries."

Patience inhaled sharply, stunned to hear they plotted to hide the truth.

The duke looked at her, eyes narrowed disapprovingly. Then, as if she were an insect—nay, as if she no longer existed at all—the duke motioned for Courtenay and Melville to join him on the far side of the room where she could not overhear.

"Come." Lady Carlyle took hold of Patience's right hand. "Let us be done with this place."

Chapter 40

Patience lay abed, unable to quell a sense of foreboding. Silence had settled over Hampton Court; a stillness that, contrary to its peaceful nature, possessed—at least in her mind—a veiled threat.

Then again, perhaps the sleeping draught Auntie Catherine insisted she drink had affected her perception. After all, none of the palace ghosts had tried to speak with her—or warn her of danger. Too, the duke said Baltharach would not return to the palace tonight.

Why then am I afraid to close my eyes?

It had to be her imagination. There were any number of explanations for the eerie sensation and sense of doom that made it impossible to relax or sleep.

Not only had an evil creature revealed itself with the intent of killing her, she'd found a body that looked like it had been turned to stone a hundred years ago.

Still, she struggled to deny the effects of medicinal herbs, despite the fact her eyelids felt heavy. Instinct told her the night was not done with her.

She must remain on guard.

Watchful.

Vigilant.

Her thoughts returned to Windermere, Melville, and Courtenay. What were they plotting? Their behavior after Anne Melville's spirit ascended had been dismissive, unsettling. Neither did she appreciate their intent to conceal the truth to protect their secrets.

One might think Charles Melville would not agree to lie about his sister's death. To claim her body was some unknown woman from a century ago. What about his parents? Were they never to know the truth?

Nay, they'd been far too preoccupied with how they should protect the *Legion* and themselves. Surely Leighton would not agree with this course of action. Then again, did he not stress she must obey whatever the duke said to do?

Patience swiped at the tears on her face.

Let them keep their secrets.

She tried to think of something else and studied the underside of the bed's carved canopy. Covered with a cream-colored silk fabric, gold, pink, and white roses were beautifully embroidered.

Her gaze then drifted to the matching bed curtains, now pulled all the way open. Elegant as the bed might be, and as chilled as her body remained after venturing into the ghost realm and encountering Baltharach, the thought of not being able to see the room…or anyone who might enter…proved intolerable.

She blinked wide, determined to remain awake. However, her body craved sleep. Truth be told, she wanted nothing more than to acquiesce to its demands. Unfortunately, there were too many shadows, too many uncertainties, and far too many unpleasant possibilities of what the morning might bring.

Courtenay was supposed to go fetch his father, the Duke of Clarence. Had they returned? What would the Duke of Windermere say to the Duke of Clarence? Or, the Lord Chancellor for that matter.

Although she understood the reason for not disclosing their supernatural powers, when lives were at risk…when people could suddenly disappear as unknown murder victims…their attitude seemed selfish and callous.

The dismissive, disapproving manner in which the duke looked at her before she left the chapel vault flashed in Patience's memory. Clearly, he did not like her. For that matter, she did not particularly like him…or trust him.

How could she marry into that family?

I know too much about them.

The duke could view that knowledge as a threat. Indeed, a powerful man like Windermere might even take steps to silence me. After all, nothing had been said about protecting her identity.

Was a member of the Royal Family—brother to the Prince Regent no less—to be told that she led them to the body? And if it were revealed the remains were Anne Melville, what if she became implicated in the girl's death?

A shudder swept down her spine.

What if they question me?

If she told the truth about ghosts, mystical Lightbearers, powers from Roman gods transferred to the sons of titled peers and respected gentlemen, as well as an evil monster released to prey upon mankind—all the rumors about her being mad would seal her fate.

No one would support her.

Who could she trust?

Leighton? He claimed to love her, but why didn't he return to Hampton Court instead of sending Melville?

No, I mustn't think that way.

Leighton contacted his grandfather to see to her safety and 'twas a good thing, too, since the duke's powers sent Baltharach away.

The duke did save my life tonight.

Still, the memory of the dark manner in which the old man looked at her in the chapel vault gnawed at her insecurities. Because he'd intervened tonight on her behalf does not mean the duke supported his grandson's intentions toward her.

One thing was certain. Much as Baltharach wanted to kill her tonight, his primary goal was to destroy the *Legion.* Therefore, in the days ahead, the *Legion* would most likely prepare for battle. Having obtained the information needed from her about Baltharach, it seemed rather obvious they'd discarded her.

There is nothing for me here.

The time had come for her to return to Scotland.

How strange the place of exile seemed a holy sanctuary now.

I could hide there.

Patience snuggled deeper beneath the blankets on her bed. Tomorrow morning, she would go to London and retrieve Henrietta. Then, quickly and quietly, they would return to the highlands.

She must admit—if only to herself—no matter what she said or did, she would never fit in or be accepted. Not by anyone. Her impulsive journey to England had been a terrifying lesson, but perhaps a necessary one.

At least she had accomplished one good thing.

I kept my promise to Anne. She is safely home.

Patience glanced at the lamp beside her bed, grateful for its constant amber glow. No doubt, Sam was lurking about, too. The lamp and Sam would both stand guard through the remainder of the night, and chase away any shadows. Keeping that thought in mind, she closed her eyes.

The sound of loud voices arguing pulled Patience from the quiet refuge of sleep. She struggled to wake, but her head felt so heavy. Indeed, it seemed as if her entire body had been weighted down. It took a moment or two before she even managed to raise her upper body and brace it upon an elbow as she looked toward the still closed door of her bedchamber.

"You have no right to come here," Lady Carlyle protested. "These are private apartments. I shall contact the Lord Chancellor forthwith."

"I have every right!" A man's sharp voice boomed forth like a violent burst of thunder. "Do not think to dissuade me from my course, madam."

Patience couldn't breathe. Panic had seized all the breath in her lungs. She must be having a nightmare. What she heard cannot be happening.

'Tis the sleeping draught, she reminded herself.

Then, her bedchamber door burst opened. In the dim light of the room she recognized the silhouette of the man standing in the doorway. It mattered not that his features were masked by shadow.

She'd heard his voice, shouting commands at Lady Carlyle as if she were a servant or lowly member of his crew. She didn't need to see the black patch he wore over his right eye to identify the man she'd feared since childhood.

The heralded naval hero who'd married her mother.

The man who despised her from the moment they met.

Lord Henley.

"There you are." He entered the room, crossing to her bedside with angry strides, much the way he once walked the distance from the terrace to the garden when she'd been six years old. He'd seen her talking to herself, he claimed. Except she hadn't been talking to herself. Not that he ever cared to hear any possible explanation.

"Get up," he ordered.

Patience looked to the doorway. Another man stood there. He said not a word but simply watched. Behind him two other men barred a struggling Auntie Catherine and Whaley from intervening.

"Did you hear me?" Lord Henley bellowed. "Get up or, by God, I will drag you out of that bed."

Patience tried as best she could to move quickly, but the blankets were so heavy and she felt terribly weak. Still, she forced her body to obey. She stood before him in her white linen sleeping gown, hastily adjusting the garment to ensure modesty about her limbs.

She stood as tall and straight as she possibly could, her bare toes curved instinctively toward the wooden floor as if doing so might anchor her there.

"*You*," he said with disgust. "Did you truly think you could deceive me? Disobey me!"

"It isn't that…" she began.

He silenced any further words when he slapped the side of her face with the back of his hand.

Patience did not cry out but tears stung her eyes and she instinctively cupped her right cheek. A burning pain rose rapidly upon her skin where, no doubt, Henley's scarlet handprint had left its mark.

"Will no one stop him?" Lady Catherine pleaded. "Whaley, quickly, find the Duke of Windermere."

The man in the doorway shifted his tall frame slightly, but continued to stare in silence.

"Leave her alone, Henley!" The countess tried again to enter the room, but was pulled back. "Do not touch that child again. I will see you locked in Newgate for the rest of your life."

At once an icy cold swept violently about the room. Sam materialized then stepped between her and Lord Henley.

"Bluidy Sassenach." Sam's vaporous face glared at her stepfather's dark features. "Touch her and I'll dispatch ye tae the gates of Hell."

Protective though Sam might be, Lord Henley had long professed himself a man of logic. He was also in a state of high temper. As such, her stepfather could not be bothered with unseen spirits or unheard threats. Besides which, cold breezes were often felt in castles.

Patience drew back her shoulders and lifted her chin, grateful for Sam's defense—however futile. Despite the quaking of her body, she inhaled quickly, deeply, determined not to cower or show fear before the man who held dominion over her fate.

"I warned you what I would do if you disobeyed me," Henley bit out. "You think me a fool? That you could sneak back into England without my learning about it?"

She said nothing in response.

"Did you think I would give you any quarter…any reprieve from what you deserve?" He placed his hands upon his hips and glared at her. "Were you a man and I still in command of my ship, I would have you keel-hauled."

"I'm sure you would," she said, surprised by her own audacity and the strength of her words.

He sneered, and the flickering light from her bedside lamp reminded Patience of the superior manner in which Baltharach had also mocked her.

She could not help but wonder how her tyrannical stepfather would have handled himself in a face-to-face encounter with such an evil, powerful creature.

Would Henley's arrogant devotion to logic and reason fail him then?

"I am not afraid of you." Patience realized a moment of satisfaction seeing Henley blink several times at her clearly unexpected response. "There are far worse things to fear in life than you. And there are far worse fates to endure than anything you try to do to me."

"Is that so?" he remarked. "Billings! Trask!"

Patience noticed the man standing in the doorway stepped aside, allowing entry for the two heavyset men who had prevented the countess from coming to her aid.

"This is Miss Patience Sinclair," Lord Henley said. "Bind her hands and feet. If she says another word, stuff a rag in her mouth. I want her placed in my carriage immediately. She has a long overdue appointment at Bedlam."

Lady Catherine entered the room, her face etched with sorrow. "Do not fret Patience. I have summoned Windermere. He will not allow this to happen."

Patience fought back tears and nodded at her elderly aunt. She would not tell Lady Carlyle, but she held little hope for intervention from anyone—especially the Duke of Windermere.

She had, at long last, recognized the man standing in the doorway.

The Earl of Hawthorne continued to stare at her, showing neither sympathy nor remorse for his contribution to her circumstances. Indeed, he crooked an eyebrow as if daring her to confront him.

Ignoring the earl, she directed her attention to the man kneeling at her feet with a coarse rope in hand.

"I will come willingly. There is no need to carry me."

The man looked up at her then directed a questioning glance to her stepfather.

"Let her walk," Henley said.

The men who aided her stepfather in his campaign to imprison her stepped back, whereupon her tearful little maid—whom she had not even seen enter the room—rushed forward and fastened Patience's favorite crimson cloak about her shoulders. She then placed soft black leather slippers upon Patience's still bare feet.

"You are so very brave, miss," the young girl whispered.

Upon hearing the kind words, a single tear escaped and slid down Patience's cheek. She wanted to scream at the fates. To howl against the injustice imposed upon her life. Instead, she raised tightly bound hands to her face and wiped the tear away.

Refusing to acknowledge Hawthorne as she crossed the threshold of her bedchamber, Patience looked steadfastly ahead. She then exited the apartments of Lady Carlyle and began a long, escorted walk from Hampton Court.

Although aware Sam remained at her side, she could not acknowledge him. Neither did she show any awareness of the many castle spirits, including a tearful Queen Jane Seymour, who had manifested to witness her forced removal from the palace.

Only when about to enter her stepfather's carriage, did she feel a slight glimmer of hope. Courtenay rushed from the palace in a great state of agitation.

"What is happening?" He directed his attention to Lord Henley and his minions. "Where are you taking Miss Sinclair?"

Henley looked down his nose at Courtenay. "This matter does not concern you, young sir."

Her stepfather then turned to the Earl of Hawthorne who, having followed them outside, now stood with his arms akimbo.

"I much appreciate your assistance in this matter, Hawthorne. Rest assured my stepdaughter will not escape again."

Receiving nothing more than a slight nod from the earl, Henley motioned for Billings and Trask, his two odious henchmen, to place her in the coach. Before she stepped inside, Patience looked one final time back at Mr. Courtenay.

He stood before the earl, and she could not help notice the great difference in their heights and demeanor.

The Earl of Hawthorne—exceedingly tall, muscular and strong, handsome as sin itself—bore no expression at all. He simply continued to stare in a condemning manner at her.

Mr. Courtney, on the other hand...slender, pale, far weaker and shorter than Hawthorne, glared at the earl, bristling with a bravery befitting his *Legion* nickname. But 'twas the heated words Courtenay said that Patience knew she would never forget.

"My God, Thorne, what have you done?"

Chapter 41

London, England

Long before Lord Henley's carriage arrived in Moorfields, Patience heard tortured screams and cries of terror. Yet she could not tell if they were conjured from her fear, cries from trapped phantom spirits, or ghosts that still haunted the asylum.

Having been prevented from looking out the window on the long journey, she had no notion of the hour. It seemed as if they'd traveled for days. However, the increasing sting of needles beneath her skin, and the painful spasms twisting at the base of her skull, confirmed they neared a place haunted by numerous spirits.

Soon, the coach came to a stop.

Patience exited after Lord Henley and the sullen behemoth of a guard named Billings. No one offered assistance. With her hands tied, the simple task proved difficult. She stumbled and fell hard upon her knees. Trask, the bald guard she'd not wanted to bind her feet at Hampton Court, stepped from the carriage after her. Rather than topple onto her, he extended his hand to help her rise.

"Do not help her." Henley ordered.

Determined to not show how disgraced she felt, Patience stood and regained her balance.

Not knowing when, or if, she would be allowed outside the walls of Bedlam again, Patience wanted one last view of blue sky, white clouds, and sunlight. A final glimpse to remember.

Instead, dense, dark clouds swollen with rain blanketed the sky. Distant thunder rumbled. The wind whined and twisted, taunting her to lose her footing and fall again. But like a protective friend, her long cloak hugged her body and kept her in place. A few stray strands of hair, however, answered the tug of the wind. Pulled free from the long braid down her back, they danced across her line of vision.

She raised her bound hands to push them aside.

"Walk," her stepfather ordered.

Nausea churned in her stomach as Patience stared at the entrance to Bethlem Royal Hospital. What would happen to her inside its shrieking walls?

Her limbs trembled with each move forward. She slowly climbed the stairs. Billings and Trask walked with her, each guard standing on opposite sides of her body. To her surprise, when a gust of wind pulled her backwards, Billings placed a hand gently on her right elbow to steady and guide her.

She almost thanked him but chose to focus on creating her protective shield. Offering a silent prayer for the angels to surround her with light, she managed to succeed. Comforted by the fact the pressure inside her head immediately dissipated, she approached the now open door her stepfather had entered.

The moment Patience crossed the threshold, she understood why the hospital was commonly called Bedlam.

Maniacal laughter, screams, foul language, and hysterical crying echoed from every direction. Her gaze fixed upon a long, dark corridor on the right—and hoped she would not be taken in that direction.

Patience turned her attention to the entry hall. Measures had been taken to make it appear welcoming, but evidence of cracked walls, peeling paint, and rotting wood gave evidence to the age and neglect of the building.

"Is this her, then?"

She pivoted and saw her stepfather approaching with a gray-haired heavyset man. Narrow, close-set eyes stared down a long nose at her. His expression held no warmth or kindness.

"Yes," Henley replied.

Patience looked down, unsure how to respond. Uncertain if she should speak at all.

"Curable or incurable?"

She looked to Lord Henley, hoping beyond hope that he'd only wanted to frighten her into obedience with this visit.

"Incurable."

The declaration by her stepfather pierced her heart.

The heavyset man moved to stand before her, resting his broad hands upon a protruding belly. "She appears docile. Perhaps she is not yet aware of her surroundings."

Her stepfather snorted with derision. "I can assure you, Dr. Monro, she is quite aware."

When her stepfather spoke the man's name, Patience looked directly at the physician. Her action caused one of the man's brows to arch, and he neared her.

"Does she bite?" Monro raised her chin with a forefinger and scrutinized her face.

"Of course, not." Henley sounded insulted by the question.

Her mouth was then forcibly opened by the fingers of the doctor, who then inspected her teeth.

"She has never been violent," Henley offered.

"How old is she?"

"Ten and nine."

"She will be our youngest patient," Monro said. "Are you certain you want her committed on a permanent basis?"

"Yes."

"Will you provide funds to ensure her care and safety?"

"A stipend," Henley answered. "I promised her mother she would not be defiled or injured. Other than that, do what you think best to treat her…madness."

"You realize incurables are where our violent patients are held. However, they are always restrained and should not be able to harm her…unless she ventures too close to them.

Henley chuckled. "She is mad, not stupid, Dr. Monro."

"Ah, but how mad is she? You claim she has been this way since early childhood. Thus, I must find not only the depth of her illness, but its cause." Monro grinned, exposing crooked, stained teeth. "Have you nothing to say, young miss?"

Not in front of my stepfather, Patience thought. *And I doubt I will ever want to speak with you.*

Monro narrowed his eyes in a calculating manner "Ah, well, we have a most effective method to encourage speech. After that, I will be better able to diagnose her treatment."

The doctor turned and motioned for a man several feet behind him to come forward. With a nod, the man stepped from shadows that had all but obscured him from view.

Shorter than her in height, he wore a soiled, dark uniform of some sort, and had an iron ring of keys attached to a belt.

"Lord Henley, this is Fincher, our chief steward."

Henley looked at the man dismissively.

As if perceiving what her stepfather thought, Dr. Monro chuckled. "He may be small in stature and slight of build, but Fincher is exceptionally strong and quite capable of handling any aggressive behavior from our residents."

Turning to the steward, Monro said, "Miss Sinclair is to be housed in the incurable wing. Find a bed for her away from the others. You may also unbind her hands. There is no need for restraints at this time. Lord Henley assures me she is not violent."

Fincher looked askance at Patience then nodded.

Patience blinked wide-eyed when the silent steward removed a knife from the cuff of his boot then cut the binds on her hands. Instinctively, she soothed where the taut, coarse rope had marred her pale flesh with angry red welts.

At once, a horrific, prolonged wailing rent the air, causing the hairs on the back of her neck to rise. She steeled herself to show no reaction, knowing the men had not heard. The wild, excruciating noise could only have been caused by a very angry ghost—perhaps in an effort to chase humans away.

"Lord Henley," Monro said. "Bid your farewell then let us return to my office to make the necessary arrangements for that stipend."

Patience looked at the man married to her mother. The man who had never shown her love or understanding from the moment he entered her life. The man who—without a shred of compassion—had kept his promise to condemn her to a cruel and unjust fate.

Would he bid her goodbye?

Say that he would pray for her?

Not surprisingly, he turned and walked away.

'Twas the middle of the night, the darkest hour, but Patience could not sleep. Horrific cries of terrible anguish and tortured pain had never ceased during the days and nights since she'd arrived at Bedlam. Indeed, at night the frightening sounds magnified.

Huddled inside her cloak—for she had no blanket to keep her warm—she studied her surroundings. Her narrow bed did not have a mattress, only loose straw that felt more like sharp daggers.

Still, she had a bed.

Many slept on the cold floor with nothing to comfort them. Locked in a large, decrepit, dank room together, they stared at her with angry, hungry eyes. Finally, she realized they were not staring at her, but her cloak.

During daylight, Patience did not look at the incurables.

She'd made the mistake of trying to smile at one old man, more out of pity than anything else. Had he not been chained to a wall, he might have killed her.

She watched them now, curled up in sleep, whimpering at times from whatever nightmare or madness tortured them at rest.

Due to limited space, there were two women and ten men in the ward with her—all shackled. Although their confinement seemed cruel, she found a sense of ease knowing any movement they might attempt toward her was limited.

The older woman, perhaps in her fifties, had gray hair which she habitually pulled out in clumps. Scabs and sores on her head marked where her scalp had bled. Her companion, chained to an iron stake in the floor, appeared to be near the same age. Her hair had been shorn. Both women never spoke and wore loose hanging gowns, torn in many places and almost black with filth.

The men were of various ages. Some wore the same type befouled gown. The others were naked, their bodies marred by bruises, wounds, open sores, and filth.

When Fincher first brought her into the room, and she'd seen the unclothed men, she stopped walking. The steward looked at her and understood the shock in her eyes.

"He ain't gonna hurt ye," he said. "Those that have no clothes is because they tear 'em off as soon as they get some. Better not to give 'em anythin' they might use to hurt someone, or themselves."

As chief steward, Fincher patrolled the incurables, and dispensed discipline. As far as she'd seen, he only did so when a patient tried to bite or attack him.

He'd also been kind to her, especially that first day. He had someone bring a bed for her and made sure it was a fair distance away from the chained reach of any incurable.

"Don't know why yer family put ye here, miss. Ye don't seem like the others." He'd paused a moment then shook his head. "Have a daughter yer age, I do. So, ye let Fincher know if anyone tries to hurt ye…anyone at all."

Patience had not spoken a word to anyone, but she'd nodded at Fincher's unexpected kindness.

She started to fall asleep when a blast of cold wind and slicing rain blew through the window near her bed. She glanced at the floor. Even in the darkness, she could see it glistened with moisture. She'd been grateful to be located near the window. A breeze provided the only reprieve from the foul stench in the room. However, situated high above, preventing any view, the window also held no glass.

Nothing to block the cold or inclement weather.

Would she still be there when it snowed?

Darkness surrounded Patience, especially at night. She thought of her living nightmare. If she fell asleep, her protective shield might falter. And the spirits haunting Bedlam were as dangerous—perhaps more—than the poor souls that were alive.

She rubbed her left side and forearm, where raised scratch marks had been inflicted upon her.

Since her incurable companions could not reach her, there was but one explanation. An angry, powerful spirit had been determined to break through her means of defense and demand attention.

Had it been the one who wailed with such fury the day she arrived? If the mad ghost had been able to hurt her with a defensive shield in place, what might he do to her without it?

I must remain awake.

Patience thought of Sam and whether she should summon him for protection. She had no doubt he would come immediately, despite her charging him to remain with the countess.

Closing her eyes, comforted by the familiar feel and scent of her cloak, Patience rocked back and forth in her bed.

Auntie Catherine will come for me, she assured herself.

Mr. Courtenay cared about her, too. She'd seen it in his eyes, and his display of outrage at Earl Hawthorne. He must have sent word to Leighton by now. This very moment, they could all be coming to her rescue.

I must be strong. I must be brave.

The ear-piercing wail started again, echoing through Bedlam. This time it traveled, racing with the ghost's movement. She looked toward the locked door, knowing it approached. No bit of iron would bar the spirit from entering the room.

Icy cold swept across her face. Her breathing escalated, yet she remained determined not to look. Not to show fear should the spirit manifest. Instead, she closed her eyes once more, and focused on maintaining her protective barrier.

She clutched her cloak tightly, continuing to rock back and forth—finding comfort in the simple act. One thought repeated in her mind.

I must not sleep.

Chapter 42

Aldebaran Castle ~ Lakes District, England

Standing in the columned Grecian folly on his family's estate, Leighton listened with unsteady breathing and rising anger as Melville informed him what had transpired at Hampton Court.

Of the manifestation of Baltharach, and how he tried to kill Patience. Of how Baltharach came to exist, and could assume the physical appearance of Courtenay. Of how they found the body of Anne Melville, and the stone-like condition of her remains.

Guilt and fury soared within him.

Everything had been triggered by the unbridled power he'd used in a cave years ago. Anne Melville had been murdered because of him. The evil at Hampton Court was there because of him. Patience had faced this monster alone, because of him. And now, this Baltharach would continue killing…because of him.

Moving away from Melville, Leighton closed his eyes. Melville kept speaking, but Leighton could barely focus on anything else his friend said, until he heard one word.

Bedlam.

He turned again to face Melville, holding fast to each word spoken about what further happened to Patience in his absence.

"How did he know where to find her?" Leighton's throat constricted, his voice raw with the certain knowledge how terrified the woman he loved must have felt when Lord Henley all but dragged her from Hampton Court.

Melville did not answer, but his expression sent warning bells ringing through Leighton's head.

"How did he find her!" Leighton repeated, stronger.

"Thorne," Melville replied.

Leighton's breathing roared through his lungs. Feeling as if his heart had been ripped out of his chest, he all but fell against a marble pillar.

"Lyon remained with the countess," Melville added. "They left immediately for London, determined to free Miss Sinclair without delay. The duke then summoned the rest of us here."

With a shaky nod, Leighton struggled to control the bloodlust racing through his body. Now was not the time to lose control of his power. But his heart pounded, echoing in his ears, drumming with an insistent rhythm.

Melville kept talking, hastily explaining why the duke ordered the rest of the *Legion* members to assemble at *Aldebaran*, his family's protected estate. Namely, his grandfather wanted them to train together and plan how to destroy Baltharach.

He heard Melville's words. He understood the importance of destroying the demonic creature that he alone had released into the world. At the same time, his conscience and love for Patience would not permit him to delay saving her.

"I cannot stay," he said in a hoarse voice. "I must leave now. I have to get her out of there."

"Lyon is already there with Lady Carlyle," Melville replied. "He will get her out."

Melville's words helped.

"Saint," Melville continued. "Even if you were to leave now, by the time you arrived, Miss Sinclair will have been removed from Bedlam. In the meantime, you will be helping her by learning how to destroy this foul creature."

Arms folded across his chest, Leighton nodded. "Your words make sense. It's just…I told her I would protect her. Had I been at Hampton Court, none of this would have happened."

"I know, but 'tis done."

"Done?" Leighton narrowed his eyes at movement in the distance. "Not hardly."

Melville turned about and swore under his breath.

Knightly and Hunter ambled across the estate's park toward the folly, and Hawthorne was with them.

Like a bolt of lightning shot by the hand of Zeus, Leighton raced out of the folly. All he could see was the Earl of Hawthorne.

"Damn you, Thorne!" Leighton yelled as he charged toward the earl. "I trusted you."

Knightly and Hunter intercepted the leader of the *Legion*, yet struggled to hold him back.

"Fighting will not help the situation," Knightly said.

"Release me!" Leighton ordered, twisting with all his might for freedom to throttle the earl.

"Release him," Hawthorne agreed.

Without hesitation, Knightly and Hunter stepped away.

Hawthorne accepted the first forceful punch to his jaw, although he fell to his knees. He spat out a stream of blood then wiped his mouth with the back of his hand.

"I'll give you that," the earl said.

"*Give* me?" Leighton sneered. "Trust me, I intend to pummel you senseless. Maybe then you will understand what you have done."

The next moment, both men came to blows. Their extraordinary strength gave otherworldly power to each contact. When one fell to the ground, the other would leap upon him, determined to give no quarter.

At one point, out of breath, both bleeding, they backed away. Still glaring, however, they circled their opponent with increasing anger, preparing for their next round.

"Why?" Leighton bit out.

"You know why," Hawthorne retorted. "You were willing to throw away your life because of her."

"How is it *not* possible for you to understand? She IS my life!" He stalked in front of the earl, his still fisted knuckles bleeding. "I told you what she meant to me. And that I intended to marry her. You had no right to do what you did."

"I had every right. I saved your life!"

Leighton glared at Hawthorne. "Is that what this is about? That you stopped me from killing myself two years ago?"

"Stopped you?" Hawthorne mocked. "I didn't stop you, Saint. You did it. You killed yourself. Because of *her*."

Leighton's blood froze. "What are you talking about?"

Hawthorne said nothing.

"What did you do, Earl Hawthorne?" said a stern voice.

The members of the *Legion* all turned to see the Duke of Windermere standing in their midst. Beside him was Leighton's father, the Earl of Strathmore. Although both men looked calm, the banked fire in the duke's eyes told a different tale.

"I did the only thing I could do," Hawthorne said. "I arrived just as I heard a gunshot. By the time I got inside, he was gone. So, I used my power to turn time back."

Victor St. Ives, Earl of Strathmore, immediately went to stand near his firstborn. Grave concern etched his features as he studied Leighton's stunned, pale face.

"Tristan," he said. "What is the last thing you remember before Thorne arrived that day?"

"Sitting in the library, looking at the pistol on my desk."

"How far did you go back?" the duke asked as he stared at Hawthorne.

"Four...perhaps five minutes."

"We must know exactly," Windermere stressed.

"No more, no less." Hawthorne looked defensively at his friends, well aware he had done something forbidden. "I wanted to be sure I had enough time to stop him."

The duke turned to the other members of the *Legion*, all of whom were clearly stunned by Hawthorne's revelation. "I must speak with Hawthorne, alone. Victor, take Tristan inside and speak with him privately.

In silence, Knightly, Hunter, and Melville departed in the direction of the stables. Leighton walked toward the castle beside his father, but paused and looked back at his childhood friend. Tall and somber, Hawthorne faced the imposing duke.

Much as he detested that Thorne informed Henley where to find Patience, he understood the fear and concern that drove him to such destructive behavior.

Unlike the consequences of his impulsive actions years ago, he prayed Thorne's use of forbidden power had not caused an aftermath they know nothing about.

"Come," his father said, resting a paternal hand upon Leighton's back. "We will talk in your bedchamber. I don't want your mother to see you have been fighting and asking questions I cannot answer."

"I didn't know," Leighton whispered. "For God's sake, he was warned. We all were warned. I would not have asked it of him. He should *not* have done it."

His father released a heavy sigh. "For what it is worth, my son, I am exceedingly grateful he did."

Chapter 43

Bethlem Royal Hospital, Moorfields

"What do you mean, I cannot see my niece? How much longer must I wait?" Lady Carlyle studied the odious Dr. Thomas Monro with her Scots temper on the verge of igniting.

"As I stated, countess, we must consult the legal guardian of a patient before allowing visitors. I regret it has taken a fortnight to receive Lord Henley's reply, but he quite emphatically said you not be allowed to see his wife's daughter. Indeed, his lordship said you are the reason Miss Sinclair disobeyed her family's wishes. That you showed no thought for their attempt to keep her safe and her illness private."

"My niece is not ill. Neither is she mad." Lady Carlyle looked at Mr. Courtenay standing to her right, grateful for his dignified, calm presence. "Please explain our position to this man. I grow short on forbearance."

"I assure you, *Dr*. Monro,"—Mr. Courtenay made a point to pause dubiously when referring to the man's professional title— "the countess is correct. And we shall do whatever necessary to remove Miss Sinclair from this *hospital* and your care, and see that those responsible for her unjust imprisonment are held accountable."

"No doubt." Dr. Monro studied his fingernails with bored indifference. "You may well try, sir. However, you are not the legal guardian for this young woman. Neither is the countess. She is, at present, under my medical care and will remain so."

"May I at least write to her?" asked Lady Carlyle.

Monro shook his head. "No communication whatsoever, countess."

"Might I be permitted to see Miss Sinclair?" Courtenay asked. "I merely want to assure Lady Carlyle and myself that her niece has not been harmed in any way."

Dr. Monro considered the question in silence. "There were no other names listed to deny visitation. However, the hospital's policy specifies only those who contribute financially toward the care of a resident are allowed to see them."

Lady Carlyle gasped with indignation, all but shaking with outrage. She looked at Courtenay. "I can well imagine how little Henley has provided for her care."

"How much?" Courtenay asked.

"Whatever you think appropriate, sir."

Courtenay slapped £3 on the desk of the Principal Physician at Bethlem Royal Hospital, a man whose family has been in charge of the madhouse and the care of the poor souls within its wall since 1728.

After pocketing the money, Dr. Monro sighed. "Unfortunately, the hour is too late to disturb Miss Sinclair now. Our residents follow a disciplined routine."

"I demand to see Miss Sinclair immediately, or I shall bring my grievance to the Governors of Bridewell."

Dr. Monro had the audacity to laugh. "Come tomorrow, Mr. Courtenay. You may speak briefly with Miss Sinclair promptly at one o'clock. Until then, I bid you both good day.

Seated once more behind his desk, Dr. Monro tabulated how much the bastard son of the Duke of Clarence would pay to continue visiting Miss Sinclair.

The young upstart had no right to question his authority as Principal Physician. Or, for that matter, any right to circumvent Lord Henley's commitment of his step-daughter.

However, if Courtenay and the countess were concerned enough about the young lady's care and comfort, they might be willing to pay a hefty sum. Hence, the longer she remained under his care, the more profit. Thus, it behooved him to prove how much Miss Sinclair needed his medical attention.

Hearing movement in the doorway, he looked up.

"Ah, Fincher," he said.

"Ye wanted to see me, Dr. Monro, sir?"

"Yes, indeed I did. Tell me, how is Miss Sinclair adjusting?

"Quiet as a mouse, sir."

"Has she spoken to anyone since arriving?"

"No, sir," the steward replied.

"I see." Monro studied the sum he'd thus far calculated. "I am told she does not sleep well either."

"Stays awake most all night."

"Ah, well, we cannot have that." He inhaled deeply and raised his gaze to the steward. "I believe it is time we take measures to pull the poor miss out of this lethargy."

Fincher did not respond.

"You know what to do," Monro continued. "See it is done without delay."

Patience stared at the bowl of gruel in her lap, determined to ignore the noise of two men yanking on their tether of chain and trying to kick one another whilst snarling like wild animals.

Neither did she want to hear the shorn woman cackling with glee at their behavior.

Unable to eat, she put the wooden bowl on the floor, closed her eyes and imagined herself in Scotland again. The wind on the loch. The blooming of the heather. She never should have left. Never should have trusted Lady Carlyle. Never should have believed Leighton loved her.

Never. Never. Never.

"I see ye still have no appetite," a voice said.

She opened her eyes and saw Fincher standing beside her bed.

"Up with ye now," he said with a smile. "Time to take a walk with old Fincher."

She stood, and started to remove her shoes from their hiding place in the straw of her bed.

"Leave yer shoes here," he said. "No one will take 'em."

Patience looked at the filthy floor; in particular, the space in the center of the room where the others had thrown their food. Not to mention their human excrement.

Biting her tongue, she put her shoes on then gathered her cloak about her shoulders. Wherever Fincher was taking her for their walk, she wanted what little belongings she still possessed with her.

Standing beside him, she watched as he picked up the bowl of gruel. Pocketing the wooden spoon, he brought it over to the older lady. She greedily accepted and raised the bowl to her mouth.

"No sense wastin' it," he said.

Fincher guided her to the door. They then walked down the corridor she had not seen since the day she came to Bedlam.

Fifteen days, she reminded herself.

Fifteen days without a word from anyone. Even Sam had not come when she summoned him over a week ago. She didn't want to believe they had abandoned her. Worse, however, was the thought Baltharach had killed them trying to find her.

If they were dead...

Tears stung her eyes, but she refused to cry.

Looking ahead she saw the ghost of a man swaying side to side, smiling at her with wide eyes. She looked down, afraid the steward might see her reaction. The spirit was harmless, sadly a former resident who did not realize he had died.

Fincher led her into another hallway, and her breath seized in her chest. She stopped altogether, realizing they had entered the corridor that so terrified her the day her stepfather brought her to Bedlam. Dark, dank, and filled with tortured spirits. She dug her heels into the wooden floor, refusing to take another step.

"Now, now, none of that." Fincher pulled her forward. "Ye need to walk, miss. Get yer blood movin'."

A moment later he unlocked a door with one of his keys. Inside was a long, narrow room with no furniture. High windows denied a glimpse of outdoors, but did afford some light. There was nothing but a wooden floor. Holding her arm, he escorted her down the length of the room and back again.

"See," he said with a smile. "Just walkin' to and fro."

Two more times he escorted her across the room and back. Then, Fincher faced her. "I want ye to keep doin' that a few more times by yerself." To her surprise he unfastened her cloak, and tried to remove it from her shoulders. She grabbed hold of its fabric.

He laughed. "What would I be doin' with this cloak, miss? I promise, no harm will come to it. When I come back, I will give it to ye. These are the rules, ye see?"

Patience eyed the man skeptically. "You promise," she said, her voice hoarse from not being used.

Clearly startled she'd finally spoken to him, the steward grinned. "Seems yer throat needs exercise, too."

She offered a small smile in return.

"I promise, miss." He folded the cloak carefully then looked down at her feet. "Can I hold the shoes, too? Ye don't want Fincher gettin' in trouble, do ye? I let ye keep 'em all this time, and no one else has shoes. 'Course they might throw 'em at me. But I trust ye."

Patience looked at the floor. Though most of it was cast in shadow, the parts she could see appeared clean. In truth, none of the incurables had shoes. And when one of the mean stewards tried to take her shoes, Fincher told him to let her keep her things.

She inhaled slowly, removed her shoes and handed them to the only person at Bedlam who had been kind to her. The only one she trusted.

With her things in his possession, Fincher walked to the door. He turned and studied her a long moment. "I'll be back in no time at all," he said. "Mind, ye have to keep yer word. Walk back and forth, back and forth."

After he left the room, she heard the door being locked.

Patience looked down the length of the room. It had felt good to stretch her limbs. Walking was good for a person's constitution. She could even pretend she was in her garden…in Scotland.

She started slowly then increased her pace a bit. Counting how many times she crossed the floor, Patience smiled. She turned for the tenth time, and had reached the middle of the room when the floor suddenly opened beneath her feet.

Screaming, terrified, Patience plummeted into a deep, dark hole, submerged immediately beneath bitter cold water. She struggled to find the surface, her throat and lungs burning from the water she'd swallowed. Over and over again, she pulled at the water.

Somehow, she managed to raise her head above the surface and breathe. Treading water, she looked up at the damaged floor far above her head. What she saw, however, was not a hole caused by aged, rotten wood, but an opened trap door.

Fincher had deliberately brought her to this room. He'd taken her cloak and shoes with the intention of keeping them and drowning her. Desperate to keep her head above water, Patience kicked her limbs and looked for a way to get out.

Distracted, terrified, hampered by the twisting, clinging length of her long nightgown about her limbs, she focused on survival. All about her was water, in a place without light. Had she fallen into a cave or well?

The water was deep, for she'd been submerged far above her head after the fall. She tried to not panic, to keep calm. If there was a trap door, there must be a ladder or other means to get out.

She started to swim away from the center, to see if she could find the wall of the well. Or, perhaps the formations of stone from a cave. In the process, she let down her guard—and control on her defensive shield.

At once, the painful spasm inside the back of her head struck without mercy. Instinctively, she tried to press her palm firmly against the pain—as she always did—but slipped beneath the water again.

Fighting against the stabbing pain, her eyes opened underwater. As she tried to pull herself up, to find the surface again, a greenish glow appeared. Followed in rapid succession by others, each green orb raced toward her, manifesting into faces of horrified, grotesque spirits the nearer they came.

With emaciated bodies, wild eyes, and gaping mouths, the ghoulish green spirits surrounded her. They seemed to number in the hundreds, and the ear-piercing screaming of their terrifying wails echoed beneath the water.

They grabbed at her limbs. Clawed at her arms. Frantically pulled her hair. Latching onto her body with such force she had not the strength to escape.

She tried to pray, to create another protective shield; her only hope of not drowning. If she could secure a means of defense, block these mad souls, she might at last break free and find the strength to live.

Yet no matter how much Patience tried—or how hard she kicked and fought to not be pulled further into the depths—she failed.

The ghosts of the well would not release her.

Her lungs burned, ready to burst.

Her body convulsed with desperate need for air.

Exhausted, she had no strength remaining.

There was nothing left to her then, but darkness.

Chapter 44

Fincher searched for Miss Sinclair, guided by light from a torch and the sound of movement in the water. He narrowed his gaze away from the center, and circled to the far end. Then, the frantic splashing stopped. Dropping the torch, he dove into the deep water.

Twice he managed to take hold of her tiny waist, but each time he tried to pull her limp body to the surface, something dragged it back down.

Somehow, on his third attempt, he managed to retrieve her. Fearing she had died, he rolled Patience Sinclair onto her stomach. Repeatedly his hands pushed upward against her back, trying to force the water out of her lungs. He'd done it before with others; some of the time it worked. He prayed this would be one of those times.

"Please, miss," he said. "Breathe."

When he'd about given up hope, Fincher heard the sound of water expelled from her mouth and some coughing. Continuing his ministrations with renewed vigor, he didn't stop until she took in a deep breath of air.

Turning her onto her back again, he looked at the young lady's face. Pale, her eyes wide with terror, she sat up and quickly crawled backwards away from him.

"No, no, miss," he said. "I saved ye."

Shivering, huddling like a small child, she stared with eyes that had lost all the trust he'd seen before he followed Dr. Monro's orders. Hearing her teeth chatter, Fincher stood, sprinting to retrieve her cloak and shoes. When he returned, he found her looking around, noting the size and dimension of the cold bath, and the walls of the hospital basement that housed it.

"Here, miss." He offered a gentle smile. "I have yer cloak and shoes, like I promised." He draped the cloak about her shoulders, and rubbed the woolen cloth quickly against her arms and back.

All the while, she stared silently at him, her body rigid with a fear that Fincher doubted he'd ever forget.

When Courtenay arrived at Bethlem Royal Hospital the next day, he was promptly directed to the office of Dr. Monro.

The Principal Physician sat at his desk, a bowl of walnuts being cracked open with swift proficiency. "Ah, Mr. Courtenay. Thank you for being prompt for your appointment."

"I wish to be taken directly to Miss Sinclair," Courtenay said.

"Yes, of course." Monro stood and brushed one hand against the other, removing any lingering walnut residue. "Afterwards, I feel we should speak again. I am confident your visit with Miss Sinclair will prove why I feel it important she remain at Bethlem."

"Very well," Courtenay said with a nod. "Now, bring me to her."

Courtenay clenched his jaw as he followed Dr. Thomas Monro down a labyrinth of corridors, dark and cold, filled with all manner of foul air.

When they reached a locked ward, a guard stood outside and promptly opened the door for Monro.

What he encountered in the room made Courtenay's skin crawl. The dregs of humanity, their minds trapped in some hopeless horror, howled and screamed. Equally disturbing, the ward held both men and women. Some of the men, wild-eyed, naked and chained, tried to charge at them.

"As you can see," Monro said, "we have precautions so Miss Sinclair will not be harmed. Her companions are manacled for their safety, the welfare of patients with them, and our staff that cares for them."

"I trust Miss Sinclair is not kept in chains." Courtenay struggled to control his fury at the inhumane, disgusting manner in which the hospital cared for its patients.

"No," Monro replied. "However, should she become violent, we will have no other choice."

Courtenay studied the physician a long moment, wishing he could put Monro in chains.

"Ah, here is Miss Sinclair."

Courtenay turned toward the direction where the physician looked, and choked back the horror he felt.

He approached the frail, young woman seated on a bed of straw in the corner. All but enveloped within the folds of her cloak, she stared blankly ahead and rocked to and fro slowly. He could hardly believe this shell of a waif was the Patience Sinclair he knew.

"I wish to speak with her alone," he bit out.

"Of course, of course," Monro said. "The steward will remain by the door. He will direct you back to my office afterwards."

Courtenay waited until Monro departed before he moved. Then, slowly, he approached the bed.

"Miss Sinclair," he said softly.

No response.

"Patience," he whispered.

Seated upon the bed before her, he studied her face. Dark circles marred the pale skin beneath her eyes. Eyes that still were a lovely shade, but now held no spark. Her lips were dry, cracked, and he wished he had thought to bring spring water or a tin of hot tea.

"Patience, can you hear me?" He paused a moment. "I am here because they will not allow Lady Carlyle to see you."

She looked at him then. "Why?"

He cringed to hear the raspy, hoarse sound of her voice. Fearing she might have a fever, he tried to feel her brow with the back of his hand. She flinched as if he intended to strike her.

Pulling his hand away, he struggled to find the right words to say. He did not want to lie to her, but she needed hope.

"Henley would not allow it as your guardian. She is fighting him, Patience. We need you to be strong. We need you to know we have not forsaken you."

She stopped her perpetual rocking motion and looked at him, seeming to understand his words. "Lyon," she whispered.

"Yes, Lyon." He smiled. "I am your friend, dear Patience."

"Leighton?" she asked. "Is he no longer my friend?"

Courtenay frowned. "He loves you, Patience. When he learned what happened, he fought with Hawthorne."

"Where is he?"

"Preparing for battle with the others."

"To fight Baltharach?" she questioned.

Courtenay nodded.

"I will never see Leighton again." Tears filled her eyes.

"You must not think like that," Courtenay touched the side of her face. "Do not lose hope."

Her body crumpled into sobs, and she hid her face behind scratched, dirty hands. "I am afraid, Lyon."

He took hold of a hand, and examined it. Deep red scratches ran the length of her delicate arm. "Who did this to you?" He looked at the other people in the room, all chained.

"Was it a guard?"

She shook her head. "They tried to kill me."

"Who, Patience? Who tried to kill you?"

"Ghosts."

"Can you not block them?"

"I try, but I am so tired. They will not let me sleep."

Patience looked about the room, fear-stricken, as if the walls could hear. Then, leaning toward him, she whispered. "I fell through a door in the floor. Into a deep well of dark water. I tried to get out, but they drowned me. I—I drowned."

She shook her head, her chin quivering. "I will tell you a secret no one here must know. Sometimes I think I am not alive."

Courtenay listened to her words, and realized Patience's sanity hanged by a fragile thread. He glanced again at her arms, at numerous bruises that looked like fingerprints. He studied the angry scratch marks from various angles and directions.

He gently stroked one long scratch.

"Did they do this to you, Patience?"

"In the water. They were in the deep water."

Pulling Patience into an embrace, Courtenay gently rocked her back and forth, realizing it comforted her as it would a frightened child. Glancing down, he saw her eyes had closed as her head rested against his chest. At least for this brief moment, he could make her feel safe.

Clearly, they could not wait any longer to gain her freedom.

Every day she remained at Bedlam chipped another piece of her heart, mind, and soul away. She looked so frail. So weak.

What if she were to die in this heinous place?

Alone, surrounded by violent, mentally ill people everywhere she looked. Attacked and perhaps killed by untold, insane spirits who had died there over the past 153 years. Tormented for centuries without end. Forced to suffer the indignity and cruelty of caretakers who knew not the meaning of human kindness and compassion.

Soon, he told himself. *I will send word to Leighton to come at once.* If we can find no other way, he must use his powers to take her from this madhouse.

Courtenay paused outside the door to Lady Carlyle's private sitting room at Carlyle House. He needed a moment to gather his thoughts before discussing his visit with Miss Sinclair.

Having seen the deplorable conditions in which Lady Carlyle's niece had been subjected, and the effect already inflicted upon her health, mind, and spirit, there was nothing he would not do to end her suffering and imprisonment.

As for his meeting with Dr. Monro, although the Principal Physician listened at length, and stated he sympathized with the distress of Lady Carlyle, Monro maintained Miss Sinclair must remain at Bethlem Royal Hospital under his medical care.

Knowing he must speak truthfully with the countess about the situation, as well as the need for immediate action, Courtenay inhaled slowly, deeply. In truth, unless Leighton helped, he doubted they would be able to rescue Miss Sinclair at all.

The countess did not want to hear such a revelation. The lady was personally determined to find a means to rescue her niece, and see Lord Henley ruined for his cruelty.

Courtenay rotated his neck a bit to release some tension. He nodded at the liveried, bewigged servant standing ready to open the door, and then entered the room.

The lady, however, was not alone.

Much to his surprise, Her Majesty Queen Charlotte was seated in a chair, sipping tea, and facing the countess. An extraordinary and longstanding friendship must exist between the two women. His father's mother, the queen consort of George III, rarely left her private sanctuary at Frogmore. If she wanted to speak with someone, they were summoned to her.

"Your Majesty, I am honored to see you again." He bowed to his Royal grandmother—a woman he had seen scarce few times in his life—usually when he'd been near death as a boy. She'd been kind to him, but they shared no relationship whatsoever.

"Mr. Courtenay," she replied with a curious expression.

He then bowed to the countess. "Lady Carlyle."

"Mr. Courtenay," Lady Carlyle nodded then indicated a seat next to her on the sofa. "How is my niece? Did you see her?"

Unsure how much he should say in the presence of the queen, Courtenay hesitated.

"Please speak freely," Queen Charlotte said. "I am well aware of the situation, and have come to aid my dear friend, if I am able. The countess has been a source of strength and comfort for me during tragic times and heartbreaking loss. Out of loyalty for me and His Majesty, Lady Carlyle has also maintained a residence at Hampton Court to ensure those we care for are safe and well. Thus, we have no secrets from one another."

"I understand, Your Majesty." Yet Courtenay wasn't quite sure he understood the queen's implication.

Had Lady Carlyle stayed at Hampton Court to not only report on the welfare of former Ladies-In-Waiting and members of the Royal Court, but *him*…the queen's sickly, illegitimate grandson?

His memory flashed back to how often the countess had made a point to visit him, or sit with him in the garden. How many times she'd conversed with him over a book, game of chess, or cards—ever since his childhood.

As if she understood his confusion, Queen Charlotte smiled. "The countess has spoken often of you. His Majesty and I remembered you in our daily prayers for good health, and were quite interested in your keen mind and intelligence. I must say, your compassion and assistance to Lady Carlyle during this terrible time is most admirable."

"Thank you, Your Majesty. I only wish I could do more."

"Please, tell us what you have learned?" the countess asked.

"Lady Carlyle, it pains me to tell you this, but if we do not remove Miss Sinclair from Bedlam—and the care of Dr. Monro—soon, I fear for her life."

"Oh, no, no," the countess whispered, a shaky hand pressed against her lips. "Have those fiends harmed my sweet girl?"

"I shan't go into a description of her state, countess. Suffice to say I was appalled and heartsick. She is much changed in appearance—weak, pale, thin. Despite her courage to remain strong, her days and nights are a daily torment inflicted by others without mercy. Thus, she is now most fragile of mind and spirit."

"Did you speak with Dr. Monro?" the queen inquired.

"Yes, Your Majesty, but other than a willingness for Lady Carlyle to pay for a private room and items to improve her niece's comfort, he maintains she must continue under his care."

"The man is insufferable." Lady Carlyle's eyes filled with tears, and she quickly dabbed at her eyes with an embroidered handkerchief.

"Indeed he is," Queen Charlotte agreed. "Neither do I believe him a competent physician. In truth, I refused permission for Dr. Monro to treat the king. His methods are barbaric."

Recollecting the bizarre reference Miss Sinclair made to being dispatched from a hole in the floor into a well of dark water, Courtenay looked at the queen. She must have seen by his expression that a horrifying incident had happened to Lady Carlyle's niece.

They both then looked at the countess, noting the woman's increased emotional distress. For certain, she must be contemplating what cruel treatment had been prescribed for her beloved niece. After all, if the queen had forbidden Monro to treat His Majesty, what must others of far less consequence suffer under his care?

"Tell us, Mr. Courtenay," the queen said in an obvious attempt to distract the frightened thoughts of the countess. "Were you able to secure better accommodations for Miss Sinclair?"

Noting the queen's question prompted Lady Carlyle to look at him, he attempted a reassuring smile. "In my presence, Monro told a steward to immediately move Miss Sinclair to a private room with a proper bed. I also told him we would deliver new bedding and clothing without delay, and that I expected her situation much improved when I visited tomorrow."

"How I wish I could go with you." Lady Carlyle clasped her hands in prayer-life fashion. "I worry when Patience sees those things arrive, she will think we no longer seek her release."

"I will tell her otherwise, countess. However, Monro must believe we not only accept your niece remaining under his care, but that you will provide funds for better treatment and accommodations."

Queen Charlotte extended an empty tea cup and saucer to the countess. "Have you contacted the Governors of Bridewell?"

Lady Carlyle poured another cup of tea for the queen, accompanied with a biscuit. "They can do nothing unless the courts appoint me legal guardian instead of Henley."

"That process will take too long, and is not guaranteed." Courtenay commented and also accepted a cup of hot tea. "I believe our best hope is to get word to Lord Leighton and the Duke of Windermere. I would travel myself to *Aldebaran*, but since you cannot visit with Miss Sinclair, I must remain here and do so each day."

Courtenay raised the cup to his lips then paused. “Perhaps your friend, Sam, can deliver the letter?”

The countess looked startled by the suggestion. She glanced at the queen, who appeared disinterested in whoever Sam might be.

“Yes,” Lady Carlyle said with a soft smile. “I daresay he will reach the duke’s estate fast as wind whistles around the sails of a ship.”

“Do you believe Windermere and his grandson will succeed where you have failed?” Queen Charlotte inquired then nibbled daintily upon a biscuit.

“I do, if one or both arrive in time,” Courtenay replied.

The queen’s expression took on a decidedly shrewd quality. “There could be another way to gain Miss Sinclair’s freedom without delay. The thought occurred to me, you may yet be able to negotiate a trade.”

“How?” Lady Carlyle asked. “Dr. Monro has refused money for her release. The wicked man prefers to extort payment on a continuing basis for keeping her prisoner.”

“True,” Queen Charlotte said then sipped her tea. “Yet, what if the trade were for an item of greater *personal* value to Monro? An item he will find too tempting to refuse?”

Lady Carlyle crooked a delicate eyebrow. “Jewelry perhaps?”

“No, not jewelry.” Queen Charlotte laughed softly. “I have this moment recalled Dr. Monro is passionate about art. Indeed, he is quite the avid collector. More importantly, I believe you have a piece by a deceased artist he would be thrilled to possess.”

“I do?” Lady Carlyle’s disposition brightened. Hope sparkled for the first time in her eyes.

“Thomas Girtin,” Queen Charlotte replied with a mischievous grin. “Remember that charming watercolor I gave you?”

“You would not object to my parting with it?”

“To ransom your beloved niece?” Queen Charlotte leaned forward and patted Lady Carlyle’s hand. “Nothing would please me more.”

Chapter 45

Aldebaran Castle ~ Lakes District, England

"You cannot leave." The Duke of Windermere declared then focused his attention on Copernicus, the family's great telescope housed in *Aldebaran's* private observatory. "The countess will obtain her niece's release."

Leighton clenched his jaw, struggling to control his temper. Summoned by his father and the duke to the castle's tallest tower, he soon realized his grandfather had no intention of discussing anything. Least of all the rescue of Miss Patience Sinclair.

"Do not underestimate the determination of Lady Carlyle," the duke continued. He paused from viewing constellations to writing notations on a chart. "Did not Lyon's letter say Lady Carlyle had a private audience with Her Majesty regarding the situation? And that this audience took place at the private home of the countess?"

"Unusual, perhaps." Leighton shrugged. "According to Lyon, Her Majesty considers the countess a friend."

"Indeed, she does," the duke replied. "You would be wise to not intrude upon that friendship, or what they endeavor to accomplish."

"You expect me to wait upon two old women who conspired over tea and biscuits about how to save the woman I love?"

"The age of these two women has nothing to do with their ability or power." After tracing an entry on the chart with an aged finger, the patriarch Lightbearer then bestowed his undivided attention upon Leighton.

"Do you believe you care more for this young woman than the countess?" Windermere asked. "That you are more distraught, angry, or determined to save her than the young woman's flesh and blood?"

Leighton raked a hand through his hair. "I do not doubt the affection Lady Carlyle has for her niece. I *do* doubt her ability to remedy this situation. How can I make you understand? This is my responsibility. Had I taken Miss Sinclair with me, she would be safe now. I vowed I would protect her. I cannot abandon her now. Indeed, not ever."

"Look above you," Windermere said. "The view may help put the situation into better perspective."

Frustrated beyond measure, Leighton inhaled deeply and looked up. Beyond the open dome shutters of the observatory, stars too numerous to count were displayed against a black velvet sky.

"Consider each star a living, breathing person gathered together amidst the vast domain of their Creator." Windermere returned to Copernicus, but kept his gaze steady upon his grandson.

"Each star is valued for the individual light it possesses," the duke continued. "Some stars are set apart, isolated. Others are arranged to form a constellation. And, as you well know, some stars are not stars at all. Does not Venus light up the night sky with great brilliance? What of the moon? Constant, illuminating greater than any star or planet above us. Yet the phases of the moon are ever changing."

Leighton lowered his gaze to study his grandfather. "Are you implying the *Legion* is a constellation, and that it is my destiny to not alter my position by leaving to rescue Miss Sinclair?"

"You are the leader of the *Legion,*" Windermere said.

"And Miss Sinclair? Where does she belong in this vast universe? Alone? Isolated? Forever? A pawn to be sacrificed?"

Windermere released a weary sign and looked at his son. "You were never this stubborn, Victor."

Leighton noticed his father rubbed his jaw and grinned. The Earl of Strathmore had remained silent since the meeting started. Now, as he always did whenever his father and eldest son disagreed on any number of subjects, the earl assumed the role of wise, diplomatic mediator.

"In my opinion, you are both stubborn," Strathmore said. "In any event, your grandfather speaks of destiny, Tristan. Each person is shaped by the choices they make; the challenges they face. Your destiny was revealed years ago in the Roman cave."

"You expect me to believe what happened in that cave was meant to happen?" Leighton asked.

"I believe so," his father replied.

"As do I," Windermere seconded.

"No," Leighton argued. "It never should have happened."

Windermere braced his hands on his hips. "The evil in that cave existed long before you boys explored the ruins of that temple. You entered at a time when the spell keeping Baltharach prisoner had weakened, allowing him to move toward you. Your power as a Lightbearer enabled you to sense what others could not."

"What if some other boy found that cave?" Strathmore asked, crossing to stand beside his father.

"Baltharach would have escaped the cave," Leighton replied, his voice haunted by the realization. "He would have used someone else until he could separate."

"Needless to say, if that someone else had been healthy,"—the duke quirked a bushy eyebrow at Leighton— "Baltharach would have been able to unleash his evil all the sooner. Who knows how many lives would have been lost by now? Or, what chaos and destruction he might have created."

"Into a world where there was no *Legion*," Strathmore added. "And no one with the necessary powers to defeat him."

Windermere rested a hand upon the shoulder of Leighton. "For years you have blamed yourself for doing what you were born to do. Each member of the *Legion* found their destiny that day, even Lyon. Doing what you did empowered them to help defeat Baltharach. The illness Lyon was born with also prevented Baltharach from getting strong enough to separate until you were adults."

"Suppose what you say is true, it does not change my decision to rescue Miss Sinclair."

"The young woman I met at Hampton Court was not weak," Windermere said. "There is a power to Miss Sinclair, I have not encountered before. I believe she is on the cusp of discovering her destiny. If you interfere before that happens, you may alter her revelation."

"She could die in there!" Leighton glared at his grandfather. "What if her destiny is with me? That is what I believe; what I have always believed."

"Tristan," Strathmore said in a quiet manner. "You do not know her destiny; neither does she. Give her the chance to find it. Do not try to change it to your will."

Leighton's throat contracted. His heart ached, and his soul burned with fear for Patience. "What if she dies?" he asked, his voice raw. "You do not know her. You do not know how fragile she is, or how being at Hampton Court affected her."

"It is when we are most challenged in life,"—the duke returned to his telescope— "that we realize how strong we are…and the reason we are here."

Leighton looked up once more at the night sky. He heard the wind softly blow whilst tears rose to blur his vision. "She isn't meant to be alone, grandfather. She isn't some distant star, alone, and fated to remain so."

"I agree," Windermere bent at the waist and looked through the eyepiece of Copernicus again. "I would say she is more like the moon. Illuminating, constant, and quite magical." He looked at Leighton with an enigmatic expression. "We cannot see the moon during an eclipse, but it is still there, part of us, part of our very existence."

The Earl of Strathmore patted his son on the back. "We know the depth of feeling you have for this young woman. There is a reason for everything, my son."

"You also know that Thorne changed my destiny," Leighton said to his father. "You said you were grateful he did, even though we were all warned not to alter time or the natural course of events."

Windermere pulled away from the telescope and looked at Leighton with a stern countenance. "Did he change your destiny? Did he alter what the end result should be? Or, did he follow what was his destiny to do? Do not doubt for one moment that *all* of you are necessary to defeat Baltharach."

"But how do you know my rescuing Miss Sinclair is not part of destiny, or what I am supposed to do now?"

Windermere crossed his arms and stared at Leighton. "Has it not occurred to you that leaving for London is exactly what Baltharach wants? He wants *you* to separate from the others. For you to run pell-mell into a situation you are not prepared for and cannot win."

"You presume he is aware she is in Bedlam?" Leighton asked. "That he is biding his time waiting for *me* to show up?"

"Do not doubt his intelligence," the duke replied.

"I daresay if he knows she is in there, you present another reason she needs my help. He may try to kill her again." Leighton crossed his arms and matched the duke's stance.

"He is waiting for *you.*" The duke's eyes narrowed with his rising temper. "If Miss Sinclair posed a threat to him, she would be dead now. He knows she is locked away, in a place where even if she speaks about *Baltharach* or the *Legion*, no one will believe her. Make no mistake, when she leaves Bedlam, *then* her life will be at risk. And that is why I wrote Lady Carlyle, advising she bring her niece here afterwards."

"You did?" Leighton asked.

"Yes," Windermere responded. "I am not a monster. Not without feeling. I do not want Miss Sinclair to suffer. Quite the contrary, I sensed greatness in her at Hampton Court. But I also believe as terrible a test as Bedlam may be for her, she will emerge stronger for it…and better prepared for any darkness which lies ahead."

Leighton rubbed the back of his neck, taken aback by his grandfather's words. Much as he wanted to ride like the wind to London, what if everything the duke said about Patience understanding her destiny proved true? Were her powers being strengthened? Then again, what if they were not?

"Three days," Leighton said. "If we have not heard from Lady Carlyle that Miss Sinclair is free by then, make no mistake, I will storm Bedlam and use whatever power I feel necessary."

"I think three days is fair," Strathmore contributed.

"How can you agree with this, Victor? Knowing your son has not the training to battle this demon alone."

"Did I say he would be alone?" Strathmore replied with a penetrating stare he'd inherited. "If the goal of Baltharach is to separate members of the *Legion*, to battle each one individually, what better means to thwart his plan than for all of them…and us…to assist my son?"

Windermere shook his head with obvious resignation. "So be it. Three days. Until then, I want you…and the others…training with your father and me from sunrise to sunset every day."

"So be it," Leighton said with a nod.

In the darkness of her private cell, Patience listened to the tortured screams, and anguished cries of now familiar spirits. They haunted Bedlam during the day, yet were often drowned out by wild laughter, nonsensical murmurings, and wild-eyed terror of the poor souls still living there. At night, however, the dead held the asylum hostage—and woe to the living.

Whether the violent spirits were mad or sane upon coming to Bedlam, they were all hopelessly insane now. Incapable of understanding, filled with rage, they were driven to lash out with unbridled vengeance at anyone they could…especially her.

Since being moved into isolation, she could not risk any sign of physical injury that might appear to be self-inflicted. Although she had not spoken again to Fincher after what he called the *drop bath* treatment ordered by Dr. Monro, the head steward did warn her to stop hurting herself—else the good doctor would put her in the *crib*. Whatever the *crib* might be, she had no intention of being subjected to another one of Dr. Monro's treatments.

Resolved to never be scratched, bruised, or drowned by anyone again, Patience stared at the locked door to her tiny room. If nothing else, isolation from the other patients—and a powerful, constant fiery current surging through her blood—now enabled her to create a stronger barricade of protection.

Thus, she focused on her new armor, waiting until the constant, violent spectral pounding stopped and the frustrated, howling spirits moved on.

Only then did Patience close her eyes. Her breathing eased, but she ignored the physical yearning to sleep. The night was not over, and the vicious ghosts often returned.

Instead, she visualized the one spirit she wanted to see.

A gentle breeze touched her face.

"I'm here, caileag." The voice and Gaelic word of endearment, gently spoken, warmed her heart.

Sam stood beside her bed, the presence of strength and goodness in a dark, frightening, and often hopeless place. Tears rushed forward, yet she smiled them away.

"Where have you been?" she asked. "I was worried for you."

He sat upon her bed, hands clasped together and studied her a long moment. "No need tae worry about me. Ye dinnae think I abandoned ye?"

"No, but I feared for your safety."

"My safety?" His brow furrowed. "I force myself each day tae do what yer auntie bids."

"What has Auntie Catherine asked you to do?"

"I keep watch for that hound from hell, back and forth 'tween here and Hampton Court. The ghosts there are watchin', too."

"Has he returned there?"

Sam shook his head. "Not since the night Windermere chased him away. 'Tis possible he's here in London town. He may ken where ye are and he may not. I keep watch outside these walls, day and night."

"Ever my protector," she said with a smile. "Thank you."

She studied his countenance and manner. His expression and the way he gripped his hands together concerned her. Knowing him as well as she did, it seemed obvious the Scots ghost struggled to contain a building rage.

"What is it, Sam?"

He looked at her then, his gaze pained with sorrow. "I ken what has happened tae ye in this foul place." His voice darkened. "Everyone says ye might be safer in here than out, leastways 'til that demon is found. Still, when I see that fat, pompous Sassenach doctor…"

"Dr. Monro?"

"I made my presence known tae him, in my fashion." Sam snorted. "The sod pays no heed."

"Not surprising. He does not heed the cries of the living; why would he concern himself with the dead?"

Sam stood, hands braced upon his hips, and looked about the squalor of her room. "Say the word, I will open every door so ye can leave now."

"Lyon visits each day." She smiled. "I cannot call him Mr. Courtenay anymore, not after meeting his evil twin. In any event, he also promised Auntie Catherine will get me out of here soon. Queen Charlotte is advising her."

"Aye, that she is."

For several moments Sam did not speak. Instead, he looked at her with a troubled expression, as if debating what he should say. Then, with a heavy sigh, he walked over to the small, high window of her cell. In profile, he lifted his face to the night air. "They found another body, same as the Melville lass."

"When? Who?"

"Some English woman. From what I ken, the lady was last seen gettin' into her coach after leavin' the house of a Mr. Knightly." Sam looked at her with a quirked brow. "Ever hear of him?"

"No."

"No matter," Sam shrugged. "They suspect the coachman, but we both ken who did it."

"I wonder why he didn't destroy her body," Patience whispered. "Clearly, he wanted this woman's body to be found. But, why?" She stood and crossed to stand beside Sam. "What was her name?"

He hesitated then spoke. "Evangeline Bailey."

"I've heard that name before." Patience rubbed her brow, as if doing so might clear the haze on her memory.

"The lady with the necklace," she gasped. "The lady who wore the necklace Anne took with her the night she ran away."

"Aye."

"Then Knightly must be a friend of…"

"Leighton."

Instinctively, Patience covered her mouth with both hands, frightened by the revelation.

"What do ye remember?" Sam asked.

Patience released a shuddering breath. "The night Baltharach tried to kill me, Anne's brother arrived. You were there, remember? He said this Miss Bailey had been wearing his family's necklace. Leighton and Mr. Knightly stopped Mr. Melville from fighting with someone named Hunter."

Sam nodded. "This Hunter and Knightly are *Legion* members. Along with that black-hearted earl that told Henley where tae find ye."

Too weary to stand any longer, Patience returned to her bed. Once seated, she situated a blanket atop the cloak she wore. Still, she shivered.

"Baltharach must have killed her that same night." She spoke in a quiet voice. "Melville said he wanted them to turn against one another. He must have left her body so one of them might be suspected of the crime. Does Leighton know? Do they all know about what happened to Miss Bailey?"

"They do now. The Lord Chancellor questioned them and Knightly's servants. Miss Bailey left alone, in her coach. Nae seen again—or her driver—after that night. The public has been told she was killed by her coachman. Nae details about how."

Patience stared at the locked door to her room. Although she'd been able to create a better defense against the thousands of ghosts haunting her at Bedlam, how could she stop Baltharach? If he were intent upon killing her, she would be trapped with no means of escape.

She caught Sam staring at her, and tried to offer a reassuring smile.

He sat beside her, shoulders rounded in a weary manner. "We never should have left Scotland, caileag. I told ye, nae good would come of this."

"Some good came of it. Anne is safe."

Clearly surprised by her answer, he snickered. "I suppose that's one way of lookin' at this mess."

"Tell me some good news. How is my sweet, Henrietta? Does she miss me?"

"Aye." Sam smiled. "She has taken a fancy to Lyon. He walks her each day."

"He is such a kind man, isn't he?"

"If ye can get beyond the fact he looks like that devil."

Patience shivered at the reminder of Baltharach. "They are different as night from day."

"He wrote a letter to Leighton. Yer aunt had me deliver it."

"You saw Leighton? Is he coming for me?"

"He had a fierce talk with the duke and his father. He fears for ye, and was determined to come at once. The duke warned of a trap. Said 'twas best to let yer auntie free ye...with the help of the Queen."

"I see." Patience considered the implications of Sam's words. She bundled herself deeper within the blanket, and tried to hide her shivering. "Do *you* think it would be a trap?"

"What do I know of traps? I'm sittin' in an English madhouse talkin' to ye when we should both be in Scotland."

She laughed softly. Comfort, reminiscent of a warm hug stirred inside her blood. "You know what, Sam? I am tempted to have you open the doors, chase away all the mean spirits, and distract the stewards. Then, I could escape and be free. We could disappear, and no one would know."

"Is that what ye want?"

"I do dream about Scotland." She sighed. "Isn't that strange? The place I thought a prison is heaven on earth to me now." She gathered her long hair and twisted it into a knot at the back of her neck. "I truly feared I would die in here. In truth, I think part of me has died in here."

"And now?"

"I can be strong a while longer. I have learned how to better protect myself. 'Tis difficult; I must remain awake each night, all night. I try to sleep during the day, but then must deal with the living."

"Ye look like a bag of bones. Do they nae feed ye?"

"I would not call it food, but Lyon is able to bring some tasty broth, tea, and fruit each time he comes. And he reads to me. They will not let me keep any books. At least they agreed to let me have a clean gown, proper bed, and bedding."

"Cursed Sassenachs."

"Lyon is English, Sam. They are not all bad."

"How ye can say that in this prison is beyond me." He quirked a brow at her. "And what of this Leighton. Ye still intend to marry him?"

"Marry?" She smiled wistfully. "I don't think I truly believed that dream would come true. Now, I dream of being free. To breathe fresh air. To walk in the sunshine. To see the sky reflected in the loch at *Ceòthar Innis*. Problem is, I have seen Baltharach. No one—living or dead—will be safe when such evil exists. When the battle is won, and he is gone forever, then we can all dream again."

"What can I do tae help ye now? Ye need rest."

"Seeing you, and talking with you tonight, has helped me more than you know. 'Tis better you watch for Baltharach. The *Legion* will need to know his whereabouts. But keep your distance. Do not get close to him. Promise me."

"Get close to him? Only if he tries to harm ye."

"Do not fret for me, Sam." Hoping to ease his worry, she grinned. "This place cannot hold a MacGregor."

“Aye, ‘tis clear yer a MacGregor. Dinnae let them win. Be strong, caileag. Even when the body falters, the spirit must soar.”

She reached out and rested her hand atop his, startling him in the process. He stared with wonderment at her mortal hand resting atop his iridescent mist-like hand.

“Something is happening to me, Sam,” she whispered. “It started at Hampton Court. I feel as if an image long shrouded in mist grows vivid and clearer. I do not yet understand what its purpose might be, but I do know—what Henley thought would destroy me, is only making me stronger.”

Chapter 46

The Prince Regent could not take his eyes off the woman. In silence, he watched Sir Henry Halford, Royal Physician, examine the stone-like remains of Evangeline Bailey, a woman long admired for her beauty. Next to the doctor, also scrutinizing the remains, stood Lord Eldon, the Lord Chancellor.

Beside the Prince Regent were his brother, the Duke of Clarence, and Mr. Edward Courtenay.

He glanced at his younger brother. "You say the body of Miss Melville was also found in this condition?"

"Yes." The Duke of Clarence looked at his son. "Edward saw the villain, as did Windermere. The coroner was summoned, as well as Eldon."

With a nod, the Prince Regent indicated for them to distance themselves from Halford and the Lord Chancellor. They exited the room where they could speak more privately.

"I agree this matter should be contained," the Prince Regent said. "I have confidence Eldon will see the matter resolved with great discretion, and Prime Minister Jenkins should be apprised. What, if anything, can be done to prevent other such killings?"

With both his father and the Prince Regent looking at him, Courtenay saw their concern and curiosity. Unfortunately, he could not tell them about the *Legion* or the powers of its members. Such a revelation would be made when deemed appropriate by Windermere, and made directly to the Lord Chancellor.

Aware he had to speak, Courtenay cleared his throat. "There is one person who can identify Baltharach. She has the ability to see beyond his mortal disguise."

"You speak of Lady Carlyle's niece?" the Prince Regent asked. "The young woman confined within Bethlem Royal Hospital?"

"Yes, sir." Courtenay glanced toward the closed door to the examination room. "Lady Carlyle is diligently attempting to have Miss Sinclair released into her custody."

"We have one witness who can identify this…creature…and she is in a madhouse?" The Prince Regent looked to his brother. "Does Eldon know this?"

"Eldon knows only Miss Sinclair was almost killed by the fiend, not that she has the ability to see through his *disguise*. For that matter, neither did I." Clarence looked at his eldest living son. "What else have you not told me, Edward?"

Courtenay released a heavy breath. "Sir, Miss Sinclair's family believed her mad because they do not know she has the ability to see and communicate with spirits. I assure you, the young woman is quite sane. She also possesses an extraordinary ability which enables her to see this evil creature with greater clarity."

The two Royal brothers looked at one another, communicating something unspoken. What would they do…or think…if he were to tell them *who* Baltharach pretended to be?

At long last, the Prince Regent returned to the examination room, followed by Clarence and Courtenay. Halford and Eldon turned about as they entered the room.

"Lord Chancellor," the Prince Regent said. "I am told Lady Carlyle seeks the release of her niece from Bethlem Royal Hospital."

"I am aware, sir," Eldon replied. "I understand Her Majesty is also concerned."

"Have the young lady released post haste. She is being held there against her will, and Miss Sinclair is also our only living witness to the murderer. Return her to…" He looked at his illegitimate nephew with a raised eyebrow.

"To Lady Carlyle," Courtenay replied.

"Ah, yes," the Prince Regent said with a knowing nod. "And see that Lord Henley be informed legal guardianship of Miss Sinclair has been awarded to Lady Carlyle by the Crown."

"As you wish," Eldon replied.

"Your Highness, we should also send word to the Duke of Windermere," Courtenay added. "He wants to be present when she is released."

"Why, Windermere?" The Prince Regent questioned.

"I know why, sir." Lord Eldon glanced back at the petrified remains of Miss Evangeline Bailey then returned his attention to the Prince Regent.

"Indeed?" The Prince Regent's face colored slightly and he puffed out his chest, clearly affronted he'd not been better informed about the entire matter.

The Lord Chancellor approached until he stood before the Prince Regent. He then spoke in a quiet voice. "Windermere may have a plan to find and destroy the creature. However, he cannot yet reveal it to Your Royal Highness, or me."

Dr. Thomas Monro looked up from his desk and glared at the man in the doorway. "I have no time for you at present, Mr. Courtenay, especially if you have come to gloat. It seems I underestimated you."

"Most people usually do." Courtenay smiled. "Much as I do not wish to disturb you, I have come to see how Miss Sinclair fares today."

"No doubt, giddy as a schoolgirl." Monro braced his hands on the edge of his desk and pushed himself to a standing position. "There is no need to speak with me. If you wish to visit her now, a steward can direct you to her room. Otherwise, she will be released at half past three in the morning, and no sooner."

Courtenay crossed his arms and studied Monro. "You *are* having a bad day. Still, I daresay you should not be surprised by this outcome."

Monro snorted with derision and shuffled some papers on his desk. "And the Girtin? I suppose Lady Carlyle will no longer offer the painting in trade."

"I hardly think so."

Raising his gaze to look upon the Duke of Clarence's bastard son, Monro glared. "Then we have nothing further to discuss. As you can see, I am quite busy."

"Yes, well, I merely wanted to thank you for being so agreeable regarding Miss Sinclair, and to confirm arrangements for her release."

"I hardly had any choice in the matter, now did I?"

Courtenay answered with a polite bow. "Good day, Dr. Monro."

Chapter 47

Patience stood beneath the small, high window of her cell, her chin raised and her eyes closed. The fresh night air, cool and damp upon her face, would help keep her awake. Even now, as the living patients of Bedlam settled down, the activity of its dead patients quickened. Another long night awaited her; she must prepare herself.

Hearing movement, she turned about. Sam stood, arms braced across his broad chest, smiling at her. "The day has come…well, the night has come."

She smiled back. "Night does follow day."

"Not much to pack, eh?" He looked at her bed, the only piece of furniture in her room. "Leavin' this beddin' behind, I hope."

"What are you talking about?"

"Yer freedom," he said. "Surely Lyon told ye about it today when he visited."

Arms hugging her waist she slowly approached her friend. "Lyon didn't visit me today. I feared he might be ill and…"

Awareness hit her the same time it did Sam.

"Och, 'twas that devil then!"

Pressing both hands against her breast, hoping to calm her racing heart, Patience struggled to catch her breath. "Is Lyon dead? Did he kill him?"

"Nae, Lyon is at Carlyle House; so are the others."

"What…others?"

"The *Legion*. They will come at half past three."

"No, no, no." She paced about the room. "Are you sure 'tis Lyon inside Carlyle House?"

"Windermere is there, and Leighton's father. The duke would know if 'twasn't Lyon. It must be Lyon."

"Warn them 'tis a trap. Do you not see? He knows! Baltharach knows they are coming for me. He wants them to come here."

"Mayhap they can destroy him? They are all together."

"Go tell them anyway. They must be prepared."

No sooner had her words been spoken than Sam disappeared amidst a swift, frigid breeze. Not knowing what to do, Patience sat upon her bed and prayed.

She'd been waiting for so long. Now, when the hour for her deliverance was almost at hand…

"I must find a way to thwart him."

Not knowing the hour, she could only guess by the sounds and activity within Bedlam that 'twas not long after midnight. Realizing she'd been too impulsive sending Sam away, Patience looked at her locked door. Her heart pounded with trepidation.

Could she do what must be done?

Could she fight her way out?

Closing her eyes, she concentrated upon minimizing her means of protection, and listened. Then, from what seemed the bowels of Bedlam, she heard the wails begin.

Bracing herself, she stood before the door.

Watching.

Waiting.

Preparing for the moment, it would open.

I can do this. I walked into the ghost world at Hampton Court and found my way out. I faced Baltharach before. I can do it again.

"I will not die," she whispered. "Not now."

At once, the door to her cell flew open and a rush of foul-smelling, icy air almost overwhelmed her. Wraith-like spirits sneered at her, their eyes wild with madness.

Clenching her fists, she charged into the fray, employing her new ability to push those in her way aside. Then, with what little strength she had in her legs, she ran down the corridor.

Skeleton-like arms and fingers propelled at her like sails of a ghostly windmill. Grotesque faces, with mouths distorted by the ear-piercing wails they made, surrounded her.

Again and again, they tried to ensnare her, to restrain her as they had so often been restrained in life. They pulled her hair, but still she ran. One man took hold of her right arm. She lashed out at him. To her surprise, he slammed against the wall, and the hue of his spectral body changed from putrid green to a gray mist-like vapor.

Upon seeing what she'd done, her other tormenters howled and screamed all the louder, continuing to chase her. The icy temperature of Bedlam proclaimed she had indeed entered their world. And, to be expected, their number soon increased.

Malicious spirits rose by the hundreds, and lined the halls of Bedlam from floor to ceiling. Some were nothing more than disembodied heads. Some were not violent, but ghosts who seemed frightened of her. Others still wore chains and tried to wield them.

Anxious, desperate, she looked for the door leading outside. If there had been one at Hampton Court to guide her into the mortal world, there must be one at Bedlam. More to the point, the entrance to Bedlam had not been changed since the asylum had been built in 1675.

The oppressiveness of the air made it difficult to breathe. Her lungs felt they might burst, and her heart might well explode in her chest. Realizing she had missed the correct corridor to take, she turned around.

'Twas then a spirit behind her managed to strike her in the eye. She immediately cupped her hand over the injured area, expecting to feel blood. Relieved she'd only been punched, she started running again.

Another spirit grabbed her from the left, holding tight to the fabric of her cloak. She jerked the material away and swept him aside with more force than she'd thought capable of possessing.

Unfortunately, the strength of her body grew weaker by the power she wielded to physically push away the spirits. It seemed she stumbled more than she ran, but the door was in sight.

Dark, heavy, and locked.

She struggled with the door handle, ignoring the pain inflicted upon her by ghosts determined to keep her prisoner.

There were no compassionate Hampton Court spirits to open this door. These ghosts attacking were either unable or unwilling to let her go free. Thus, like Catherine Howard, she pounded on the door, yet the name she screamed was, "SAM!"

The moment the door opened, Patience collapsed at his feet. Unable to lift her, Sam knelt beside her.

"Caileag, you must stand. Step out of this hell with me now."

Too weak to move, Patience lay crumpled on the mist-covered floor. She looked at him through the only eye that seemed to be open. With shaking arms, she attempted to push her body upright, only managing to raise her torso.

At once, the hostile spirits of Bedlam swarmed, determined to pull her deeper back into their world. Sam stood and towered over her body, yelling and fighting hand-to-hand with the multitude of savage spirits rushing toward the doorway.

"Leave me, Sam." Her throat felt raw enough to bleed.

"Get on yer feet!" Sam shouted. "Step over the threshold, and we can leave this madness forever."

Again, Patience pushed her seemingly weighted body, this time into a position whereby she might crawl from the doorway. Before she could inch her way forward, someone lifted her body. Between locks of hair in her face, her swollen eye, and the position of her body, she could not see who had come to her rescue.

Then, like a long sealed entrance to a tomb, she heard the door slam shut behind her. She struggled to twist out of the man's arms, to make sure Sam was safe.

"Sam," she cried. "I cannot leave him."

"You didn't," said the unfamiliar voice.

He shifted her body over like a small child being tossed high in someone's arms. For the first time, she saw who rescued her from the ghost world of Bedlam.

Patience stiffened in the arms of Marcus Hawthorne, the earl who told her stepfather where to find her. The man responsible for her being committed to Bedlam.

"You," she managed to whisper.

"Me," he replied then put her effortlessly in the arms of another man. "We best get the blazes out of here," Hawthorne called in a louder voice.

Patience looked to see the other members of the *Legion* standing beside horses and a waiting carriage. She glanced up at the man who now held her, and saw the angry face of Leighton.

"How did he do that? she asked. "How could he go into their world and get me?"

"I will explain later." Leighton gently placed her inside the carriage, where she saw Lyon waited. Leighton kissed her hand and looked at his friend. "Hold her safe. I am about to drive this coach like the devil himself will be chasing us."

"He may well be," Lyon replied.

Chapter 48

Leighton's Town House, London

"I daresay I will never forget the sound of Miss Sinclair pounding on the door, screaming for her friend." The Earl of Strathmore handed his father a glass of brandy. "Or, my son's reaction when we charged inside Bedlam and she wasn't anywhere to be found. The stewards came rushing toward us like we were mad. Yet we all heard her screaming from that other world, even Dr. Monro."

"Not an experience he will likely forget either," the duke replied.

Both father and son looked up when Leighton entered the room, his expression fraught with worry, his manner agitated. Behind him, Courtenay entered.

"Where are the others?" Courtenay asked.

"Stationed about the house," the duke replied. "We should be safe here from Baltharach. We are well protected against evil."

"Tristan, how fares Miss Sinclair?" Strathmore studied his son, noting his hands shook when pouring himself a drink.

"Battered. Bruised. Exhausted. A hot bath has been prepared and the women are tending her." Leighton faced his father. "Blast it all, we waited too long. For what? We could have all come to town at once and saved her from enduring that terror."

"Perhaps," the duke said. "However, the young lady found her own way to escape Bedlam, one that proved most enlightening."

"Enlightening?" Leighton glared at his grandfather. "This is your fault. I never should have listened to you. She has a black eye. She has lost so much weight, she felt like a child in my arms. Did you see her? Did you see how weak she is? How fragile? And where exactly is Baltharach? He wasn't there. No doubt, he toys with us yet again."

"Because of the bravery and ingenuity Miss Sinclair took, the timing of our plan changed." The duke looked at the longcase clock, noting the hour. "He may be there in two hours, at the designated time, only to find she is gone…and so are we."

"Admittedly, what she did was very brave," Courtenay stood before the hearth, arms folded across his chest. "Having said that, if Thorne had not been with us, would we have been able to get her out from that hidden realm?"

"Perhaps," Windermere murmured.

"And perhaps not." Courtenay shot a knowing look to Leighton.

"Alright, Lyon, the irony of Thorne being able to get her out does not escape me." Leighton downed his drink and poured another. "Then again, she would not have been there, if not for him."

"Is Lady Carlyle sitting with her tonight?" Strathmore asked.

"Yes," Leighton replied. "She is in the bedchamber next to Miss Sinclair, and the little maid, Gates, will be sleeping in an adjoining dressing room. The countess agreed it would be safer for her niece at *Aldebaran.* She will, of course, accompany Miss Sinclair, and insisted her servants be protected. They are all here now."

"Should be quite the caravan," Strathmore mused. "You realize the greater our number of travelers, the more delays we shall likely encounter."

"I admire Lady Carlyle's concern for her people," Courtenay replied. "Having been a guest of her home, I am most impressed. They are family to her. We cannot risk them being harmed."

"Finding Miss Sinclair removed from Bedlam, and Carlyle House empty should quite irritate Baltharach." The duke stood and stretched his long arms.

He then proceeded to retrieve a wooden case from his coat pocket, and removed two pieces of carved ivory that, when interlocked, became a long pipe. Returning the case to his pocket, Windermere removed a drawstring leather pouch from another, and filled the pipe's bowl with his favorite fine tobacco.

No one spoke whilst the patriarch of the St. Ives family, and Elder Lightbearer prepared and lit his pipe. The simple and familiar task, in the quiet of Leighton's library, seemed to provide a sense of normalcy in the midst of upheaval.

Windermere took a long draw upon his pipe then noticed his audience. "We cannot delay too long before starting for *Aldebaran.* I realize Miss Sinclair needs rest, but we can spare two days, no more. As it is—weather permitting and with our travel party—we will not arrive for near a fortnight."

"I will go and tell the others," Strathmore said.

Leighton nodded and watched his grandfather and father leave the library. He then took the chair the duke had been occupying and looked at his dearest friend. "Lyon, how can she ever forgive me, when I cannot forgive myself?"

"You have done nothing that needs forgiveness," Courtenay replied. "She understood why you did not come, and she agreed with the reason. What needs to be done now, is to look forward."

"She will be safe at *Aldebaran*," Leighton said with a nod. "I depend upon you to remain with her in the carriage, since I must act as outrider with the others. Much as I would prefer to talk with her, I must be on guard for Baltharach and ensure our safe journey."

"Of course," Courtenay said. "I shall sing your praises, Saint. I only wish I could do more."

"You have done far more good than you realize, Lyon. I should warn you, Lady Carlyle may ride in your carriage from time-to-time. You can also expect that invisible Scotsman."

Courtenay laughed. "Ah yes, Sam. He'd make a good member of the *Legion*, eh?" Standing, he crossed to where his friend sat, and rested a hand upon Leighton's shoulder. "Go and rest while the others are on watch."

"I cannot."

"Saint, listen to me. Patience Sinclair is stronger and braver than you think. And she loves you. Never forget that."

A whirlwind of activity had happened since Patience's escape from Bedlam. Now, as she looked about her surroundings, she had the numbing sensation of feeling safe for the first time in months.

After being carried by Leighton to a guest chamber, she was reunited with her aunt, who wept with joy. Her beloved Henrietta, who cried in her own fashion, had licked Patience's face. Gates was there as well, smiling through happy tears.

A hot bath scented with lavender chased away the constant cold from Bedlam. Aches and pains were soothed, and what remained of filth and stench had been washed away. Her long, tangled hair was cleansed then treated with what looked like whipped egg whites and smelled like brandy.

Afterwards, attired in one of her linen nightdresses, Patience sat before the hearth and listened as Gates hummed whilst combing her still drying hair.

Comforted by Henrietta's head resting upon her lap, she stroked the coarse fur of her dog, and tried to push the desperate flight from the ghost realm of Bedlam out of her thoughts. No one would understand being physically attacked by ghosts, or the terrifying thought she'd be trapped with them forever.

Henrietta's brown eyes kept looking at her in a curious manner. Patience smiled then remembered her swollen eye. She gently touched the area, wincing slightly from the pain.

Thank heaven, Sam had come to open the door when he did. Hearing him fighting bravely, overwhelmed by ever-increasing violent spirits, had frightened her more than anything. Then there was the fact, Earl Hawthorne had carried her out of the ghost realm. His manner may still be abrasive, but he'd made amends for his part in having her committed.

Her heart rejoiced, remembering how it felt to see Leighton again. The love and concern in his eyes embraced her very soul. She could not bear it if anything happened to him.

All the members of the *Legion* had gathered to help her leave Bedlam—as well as the Duke of Windermere and Earl Strathmore. They were concerned not only for her safety, but for the safety of Lady Carlyle and her servants. How would she ever be able to thank them?

"Time for you to rest in bed now, Miss Patience."

Patience opened her eyes, realizing she had drifted off to sleep in the chair. She stood, balance unsteady. In understanding, Gates helped her walk to the tester bed. Once settled beneath the comfort of fine linens and warm blankets, she took hold of Gates' hand.

"Thank you, Gates. Do you have a place to sleep?"

"Yes, Miss Patience." Gates' hazel eyes glistened in the dimly lit room. "Lord Leighton made sure we were all taken care of here. I shall be in the dressing room,"—she pointed to another door— "close at hand should you need me."

"This is a bachelor's home," Patience said. "I doubt other women have been guests here. Lord Leighton must feel invaded. I do not want to be of trouble to him."

"You conquered his lordship's heart long ago, Miss Patience."

Patience closed her eyes, savoring the peaceful quiet of the house. "Is Henrietta still sleeping before the fire?"

"Yes, Miss Patience."

"Good…I want her to…stay…with me."

Chapter 49

Kirkstone Pass, English Lake District

The wind whistled, loud, forceful. It soared across the *fells* and rose against the mountains and crags. Somewhere close, a hawk cried, no doubt in search of its morning meal. Yet what woke Patience after drifting to sleep was the stillness of Leighton's coach. She looked out the window. Their long procession had stopped.

A light dusting of snow on the ground muted vibrant shades of greens and intermittent tufts of taller brown grass. Here and there some of the dry, white ice crystals collected in crevices on drystone walls bordering either side of the narrow road.

Much like Scotland, the weather in northwest England could be unpredictable, especially in the high, remote area they now traveled.

Still, why had they stopped?

They'd been traveling an hour, no more—not long enough to rest the horses. Besides which, from what Leighton had told her when next they stopped, they would be at *Aldebaran*. Eleven days after their journey began, this last mountain pass would end their journey.

Patience gathered her cloak about her shoulders. Perhaps walking Henrietta might prove a good excuse to investigate the delay? Having adjusted the leather lead about her dog's collar, she touched the door latch when a hand stopped her.

"What do you think you are doing?"

"We've stopped moving," she answered.

"I realize that," Courtenay replied. "Most likely another traveler comes from the opposite direction. We will start up again in a moment."

"Henrietta needs to be walked."

"I walked her this morning before we left the inn."

She looked out the window again. "What are they doing?"

Courtenay quirked a brow. "Do you want me to investigate?"

"No, *I* want to investigate."

With an exaggerated sigh, he extended his gloved hand for Henrietta's lead. Once the three of them exited the coach, they noted the Duke of Windermere's coach at the head of their procession had stopped for a large flock of black-faced sheep blocking the road.

"Aren't they sweet?" She moved toward the woolly creatures. "I love sheep."

"Of course, you do." Courtenay chuckled and followed dutifully with her dog in tow. Unfortunately, at that point, Henrietta bolted free, racing toward the animals.

At once, she and Courtenay gave chase, until a tall gentleman single-handedly stopped Henrietta's flight. Standing in the midst of the road where he'd obviously been trying to move the stubborn flock, Leighton frowned.

He always frowned whenever he saw her now. In truth, he'd been surly and distant since they'd started on this journey. The only times he spoke were to tell her to eat more or rest. Then he and the other men huddled together and talked about how far they would travel each day. What precautions must be taken, and what arrangements had been made for coaching inns along the way. At times they argued. Some complained the journey was too slow, and they should not have taken the Great North Road out of London.

It soon became obvious—at least to her—the duke had chosen the route. She had to admit the man had considerable influence over others. Never had that been more apparent than when their entire party was hosted as welcomed guests at a grand manor house in Kedleston.

Unsure whether she should continue toward the adorable but clearly dimwitted sheep, Patience paused. The man who had become like a brother to her had refastened Henrietta's lead and allowed her to further intimidate the sheep. Indeed, Courtenay encouraged Henrietta.

"Well done," he said. "Tell them to move along."

Mr. Melville and Mr. Knightly were more afield, trying to herd the sheep off the road. She glanced behind to see if anyone else had decided to stretch their legs. Lady Carlyle's coach rested third in the procession. No doubt, she conversed with an invisible spirit named Sam.

Whaley, first footman Nicholas, as well as Lady Carlyle's maid, and Gates rode in the fourth carriage. The other Carlyle live-in servants were traveling to *Aldebaran* by post chaise—and may already be there.

Fifth in line, Mr. Knightly's beautiful sapphire blue coach completed their line of carriages. Intended as an extra conveyance should they need it, the coach also provided shelter for the *Legion* during inclement weather.

Then there were the fine horses the gentlemen used as outriders. She squinted and saw Lords Hawthorne and Hunter conversely rather heatedly. Either Hunter voiced concern about the restless horses waiting for their riders, or Hawthorne had said something disagreeable.

Inhaling deeply of the fresh, clean air, Patience studied their surroundings. Leighton called this road the Kirkstone Pass. Much as she enjoyed being in the country, and the beautiful scenery, this isolated, remote stretch of road disturbed her.

"You need to return to my coach," said a familiar voice.

She looked at Leighton. "Are you angry with me?"

"No." His brow furrowed. "Why would you ask me that?"

"You always seem out of sorts; I was concerned."

A gentle smile came to his eyes. "I could never be angry with you." His gaze drifted to the other coaches. "When we get to *Aldebaran* today, you and I will have time to talk about everything."

She returned his smile, but a distraction caught her eye. A heavyset man approached Lyon and her dog. Cap in hand, he had unkempt brown hair and walked with a slight limp.

"He must be the owner of those beasts." Leighton started to walk away, but Patience tugged on his arm.

"It's him," she whispered, her throat constricted.

Leighton eyed her warily then looked back at the stranger. "Are you sure?"

"Do you not sense evil?"

Leighton paled and shot off after his friend. "Lyon!" He then shouted for Melville and Knightly, but they had moved too far away in their attempt to clear the road.

Patience ran as well, unsure what to do but hoping she might be able to help in some way. She had neared enough to hear Courtenay ask the man a question, but Henrietta's wild barking drowned out the words.

As Courtenay struggled to restrain her dog from attacking the stranger, and distance himself at the same time, Windermere and Strathmore exited their coach and stood with Leighton.

"We cannot strike Lyon." Leighton said.

"We may have no choice," Strathmore replied.

At that point, the stranger stopped speaking with Courtenay and smiled, as if he'd heard their words, or perhaps their thoughts.

Undeterred, no longer concerned with whatever the St. Ives Family Lightbearers planned to do, Patience sprinted forward, darting around any sheep blocking her path.

She alone understood how quickly Baltharach could strike. She'd seen it before. And the closer she neared, the more she saw the signs of

Baltharach's face emerging. Terrified for Lyon, and her sweet Henrietta, she tried to create her iron shield—the one that had helped protect her in Bedlam. If she could get close enough...

"You think you can stop me?" Baltharach shouted at Leighton, but then directed his attention upon her.

"Hurry," he teased then laughed. "Who do you want to save, Miss Sinclair?"

Out of breath, she stood beside Courtenay. "Both of them."

"What are you doing?" Courtenay asked. "I'm half-dead already. Take Henrietta and leave me."

She looked at her friend, noting how weak and pale he appeared—as if all the blood in his body had been removed. Yet Baltharach hadn't transformed. How could Courtenay be hurt? Then she noticed one lethal talon visible on Baltharach's hand, dripping with blood.

"No, no, no." Tears rushed to her eyes, cascading down her cheeks. "You cannot die, Lyon. Please."

She turned on Baltharach. "WHY?"

He shrugged, still maintaining his disguise as a drover. "It had to be done, despite the fact he proved useful to me at one time. In my own way, I was merciful."

Baltharach glanced at the others. "Look at them. They are useless. You showed more bravery than they."

Courtenay stumbled, and fell upon the ground. Releasing his hold on Henrietta, he then pressed a hand against his side where dark red blood saturated his coat.

"Go, Henrietta!" Patience commanded then dropped to her knees. Trying to comfort a now shivering Courtenay, she removed her cloak and pressed the wool fabric against his wound.

Suddenly, what felt like a wall of flames came from out of nowhere. She looked over her shoulder and saw the mysterious fire had struck Baltharach in the back.

At the same time, wave after wave of blinding rings of light struck the demon's chest with such force he howled and changed into black granules that lifted, changed direction, and flew away.

How and what had happened, she knew not.

"See,"—Courtenay looked at her and shuddered with pain— "I told you she was brave."

Patience realized Courtenay was talking to someone else, and looked up to see Leighton, his grandfather, his father, and the *Legion* stood about them. United in their grief, all of their expressions were stunned, devastated, and…lost.

Leighton knelt beside her, and grimaced at the wound inflicted upon his friend.

The other members followed suit around their fallen comrade. They spoke words of assurance. Promising he would survive, that they would take him to the coaching inn and tend his wound.

Patience knew the truth, and so did dear, kind, *Lyon.*

Struggling against emotion, Leighton held the hand of his dying friend. He watched as his grandfather rested a hand upon Courtenay's pale brow and recited a soft prayer.

Opening his eyes, Courtenay looked at all of them. "I am not dead yet." His attempt at humor conjured no smiles.

"We should move him," Thorne said. "Take him to that coaching inn. Where is it?"

"No," Courtenay said, his voice calm. "Death wins this time."

"Death did not do this to you," Melville charged.

Courtenay coughed. Speckles of blood appeared on his lip. Leighton wiped them away with his hand.

"You must all promise me…" Courtenay struggled to remain focused and speak. "I want Miss Sinclair to take my place in the *Legion.*"

Everyone stared, confused by his words.

"You need her," Courtenay continued. He looked at Leighton. "You always said I reminded you of your humanity. To remember you are not…"

"Gods," Leighton answered.

"She will do…the same." His brown eyes sought the duke's attention. "Powers…she does not realize. He knows it."

Wracked with a spasm of coughing, Courtenay fought for air, not ready to depart their midst. "Promise me." He looked at Hawthorne. "Promise… *me.*"

"I promise," Hawthorne replied, the words gruff with emotion.

"We all promise," the duke said. "Miss Sinclair will join the *Legion*, and we *will* destroy Baltharach."

Leighton glanced at his grandfather, stunned the duke had voiced his support as well. If he spoke the words, they became a sacred vow—one he would forever defend.

"Patience…" Courtenay whispered.

Leighton called for Patience. Standing beside Lady Carlyle, she returned quickly and dropped to her knees. "Yes, Lyon."

"He didn't… kill… my soul."

"No." She gently brushed strands of windblown dark hair out of his eyes.

"I may haunt…you."

She smiled through her tears. "No, sweet Lyon, you will find peace. The angels have come for you. See. They are here now."

His gaze lifted to the sky with a look of wonder. "So they are."

Chapter 50

Aldebaran Castle ~ Lakes District, England

The funeral was over. A month after his death, Edward FitzWilliam Lyon Courtenay had *officially* been laid to rest in the St. Ives family chapel at *Aldebaran*. Now, as the Prince Regent, the Duke of Clarence, the Lord Chancellor, and even Prime Minister Jenkinson, met in private with his grandfather and father, Leighton wanted nothing more than to clear his head.

He didn't want to consider what the duke told men—whose lives revolved around power—about the *Legion*. He didn't want to relive what happened in the ruins of a Roman temple years ago. Or, to demonstrate abilities they could never understand. For that matter, neither did Thorne, Hunter, Melville, or Knightly.

Instead, all Leighton wanted was to ease the pain in his heart. He wanted to find some measure of hope for the future. To feel undeniable certainty that good still existed in the world. That light would always conquer darkness.

He wanted to…believe.

Who can I confide in now? Leighton asked himself.

He thought upon his friend's dying words, and his request that Patience Sinclair replace him as a member of the *Legion.* Much as he wanted to honor that request, how could he consciously put the woman he loved in a position of unknown danger?

And yet, had she not consistently demonstrated a strength and courage that astonished even his grandfather? At a moment when he wasted precious moments strategizing with his father and the duke when to strike Baltharach without harming Courtenay, Patience had raced toward the murderous fiend and faced him.

What might he have done differently that morning in Kirkstone Pass? So close to the end of their journey, did they become reckless? Less guarded? God help them. They'd been distracted by a flock of bleating sheep.

Every member of the *Legion* had been separated.

If they had been more vigilant, could they have prevented Courtenay's death? Standing together, side-by-side, could they have destroyed Baltharach?

He stood alone on the grand terrace overlooking the formal garden at *Aldebaran.* Inspired by the gardens at Versailles, two adjoining parterres with circular reflecting ponds featured stone fountains. In the distance, sunlight glistened on the waters of Lake Windermere. Reminding himself that grown men do not cry, he blamed the sunlight for the tears gathering in his eyes.

Using the heel of his hands, he wiped them away.

And then he saw her. As stunning as the garden appeared with its emerald green turf and flowers in brilliant bloom, nothing compared to the vision of Patience Sinclair in the garden with a book and her faithful Henrietta.

She is stronger and braver than you think, Leighton said to himself, remembering what Courtenay said about Patience before they left London.

"And she loves me," he repeated aloud.

He watched as she selected *his* favorite spot to sit—facing the distant lake—then opened her book.

Try as she might to concentrate on the third volume of *The Faerie Queen*, Patience Sinclair could not.

Someone was watching her.

Seated next to her, Henrietta turned her head, then stood and rushed toward whoever approached.

Standing, Patience turned and saw Tristan St. Ives. He had paused to pet her wolfhound then raised his gaze to her. From a distance, she could see his eyes glistened and were more turquoise than green. She had watched him closely during the funeral. How beautifully he had read from the Scriptures, never once faltering in voice or composure. Never once showing the depth of his pain.

She saw it now.

Noting uncertainty in his expression, she approached. Then, standing before him, she gently touched the side of his face. "You are in pain. But he is not far from us. Lyon will always be with us, and we will keep his memory alive."

"Yes," he replied, and kissed her palm. "Will you walk with me?"

Taking his arm, they wandered toward the far end of the garden. From there they looked back at the castle with its turrets, towers, and steeped terraces. Radiant in the sunlight, the cream-colored stone looked almost white. Yet they turned their faces toward the water, and let the breeze rising off Windermere soothe their sadness.

He squeezed her hand gently. "We need to talk about the *Legion.* Lyon wanted you to take his place, Patience. Will you? We need you. *I* need you."

She considered his words. "And the others? Do they agree with allowing me…a woman…to join their secret group?"

He smiled for the first time. "In truth, I think we will be lost without you."

"I will join, on one condition."

"What condition?" He quirked an eyebrow.

"That you all no longer hide your abilities, but use them to help others. And I shall do the same."

COMING 2016

THE LEGION OF MITHRAS

Echoes from the Darkness

Glossary of Terms, People & Places

[F – Fiction, NF – Nonfiction, D - Dialect]

Aldebaran – [F] Family seat for Duke of Windermere, located in the Lakes District. *Aldebaran* is a 17th century castle and fortress protected by the St. Ives family's *Lightbearer* mystical power. Situated in one of its towers is an astronomical observatory with shuttered dome.

Bethlem Royal Hospital – [NF] Originally a religious priory (1247), became a hospital for the sick (1330), controlled by the City of London. Mentally ill patients first admitted (1337). In time, the hospital only admitted mentally ill individuals, and patients were called inmates. After 1557, management of hospital transferred to Governors of Bridewell; Keeper hired to operate facility. Keeper replaced by a Keeper-Physician (1619). King Charles I ordered investigation into allegations of mismanagement, embezzlement and neglect (1634), after which, Keeper-Physician position was eliminated. Apothecary, non-resident physician, and visiting surgeon then hired by the Governors. In 1675, due to complaints regarding noise, stench, and unsightliness of facility, hospital relocated from Bishopsgate to Moorfields, just outside the city. In 1700, inmates were finally referred to as "patients". Most patients were kept in form of restraint; patients considered violent were left manacled day and night. Requirements for admittance was someone's word against you, family member, friend, acquaintance, stranger, etc. Getting into the hospital now notoriously known as ***Bedlam*** was easy; getting out proved nearly impossible. In 1728, team of three caregivers was replaced by James Monro as Principal Physician. Monro had total control of facility and patient care. The Monro family would thereafter retain control of facility for 135 years. Patients were categorized as "curables" or "incurables"; however, wards to separate the groups did not occur until 1725-1734. Corruption, inhumane treatment, neglect, and unsanitary conditions continued. For more information, visit AKB blog post at:
http://ashleykathbilsky.com/2015/05/21/bedlam-a-historical-perspective-of-englands-first-institution-for-the-mentally-ill/

Bedlam - [NF] See Bethlem Royal Hospital.

Bridewell, Governors of – [NF] Bridewell Prison and Hospital created for the "punishment of the disorderly poor" and to provide housing for homeless children in the City of London (1553). A Court of Governors governed Bridewell, as well as Bethlem Royal Hospital.

Brunswick, Dowager Duchess – [NF] The Princess Augusta Frederica of Great Britain was the daughter of King George II; elder sister of King George III. (b. 31 Jul 1737; d. 23 Mar 1813). Married Charles William Ferdinand, Duke of Brunswick-Wolfenbüttel (16 Jan 1764). Their daughter, *Princess Caroline of Brunswick* later married Prince Regent, and became Queen Consort of the United Kingdom when he inherited throne as George IV. [Fact: On Thursday, 01 Apr 1813, while attempting to prepare for the burial of the Dowager Duchess of Brunswick at Windsor, a wall was broken, revealing another burial vault. By command of the Prince Regent, an investigation was made to enter this vault and identify the coffins, and if one of them contained the missing remains of King Charles I. The Prince Regent was present when entering the vault, whereupon the coffins of Henry VIII, Jane Seymour, and Charles I were located. Also present was Sir Henry Halford. Halford later provided a full accounting of the investigation to the Royal College of Physicians, detailing the event and positive identification of King Charles I.]

Bushy House – [NF] Royal residence, Duke of Clarence. Situated in Teddington, South West London, overlooking Bushy Park, the residence was granted to William, Duke of Clarence, in 1797 along with his appointment by King George III as Ranger of Bushy Park.

Bushy Park – [NF] Approximately 1100 acres situated in London Borough, Richmond Upon Thames. In 1529, when Henry VIII seized Hampton Court Palace from Cardinal Wolsey, he also seized control of three adjacent parks (Hare Warren, Middle Park, and Bushy Park), thence creating a vast deer-park for hunting. King Charles I created 19-km canal called Longford River, directing water to Hampton Court Palace and numerous ponds. The Arethusa Fountain, designed by Sir Christopher Wren, was also created at this time.

Caileag – [D, NF] Scots-Gaelic for lass, little girl, daughterling, term of endearment. (kalag)

Carlyle House – [F] London residence of Catherine MacGregor, Lady Carlyle.

Ceòthar Innis – [F] Ancestral home of MacGregor clan located in Western Highlands; inherited by Patience MacGregor Sinclair from her paternal grandmother, Margaret MacGregor Sinclair. Name translates from Scots-Gaelic into English as "misty island".

Charlotte, Queen – [NF] Sophia Charlotte of Mecklenburg-Strelitz (b. 19 May 1744; d. 17 Nov 1818), married King George III 08 Sep 1761. Queen consort of Great Britain and Ireland. After 1801, and the union of the two kingdoms, she became Queen of the United Kingdom of Great Britain and Ireland. Amateur botanist, patroness of the arts, she had 15 children, 13 of whom survived to adulthood.

Copernicus – [F] In relation to The Legion of Mithras novels, Copernicus refers to the Great Refractor Telescope at *Aldebaran.*

Cosway, Richard – [NF] Noted for his miniatures, Richard Cosway was a leading portrait painter during the Regency period. (b. 05 Nov 1742; d. 04 Jul 1821)

Courtenay, Edward 'Lyon' – [F] Edward FitzWilliam Lyon Courtenay, known as 'Lyon' to his close friends (b. 14 Aug 1788) Member, Legion of Mithras, illegitimate son to Duke of Clarence; younger brother to William Henry Courtenay.

Courtenay, William Henry – [NF] William Henry Courtenay (b. 1784; d. 1807); illegitimate son of HRH Prince William Henry, Duke of Clarence. Joined Royal Navy as child; was drowned off Madagascar in 1807 with the crew of the HMS Blenheim.

Clarence, Duke of – [NF] HRH Prince William Henry (b. 21 Aug 1765; d. 20 Jun 1837), 3rd son of King George III (House of Hanover) and Queen Charlotte (Mecklenburg-Strelitz). Joined Royal Navy as Midshipman at 13. Lieut. Royal Navy (1785). Captain Pegasus (1786), Commander, Andromeda (1788), Rear-Admiral, Commander, Valiant (1789). Created Duke of Clarence and St. Andrews, and Earl of Munster, by King George III on 16 May 1789. Resided at *Bushy House* with mistress, Mrs. Jordan and their 10 illegitimate children. In 1811, relationship with Jordan ended. He continued to live at Bushy House with sons. Mrs. Jordan had custody of daughters, provided she not return to the stage. In 1814, she returned to the stage; the daughters returned to Bushy House and the duke's custody. On 11 Jul 1818, Duke of Clarence married Princess Adelaide of Saxe-Meinengen. Upon death of George IV (1830), the Duke inherited throne as William IV.

Deamhan – [D, F] Scots-Gaelic for fallen angel, evil spirit, demon. Patience Sinclair refers to *Baltharach* as such after her first encounter.

Droch Dubhar – [D, F] Scots-Gaelic for Evil Shadows. *Droch* translates to bad, possibly evil or intending to harm. *Dubhar* means shadow or darkness. See: Shadow Figures.

Droch Tannasg – [D, F] Scots-Gaelic for Evil Spirits. *Droch* translates to wicked, evil and/or intending to do harm. *Trannasg* translates to a wraith, phantom, the shadowy semblance of a disembodied soul. Sometimes used by Patience Sinclair when referring to soul-less, inhuman-looking phantom spirits. See: Phantom Spirits.

Eldon, The Lord – [NF] John Scott, 1st Earl of Eldon (b. 04 Jun 1751; d. 12 Jan 1838. British barrister, politician. Served as *Lord Chancellor* of Great Britain (1801-1806) (1807-1827). Chief Justice for Court of Common Pleas (1799), Entered House of Lords as Baron Eldon (1799). Created Viscount Encombe and Earl of Eldon (1821) by George IV.

Fell(s) – [D, NF] Mountains, moor-covered hills; a high, barren landscape. From Old Norse *fjall* for mountain.

Frogmore – [NF] Situated on 33 acres with private gardens in English county of Berkshire; adjoins Windsor Castle, Frogmore was country retreat for Queen Charlotte, purchased by King George III in 1792.

George IV – [NF] HRH George Augustus Frederick, eldest son of King George III and Queen Charlotte. (b. 12 Aug 1762; d. 26 Jun 1830) Became Duke of Cornwall, Duke of Rothesay at birth; created Prince of Wales. Earl of Chester a few days later. Married Caroline of Brunswick (1795); after birth of daughter, Princess Charlotte (1796), the couple separated. Named Prince Regent 05 Feb 1811 when George III's illness proclaimed him unable to act as king. The Regency Act of 1811 provided for regent to be named should a reigning monarch become incapacitated or under the age of 18. Upon the death of King George III in 1820, the Prince Regent officially ascended the throne as King George IV. George IV's daughter, Princess Charlotte, preceded him in death (1817). Thus, upon his death, his brother, William, Duke of Clarence, succeeded him, becoming King William IV.

Girtin, Thomas – [NF] English Artist (b. 18 Feb 1775; d. 09 Nov 1802) Highly respected influential etcher, English painter who played significant role in using watercolors for his paintings. A friend and rival of J.M.W. Turner, Girtin's exceptional reputation was established by his unique, romantic style capturing architecture and landscapes.

Halford, Sir Henry – [NF] MD, Royal Physician, Society Physician, Fellow and President, Royal College of Physicians (b. 02 Oct 1766; d. 09 Mar 1844) Born Henry Vaughan, second son of Dr. James Vaughan of Leicester. Graduated Christ Church, Oxford with a B.A. (1788) and M.D. (1791). After practicing medicine in Edinburgh, and also with his father in Leicester, Dr. Henry Vaughan moved to London. Elected physician to Middlesex Hospital (1793). Appointed Physician Extraordinary to King George III (1792), Elected Fellow, Royal College of Physicians (1794). Married Hon. Elizabeth Barbara St. John, daughter of Lord St. John (1795). Inherited large property upon death of Lady Denbigh (widow of his mother's cousin), Sir Charles Halford, 7th Baronet (1800). Changed surname from Vaughan to Halford by Act of Parliament (1809). King George III created him Sir Henry Halford, 8th Baronet, the same year. Sir Henry Halford served as personal physician to the Royal Family, including George III, George IV, William IV, and Queen Victoria. Elected President, Royal College of Physicians (1820), a position he held until his death in 1844.

Hampton Court Palace – [NF] Historic Royal Palace situated on the north bank of the River Thames in present-day Richmond-Upon-Thames. Thomas Wolsey acquired the property from Order of St. John of Jerusalem (1514). Wolsey spent 7 years building Hampton Court as Renaissance palace. Cardinal Wolsey fell out of favor with Henry VIII; king seized ownership of palace (1529). Extensive remodeling and expansion to palace and grounds made by Henry VIII and each Royal resident thereafter. Hampton Court remained Royal Palace where English monarchs often resided. King George II was last king to spend time there. George III did not inhabit or frequent Hampton Court.

Hawthorne, Earl – [F] Marcus 'Thorne' Hawthorne (b. 13 Nov 1788) Member, Legion of Mithras, Member, House of Lords. Son of Anthony Hawthorne (b. 1766/d. 1796) and Lady Elizabeth Marcus (b. 1770).

Hunter, Viscount – [F] Adam Aldrich (b. 01 Dec 1788). Member, Legion of Mithras. Son of Nathaniel Aldrich, Earl Asbury.

Jenkinson, Robert - [NF] 2nd Earl of Liverpool (b. 07 Jun 1770; d. 04 Dec 1828), son of King George III's close advisor, Charles Jenkinson, later 1st Earl of Liverpool. English politician; longest serving and youngest Prime Minister of United Kingdom (1812-1827). Served as

Prime Minister through War of 1812, End of Napoleonic Wars, Congress of Vienna, the Corn Laws, Peterloo Massacre, and the Trinitarian Act of 1812. As Prime Minister, Jenkinson dealt well with the Prince Regent when George III was incapacitated. Steered country through radicalism and unrest after Napoleonic Wars. When his father became 1st Earl of Liverpool (1796), Jenkinson took courtesy title of Lord Hawkesbury and served in House of Commons. Elevated to House of Lords as Baron Hawkesbury (1803).

Kirkstone Pass –[NF] Mountain pass, English Lake District (alt. 1,489 ft.) connects Patterdale (Ullswater Valley) in north to Ambleside, (Rothay Valley) in south. Kirkstone Pass often used by drovers taking livestock to market. [Now A592.] *The Kirkstone Pass Inn,* located at the 1500 ft. high summit, has a 500-year history servicing travelers.

Knightly, Peter Cavendish – [F] Peter Cavendish Knightly, a gentleman. (b. 07 Oct 1788) Member, Legion of Mithras.

Leanaban – [D, NF] Scots-Gaelic for little one, tiny, small, or baby under one; also a term of endearment for children.

Leighton, Viscount – [F] Tristan 'Saint' St. Ives (b. 29 Oct 1788). Founder and Leader, Legion of Mithras. Eldest grandson to the Duke of Windermere; son and heir to Earl Strathmore. Lightbearer.

Lightbearer – [F] Mystical beings believed to be descendants of wizards or offspring of angels (Sons of God) who mated with mortals (Daughters of Men). A spiritually, devout race of beings that radiate light, have magical abilities, and detect as well as incapacitate evil.

Lord Chancellor – [NF] British officer of state, also known as *Lord Keeper of the Great Seal of the Realm* and *Lord High Chancellor*. The '*Seal'* symbolized Sovereign approval on state documents. Appointed by the monarch upon advice of Prime Minister. Historically, Speaker of the House of Lords, and head of the judiciary. All petitions addressed to king must be directed to *Lord Chancellor*. The Lord Chancellor also had many Ecclesiastical responsibilities for the Church of England.

MacGregor, Sam – [F] Lachlan Samuel Tyree MacGregor (b. unk; d. unk), Ghost Guardian of Ceòthar Innis of the Western Highlands and the MacGregor Clan.

MacGregor, Margaret – [F] Margaret Isobel MacGregor Sinclair (b. 03 Nov 1742; d. 01 Nov 1800) Paternal grandmother of Patience Sinclair, mother of John Malcolm Sinclair, wife of Sir Malcolm Sinclair of Caithness. Eldest daughter of Alistair MacGregor; twin sister of Catherine MacGregor, Lady Carlyle.

Melville, Anne – [F] Anne Elizabeth Melville (b. 10 Feb 1793; d.1813), sister of Charles Melville, only daughter of Arthur Henry Melville and his wife, Mary Wynne Melville.

Melville, Charles – [F] Charles Arthur Pendragon 'Dragon' Melville, a gentleman. (b. 22 Apr 1789) Only son of Arthur Henry Melville and his wife, Mary Wynne Melville. Member, Legion of Mithras.

Mithras, Legion of – [F] A secret group comprised of Earl Hawthorne, Viscount Leighton, Viscount Hunter, Mr. Peter Knightly, Mr. Charles Melville, and Mr. Edward Courtenay. Created by Viscount Leighton. The Legion was initially created to study, control, and conceal supernatural abilities of its members. The Legion also includes the Duke of Windermere and the Earl Strathmore as advisors.

Mjölnir – [NF] The hammer of Thor the Thunder God, in Norse mythology; one of the fiercest weapons, capable of leveling mountains. When thrown by Thor, into the sky, lightning is conjured.

Monro, Thomas – [NF] Dr. Thomas Monro (b. 1759; d. 13 May 1833), 5th son of Dr. John Monro and Elizabeth Culling Smith. Graduated 1787, Doctor of Medicine from Oriel College, Oxford. Employed 1787, Assistant Physician at Bethlem Royal Hospital (aka Bedlam). Admitted 1791 as Fellow of Royal College of Physicians. Succeeded his father in 1792 as Principal Physician, Bethlem Royal Hospital (aka Bedlam). Note: Dr. Thomas Monro resigned as Principal Physician due to scandal in 1816.

Mór – [D, NF] Dialect: Scots-Gaelic for big, large, great.

Netherworld – [F] Dimension between the spirit world and the mortal world; where phantom spirits are trapped.

Phantom Spirits – [F] Trapped spirits, ghosts doomed to repeat events or choices made in life. Unable to interact with the living, they manifest intermittently and without warning. (A residual or recurring haunting.)

Prince Regent - [NF] See George IV.

Royal College of Physicians – [NF] Established 1518, upon receiving Royal Charter from King Henry VIII, the College is a professional British organization of physicians of general medicine, as well as subspecialties. Charter affirmed (1523) by Act of Parliament. The primary function, as stipulated in its charter, created authority to examine and grant licenses to qualified physicians. They could punish physicians (and apothecaries) deemed unqualified or who engaged in malpractice. College conducted medical research, published findings, and created standards for classification of diseases. Also conducted lectures regarding medical matters, and became licensing body for publication of medical books. Candidates for membership must have passed examinations for the *Diploma of Membership of the Royal College of Physicians of the United Kingdom.*

Shadow Figure – [F]An undulating black mass or dense shadow that has no physical resemblance to a human or sense of its former self; an inhuman essence that remains earthbound after its spirit or soul has somehow disintegrated. Sometimes called the *Droch Dubhar* in Scots-Gaelic by Patience Sinclair.

Sinclair, John – [F] John Malcolm Sinclair (b. 25 Aug 1764; d. 31 Oct 1794), son of Sir Malcolm Sinclair and Margaret Isobel MacGregor. Father of Patience Sinclair.

Sinclair, Patience – [F] Patience MacGregor Sinclair (b. 19 Sep 1792), Visionary, Member, Legion of Mithras. Daughter of the late John Sinclair of Caithness, Scotland and Miss Juliana Randolph of Warwickshire, England (b. 1774).

St. Ives, James Matthias – [F] See Windermere, Duke.

St. Ives, Tristan – [F] See Leighton, Viscount.

St. Ives, Victor – [F] See Strathmore, Earl.

Strathmore, Earl – [F] Victor James St. Ives (b. 25 Aug 1764), firstborn son and heir to James Matthias St. Ives, Duke of Windermere. Father of Tristan St. Ives, Viscount Leighton. Married Lady Eleanora Warren, 1788. Member, House of Lords; Lightbearer.

Tisane – [NF] Term from the 14th century, an infusion of dried herbs used in a tea for medicinal purposes.

Transition Haunting – [F] Ability to cross the veil that separates the present from the past, a dream from reality, and the boundary between realms of life and death.

Veil – [F] Undetectable thresholds separating realms of life and death, past from the present, other dimensions, and doors through time and space.

Verrio – [NF] Antonio Verrio (b. c 1636; d. 15 Jun 1707) Italian-born artist, known for introducing Baroque mural paintings to England. Verrio served the Royal Family over a 30-year period. Commissioned by King William III, Verrio's work at Hampton Court Palace includes the King's Great Bedchamber, the King's Great Staircase, the King's Little Bedchamber, the Queen's Drawing Room, and the Banqueting House. In 1705, Verrio was granted an annual pension of £200 by Queen Anne and permission to keep his lodgings at Hampton Court Palace. He would later die there.

Visionary – [F] According to legend, individuals possessing this extraordinary, ancient magical power are rare. Among their powers are the ability to traverse worlds of the living and dead, to move beyond the fabric of time, to see visions, and communicate with spirits. It is believed their power originated with the Fey or *Faerie* folk.

Windermere, Duke – [F] James Matthias St. Ives (b. 14 Feb 1743), 6th Duke of Windermere, Member, House of Lords. Father of Victor St. Ives, Earl of Strathmore, grandfather to Tristan St. Ives, Viscount Leighton. Elder Lightbearer.

ABOUT THE AUTHOR

International best-selling, award-winning author, Ashley Kath-Bilsky writes Timeless Historical Romance and Historical Literary Fiction with Mystery, Suspense and/or Paranormal elements.

Woven like a delicate thread into the fabric of each Ashley Kath-Bilsky book are unforgettable characters, beautiful imagery, compelling, suspenseful plots, as well as a timeless romance and enduring love story you'll always remember.

Interested in genealogy and historical research, as well as historical and environmental preservation, Ashley is also a proud member of the Daughters of the American Revolution (DAR). Happily married and the mother of three sons, she lives with her family in Texas.

For more information, please visit:
http://www.ashleykathbilsky.com
http://www.amazon.com/ashleykathbilsky
https://www.twitter.com/AKathBilsky
https://www.facebook.com/AshleyKathBilsky?ref=tn_tnmn

OTHER AKB TITLES

THE SENSE OF HONOR
Best-Selling, Award-Winning
Historical Romance
with Mystery & Suspense
Setting: Regency England

WHISPER IN THE WIND
Best-Selling, Award-Winning
Historical Time-Travel Romance
Setting: American West

Ashley Kath-Bilsky

Ashley Kath-Bilsky

51019643R00176

Made in the USA
Charleston, SC
08 January 2016